The Life and Times of the Traitor Killean Onryn

The Relics Saga, Volume 1

A.R Cunningham

Published by A.R Cunningham, 2024.

This is a work of fiction. Similarities to real people, places, or events are entirely coincidental.

THE LIFE AND TIMES OF THE TRAITOR KILLEAN ONRYN

First edition. November 5, 2024.

Copyright © 2024 A.R Cunningham.

ISBN: 979-8227982148

Written by A.R Cunningham.

Dedicated to my dad. Because he is awesome. And my cats, who are also awesome but less interested in this book.

Map of the Lands of Magic

Chapter One

The massive fireball hurtled through the air, blazing like a green-gold comet. Killean vaulted over the broken spine of an old stone wall and hit the dusty ground on the other side with a bone shuddering thud. He rolled over the parched soil, pricked and poked by the stubble of broken stone and pottery littering the ground. Evidently, it was going to be one of *those* days.

The fireball smashed into the wall, the magic shattering against the old stone. Spatters of greenish fire leapt over the wall to set the dry stalks of dead grass alight before sputtering out just as quickly.

Interesting. Having immolated his fair share of inanimate and not-so-inanimate objects with fire magic, Killean knew that true adepts could keep their fires blazing for a lot longer than that.

He rolled into a crouch behind the wall and waited. He heard heavy footfalls and a moment later a figure in a dark, hooded cape, appeared, saw Killean, and leapt over the wall with a wordless roar of inchoate rage. Killean was familiar with the sound. A not all that surprising number of people tended to roar in murderous rage on seeing him.

Unfortunately for this particular would-be murderer, Killean knew exactly how to deal with him. Snatching up a piece of pottery and a fistful of dry dirt he threw the dust into his attacker's face as he straightened out of his ill-advised leap. Time slowed and Killean caught a glimpse of an oval of brown skin covering a painfully young face and a pair of wide, wild eyes inside the hood before the cloud of grit and dust hit. Blinded, the figure lost his balance, batting at his face.

Killean could have been sporting about all this. His assailant was obviously an amateur and very possibly a child. But if Killean was the type to be sporting, he wouldn't have nearly as many people trying to kill him. Snatching the hood from his assailant's head, he shimmied behind him, jerked his head back and notched the sharp edge of pottery against the soft and tender skin just under his jaw.

His attacker was a boy somewhere between a well-built twelve and an underfed fifteen by Killean's reckoning. The boy had the sense not to struggle. His muscles were coiled like high pressure springs as he held very still, throat working soundlessly. Grimacing to show all his teeth he kept trying to see Killean out of the corner of his eye, as if that would do him any good.

He looked like a panicked colt; a creature of wild, twitching nerves barely held in check. His soft, tightly curled black hair was shorn close to his skull. He wore no marks of affiliation to any country or clan, but that meant little. Only the profoundly foolish or, conversely, the immensely competent would challenge Killean openly. This boy may well be a fool but competent he was not.

Catching the boy's gauntleted wrist, Killean twisted his arm behind his back. The gauntlet was part hardened leather and part plate armour. It was a very nice piece of work. The kind that no arcane armourer worth his salt, would waste on a skinny twig of a boy like this.

Metal studs over the knuckles had been set with pale green peridot stones Killean noted, interest well and truly piqued. He had seen the design before. The fire was new however, and it made him curious. It had been a while since anything had stirred his curiosity, which was why he decided to show mercy.

'Why are you trying to kill me?' he asked the boy withdrawing the shard but keeping a firm grip on his captive with one arm braced over his chest.

'You murdered my father,' the boy gritted out through his teeth.

Killean nodded slightly. That was more than likely. He'd killed a lot of people. 'Name?' he asked, glancing around for something he could use to knock the boy's brains out if it proved necessary. Mercy, after all, was a matter of definition.

'Ashinue Rogu of the Dancing Deer clan,' the boy declared proudly.

Killean cocked his head in thought. 'Doesn't ring a bell,' he said finally. 'I killed a lot of warriors in the war. Dancing Deer. Manic Monkeys. Annoyed Aardvarks. And others from clans even more ridiculous. I was on first name basis with very few of them.'

'You're a monster,' the boy accused fighting against Killean's hold.

Killean rolled his eyes, released the boy, allowed him to upset his own balance by trying to twist around to face him, and then shoved him over into the dirt and planted a knee into his back. 'You are not the first to tell me that,' he said conversationally. The boy wriggled like a squashed bug, unable to stop Killean wrenching his gauntlet off and flinging it aside. Whoever had trained and dispatched this child should be ashamed of themselves.

'Boy, answer my question,' he said when it became apparent the Dancing Deer wasn't going to give in. 'Where was your father slain?'

The boy twisted his head and spat at him. At least, he tried to, gravity was not on his side. Killean did him the courtesy of ignoring the fresh spray of spittle liberally covering the boy's face. Snarling through his embarrassment the boy saw fit to criticise him. 'You don't even remember all the people you've killed, do you?'

'Of course, I don't,' Killean replied irritably. He was sure he'd said that already. 'I commanded an army. I besieged towns and cities. Do you think I asked for a census before I put each one to the torch?'

Why was this so hard for people to understand, he wondered tiredly. It had been war. A very personal war, true, but one with impersonal casualties. Which, he supposed made it a fairly ordinary war at that. Killean respected revenge, he'd have to be a hypocrite not to, and he accepted responsibility for the deaths he'd ordered and the lives he'd dispatched personally. He had never asked anyone he'd deprived of a relative for forgiveness. He had earned their hatred. Still. Expecting him to know the names of every person who had fallen in the name of his war was ridiculous. He wished the righteous fools who came looking for him would grasp this point. He could give them a fight, but he could not give them closure.

'You're evil,' the boy told him.

Killean nodded. He didn't consider himself evil, but what did that matter? He had done terrible things, he would not deny that, and any righteousness he'd claimed in the beginning had been well and truly spent by the time the war was done. He made no bones about his sins. Had his side won, he'd be a hero now. Instead, he was a villain forever more. Those were the wages of war.

'The consensus suggests I'm also mad,' he told the boy. 'I've heard rumour the good and just in the Land of Three Rivers believe my madness exonerates me of evil. It wasn't my fault, you see. I was too mad to know better.' A bitter smirk twitched his lips.

The boy grew still. His eyes were very wide as he strained his neck to look at him. 'Why would Three Rivers defend you? You tried to raze their land to the ground.'

Very true. It was a sore point for Killean that he'd ultimately failed. He sighed. 'Have you heard of Nadil Shiny Scale?' he asked.

'Of course. He's the legendary hero who defeated you.' The boy scoffed, '*Everyone* knows that.'

Killean glanced up at the purple striped sky. Dusk was fading into true night. It would be too dark for this nonsense soon. 'He likes me,' he said.

There was a beat of silence before the boy bleated, 'How can the great hero *like* you? You're enemies.'

Killean's lips twitched again. 'I've tried to tell him that. Many times. He doesn't believe it. Personally, I think someone dropped him on his head as a baby. Possibly repeatedly.'

It would fit perfectly well with the rest of his trite, rags to riches tale. In fact, he wouldn't be at all surprised if the head bashing had been on purpose. If Nadil were here now, Killean would happily bash his head in. He'd always had that effect on him.

'You were going to slaughter everyone in the land of Three Rivers,' the boy complained. He seemed inordinately hung up on stating the obvious. Killean knew the rumours people told about him as well as anybody else. And for the stuff that was actually true? Well, he'd been there. It wasn't like he was going to forget anytime soon.

'My goal was to capture the capital,' he told the boy. 'I wanted to break their military and destroy their economic base, indiscriminate death and destruction wasn't essential to that goal,' – although it had been a common side-effect – he sighed and admitted, 'I understand your point. Sadly, Nadil has never been moved by logic. He thinks we're friends.'

'That's madness,' the boy declared.

'I agree,' Killean said. 'But as I'm a publicly acknowledged maniac my opinion doesn't hold much weight.'

Of all the punishments his enemies could have inflicted on him after his defeat, all of which he had earned to one degree or another, the label of mad was without doubt the most irritating. True, irritation should not be on a level with death by lava, or having his soul ripped out and tossed to the four winds so his spirit could never know peace, but the virtue of incineration was that it didn't last long, and spiritual oblivion was at least definitive. The accusation of madness rendered all his deeds, good and bad, suspect, and declared Killean a victim of his own mind. He'd rather be hated than pitied, and Killean wondered, not for the first time, if that was why the High King of Three Rivers had let the rumours spread. Torvin had always been a tricky bastard.

Gaze roaming over the lonely plain as his attention wandered, Killean let his eyes track over the broken pillars of old stone and the crumbling remains of a once vast settlement laid out like a patchwork of rubble and shattered tile in front of him. Had he been of a more poetic state-of-mind he might have found a metaphor for life amid the ruins. Instead, Killean's gaze focused on the enormous stone arch rising taller than the rest of the ruins. It was formed of two massive standing stones with a shorter stone laid over the top like a lintel.

The archway was a transportation portal to one or several of the other lands. It connected the lands of the temporal world to the wild and mostly ungoverned Timeless Realm. Unlike the cultivated portals in civilised countries, only the brave and desperate ventured into the Nameless Plain to use the archway. Killean had been contemplating whether he was desperate enough to risk the magic of the Timeless Realm as a shortcut when the son of Ashinue Rogu attacked him.

The boy spoke, finally answering the question he'd almost forgotten asking. 'You attacked the Land of Green Peaks. My father was one of the castle defenders you slaughtered.'

'Ah.' Killean breathed out carefully. He released the boy and stood.

The boy rose warily. Killean retrieved his gauntlet from a patch of thistle growing around the base of the wall and threw it to him. 'I'm going to give you one shot.' He pointed to the stone arch. 'If you can hit me before I reach the portal, I'll give you the fight to the death you want.'

The young buck of the Dancing Deer clan gawped at him. 'That's not how this is supposed to work,' he objected. 'This isn't a duel. I'm here to *kill* you.'

'And I'm neither suicidal nor looking to kill you, so that option is off the table. Next time you go looking to ambush a man, do it right.' Killean told him frankly, 'I do respect your right to vengeance, however, so if you can prove your magic is up to the task, I will give you the chance you seek.' Or enough of a thrashing to convince the boy to never again pick fights with insane war criminals in dark and isolated locales. Killean had never been that stupid at this boy's age.

The boy's face scrunched in confusion. 'You're patronising me,' he said.

'I'm really not,' Killean said pushing his hair out of his face as a whispering breeze swept across the plain.

Patronising the boy would be braining him with that gauntlet of his and dumping his unconscious body on the doorstep of the nearest healing mission he found. Killean should know. He'd had to do exactly that to several war orphans when their skills proved unequal to their bloodlust.

Killean was not always guilty of the crimes he was accused of. One man could only do so much, and it wasn't as though he'd fought the war alone, but the attack on the Land of Green Peaks he remembered well. Green Peaks had been neutral in the war and his mission to infiltrate the treasury had been an unmitigated disaster. He'd been impatient and under pressure that day. He'd let his rage get the better of him and that was shameful.

'One shot?' the boy asked, pulling on his gauntlet and extending his arm toward Killean.

'Yes.' Had the boy been serious, or half-way competent, he'd have already taken his shot while Killean stood far too close to find cover.

But this boy wasn't a seasoned warrior or a hardened killer. He was just a boy whose happiness had been destroyed by war. Killean could relate. He'd been one of those once.

The boy sucked in his bottom lip. He adjusted his stance. His movements too deliberate and stiff to be well-practiced and Killean suppressed a wince. He estimated that this boy had less than three years true training behind him. All the same that fireball had been impressively large. It had eaten the distance between them swiftly and would have had no trouble devouring flesh if the dumb kid had only known how to aim.

He wouldn't dismiss the boy out of hand just yet. His control might be lacking but the magic fire he commanded wasn't to be taken lightly. Killean was in a position to know. He'd been able to wield magic fire before the gift had been stripped from him after the war. He eyed the boy's gauntlet speculatively, the barest inkling of a plan forming around the edges of his thoughts.

'Run,' the boy said, his arm quivering.

Killean did not run. Instead, he dropped to his hands and knees on the ground. Stretching his spine, he felt his flesh flow like water and warp like air as he claimed his wolf skin. It was only then that he deigned to run – and it was more an ambling gambol, at that. He heard the boy shout behind him, half-surprise and half-outrage, and his ears pricked. Either the boy had forgotten Killean was a shapeshifter or he'd never been told, which was, again, more evidence he shouldn't be roaming around picking fights alone.

Killean's paws pounded over the uneven ground nimbly as he picked up his pace and loped toward the giant arch. It was good to run again. He heard the sizzle of air and a scream of magic and dove to the side, rolling over and leaping to his feet just clear of the impact point.

The ground he'd been running on exploded in green fire. Hot splinters of rock and pottery struck his flank but failed to penetrate his shaggy coat. Killean launched forward, increasing his pace to a full sprint. He wasn't surprised when the boy broke the terms of their agreements and fired again. Killean ran in a zig-zag path, occasionally giving the boy a good shot at his flank, but only because he was enjoying himself.

The boy pelted his path with a barrage of smaller fireballs, all of which missed. Green fire ate across the ground, leapt into the air and formed a wall between him and the arch. Killean's tongue lolled between his jaws in a wolfish grin. Clever boy. There was hope for the young buck yet.

Pretending to stumble just ahead of the firewall, Killean let his front legs crumple under him and rolled tail-over-head. His second form shift took him like the snap of fresh linen shaken out on a cool spring morning. His body collapsed in on itself, fur melting into feather as broad wings burst from his back. He took off into the air, sailing over the fire.

'Not fair!' Killean heard the boy yell as he circled above in his hawk form before arrowing through the night toward the archway.

He landed on top of the lintel and immediately set about preening his breast. The air lit up with a wash of green fire. Killean took wing as the fireball smashed into the lintel, dripping trails of emerald flame to the ground.

The boy had a job getting across the burning plane, but finally made it to the base of the archway. 'You have to come down eventually. Then I'll get you,' he shouted, narrow chest heaving under his homespun shirt and the tatters of his cape. His gauntleted fist spat sparks of green fire. Killean circled the arch lazily, enjoying the updraft, waiting for the fire to burn itself out before he landed.

He did not realise there was anything wrong at first. The magic of the arch was subtle, whispering up through the stone in a gentle murmur as Killean perched on the rim. A sudden surge of energy under his feet was his only warning as the air between the vertical pillars shivered and broke into a rippling wall of haze. Killean cree'd a warning to the boy but it was too late. The magic bowed out from between the pillars, ballooning like a soap bubble, catching the boy instantly. Killean dove toward the portal, chasing the magic as it spilled back from whence it came. He smashed through the bubble after the boy.

He had never liked portal travel. It was *almost* instantaneous, but therein lay the rub, because that split-second lag between here and there made all the difference in the Timeless Realm, ironically. In every portal jump there was a moment where the traveller was held suspended outside of time and place, trapped in a realm where nothing and everything happened at once.

Some parts of the Timeless Realm were ruled by rampant chaos, but the partially tamed landing sites connecting the portals were places of still, sensationless sterility that he could almost believe had been designed to drive a shapeshifter mad.

The time spent actually in the Timeless Realm lasted barely longer than a slow blink, but for a being like Killean who lived to feel the ground under his feet or the currents of the air under his wings that moment was entirely too long, which summed up the Timeless Realm entirely. Too much and not enough, in perpetuity.

He and the boy were spat out inside a large, wood and paper walled room, made cloudy by a mixture of pipe smoke, the fireplace set into the backwall, and the fumes from the lamps hanging from the low ceiling. Killean reclaimed his man form and his enchanted coat and trousers as he hit the ground. He rolled with his momentum and landed in a predator's crouch, arms extended and a slender blade in each hand. The boy landed in a sprawl of limbs, his chin hitting the rush matting like it hurt.

A group of men stood clustered in a semi-circle in front of Killean. Half of them were old, with wispy greying beards hanging from their chins and arms folded across their chests so their hands were hidden in the hang of their ornate sleeves. The rest were obviously soldiers. The points of several sword blades jabbed in his direction and the men behind them wore elaborate helmets and masks moulded to resemble the sour faces of aggrieved carp. Their white tunics were overlaid with scale-like armour made from magic hardened chips of mother-of-pearl, the smooth surface reflecting the dim light from the lamps.

Killean looked beyond the men to the emblem of the nation of Jumping Carp painted on the back wall and dropped his blades with a sigh. 'I know for a fact that I have never attacked any of you,' he said. 'Why have you kidnapped me?'

'You are Killean-the-Swift,' one of the wizened elders said. He wasn't sure if that was meant to be answer or greeting.

'Onryn,' he corrected in a low voice. 'I am Killean Onryn of the Striking Talon clan.'

'A clan that no longer exists,' scoffed one of the other old men.

Killean stared him down. He had pouches under his eyes deep enough to hold his small change. 'I'm aware,' he replied evenly. 'I was there when they were slaughtered to the last man, woman, and child.'

'Not the last child. *You* survived,' a querulous female voice called out from the back ranks. 'And you've certainly caused enough trouble for the rest of us in the fifteen years since.'

Killean narrowed his eyes trying in vain to see through the wall of old men. 'Mamie Cat, is that you?' he asked.

Mamie Cat elbowed her way through the press of flesh. Short, fat and redoubtable, Mamie Cat wore robes of deep blue with a broad sash of lurid pink patterned with some kind of flower never seen in nature. Her hair was a froth of tight corkscrew curls that framed her face. That face was round with heavy jowls and her rich brown skin was grooved with laugh lines.

Her small, shrewd eyes peered at him. 'Of course it's me, boy, who else would it be?' she demanded.

Killean deemed that a foolish question and didn't answer it. He studied the men again with more interest. Since the inexplicable commutation of his execution to ten years imprisonment, of which he'd only served five before the High King decided to pardon him – a decision that baffled many to this day – he'd spent far too much of his time being kidnapped by men just like these.

Most of those other men remembered his war record and that he'd served another man for most of that time – which they assumed made him eager to serve them – but conveniently forgot that he had lost his war in the end. He'd been planning to do to these men what he'd done to all the others. Put on a show of force and break out before they could tell him what they wanted. Mamie's presence changed his plans.

Killean did not have friends. He was, after all, varying degrees of evil and insane, neither of which enhanced a man's social life. He was also a recently released prisoner and a convicted war criminal. Traits that did not endear him to anyone. But Mamie and her clan of smugglers might be the closest thing he still had to an ally. The Silk Paw clan had once been allied with the Striking Talon, but more than that, Mamie had been his mother's true friend.

There were so few people alive who remembered his parents fondly. Mamie might be the last to remember the Onryn with kindness, and she had used that old connection mercilessly to take advantage of Killean since his release. Mamie knew as surely as he that he'd preserve her life merely to keep the memory of his parents alive and with Mamie here, he had no choice but to listen to these old men.

He decided that the bearded old man in the conical hat with the wide brim shadowing his face was the leader of the group. Wisely, he had chosen to stand to the far left of the semi-circle of men and had not drawn attention to himself by speaking. His unadorned golden robe, bound by a thick sash of fine white silk, marked him as a man of means and discernment among the nobility of the Jumping Carp.

'Obawai and his consortium have use of your services. You'll be a good boy and listen to what the nice men have to say, won't you, Ilin?' Mamie asked sweetly using his old boyhood nickname.

As a child he'd struggled with the flowing syllables of his name and only been able to pronounce "Ilin". His mother had thought it sweet and funny and picked up the naming convention. His older brother, Kindean, had become "Indin", his father, Tinnian, had become "Inan". Reminding him of that happier time, Mamie twisted the knife expertly. Killean would admire the manipulation if he wasn't on the receiving end.

He pasted a sharp toothed smile on his face and simpered, 'Of course, Mamie, anything for you.'

'You see, gentlemen?' Mamie turned to the men triumphantly. 'I told you my boy would be reasonable.'

'Who is the youth,' one of the armed men demanded, pointing the tip of his blade toward the young buck.

The boy, who had so far proved he possessed an iota of intelligence by staying quiet, straightened his spine and drew breath to speak. Killean beat him to it. 'A thief from Green Peaks,' he said. 'I captured him for his bounty. The spell you put on the portal drew him in with me.'

'Green Peaks is no friend to you. Why would you stoop to catching petty criminals for them?' Obawai asked.

Killean smiled thinly. 'No one is a friend to me, nor I to them,' he replied. 'I intended to deliver him to the outpost in Frolicking Squirrel.'

A shiver of relief ran through the gathered consortium. Frolicking Squirrel was a mostly lawless country with a weak High King but several powerful assassin clans who made their money hunting down criminals for other countries. Killean had come to an agreement with the clan leader of the Sly Fox after he'd taken several commissions against Killean that had left the clan facing a personnel shortage and Killean with a bad mood. He worked for the clan occasionally in exchange for the leader's solemn oath not to take any further contracts on his life. If the men of the consortium had dragged him here then they had most likely done their homework and knew about his agreement.

'He must be a better thief than he looks, to command a bounty high enough to warrant your skills,' one of the other old men said.

Killean roughly snatched the boy's gauntleted arm, pulling down his sleeve for the men to see. 'A gauntlet stolen from the royal guard,' he said. 'Green Peaks have offered a substantial reward.'

The boy wrenched his arm back and huddled into himself, glaring at Killean. Which was fine, so long as the boy kept his mouth shut. Killean *was* trying to save his life but if he got it into his head to use the gauntlet, he'd leave him to the Jumping Carp soldiers.

'How did you know where to find me?' he asked Obawai, changing the subject to something more interesting.

It took precise magic and a lock of hair or drop of the target's blood to pull a target through a portal deliberately. Killean knew Mamie Cat had supplied the necessary items, although how and when she'd acquired them, he'd soon enough leave a mystery. All the same, unless Obawai and his men had primed every portal on the main continent – an improbable feat – they had to have known he'd cross the Nameless Plain tonight. He'd intended to head west, crossing through Red Mountain, but flooding on the border had turned him back, forcing him to head north to the portal site. As he was hardly in the habit of advertising his movements the pileup of coincidences made him suspicious.

Killean narrowed his eyes in suddenly understanding. 'You flooded the river to divert my path.' He shook his head, 'You must be desperate.'

The men puffed out their chests like a group of spiny fish. 'Do you have any idea who you are talking to, boy?' said a man with liver spots and skin the exact shade of a rotted lemon.

'No,' Killean told him honestly. All he knew was that he faced a group of old, self-entitled men who wanted something from him but were taking their sweet time to get to the point.

'You speak to the patriarchs of Jumping Carp's most influential mage families,' Mamie told him, voice quiet and serious. 'These men own most of the wealth in the country. They have the ear of the High King.'

'Had,' Killean corrected her with a smile. 'If they still commanded so much power, they wouldn't need me,' he said confidently.

'How so?' Obawai asked, cocking his head inquiringly.

Killean let his gaze sweep over the assemblage. 'My reputation proceeds me, gentlemen,' – far more than theirs at any rate – 'I made my name overthrowing kings. My reputation was forged in revolution and the quest for revenge. People happy with their king do not seek me out.'

Chapter Two

'We have no quarrel with our king,' Obawai said, pulling one hand free of his sleeve. His gnarled fingers plucked at the hem, revealing a hint of silver thread. His nails were long and yellowed.

'Which king do you have quarrel with?' Killean asked, too familiar with this game to be caught out by guarded words. He knew what people believed about him. Moreover, he knew that monied men did not go to the trouble of dragging him halfway across the known world without wanting someone dead.

'Obawai, are you sure this is the right course of action?' One of the men asked. His face was round as a copper coin and he wore a band of knotted cloth over his brow. He was the only beardless elder. Under his brown robe with its pattern of white chrysanthemum flowers, his body was straight backed and strong. Despite his tremulous question, Killean marked him as a man with martial experience, perhaps the master of the armed men seeded through the group.

'We have gone to much trouble to bring the Striking Talon here, Tana,' Obawai said. Killean noted the use of his clan title with interest. Clearly, Obawai remembered what his clan had been, once upon a time. Either that or he honestly thought flattery would sway Killean. Who knows, it just might. As well as evil, mad and vengeance-obsessed, more than a few people had called him proud in the past.

'But can we *trust* him?' Tana demanded.

What a ridiculous question. Killean shot an impatient look toward Mamie Cat. She responded with a slight shake of her head and clucked her tongue at the elders. Such an obvious show of dissention in the ranks was unprofessional. They should have sorted all this out before they set their trap for him and Mamie knew it.

'We brought you here to resolve a delicate matter for us,' Obawai told him, ignoring Tana's question. There was an edge to his voice that was not meant for Killean. 'We wish you to travel to Shipwright Island. There you will hunt down a defector named Rhodu Gakai. He is being held by the Blue Crab pirates.' Tilting his chin the old man instructed, 'You will find Gakai and his captors and you will kill them.'

'The Blue Crab are powerful,' Killean said thoughtfully. 'They have a great deal of influence in the Fish Archipelago. An attack on them will have far reaching consequences.'

'That is not your concern,' Obawai snapped.

It wasn't, but it should be Obawai's. Jumping Carp was the largest in the chain of islands making up the Fish Archipelago, but their dominance had been waning for some time. In part because of the expanse of organised piracy led by enterprising men calling themselves Sea Lords, but also because of the war on the mainland.

Jumping Carp had remained neutral, refusing to take any part in the conflict beyond employing her impressive navy to defend her waters. On the one hand, this had been a sensible decision, but the choice to take no part in the battles that had decided power on the mainland meant Jumping Carp had lost any chance of increasing her influence with the other nations.

Was Jumping Carp trying to change that by removing the strongest of the pirates from the archipelago? But that begged the question of why they'd employ a war criminal to do the job and not dispatch their own impressive fleet. And then there was also the matter of the defector, Rhodu Gakai. Defectors came in two flavours, sell-out traitors and conscientious objectors. Killean was interested to know Gakai's flavour.

'Imui, let us show our guest his recompense for undertaking this task,' Obawai gestured to one of the armed men.

Replacing his slim blade in its glossy black lacquer sheath, Imui turned and walked across the matting to a white sliding door at the back of the room near the fireplace. Killean glimpsed a fall of diffuse grey light filling the room beyond and then Imui returned, pushing an elaborate wheeled cabinet of shiny red lacquer with the emblem of the Jumping Carp embossed in gold on each of its doors.

Inside was a stack of gold bars, six in total, nestled alongside a small pile of pale green papers. Imui showed him the front of one of the certificates. Killean recognised the crown seal of Jumping Carp printed on the intricately decorated page.

'Bearer bonds,' Obawai explained. 'Here is one hundred thousand Carp roe. Yours, if you agree to be our instrument in this matter.'

Beside Killean, the Dancing Deer boy sucked in a sharp breath. Killean didn't blame him. The gold bars had a dull lustre, not shiny, but impressive all the same. Jumping Carp currency had a good rate of exchange throughout the mainland. He would not lose much transferring the currency into Three Rivers groats or Squirrel kernels. Assuming the gold was pure and the bonds were not forgeries, which Killean would be foolish to do.

'I need to know what Rhodu Gakai took from you,' he said.

Imui glanced at Obawai who waved one long nailed hand. Without a word, Imui closed the cabinet and wheeled it aside. 'That matter is no business of yours,' said Obawai.

Killean cocked an eyebrow. 'You don't pay a man like me a small fortune to hunt down someone whose only crime is vacationing-without-leave,' he pointed out mildly. 'Gakai stole something from you or else he knows something you don't want him telling anyone else. Which is it?'

Obawai stuffed both hands back into his sleeves. 'It is easy to forget that you were once more than the filthy sell-sword who kneels before me,' he muttered peevishly.

Killean was not offended. He knew what he looked like. His ragged brown hair bound in a loose tail behind him, his enchanted coat and trousers torn, stained and frayed, his face coated in road dust and his upper body naked under his coat because his last enchanted shirt had been shredded beyond repair. 'I've never used a sword,' he commented drily. 'And you're stalling. Any man held by the Blue Crab is in possession of something valuable. Killing him might not be enough to secure your losses,' he pointed out reasonably.

'I have the details, boy. I will tell you what you need to know once we're away from here,' Mamie Cat told him curtly. 'No need to waste these illustrious gentlemen's time with endless questions.' She smiled as she spoke, her cat grin no more than surface deep.

Killean frowned at her. The Silk Paw had no particular ties to the land of the Jumping Carp. Which meant her interest was in Rhodu Gakai or the Blue Crab. Or possibly, someone or something else entirely. Anyone less well acquainted with Mamie Cat might think money was her only consideration, but Killean knew better. The Silk Paw had plenty of money and many more avenues available to them on the mainland to earn more. But what Mamie loved best was intrigue. She was playing politics. But with whom?

'You will take this commission and tell no one of what has occurred here,' Obawai said. 'If you are captured—'

'—I will tell my captors nothing,' Killean finished for him. It was a futile vow. Torture was torture and Killean had no bond of loyalty to these mostly anonymous men. He would talk to avoid needless suffering for himself, but he doubted it would make much difference. Obawai and his men would deny everything and accuse him of stealing the bonds and gold. They would be believed. Killean's reputation really did proceed him everywhere, and its shadow was large enough to encompass any crime.

Still if he wanted to get out of here any time soon, he'd have to feign obedience. 'I will do as you ask.' He stood, ignoring the nervous shuffling of the men in front of him and offered a shallow bow. 'Mamie Cat, I leave my payment in your hands. I trust you will hold it in safe keeping for me?'

'For a two percent holders fee,' she said.

Killean turned so he could study the portal arch behind him and hide his smile. Two percent was Mamie being generous. She must know how close to snapping his leash he was. It was nice to know she still feared his wrath.

The consortium's portal arch was far more elegant and delicate than the great stone edifice back on the Nameless Plain. The portal was the width of an ordinary door and reached to the ceiling. The two vertical poles were painted a cheerful sky blue. Magical script had been applied to the paint work with gold leaf, a casual reminder of the wealth of this ancient island nation.

Beyond the arch the same grey light he'd spied from the antechamber glowed through the screen doors set into the backwall. Killean suspected they slid aside to reveal a porch and interior garden. There was a chill wafting under the screens and a murkiness to the light that made him think of snow.

Killean hauled the boy to his feet. 'You will return us to the portal on the plains,' he told the men at his back, 'so that I may deal with this boy.'

'Agreed,' Obawai said quickly. So quickly that Killean smirked. Evidently, Obawai was nervous about their adolescent witness. Equally obvious was the fact that he expected Killean to kill the boy as soon as he reached the mainland. If he hadn't implied the boy was enroute to a hanging, Obawai would have insisted he die here. These were not men to suffer a witness to live, even an insignificant one with no chance of being believed. Somehow, Killean still doubted the boy would appreciate the lie he'd told to save his life.

A trio of soldiers came forward to activate the portal, pricking their fingers before tracery the goldwork with their blood. Killean watched the men work, observing the pattern and committing the script to memory. The soldiers stepped back quickly as magic sounded a clear, melodic note through the air.

'I will see you in Cockle Shore in two days, Mamie,' Killean told the smuggler as he hauled the boy toward the portal.

He heard Mamie Cat cackle behind him as he stepped through. 'That's what I like about you, boy. You love to live dangerously. I'm sure Kindean will be thrilled to see you.' Her laughter chased him through the doorway.

The portal spat him and the boy back onto the Nameless Plain. The darkness was complete, the only light coming from the spill of stars in the sky. Killean's enhanced eyesight adapted quickly, but the boy was night-blinded. A whistling wind swept the debris of burnt grass stalks into wild eddies and tossed rock dust into their faces. Killean raised an arm to shield his eyes. He heard the unmistakable crackle of magic at his back and sighed loudly.

'Don't,' he warned.

The boy had activated the gauntlet. Green fire curled around his fist and underlit half his face. He looked demonically furious. 'You agreed to kill that man and you don't even know what he did. He could be innocent,' he exclaimed.

THE LIFE AND TIMES OF THE TRAITOR KILLEAN ONRYN

'He probably is,' Killean agreed. 'Shipwright Island has no extradition treaties with any of the major powers. It's a good place for a man to run if he fears for his life and can't trust the law to protect him.'

The boy shook his head angrily, firing off another question. 'You told them I was a thief. Why?'

'Because you are,' Killean answered. 'I might not remember the defenders I killed in Green Peaks, but I know that gauntlet is worn by mages of the Royal Guard, which you most certainly are not.'

The boy gaped at him. The flames wreathing his arm died out. 'How do you know so much about the honoured guard?'

Killean thought about reminding him he'd killed a lot of them, but that seemed crass. 'My uncle told me,' he said instead. Now the boy goggled at him. He smirked and confirmed, 'Yes. *That* uncle.'

Killean had exaggerated a little when he told Obawai every member of the Striking Talon had been slaughtered when he was a boy. There had been three survivors. Killean and his brother Kindean and their uncle Dadarro. His uncle had started the war Killean had eventually lost but before that he'd been his teacher and mentor on the road to rebellion. And madness. Because his dear uncle had most definitely been mad. You didn't tilt the entire mainland into all-out war for the soul purpose of turning yourself into an immortal dragon otherwise.

His uncle had fashioned himself a High King in the mould of their Onryn ancestors' dead and past, wishing to reclaim their ancestral home of the Barley Lands from Three Rivers. Or at least that's the story he'd sold Killean in the beginning. Kings took an interest in the wealth and power of their fellow monarchs, and his uncle Dadarro had passed on this interest to Killean, which meant he was very well versed in the powerplays of the petty lords and minor kings on the continent even now.

He told the boy, 'Obawai would've killed you if he thought you destined to live. Had I refused his proposal the soldiers would've tried to kill me too. Evading assassination attempts gets tedious after a while. It's generally easier to feign compliance, leave, and come back later to stab them in the back.' He shrugged, 'It's just common sense.'

'I don't believe you,' the boy said. 'You're a villain. Why would you protect me?'

'I told you. I respect your right to revenge.' The wind picked up again, tugging through Killean's hair. Turning his back on the breeze he started to trek toward the broken wall where he'd stashed his pack.

The boy dogged his steps, cursing softly as he tripped over loose stones in the dark. 'I'm not going to let you hurt anyone else,' he declared boldly. 'As soon as we get to Cockle Shore I'm going to report you to the Rivers Guard.'

Killean glanced over his shoulder. '"We?"' he asked.

The young buck's voice was reedy and fluting, 'Watching you die at Rivers' hands will be almost as satisfying as killing you myself.'

'Are you sure?' Killean asked, curiously. 'I've always found more satisfaction in killing my enemies personally.' It was the best way to make sure they truly ended up dead, he'd found. The old adage about wanting a job done right was never truer than when at war.

'That's because you're evil,' the boy told him, with the confidence only a fourteen-year-old boy could muster.

Killean smirked. Of course. How silly of him to forget. He found the nook where a corner of wall remained, creating a wind break for the straggling patch of weeds that had grown up around it. Fishing in the bush Killean found his pack and shrugged into it. 'You'd be better off going home,' he told the boy. 'I don't think you can keep up with me on the road.'

'I won't go home. Not until you're dead. I've staked my reputation on it.'

'Ah,' Killean said. 'You think killing me will exonerate your theft.' He ignored the boy's spluttered denials. 'Suit yourself. But know this. Our deal is done. I gave you a chance to strike me dead and you failed. I won't give you another.'

'Next time, you won't see me coming,' the boy insisted.

Killean cast his gaze heavenward, looking up at the starry sky. 'What's your name?' he asked.

'I already told you. I am Ashinue Rogu of the Dancing Deer clan.'

Killean twisted back to look at him. 'I thought that was your father's name?'

'It was.' The boy looked away sharply, fiddling with the strap on his gauntlet.

Killean sighed. Either the boy was lying or his mother was unimaginative and his late father a raging egotist. 'I'm going to call you Ash,' he said.

'I don't want you calling me anything,' the boy told him.

'Clear off, then.' Killean set off with long strides across the plain toward the border with Potbelly Hills. If he squinted he could just make out the distant hills, rising like a slightly blacker outline against the horizon.

The boy did not clear off. He hurried to keep in step, igniting his gauntlet to light his way in the dark. 'I'm not a thief,' he panted after about forty minutes of the punishing pace Killean set.

'I don't care,' Killean replied, noting with keen interest that the boy's wick of flame was stronger the closer he was to Killean. His lips twitched, somewhere between a sneer and a smirk. Oh, yes. The game was definitely afoot.

Other than late, he had no idea what time it was. He did not own a time piece and for all the nights he'd spent camping under the stars he'd yet to master the art of keeping time by their movement. It was cold on the plain. The wind buffeting them first from one side and then the other, changing direction constantly as they trekked. Aside from the whistling wind and Ash's muffled curses as he blundered along, there was no sound. No animals hunted the plain and few people would come out here by choice. The Nameless Plain really was a desolate, miserable place; a scar on the landscape that would never heal.

He'd learned as a boy that there had once been an affluent, independent city state on the Plain, but long ago some manner of magical calamity had destroyed it, leaving only ruins behind. The magic unleashed on that day had ruined the landscape permanently, preventing any new settlers from reviving the old city. Many speculated that a portal accident had caused the wilder magics of the Timeless Realm to invade the Plain and that was the reason no one could remember the city's name. The name had been snatched from memory and over time, the records lost.

Killean wondered if the once fertile Barley Lands looked like this now. He hadn't seen his homeland since the end of the war. Had the magic unleashed in that final decisive battle left the land arid and ruined, he wondered, or were the Barley Lands even now providing food for his enemies in Three Rivers?

He'd find out in two days. Cockle Shore sat on the banks of the Uswe River, one of the three waterways that gave Three Rivers its name. The river also denoted the border with the Barley Lands. There were many countries and territories Killean was barred from entering, but strangely, Three Rivers wasn't one of them. His pardon held, and while he was sure the High King's guard would take an immediate interest in his presence in their territory, they couldn't arrest him for being there. Not according to their own law.

Privately, Killean suspected none of the guards would be prosecuted if they blasted him with magic or punched him through with arrows on first sight, but Three Rivers had always been enamoured with her own moral superiority. To kill a traitor in cold blood after having pardoned him would make the High King look two-faced, something to be avoided at all costs by the image conscious elders. Torvin, who had claimed his throne by murdering the previous incumbent, would be more sanguine about being called two-faced. He knew exactly what a bastard he was.

All the same, in the six months since his pardon, Killean had avoided Three Rivers. Defeat and prison had quenched the fire in him to wreak havoc. He did not long for more war. He thought it would probably surprise his enemies to know he hadn't enjoyed the last one. He'd fought because he'd believed his cause was just and when he could no longer believe that he'd fought for the cause he'd chosen regardless – because if he didn't, who would? Revenge and justice were a double-edged sword and as he could not claim the former on his family's behalf, he'd sought the latter instead.

His clan had been killed on Minuidon's orders. The former High King of Three Rivers and a member of a clan long at odds with the Onryn, Miniudon had been just as mad as Dadarro, in his own way. Kings stood above their laws, so Killean had had little recourse but to try and rip him off his throne and stamp his kingdom into the ground. Minuidon was gone now. His legacy thoroughly disgraced. But Three Rivers remained.

Words could not describe how much he hated the land of Three Rivers. He'd been raised there, after his clan had fallen. He and Kindean. He'd been too young to understand at the time, but they had been brought to the High King as political prisoners. Kindean had been older, fourteen to his nine. A gifted mage even as a child, Kindean had been placed with the King's Guard and swiftly found happiness in their ranks, appearing almost eager to forget their clan.

Killean, not especially gifted at anything at that age, had been placed in the care of the man who would go on to be crowned High King after the war, Torvin-the-Spark, arguably Three Rivers greatest battle mage.

He had not been Torvin's only ward. Nadil Shiny Scale had been with Torvin two years by the time Killean was dumped on his doorstep. Two orphans no one else wanted, one with a lineage that marked him as both victim and potential traitor and the other a boy with no acknowledged parentage, born with a power to shapeshift that had once been thought exclusive to the royal line and the Onryn. Nadil would go on to become the hero of Three Rivers, loved by one and all, while Killean would realise all Three Rivers private fears about him.

It had taken him years to realise putting him and Nadil together had been strategy not accident. Minuidon had hoped that by claiming the spoils of war, he could harness the dragonborn heritage that slumbered in both his and Nadil's blood. Which only proved his madness. The Onryn had never been happy vassals of any High King, and Killean was no better, and as for Nadil...well. He was a whole other kettle of fish.

But Minuidon had been desperate. His family line of Camry and the Striking Talon clan had both been dragonborn. An attribute that gave certain members of the bloodline the ability to shapeshift. The most remarkable of both families were able to shift into dragons and dominate the skies, but it was a rare ability and one that hadn't been seen in the Onryn for several generations before first his uncle Dadarro and then, much later, Killean himself, had turned scale. The royal Camry bloodline had bred for the scale more freely, at least until Minuidon's father and then Minuidon himself had been born with no magic at all.

Always equals in power and esteem, war between Onryn and Camry had ended in costly stalemate a century before, necessitating a permanent peace. Yet, when the ability to turn scale left the High King's bloodline the monarch started to fear the Striking Talon clan more than ever, especially when Dadarro proved he possessed the ability and the inclination to use it. Recognising that the balance of power had shifted in their favour, Dadarro pressed the clan to attack Three Rivers. The clan refused, and tired of war, they exiled Dadarro.

It did not save them. Dadarro's rabble raising had only legitimised Minuidon's fears. He orchestrated a massacre that could not easily be traced back to Three Rivers, but that everyone with any political acumen knew could only have occurred on his orders. Especially when Minuidon had swept in and claimed the youngest and weakest members of the bloodline as his "honoured" guests along with young orphan Nadil, who even to this day, no one publicly acknowledged as Minuidon's bastard-born son.

Nowadays that was because no one in Three Rivers wished to remember the disgraced former king, but in the beginning, it had been because no one would dare suggest Minuidon was anything but unfailingly devoted to his sickly and barren queen.

Minuidon no doubt thought he'd arranged things very nicely for himself in the beginning. Kindean was happily loyal and Killean and Nadil were well-managed by Torvin. But Killean was never able to accept that his family's killers remained at large. Frustrated that no one in Three Rivers appeared interested in pursuing justice, or the strategically vital fact that mercenaries strong enough to wipe out a powerful magical clan remained free to do it again, Killean abandoned Three Rivers at age fourteen, determined to find them himself.

Which made him not entirely unlike his current tagalong. A fact Killean was fiercely ignoring. At least *he'd* had the sense to find adequate training before rushing off to his doom. Say what one will about Dadarro, his uncle had given him all the education in power and rebellion he could ever want.

'Are we going to walk all night?' Ash whined.

Killean set his gaze on the almost invisible bumpy black line of the horizon. 'No one is forcing you to come,' he reminded the boy.

'Go home. Give up on revenge for the nonce. The magic in your gauntlet will open the portal.'

'Would you?' Ash asked shrewdly.

'No,' Killean admitted. 'But I'm evil, remember?' And a failure. Let's not forget that.

Chapter Three

Dawn on the border was a pretty affair. The sky was watermelon pink traced with gold behind the shadowed humps of the hills that gave Potbelly its name. Goods carts trundled up the road laden with produce headed for market even at this early hour.

'I'm hungry,' said Ash, voice subdued with fatigue as his eyes tracked a cart laden with caged chickens.

Killean handed him a cloth wrapped package of oak cakes from his pack. 'Here. Be warned, I can't remember how long I've had these so they're probably stale.'

Ash shot him a look, taking the package warily. 'Are they poisoned?' he asked.

Killean fought a smile. 'If I wanted to kill you, I'd just eat you,' he said.

Ash's skin greyed and his eyes went wide. He shovelled the oak cake into his mouth and chewed around a grimace. Killean turned away and coughed into his fist. It was probably a testament to how well-earned it was that he enjoyed his terrible reputation and effects immensely. So long as he was willing to put up with the occasional armed mob or mercenary assassin, it proved incredibly useful for brow-beating annoying kids.

They found a mob later that day outside a run-down inn halfway up one of Potbelly's omnipresent hills. The heat had been rising throughout the day and the song of cicadas in the trees and long grasses skirting the winding road had swiftly become close to maddening.

By the time Killean and Ash had reached the ramshackle inn they were both sticky with sweat, the humidity making the air feel as viscous as water. Dust clung to Ash's bare legs under his knee-length, dull green robe and Killean's sinuses were clogged with road dust and the riotous scent of Camillia and rotting cherries fallen from the trees.

The mob had gathered in the coachyard in front of the dark roofed inn Killean had been hoping to stop at. With its lop-sided, black tiled sloping roof and air of shadiness it was the kind of place where random mobs were commonplace. When a buggy disgorged a group of travellers, they hurried inside quickly, barely sparing the mob a second glance.

The mob were all culled from yokel stock. Wood cutters, trappers, fur traders and poachers, with a few brave farmers who had climbed the hill to wet their whistles at the inn. Ages ranged from sixteen to sixty, the men were all lean, rangy and strong from hard work. But not a one of them was a trained fighter.

Which was probably why several lay on the ground, groaning and cradling broken limbs. Killean smelled the tang of blood on the air. Whoever it was the mob had cornered, they were too much for these peasants to handle. The stumbling collapse of one man, flung backward out of the circle by a powerful blow, revealed their quarry. Killean nearly choked on his tongue. *Oh, no.*

The woman was tall and stunning. Sunlight glinted off the dulled scales of her chest plate and the vicious edge of the spear she held across her body. She wore a short, voluminous red skirt under her armour. Her long legs were encased in thick leather boots, scaled with iron. The gauntlets on her hands were leather and knuckled with spikes. She wore no helmet and her riotous black hair was braided tightly to her head, taming it. Her brown skin was luminous, flawless under the sun, her beautiful face was scrunched in anger, but even rage couldn't hide the fact that her features had been carved by a loving god. She wore a protective armoured neck plate covering her throat and her lips were skinned back from her teeth in a silent sneer.

Conveniently hidden under the shade of a cherry tree across the dusty road, misery gripped Killean. He harboured few hopes, but one he had clung to was that he would never have to see this woman again. He'd heard that heartbreak felt like having your heart ripped from your chest, and while Killean had always found romantics tiresome, he was definitely experiencing chest pains now.

A large man, half-a-head taller than the woman, whose shoulders strained against his dull brown shirt, began to circle. The man looked like he could fell a tree with a hug. The fingers of his meaty right hand flexed in the air as if he could barely wait to grapple. He was ruddy with good health and moved well on his feet. He had a makeshift cosh — no doubt with a good-sized rock inside the sackcloth— in his left hand. He feinted right, swinging overarm with the cosh. The woman ducked to the side and swept low with her spear, cutting his legs out from under him. The man landed with a pained grunt and a hard thump.

Wielding the spear like an extension of her body, the woman moved in for the kill, slamming the spear tip down toward his neck, two-handed. One of the man's friends threw a rock at her head. He had excellent aim. The palm-sized rock hit her left temple. Eyes rolling back, her knees crumpled and she collapsed to the ground. She was mobbed instantly, disappearing from view as the men closed in.

Ash surged forward. Killean hauled him back with a grip on his cape. 'We have to help her,' Ash insisted angrily. 'Did you see that armour? She's a soldier of Green Peaks and she needs our help.'

There were a lot of things Killean could have said. For a start he could have pointed out that he was evil and a criminal and therefore not honour bound to help anyone. He might also have asked Ash what he thought a noble soldier of Green Peaks was doing brawling with drunkards in middle-of-nowhere Potbelly. But all that took time and he was tired. So, what he said was, 'Sammia, Child of Death, doesn't need our help.'

Ash stopped straining forward. He turned very large eyes on Killean. 'Did you say Child of Death?' he asked, making sure to emphasise the capitalisation. As well he should. Any man who dared speak of Sammia, should do so with respect.

In the coachyard the thicket of men exploded outward in a shower of bodies as Sammia popped to her feet, blood drying down the side of her face. Her nose was bleeding and one eye was swollen shut. She was still beautiful. Inflicting violence had always been a good look on her. Sweeping up her spear Sammia whirled it in a controlled arc through the air, slashing open the bellies of two men. She smiled through the blood staining her face and stepped on the groin of one of the men on the floor with her booted foot. The man gasped, flailing like an upended beetle.

Sammia smiled wider, musing, 'Which one of you should I castrate first?'

Killean looked around. The branches of a blossoming persimmon tree hung over the road, creating a canopy of shade that would allow them to slip passed. Snagging Ash's sleeve, he towed the boy along, quickening his pace. If they could just make it past the inn, he'd be fine. Sammia would be too busy emasculating the men at her feet to notice him.

'Wait. Aren't we stopping? I thought we were stopping,' Ash whined. 'You said we could get something to drink here.'

Killean was ready to clout the brat into next week when a husky female voice stopped him dead. 'Killean Onryn, is that you?'

He groaned silently and briefly considered taking wing, abandoning Ash, and escaping into the clear blue sky, but it was too late. Even if he ran, it would do no good. Plus, he didn't want to gain a reputation for cowardice along with everything else. He turned around slowly and greeted her with a stiff bow. 'Sammia.'

She stepped on the man on the ground, walking over him like a carpet. Smile spreading wide as a yawning tiger she purred, 'It *is* you. The goddess of the Starless Night blesses me this day.'

Killean was glad She blessed one of them, because it was obvious the dread goddess hated him. Considering the life he'd led and the laws he'd broken, there were few things Killean truly regretted, but his last parting with Sammia came close to topping that list.

Squaring his shoulders, he stepped out from the shadow of the overhanging persimmon, noting that Ash did not. In fact, the boy shuffled further into the gloom under the tree as Sammia approached. Evidently, he thought he knew the Child of Death by reputation. He was wrong. Sammia was greater than her legend.

One of the men on the ground had discovered his second wind. Flexing like a leaping salmon from a prone position on his back, he lunged forward and plunged a stubby-looking knife into Sammia's flank, finding the sweet spot where her armour parted. Sammia hissed through her teeth, snatched the man by his hair, wrenched the knife out of her side and sheathed it in her attacker's right eye all in one smooth motion. The man sank to the ground, stone dead. The whole thing took mere seconds.

Sammia glared at the blood slicking her palm and hissed, low and venomous, before kicking the dead man in the head. 'You clod. This was my favourite shirt.' The under shirt in question was rapidly turning crimson with her blood. It didn't faze her.

It did faze the mob's survivors. The men scattered like the cherry-scented breeze, many taking refuge in the inn. Killean wondered what the fight had been about and whether it had been worth four men's lives. But not enough to ask.

There was a dangerous glitter to Sammia's narrowed eyes when she looked across at him. He stared back, flatly. 'Well met, General,' she said, voice low.

'Not a general,' he replied. 'Not anymore.'

Continuing to ignore the wound in her side, she leaned casually against her spear and asked, 'Should I pity you?'

No, she should go and leave him be before things got even more awkward. 'I'm just passing through,' he said. 'Don't let me keep you.'

Sammia grinned at him. 'Nice try, but I'm not done with you. You may not be my General anymore, but we still have unfinished business.'

Oh, he knew. That was the problem. Starless Night, but he'd missed her. The realisation hit him like a rock to the temple. It did not make him happy. Very little about his past did. Sammia had been a terror on the battlefield, worth the weight of twenty ordinary men. She had always been his equal, even if he outranked her in his uncle's army, and over time, they'd become lovers.

Along with his two other lieutenants, Bodai of the Killing Breeze and Juri-the-Cursed, the four of them had performed many covert operations, becoming known to their enemies as the Dread Four. Some of his happiest times had been when the four of them, far inside enemy lines, scraped through their missions by the skin of their teeth. But remembering those times forced him to remember that they were well and truly over now.

Sammia had been captured in battle in Three Rivers territory toward the end of the war. She'd escaped on her own with no help from him and gone on to abandon the war effort. After his own defeat and imprisonment, he'd heard that she'd found work with mercenaries on the southern coast. He had never tried to seek her out. He'd told himself there was no point. He had nothing to offer her anymore. As excuses went, it masked his shame well enough.

'What are you doing here, Sammia?' he asked tiredly. Potbelly was surrounded on three sides by Three Rivers. It was hardly the safest place for a woman with her reputation. The only reason to come here was as a provocation – or to find someone.

Absently poking at the wound in her side, a distracted frown on her face, Sammia said, 'I could ask the same of you. Last I heard you were hiding out in the Lotus swamps.' She wrinkled her nose. 'Lotus is a crap hole. I knew the rumours couldn't be true.'

The rumours were true, as it happens. He'd spent seven blissful weeks immediately after his pardon shifted into the form of a cormorant working with the fishermen in Lotus' wetlands. He'd enjoyed it. The fishermen had worked with birds to fish for generations and, penniless and universally reviled, Killean had managed to keep himself fed on his share of the fish he helped catch without anyone recognising him. Hiding in feathers had given him a chance to adapt to the world after five years imprisonment in a nearly timeless void. There was little to be gained in telling Sammia that, however.

'I know that look,' she said shrewdly, extending her spear playfully as if pointing a finger at him. 'What are you up to now, Killean-the-Swift?'

He really did hate that name. 'I'm headed for Cockle Shore,' he told her, lips twitching up in expectation.

She didn't disappoint him. Throwing back her head, she brayed with laughter. Killean noted that blood from her wound had soaked into her skirt, darkening the scarlet material into a true crimson. It didn't bother her in the least, but then Sammia, Child of Death, had earned her name honestly. It was about the only thing she ever had earned honestly.

There were many rumours as to how Sammia had gained her resistance to pain and miraculous ability to heal any wound. The most well-known was that she was the illicit child of the goddess of the Starless Night and a mortal man, granting her immunity from death. Sammia was particularly attached to that story and proliferated it happily. It was only to him that she'd admitted she had no idea where her power came from. She'd simply been born a freak.

'You always did like to live dangerously,' she told him echoing Mamie Cat's words from earlier. Her eyes glittered with wicked glee. 'Going to pay that brother of yours a visit?'

Killean's good humour plummeted. 'Not if I can help it,' he said. 'I'm meeting Mamie Cat.'

As he'd thought she would, Sammia scowled. 'What does the flea-bitten old bag want with you this time?'

'That's my business.'

Sammia's scowl deepened. She'd never liked being left out of the loop. It amazed him that after all this time, things could still feel so normal between them. 'Are you holding out on me?' she asked.

'You're not my vassal anymore,' he reminded her, wondering why he was trying to provoke her. The last time he'd called her his vassal she'd threatened to castrate him and meant it.

Now she said, 'Don't tell me you've replaced me with that little stripling.' Peering around him at Ash, she studied the boy critically. 'I didn't think you were into boy-flesh, Killean. Prison must have changed you.' Cocking her hip, she paid no mind to the fresh wash of blood spreading over her skirt. 'Whatever that kid's got going for him, I can do you better. I know you can't have forgotten our time together already.' Sultry was a look that should not have worked with blood drying on her face and staining her clothes, but then again, Killean was a freak too. It worked very well.

'The boy isn't your concern,' he said, gruffly, clearing his throat.

'Perhaps I'm making it my concern.' She sashayed into his arms, as much as she could with her spear in hand.

Killean held her at arm's length by the shoulders. Wouldn't help much with that spear of hers poised, but she didn't want to kill him.

Not today. If she did, he'd be in a lot of trouble. 'Try and steal my wallet and it will be the last thing you do,' he warned her mildly.

Sammia puckered her lips in an obviously false pout. 'Well, if you're going to act like that, I'll go,' she sulked. He didn't believe her for an instant. Everything about this accidental meeting was suspect. If it wasn't for the fact that she truly hated Mamie, he'd think she and the Cat had arranged for her to cross his path.

Ash blurted out, 'Is it true? Are you really immortal?'

Sammia cocked her head and put her hand to her ear in exaggerated fashion. 'Are those the dulcet tones of home I hear?' she asked. Swaying toward Ash she planted the base of her spear into the ground at his feet, kicking up a few pebbles and making him flinch. 'Do you know what I do to lost little Peak boys I find wandering the hills?' she asked sweetly.

'Don't,' Killean warned but it was too late.

Ash balled his fists, his gauntleted arm igniting in green flame. 'I'm not afraid of accursed traitors like you,' he said.

Sammia stared at his arm, eyes wide. A huge and gleeful grin spread over her lovely face. 'Oh, my. Oh me,' she chortled. She looked at Killean and asked, 'Is that what I think it is?'

Killean grabbed Ash's shoulder and pulled him out of reach. He blocked Sammia's view of the boy, braising his backside against the boy's fire. 'I've been paid one hundred thousand in Carp roe to kill some pirates. I'll give you ten percent for your help and your silence.'

Sammia's smile was almost bigger than her face. Pulling her spear in she leaned into his left side and whispered, 'I know what that gauntlet is. When you take what you need from the boy, give him to me and you can keep your money.' Her free hand snaked under his open coat, fingers tickling the bare flesh of his side.

He pulled her hand away. 'Ten percent is my final offer,' he said. The days when they traded in favours for favours were over. If she wouldn't take money they'd have to fight. It would a fair fight. For all her inability to die, Sammia wasn't any stronger than a normal, well-trained warrior woman, and he could turn into a bear if he wanted.

She looked at him sharply. Intelligence glinting in her gimlet eyes as she threw off the act she'd been pulling. He knew she heard the threat he wasn't making. He didn't know what she saw in his face but whatever it was she drew away with a secretive smile. Grasping her spear in both hands she held it in front of her and thrust the end into the ground. 'As my General commands.' She tapped her forehead to the long spear's shaft, in mocking salute.

'This is outrageous,' Ash exclaimed. 'Did you bring us here on purpose to collect your monstrous whore?'

Faster than thought, Sammia slammed the blunt end of her spear into his stomach. Ash toppled flat on his back in the dirt, more than just his vitriol punched out of him. He lay there gasping and wheezing for air. Sammia nudged him with her foot and he groaned. 'The moral indignation is cute, kid, but call me that again and I'll gut you like a trout.'

Killean reached down and hauled the boy to his feet roughly. He leaned down and reminded the boy, 'You can still run.'

Ash couldn't answer at first, too busy retching, but when that was done, he turned on Killean, cheeks mottled, eyes bright with pain and lips white with strain. 'I'm not going anywhere,' he insisted furiously. 'I'm going to be the mage that brings down two of the Dread Four. My name will be revered forever.'

Killean sighed. He'd tried. 'Be that as it may, insult Sammia again and I'll make sure she leaves you for the birds after she guts you.'

Ambition was well and good, but rudeness was never acceptable. He reminded himself that he'd been like Ash not so long ago – he was only a decade his senior – he knew well there would no telling him. He'd have to learn the price of his ambition on his own, and

THE LIFE AND TIMES OF THE TRAITOR KILLEAN ONRYN

when he did Killean would remind him that he'd warned him all the same.

Chapter Four

They found a fruit seller in a river valley and gorged on fat wedges of fresh watermelon and late season cherries while soaking their feet in the river. A highly decorated wooden bridge spanned the water. The bridge was carved like the back of a round fish and painted silvery-grey. The support posts had ornate fins. Carved fish heads decorated the pillars on each bank of the river.

An offertory box with a backboard painted with shiny silver fish had been placed beside the small shrine next to the road. Someone had left a pile of cooked and skewered sweet fish stacked on a plate in front of the shrine and the afternoon flies swarmed so thick they looked like a tiny hovering rain cloud. What a waste. Who in their right mind would think an offering of charred and impaled fish would please a water deity? He hoped whoever had left the offering had been cursed good and true.

Sammia nudged him and murmured, 'Brings back memories, doesn't it?'

Killean grunted and spat a cherry pit into the river. The water was not very deep, no more than waist high, but the current was fast moving. The water was crystal clear. Killean could see the rocky river bottom and the darting silver fish flowing downstream with the current. He noticed that the rocks were clean. No trace of ash or scorching. He wondered how long it had taken to refill the riverbed after he'd scorched it dry.

The drooping branches of a weeping willow on the opposite bank dangled into the water, only some of its branches still burned bare, and tiny leaf boats braved the rapids, spinning and tumbling on top of the fast-moving water. It was an idyllic scene, so different from the last time he had come here.

'Not sure about the new paint job,' Sammia continued, studying the bridge. 'I think I liked it better before.'

Killean said nothing, leaning forward to wash his hands in the deliciously cold river. He watched the fish. He'd never dared transform into a fish before. His uncle and his brother had told him more than once that aquatic forms were the hardest to shift into and he'd always feared he would drown if he did, but the thought of shedding his skin for smooth scale and slipping under the water was a tempting one. Blasphemous as well. Fish were sacred among the Great Nations of Magic.

Beyond the line of willows on the opposite bank, set back from the road, was a temple dedicated to Sakmon the Great Salmon. Or maybe it was still a ruin? The last time Killean was here he'd ordered the temple sacked and burned and the bridge destroyed. He'd dammed the river further upstream and used magic to set fire to the riverbed. He'd had his reasons. Intelligence had told him that the priests had been harbouring the Golden Firefly, a powerful relic his uncle Dadarro wanted badly enough that he'd risked their conquest of Three Rivers to divert a portion of their forces to Potbelly.

The Firefly was one of three sacred relics created by the Great Mage, Myron, the father of all dragonshifters, a skilled maker of magical objects and ancestor to both the Onryn and Camry bloodlines. He was revered among the mainland nations almost as much as Sakmon and his relics had been closely guarded by the Salmon Priests for centuries. Or at least that was the rumour. Another rumour said that any of Myron's descendants who could acquire all three relics would ascend to godhood. Which should make Dadarro's interest in them clear.

His uncle had ordered Killean to reclaim the relic by any means necessary. He'd taken the Dread Three with him to negotiate with the Salmon High Priest for a bloodless handover, stationing his battalion of two thousand men in front of the capital, the irritatingly named Pork Cutlet City — Killean had absolutely no respect for a nation that would name its capital after food — alas, the chief Salmon had proved obstinate.

The man rallied the locals to his defence, arming them and the small body of temple guardsmen with whatever he could find. His militia had been ill-trained, ill-equipped, and undisciplined and Killean and his lieutenants had resisted their ambush attempts easily, routing their resistance and sending the Potbellies running home.

Still, the High Priest had succeeded in annoying him and that was never a good idea. Resistance he understood. Defiance was to be expected. Honouring one's duty was admirable. But if the priest was determined to stand firm against the Dread Four and an army of two thousand, he should apply good strategy. Instead, he'd sent ill-equipped civilians off to their would-be deaths with nothing between their ears but religious rhetoric. If there was one thing guaranteed to irritate Killean, it was wilful incompetence. Priests should meditate, engage in landscape gardening, indulge extreme fad dieting and leave war to the experts.

To avoid the needless deaths of more hapless civilians, Killean had destroyed the bridge and choked off the sacred river to give the locals something else to worry about than answering the High Priest's call. His battalion dug in outside Pork Cutlet would keep the capital from sending reinforcements. In a stroke of bizarre luck that really couldn't have been less useful to his cause, it turned out Pork Cutlet's garrison had not heard the holy pescatarian call to arms, and the town had surrendered thirty-two hours into a siege that mostly involved his troops digging a few earthworks and parading outside the city gates.

It was ironic that the conquest of Pork Cutlet should be declared one of his greatest military conquests, considering he'd never wanted the city in the first place and seizing Pork Cutlet had not in fact made acquiring the Firefly any easier.

So, it could be said he wasn't in the best of moods when he'd entered the temple precincts almost seven years ago, the riverbed still burning merrily a short distance away. The High Priest further annoyed him when he ignored every one of Killean's polite requests to negotiate and barricaded himself behind the massive, spelled-doors of the main temple building, leaving his young acolytes —a group of boys between the ages of ten and seventeen — to face the Dread Four alone.

Killean had spared the boys and ordered Bodai and Juri to rip the centuries old temple complex apart, piece by piece, until the High Priest was delivered to him. To the priests' credit they'd lasted a whole hour before giving themselves up.

By which time the choking smoke from the riverbank had filled the sacred grounds and a tornado of destruction had torn the copper tiles from the rooftops, bringing several roofs down entirely. The great prayer bell was in pieces, there were holes in the walls and the jade statue of a leaping salmon that had held pride of place in the courtyard was in two pieces, one of which had been hurled through the spelled doors to smash them open. And to think, all of this destruction could have been avoided with a simple conversation.

Killean had been reluctant to kill the High Priest outright. Not on personal or moral grounds. The man was a coward and a nuisance. Killean very much wanted to have him salt baked for all the trouble he'd caused. His concerns were strategic. His uncle's campaign was still gathering momentum and while support was growing, alliances with their allies were tenuous. This was mostly due to the difficulty arising from his uncle's increasing lunacy. Dadarro did not care much for the logistics or technicalities of war, which meant it became Killean's job to think practically.

Killean had been thinking practically that day in the temple. He'd mostly been thinking about the exorbitant cost of holding Pork Cutlet, and by extension, the rest of the country. Going around killing beloved clerics on a whim was bound to rile the locals. Locals who might otherwise tend their farms and send their cured meat products to his army if he showed a modicum of mercy.

While neither he nor his uncle cared much for Sakmon, the Great Salmon was a very popular holy fish among the lesser kings who supported the war against Three Rivers; petty lords and wealthy city merchants in Frolicking Squirrel, the Cow Lands and Past Tiger who might look poorly on sacrilege without just cause.

These were the sorts of considerations his uncle viewed as beneath him, and so it fell to the then eighteen-year-old, Killean to think about them for him. Of course, at eighteen he'd had a temper, and for all his careful thought, he was rarely able to act the part. Which, honestly, was the reason for all the fires. Still. He really had tried.

He'd held Bodai back from summoning a hurricane strong enough to reduce the temple to toothpicks and kept Juri's murderous rage to a gentle, manageable simmer as Sammia herded the priests of the temple out to meet him in the shattered precinct. The High Priest, a shrivelled peanut of a man named Geppi, should have been grateful for Killean's restraint. Instead, the man had suffered from an inflated sense of his own importance.

Whether he truly believed the spirit of the sacred salmon would dive down from the heavens to save him, or he'd just been fatally unaware that Pork Cutlet's garrison had already turned coat, it was impossible to tell. He might simply have been a raging idiot. Whatever the case, he proved to be an infuriating one.

At first, he and his terrified attendants had insisted the Golden Firefly was not on the grounds. Then, when Killean pointed out he had excellent intelligence that said otherwise, gleaned from sources who had seen the thing wheeled out in a reliquary box on holy days, Geppi and his people had changed their tune. They did have the Firefly but they would not tell a blasphemous renegade like him where it was.

Idiots. The lot of them.

Killean had never claimed to have a tremendous amount of patience, and while he could appreciate the importance of diplomacy better than his uncle, this did not mean he was gifted in the art form. Looking at Geppi in his shimmering pink robes, decorated with silver-leaf fish and embroidered with expensive seed pearls at the sleeves and hem, his bald pate shiny with sweat, Killean had turned and nodded wordlessly to Bodai.

His lieutenant, anaemically pale, his fine white hair whipping around his head in a perpetual magical breeze that rippled over his purple-black storm cloud robes, had raised one negligent hand and summoned a great gust of wind. The gust had picked up a hail of dust and debris from the destruction all around and flung it at the shivering priests.

Broken tiles are sharp. The flaying breeze swept Geppi off his feet, blasting him backward before driving him along the littered ground with enough force to tear through his robes to the flesh beneath. Killean ambled toward the downed priest, who looked a bit dazed as he flopped on the ground. Dazed *and* shredded.

He'd smiled and asked, 'Can I have my Firefly now?'

Geppi was a proud man. Proud and very stupid. 'I am a servant of Sakmon. I will never break,' he declared, thrusting his chin out like a cranky turtle.

Killean hunkered down in front him. 'Yes, you will,' he said pleasantly. 'And when you are broken, I will move on to the next in your order and do to him what I will first do to you. And then the man after that, and the next after him until I reach the last man. He will tell me what I want to know, while the rest of you broken priests watch on, powerless to stop him.'

Geppi had boggled at him. 'You are a fiend.'

'No. I'm on a deadline,' he retorted. 'Believe it or not I have better things to do than fillet stubborn salmon. Give me the Firefly and keep your skin.' There. That was a reasonable request, wasn't it? These men had to realise they'd lost. Why be stubborn about it?

'I don't have it,' Geppi had told him, voice loud and proud, as if he was declaring holy truths. 'I swear by Sakmon and the Knowledge of All Things, the relic we have is a fake. The real Firefly is a myth. It doesn't exist.'

Uncle Dadarro would not be happy to hear that. Killean glanced back at Bodai. Bodai was only half-human. His father had been a minor deity of air and storms who had passed through a portal from the Timeless Realm to cause mischief and enjoy a little time in the flesh. No one who had met Bodai would ever call the Killing Breeze wise, nor his father for that matter, all the same, air spirits had a knack for telling truth from lies and Bodai was excellent at sniffing out bullshit.

'Well?' he asked.

Bodai gave him a pointy smile. Not a pointed one. He just had a lot of very sharp teeth. 'He's lying,' he said, his nasal voice a smug whine. His pale eyes fixed on the battered Geppi hungrily. 'Points for effort, but I can hear his thoughts screaming on the air. What he has isn't a fake. At least, he doesn't believe it is.'

Gasps rang out among the lesser priests in their pale robes, the colour of orange salmon roe. This was clearly news to them. Killean wondered if they'd been sold the same lie. Sammia smacked one of them around the head. 'Got something to say, fish bait?'

'N...no.'

'Then shut your mouth before you lose your tongue.'

Killean weighed his options. The prospect of failure rankled. His uncle was an obsessive man with a weakening grip on sanity. He would not be pleased if Killean returned empty-handed. Killean was not afraid of his uncle's moods. He was used to them by now and his uncle wasn't so far gone that he failed to realise he needed Killean. If he killed him, he'd land himself with more work to do. Still, he did fear that his uncle's tantrums could throw them off schedule. What's more, if Dadarro decided to take his anger out on Potbelly Hills, he might lose them the war and the chance to topple Minuidon.

Choices, choices. Killean turned slowly, taking in the precinct. The temple complex was built in a quadrangle design. The main temple building, housing a massive salmon statue was positioned to the north, directly opposite the gates. There was a smaller shrine building to the east and the priests' dwelling to the west, with a guard house built into the wall near the gate. Now, if he was hiding a relic, where would he put it? He narrowed his eyes. The Dread Four's earlier efforts had caved in the main doors of the statue building and brought some of the roof down, exposing the top half of the giant salmon statue's ugly mug.

'Bodai, Juri, see if you can smash that statue,' he ordered.

At seven and-a-half feet tall, Juri was a giant among men. He was also madder than Dadarro. Twitching with nervous energy, Juri had taken up his usual pose, lurking near a broken pillar across the precinct, almost hidden from view. His strong arms were wrapped around himself and his fingers plucked nervously at the sleeves of his short red robe. His brown hair hung limply over his eyes.

In his calmer moments, Juri tended to look sad and lost, despite his height and obvious strength, but his calm moments never tended to last long. When he wasn't homicidal, he was anxious. The only time he wasn't anxious was the rare fifteen minutes he managed to sleep. He and Bodai were both Accursed, but while Bodai was mostly a curse inflicted on others, Juri lived up to his name.

Shuffling forward on huge, bare feet, he looked deeply reluctant. 'Smash?' he whispered. Head down, shoulders hunched and spine bowed, his chin angled toward his chest, he looked up at Killean woebegone.

'Yes, smash,' Killean repeated firmly.

A change crept over Juri. One side of his mouth jumped, twitching into a sickly, lop-sided smile. 'Smash,' he repeated, voice a little firmer. And then again, with relish, '*Smash*.' He rocked on his heels, an unhinged grin spreading over his face like a rash. 'Smashy-smash. Smashy-mashy-dashy-lashy-kashi —'

'Starless Night,' Sammia groaned. 'Shut him up already.'

'Yuri,' Killean snapped, cutting him off. Sad Juri could drain the vitality from a group outing faster than a bout of cholera but at least they were spared his manic babbling. It was vital for the sanity of all to shut him up before he really got going.

The smile vanished from Juri's face. 'Sorry, sorry,' he mumbled. 'Didn't mean to get carried away. Didn't mean it. No, no, I didn't.'

'The statue, Juri,' Killean reminded him tiredly.

Juri was light on his feet for such a big and awkward man. He scuttled across the courtyard, much to the horror of the watching priests, and set about clearing the door in no time. Even Bodai would struggle to brush aside the wreckage faster.

Killean could just make out the five-foot-high marble statue base in the gloom. The statue itself was closer to thirteen feet high, carved from pink marble. The statue had been shaped as though it was leaping up a waterfall, powerful body frozen in stone. Clear gemstones gave the salmon a slightly mad-eyed look, as if this version of Sakmon was aware of His precarious position, caught forever between rising and falling, and didn't much like it.

THE LIFE AND TIMES OF THE TRAITOR KILLEAN ONRYN

Leaving Sammia to watch the priests, Killean followed Bodai over to the door for a better look. The top relief of the black marble base was elaborately carved with a curving wave pattern, picked out by a tracery of gold leaf. Killean had been to temples to the Great Salmon in other lands. They tended toward reflective pools and discrete waterfalls hidden behind careful landscaping. This statue looked vulgar in comparison.

His uncle's intelligence, gleaned from mystics and eccentric academics, said that the Firefly had been forged to contain a spark of the eternal flame, the essence of fire. It was said that when wielded by Myron's spiritual successor the Firefly could produce a flame that no force on land or sea could put out. Eyeing the base of the statue, Killean wondered if there was some significance to the fact that there wasn't a drop of real water in this temple.

'Juri,' he said. 'Smash the base. Bodai, keep the fish from falling and crushing him.'

'Bossy,' Bodai muttered, under his breath.

'Just do it,' Killean snapped, turning and walking back across the precinct.

Geppi was upright and standing among his priests. All of them gaped at him like landed fish, choking on air. 'You can't do this,' Geppi cried, outraged. 'Have you no shame? No fear? Are you truly as corrupted as they say?'

'Probably,' Killean admitted, tossing him a look. 'Who are these people and what do they say about me?'

Geppi's throat throbbed as he swallowed. 'That you sold your soul to your uncle for power. That you are consumed with unjust vengeance. That you have forsworn all who love you to wage your unholy war on Three Rivers.'

Killean nodded solemnly. 'All true,' he said flatly. 'Even the parts that are clearly ridiculous. But tell me, is this Three Rivers nonsense, or are others spreading rumours behind my back?'

Geppi pressed his thin lips together. 'It is spoken all over. Even in Past Tiger they say you are as brutal as lightning and just as fickle.'

Killean cocked his head thoughtfully. 'I'm not fickle.' Still, he liked the part about the lightning. When he sent spies out to tell exaggerated stories to scare the peasantry in enemy lands, he'd be sure to insist they include that line.

'By Sakmon's scales, what is he doing?' shrieked one of the more hysterical priests.

Killean looked over his shoulder, already knowing what he'd see. Juri's bloodline was cursed. Long ago one of his ancestors, a warrior of some renown, had passed a sacred shrine dedicated to a long-since forgotten deity of the mountain without leaving an offering. The deity, viewing him as an uncivilised and brutish man, had cursed the warrior and his progeny with the attributes of tremendous physical strength and the unthinking rage of a demon. A curse that had passed down the male line long after the deity had faded from the world, ensuring that there was no way for the curse to be lifted.

Juri was still standing in the ruined doorway. Activating his curse, he began to shake violently. His limbs spasmed, his head jerking back and forth on the thick stalk of his neck. The muscles of his back and shoulders writhed like snakes under his skin. A deep red hue bloomed to life over his skin, as if he'd been broiled all over. His hair grew shaggy and wild, rising around his head in a wild mane.

Killean knew that his jaw would broaden and distend, his nose widening and flattening into his face and the snub horns, usually hidden by his hair, would grow in size, erupting from his brow in lethal points, even if he couldn't see it happen. Unleashing a bloodcurdling howl, Juri threw back his head and beat his chest with his massive fists. Even at a distance and with his back to them, it was an impressive sight.

'Abomination,' Geppi hissed. 'Accursed creature.' He fluttered his hand in a simulated wave, the gesture meant to wash away evil before it could spread to the priest. Sammia laughed at him.

Rushing forward, Juri threw himself through the broken doorway and set about smashing the statue with great enthusiasm. Bodai lingered limply just outside. Killean shouted, 'Get in there and help him.'

The sprite pivoted around to glare at him, his feet floating off the ground. 'Too much effort,' he complained, not needing to raise his voice as the air carried his words to Killean's ears effortlessly. 'Besides, Juri likes to work up a sweat when he's like this.'

Killean didn't bother to shout this time. 'Do it, or I'll set you on fire.' Holding up one hand, he ignited the tips of his fingers in cheery orange flame.

Fire liked air, but air did not like fire quite so much. Bodai eyed his fingers warily and gave in. 'Fine. But I don't see why you asked Juri to transform if you're going to make me do all the work anyway.'

'Because you two come as a pair,' Killean reminded him. It was what Bodai had told him when he'd travelled to the Icicle Lands to recruit him. Bodai and Juri had been roaming the frozen valleys robbing goods caravans and terrorising travellers since their schooldays, had either of them ever gone to school, and every bloody tale he'd heard about the pair said they were inseparable, sharing a bond few wished to understand.

All the same, at first, Killean had thought Bodai made the boast because he assumed Killean would refuse to quarter a half-mad, demon-cursed maniac with his soldiers. He had gravely underestimated Killean. He immediately saw the value in a half-mad, demon-cursed maniac on the front lines and jumped at the chance to have them both, essentially trapping Bodai into the role of Juri's keeper.

Bodai might whine, but Killean had never known him to shirk in his duty to the other Accursed. Juri was more than likely the only thing between here and heaven Bodai actually cared about. Working together, it didn't take Juri and Bodai long to fell the salmon.

Clouds of thick dust rushed the ruined doorway and the sounds of shattered masonry and cracking wood beams wailed through the precinct. As did the priests, who took the desecration of the statue about as well as the average soldier handled a field amputation. Through the weeping and wailing, he heard Bodai alert him to a curious find.

Pushing through the thick dust, he stepped around the shattered pieces of the statue and peered into the depression left by the statue base. The base must have had a hollow built into the mould, because there was now a wholly intact palm-sized orb quietly glowing amid the wreckage.

'Huh,' said Bodai at his shoulder. 'I expected the Golden Firefly to look like a real bug.'

'Me too,' Killean admitted.

The mythical relic was neither made of gold, nor did it look anything like an insect. But there was no doubt what it was. The relic radiated power when Killean scooped it out of the dust. The orb was perfectly round and smooth, but when he touched it, it didn't feel like glass or stone. It was faintly warm, as if a globule of magical flame had been sealed inside a bubble of frozen time. The pulse of heat buried under its surface called to the fire in Killean's soul.

He smiled and dropped the relic into the satchel he wore. 'Good work,' he told the others. 'We've got what we came for. Let's go.'

'What about the priests?' Bodai asked.

Killean shrugged. 'I'm sure they'll have the sense to run before the precinct burns down around them,' he said, slipping his hand inside the satchel.

THE LIFE AND TIMES OF THE TRAITOR KILLEAN ONRYN

Uncle Dadarro would appreciate him taking the time to field test the relic, he decided, and if not, then at least he'd have the pleasure of watching the temple burn before he faced censure.

Chapter Five

They spent the night in a climber's hut on top of one of Potbelly's many hills. Sammia spit-roasted the trio of rabbit Killean caught in his wolf form and they ate the meat with the last of the oak cakes. Ash was quiet, drowsy from the long trek and disinclined to ask awkward questions, which was a small blessing. It had been more than strange retracing the path he'd walked with an army at his back years ago. Although thanks to his imprisonment it didn't feel that long.

No one had recognised them, even in the villages he remembered raiding. It was like they were cloaked in a spell of invisibility. The civilians they passed eyed Sammia's spear and armour warily, but no one sounded an alarm. Had he and Ash been travelling alone they would have gone completely unnoticed.

Was five years of peace in the region really enough to forget, Killean wondered. More probably, the civilians he passed failed to recognise him because no one expected a war criminal to stroll into their village in a ragged coat and frayed trousers covered in road dust and looking more like a beggar than a barbarian. Once, everyone had known his name, whispering it in terror. People had run from the sight of his emblem flying in the wind. Now they crossed the street to avoid the smell of his unwashed body.

It took some getting used to, and the result was a sense of distinct unease. He felt out-of-step with reality. His thoughts were lodged firmly in the past, back in times that felt simpler but never had been, his skin itching as he watched every civilian for the gleam of an assassin's knife or the moment when their gazes shifted from blank indifference to smouldering hate. He tensed in anticipation every time, not sure whether it was relief or disappointment he felt when each stranger passed him without incident.

'You're quiet,' Sammia nudged him, settle on the ground beside him as the small fire crackled, sending sparks up into the air.

The view from the naked hilltop was spectacular. The indigo sky striped with fading hints of gold from the sunset, the surrounding hills rising and falling away in the distance. The hill they were on was heavily covered in pines everywhere except the rocky peak and Killean could hear the boughs groan in the breeze that swirled the air this high up. An owl hooted and Killean scowled.

'I'm always quiet,' he said. He'd been known for many things in his day, his skill in conversation wasn't one of them.

'Hn.' Sammia tossed rabbit bones over her shoulder and reached out to poke the fire with her skewer. The flames jumped and hissed, reacting to the slick of animal fat coating the skewer. 'Tell me about these men we're killing,' she said.

'I don't know much. A group of elders from Jumping Carp want me to hunt down a defector on Shipwright Island. They claim he's being held by the Blue Crab. They want the defector and his captors killed.'

Sammia buried her skewer in the flames. 'Blue Crab own those waters. Attacking them could spark a war.'

Killean nodded. 'I'm guessing that's what Mamie Cat wants. Or at least, whoever is hiring her to meddle in Fish affairs,' he added thoughtfully.

'What's Jumping Carp's angle?' Sammia asked sitting back so that the line of their bodies touched shoulder to hip. 'Dragging you into their mess is a lot of risk for one defector.'

Killean smirked humourlessly. 'I don't know. I was told it wasn't my concern.'

Sammia snorted. 'They're going to try and kill you when this is done.'

Killean's smile bloomed wider. 'I know.'

Sammia rested her head on his shoulder, cuddling around his arm. 'What about the kid?' she asked. 'What's he want with you?'

'I killed his father.' Killean told her about Ashinue Rogu senior.

Sammia snorted and sat up. 'The kid's having you on,' she said. 'I know the Dancing Deer clan and they're not soldiers. Igo Kethi runs the Pink Rabbit Circus in Jade City. His clan are all thieves, fire eaters and acrobats.'

Across the fire, Ash slept curled on his side under a rough blanket Killean had dug out from his pack. He slept like a child, with his fist pressed to his mouth. The fire painted tiger orange stripes across his face, which was scowling even in sleep. 'Maybe he takes after his father,' Killean suggested. More confidently he asserted, 'The gauntlet he's wearing is not a fake.'

'No, it isn't.' Sammia agreed. 'Why don't you steal it from him?' she asked. 'It's the fire you're after. I know you lost yours. The gauntlet could make up for the loss.'

He hadn't lost his fire. Saying he lost it made it sound like he'd set his magic down somewhere and a thief had come by and stolen it. His fire was still a part of him. It was just locked away behind a curse he couldn't break on his own.

'The gauntlet's no use to me,' he said. Even if he had the gauntlet on his wrist, it would be nothing more than deadweight on the end of his arm. Torvin's curse was clever, like the man himself. The only way Killean could regain his magic was through the touch of his own magic. Outside of time travel, his chances of regaining his magic were almost non-existent. Almost.

He could feel Sammia's eyes on him. She knew he wasn't telling her everything. 'Take the gauntlet from the kid anyway,' she insisted. 'It'll command a good price on the market. I've never known you to pick up strays unless you wanted something from them. And this kid is obviously useless.'

'Leave the boy and his gauntlet alone, Sami.' Killean tilted his head back and leaned against the weathered stone at his back, ignoring her attempts to fish for information. The problem was, she knew him. If anyone could figure out his plan, it was her.

He sighed. Behind him, the dilapidated climber's rest hut created a wind break, the night breeze whispering noisily around it. The owl hooted again in the distance. Killean hunched his shoulders, drawing his head up.

'If the owl is bothering you take wing and kill it,' Sammia mocked softly. 'Unless you think it's your brother? We are near the border with Barley Lands.' Killean glared at her. She smirked. 'You can't hide from me, Killean Onryn. I know you too well. And I will figure out what you want with the boy,' she warned.

'Think what you like,' Killean told her turning away to look out at the night beyond the drop off. The fire popped, dancing in the wind. The damn owl hooted again.

Unlike him, his brother Kindean could only shift into the form of man or owl. He'd favoured the form of a large white owl for as long as Killean could remember. There were few such owls native to the southern regions meaning that if Kindean was here, Killean couldn't fail to spot him. There was no reason for his brother to be here, however. News of Killean's approach could not have gotten ahead of him, assuming his brother tracked his movements in the first place. Which he probably did. They were enemies after all.

After the war, one of Torvin's first acts as High King had been to grant Kindean stewardship of the Barley Lands, their clan's ancestral home, in gratitude for his loyalty. The fact that granting Kindean the land Killean had fought a bloody war to liberate would infuriate him was no doubt an added bonus.

Or maybe not. Torvin had granted Kindean a great deal of freedom to run the lands as he saw fit, stopping just short of abdicating Three Rivers claim on the territory. It was a surprising political move for the victor to make, seeing as Three Rivers had won a resounding victory against Killean, his uncle and the rest of Three Rivers' many enemies.

Killean toyed with the idea that in his own way giving the land back to Kindean was Torvin's way of making amends for what the previous High King had done, but the thought made him uncomfortable. It was easier to think of his former caretaker as nothing more than an enemy. The figurehead of the nation he despised, not the man who had cared for him almost like a father.

There was another reason to give the land back to Kindean. Three Rivers might wish to use his brother as a stalking horse, setting him up to be the target of Killean's rage. If the two brothers killed each other battling over the Barley Lands then the last of the Onryn bloodline would finally be expunged from the world, an outcome Killean was sure many in Three Rivers would celebrate. He couldn't even blame them. There was a time when he'd wanted nothing more than to wipe out every last trace of the Camry line. Sadly, for him, the last scion of that bloodline happened to be fiendishly difficult to kill and terminally optimistic, Nadil Shiny Scale.

'There's no fate, Ilin. Only choices. And I gotta say, your choices really aren't the best right now,' Nadil had told him once, shouting across the battlelines on the verge of battle, stupidly determined to talk it out when any sane person would know the time for talk was long past.

It had been one of their last encounters before things had well and truly slid out of control and the war had descended into magical carnage neither side wanted. His army of five thousand had faced off against a rump of three thousand Three Rivers' men cut off from the main battle along the banks of the Uswe River. They had faced each other on fertile arable lands not far from Cockle Shore. The air had been spiced with the heady scent of gunpowder and alive with the rippling of dozens of banners.

Killean had mounted cavalry at his back. Pikemen in front of him and men with cannon higher up the rise. His soldiers were well drilled and better equipped than the enemy. They had superior numbers and the advantage of holding the higher ground. Killean had ordered his men to bombard the enemy and had already routed their left flank when Nadil appeared from nowhere. He'd been in his dragon form and from a distance he looked like one of the enemy's streaming banners, his shimmering serpentine body twisting in the gunpowder clouds high above.

Nadil had spat white hot jets of fire down from the clouds and destroyed some of his cannon, but Killean's soldiers were not easily frightened. They were guerrilla fighters from the rainforests of Past Tiger, the vassals of petty lords from Cow evicted from their lands by the Three Rivers High King, and they were Accursed, who had dangerous power all their own. Some were handsomely paid mercenaries from Squirrel, who knew it would damage their reputation to turn tail and run from a dragon. They were the flotsam and jetsam of the magical kingdoms, the freaks and cursed children of liaisons with fallen deities or the by-product of failed spells. Hunted by some and shunned by all, Killean gave them purpose and an outlet for their rage. When they saw a dragon they jeered for his blood.

Nadil's white dragon was soon chased from the sky by storm bringers and mages and a torrent of abuse for the bastard-heir to a bloodline that had caused irreparable pain to many. Killean could have ordered a frontal charge straight at the enemy line while the Three Rivers forces had watched on in dismay as their talismanic hero was forced to retreat. He didn't. He was never able to find a satisfactory reason as to why.

Instead, he let Nadil reclaim his human form and agreed to meet him in the no-man's-man between their opposing armies — to *talk*. A fact that disgusted him to this day.

Blond hair flattered to his head by the helmet he stupidly took off immediately, Nadil had beamed at him as if they were long lost friends meeting by chance on a peaceful street corner. His cornflower blue eyes were wide and annoyingly earnest. 'That's a colourful bunch of people you got there,' he said cheerfully, nodding to Killean's waiting army. 'I think I saw an ogre. He hit me with a boulder.'

'She,' Killean corrected him absently, his voice muffled by the mouthpiece of his helmet moulded to resemble the snarling jaws of a wolf. The upper piece of his helmet hung low over his eyes, shaped like the beak of a hawk. The chimeric effect was supposed to instil fear in his enemies, but the stupid helmet was torture to wear. Sweat trailed down his cheeks to dribble out of the hole drilled under the chin piece of his armour. He wanted to finish this and get back to the battle.

The only reason he was indulging this nonsense – at least the only sane reason he was willing to admit to – was that his orders had been to keep the rump from joining Three Rivers forces fighting his uncle further downstream. Parley did that as effectively as a bombardment and allowed his troops time to tend the injured and bring forward more supplies while he humoured Nadil's idiocy. That his was his excuse, anyway. The truth was, he was probably the only person in his army who didn't want to kill Nadil.

Nadil sighed deeply as he looked at him and Killean had taken the time to study his old childhood friend in turn. He was barely armoured, dressed in spelled leathers for ease of movement and a cloak that had once been white but was now smeared with the dirt of battle. Yet somehow, he still gave off the impression of being incredibly shiny. Killean imagined shifting right there and biting his head off. It was a nice thought, except for the part where he knew he'd never go through with it.

'Are we really going to fight?' Nadil asked him, a hint of whine in his voice.

'Yes,' Killean hissed. 'This is war. That's what happens in war.'

'It's stupid,' Nadil had argued. 'Killing people isn't going to bring your family back.'

Killean growled in his throat. 'Is this the part where I'm supposed to act contrite and give up?' he asked irritably. 'Moralising at me isn't going to work. This is war. We're enemies. Go back to your people and prepare for battle.'

Nadil shook his head frustratedly. 'It doesn't have to be this way. We're working on forcing Minuidon to abdicate. Everything will be better once he's gone,' he added brightly.

Killean shut his eyes. 'Are you high?' he demanded. 'Did that boulder hit you? Why would you tell me that?'

He'd always known Nadil subscribed to a logic all his own, but he hadn't believed his old friend was a *complete* idiot until now. If what he said was true and Three Rivers was in open revolt against its High King that only made his side's chance of success all the greater. This information was too important to be handed out so freely.

Nadil had merely shrugged. 'I figured you have spies in the capital already,' he said blithely. 'But in case you didn't, I wanted you to know we're not all like Minuidon. He admitted what he did,' he added quietly. 'The Onryn aren't the only clan he's destroyed.'

'I know. I recruited most of the other survivors,' Killean replied drily. 'Minuidon should have done his own dirty work. That way there'd be fewer witnesses.'

'You know he's crazier than a cat in a bathtub, right?' Nadil squinted at him. 'Your uncle as well. They both want to use Myron's relics to destroy the world.'

Killean had not known the High King had an interest in the relics. His uncle's insanity, on the other hand, was hardly news. 'Uncle Dadarro only wants to be a god,' he said.

Nadil cocked his head giving him a flat look. 'And you don't think that might be a bad idea?' he asked incredulously. 'Your uncle's hinges are looser than ol' Itogan's garden gate. Do you really think giving him more power is a solid plan?'

Killean sighed. 'Please stop talking in metaphor. You're really bad at it.'

Distantly, carried by the wind, he could hear the sounds of battle raging miles away. Turning his head, he looked out over the golden fields. He could see black belching smoke rising above the horizon and realised Cockle Shore was burning. Damn it. Those new walls he had built better be holding. 'There are many gods,' he said flippantly, hiding his annoyance. 'What harm could one more do?'

'Weren't you listening?' Nadil snapped. 'He could destroy the world.' Propping his gauntleted fists on his hips, Nadil struck an unconsciously stubborn pose and claimed, 'I don't believe you've sunk so far that you want the whole world to burn. This isn't you. You were always...well, a bit intense,' he admitted wincingly, 'and you could hold a grudge like your life depended on it. Which,' he added quickly, 'I realise it kinda did. But you still knew right from wrong. You had honour. Restraint.' Nadil's blue eyes were very solemn when he asked, 'What happened to you, Ilin?'

'I grew up,' Killean snapped, turning on his heel and striding back toward his troops. Or clanking back. Seriously, if Nadil was going to fight in leathers he might as well strip this damn plate off. He couldn't breathe like this.

THE LIFE AND TIMES OF THE TRAITOR KILLEAN ONRYN

He had no fear that Nadil would stab him in the back. He'd broken the parley before his temper snapped and he burned off Nadil's stupid face. He felt his ex-friend's eyes on him the entire way back to his line. His silent judgement struck deeper than Sami's spear thrusts. He ordered another bombardment as soon as he reached his men and soon Nadil was lost amid the explosions as the two armies met.

Killean's forces won that day, taking many valuable prisoners, but Nadil got away, taking wing and escaping toward the battle at the river bend. It was only later that Killean realised that Nadil's plan all along had been to distract and delay him so he could not make it to his uncle's side.

Because as it turned out, for all his uncle's considerable power, his arcane knowledge and his unshakable self-belief, Dadarro was not the tactician Killean was and he'd only narrowly avoided losing Cockle Shore to the enemy. The city had held because of the fortifications Killean had insisted on, while his uncle's army had taken massive casualties. And all of it was because of Nadil.

Eager to show himself the greater dragon, Dadarro had left the field to fight Nadil in the air. Without their general, Dadarro's army had floundered and lost ground allowing Three Rivers to push them back behind Cockle's walls. Had Killean been there he could have marshalled his uncle's forces.

He'd learned three valuable lessons that day. The first was that his uncle couldn't be trusted. The second was that his old friend was not, in fact, a complete idiot. But it was the third that kept him up at night. Swift on the heels of the realisation that Nadil had tricked him was the knowledge that the ploy had only worked because, deep down, Killean had wanted to be distracted from a battle to the death.

The owl hooted again and Killean blinked out of his light doze. Sammia was asleep with her head on his shoulder, her body curled into his, her spear stuck into the ground in front of her feet. Ash was tucked under the blanket on the other side of the smouldering remains of the fire. Killean looked up at the sky, watching the stars wheel above. There was a tension in the air, he decided, he felt it in his own muscles. His instincts screamed at him.

The distinct flap of wings drew his attention to the branches of one of the shaggy pines growing on the hillside. The uppermost branches formed a peak that poked over the top of the hill. A white owl blinked at him from the branches.

Killean swore, loudly. 'Oh, for fuck's sake. What the flying fuck are *you* doing here?'

Chapter Six

The owl burst from the tree and swooped toward the crest of the hill. Elegant to a fault, Kindean transformed before hitting the ground, appearing to step out of the air with the ease of a man descending a low stair. Clothing formed around him like coloured air condensing around his body, materialising as a long green cloak patterned with leaves and a knee-length white robe with a pattern of barley stalks hemming the bottom and the sleeves. His glossy dark hair was swept back from his brow and tied at the base of his neck.

Killean realised in dismay that their hair was now exactly the same length and vowed to get a haircut in Cockle Shore. Face lean and long and features even, Kindean looked every inch the aristocratic lord. Killean wanted to break every bone in his face. But that wasn't a new sensation. Their relationship had always put the homicidal into sibling rivalry.

'It is good to see you brother,' Kindean dropped him a shallow bow.

Ash was awake, struggling to unravel the blanket around his legs. Sammia stepped up beside him, her spear extended. 'Who told you I was here?' he demanded flexing his fingers around the hilts of the daggers in his hands.

'Mamie Cat,' Kindean replied. His thin lips twisted in a wry smile. 'I promised to pay her five thousand groat to tell me when you were near our borders.'

So that was several thousand the Silk Paw matriarch had made out of both of them. After Killean collected the rest of his money he was going to pluck the fat cat's whiskers. He expected treachery from the tricky woman but squealing on him to his brother was beyond the pall.

'I'm meeting Mamie in Cockle Shore on business. It has nothing to do with the Barley Lands or Three Rivers,' he told Kindean, sheathing his blades. He wasn't going to use them this night and he had better discipline than to stand around with naked blades.

Kindean watched him. His pensive expression gave nothing way. It was the expression he always wore. He looked curiously over at Ash, and then his gaze hardened when he looked at Sammia. His expression softened again when he met Killean's eyes and asked, 'If not war, then what business brings you back home, brother? You have shunned Barley since your release.'

A fact his turncoat brother should thank him for, but all he said was, 'I'm not a rat to run into the elders' trap. Three Rivers would love it if we killed each other.'

Kindean sighed deeply. It was the same sigh he'd used when they were children and Killean would change into a wolf pup and chase his heels as Kindean went out to the training grounds. 'Do you want to kill me, brother?' he asked softly.

'Now specifically, or in general?' he asked.

Kindean looked at him curiously. 'Would the answer change either way?'

'That depends on whether you're going to leave me alone,' Killean admitted. 'If you do, I'll return the favour.'

Kindean nodded again, as if Killean had said something profound. Another habit he remembered from childhood and found just as annoying now as he had then. Kindean might well be smarter than him. He was certainly the better magician, which was why any fight between them would be a fair one. Still as smart as Kindean was, he liked to pretend he was smarter still. He used silence and knowing pauses to imply he had all the answers. Killean eyed the tip of Sammia's spear and speculated on their chances of taking him down together, just for the hell of it.

'I don't like the company you keep, brother,' Kindean said reprovingly.

'I don't like you,' Killean shot back as, beside him, he heard Sammia mutter, 'Oh, no, he didn't.'

Kindean smiled, a tight flex of his lips. Killean didn't know why he bothered. He hadn't been joking. 'I want you to come home with me,' he said.

'And I want to level Delta City,' Killean retorted. 'I don't get what I want so you don't either.'

His brother blinked, a flash of relief loosening the set of his shoulders. 'Does this mean you've turned your back on revenge?' he asked hopefully.

Killean frowned at his brother. 'You're not listening to me at all, are you?' he accused. 'I just told me I'd like to crush the capital.'

'Yes, but you also implied you wouldn't,' Kindean said quickly. 'That's progress. Five years ago you very nearly did it.'

Killean pinched the bridge of his nose. 'Please go away,' he said sincerely. 'I don't want to deal with you right now.'

'If I waited until you felt like dealing with me —as you put it—I'd have to wait the rest of our lives,' Kindean snapped. 'We haven't talked since the battle of Shrimpton,' he added voice softening.

Killean scowled. Shrimpton had not been one of his success stories. 'We didn't talk then. We were trying to kill each other,' he reminded Kindean.

'You had to be stopped. Your dragon heritage had warped your mind. Encasing you in ice was the only way to get you to see reason.' Kindean waved a hand and both he and Sammia pulled back, but his brother wasn't casting a spell. He was gesticulating, another of his habits Killean found irritating.

'Since when has inducing homeostatic imbalance made anyone saner?' Killean asked disgustedly.

Kindean looked at him sharply. 'So you admit it? You recognise that you weren't in your right mind?'

'I admit that I wasn't at my best in Shrimpton,' Killean replied carefully.

Things had been going badly for a while at that point. His uncle had proved to be not merely insane but unmanageable and people like Nadil and his brother kept interfering with all Killean's plans to rescue the war effort from his uncle's egomania. This had resulted in him being generally impatient and perhaps a bit reckless in his response to setbacks. It had certainly resulted in him setting a lot more things on fire. Including most of Shrimpton. But whether that was a result of his brain being warped, or just a profound character flaw, he probably wasn't qualified to say. After all, weren't the mad usually the last to know it?

Beside him, Sammia snorted softly. He winced, remembering that Shrimpton had been where he'd lost her. Caught up in the wreckage of a building he'd – somewhat accidentally – brought down she'd been captured by Three Rivers forces.

'Are you at your best now, brother?' Kindean asked him pointedly. 'Look at you. You don't even have a shirt on.'

Killean looked down at his naked chest under his open coat. It was true he hadn't bothered to buy a new shirt after his last enchanted robes had been ruined beyond repair in a skirmish with Squirrel bounty hunters, but that said more about his finances —or lack thereof—than it did his sanity and moral equilibrium.

Sammia murmured, 'I like the rugged look. It makes you look very piratical, which will be useful later.'

'You're not helping,' Killean murmured back, though honestly, he did feel a bit better. He turned to his brother. 'I'm not going home with you, Kindean. Leave now before I show you how unbalanced I can be.'

To his surprise Kindean bowed again. 'Very well brother, I will see you in Cockle Shore.' Shifting form in an explosion of showy magic and a fall of white feathers, Kindean took wing and dropped below the hilltop.

Killean swore softly this time. Sammia chuckled. 'Shouldn't have told him where we were headed,' she said.

'He already knew,' Killean replied tiredly. 'At least if he's there the guards will leave us alone.'

'So, you planned this?' Sammia asked not hiding her scepticism.

'No. But I can use it to my advantage,' he admitted.

Sumie huffed quietly. 'Now there's a certain fact. I've never known you to let an advantage slip through your fingers.'

'It's been known to happen,' Killean said softly. 'I lost you.'

Sammia's defection might have been for the best, but it had still hurt. The war had been lost already even if he hadn't known it then, but he could admit it felt good to have her back at his side. Far more than he'd expected it could on that winding road where he'd tried to sneak away without her noticing him.

Sammia looked at him sharply, and even in the dark Killean's night attuned vision could see how her lips parted and her expression softened in surprise. He couldn't blame her. He couldn't remember the last time he'd complimented her either. Which was why he'd never blamed her for leaving. He should have known losing her loyalty was the beginning of the end. Instead, he'd charged toward defeat like a stampeding horse. Perhaps Kindean was right about him after all. He had needed to be stopped. Just not by *him*.

From the dead fireside Ash piped up. 'That was your brother? He seemed...almost decent. For an Onryn,' he added in a dark mutter that Killean heard just fine.

'I'm sure he'd appreciate the sentiment,' he replied drily. 'He's never much liked being an Onryn.'

His family seat had been well defended by ancient magic and strong walls. His clan had been capable. No group of outsiders, no matter how skilled, could have taken them all by surprise without inside help.

Kindean had betrayed his blood in favour of Three Rivers. He'd been tricked, or so he claimed. Minuidon had convinced him that the clan intended to align with Dadarro and start a bloody war that would kill thousands. Kindean thought he'd be acting the hero when he brought down the Onryn defences and convinced Killean to run off into the night with him, oblivious to what was happening inside the keep.

Kindean had confessed everything to Torvin during the war and the story had eventually reached Killean's ears – almost certainly on purpose – as an attempt to break his resolve, or perhaps, make him reconsider his own position as a tool to a man seeking war. The attempt had failed on both counts.

His brother had never stopped believing they were the same. Two boys manipulated by powerful men, but it had never been true. Killean hadn't been some naïve, wide-eyed kid with heroic dreams like Ash. He'd given Dadarro more credit for strategy than he should have, but he'd never deluded himself as to his uncle's character. Dadarro had been ruthless, deceptive and megalomaniacal. He'd also been powerful, charismatic and far better connected politically than Killean. Hitching his wagon to his uncle's mad horse had been his best chance of unseating Minuidon and getting his revenge on the complacent, self-righteous hypocrites in Delta City who had stood by and watched as Minuidon broke treaties, started proxy wars and had innocent people murdered across the lands with impunity.

Killean wasn't making excuses, his campaign had not been a bloodless one. Between him and the men and women who deserved it lay the unmarked graves of hundreds of innocent people killed in his war. He knew that. He'd known it when he took up his uncle's cause. To unseat a tyrant, you needed to be one. At least, he'd thought so at the time. Now, he found he'd lost his taste for tyranny and grand causes. He was sure there were people out there who could make it work, he just wasn't one of them.

Most of Three Rivers thought he hated his brother because of the massacre. They were wrong. He'd never blamed Kindean. His brother had thought he was acting the patriot. He'd thought he was protecting the lands from uncle Dadarro. He might even have believed Minuidon would show their parents mercy, if he helped him. All that Killean could forgive easily.

He could even forgive Kindean serving Minuidon in the aftermath. He was fourteen and a self-made orphan with a talentless little brother to protect – what choice did he have but to pretend the king was just and kind? He couldn't speak out against the tyrant who had made him complicit in the murder of their clan. Even if he'd been believed, he had no proof and no clan to support him. Minuidon had stitched him up, but good. If Kindean wanted to live, he needed to act the happy turncoat. And he had, masterfully.

That was the problem. What he could not forgive was Kindean's refusal to admit the truth. The act had become reality. He'd chosen his side and become a willing traitor to his blood. He and Killean had each picked a crazy horse in a two-tyrant race. Minuidon and Three Rivers on one side versus Dadarro and an uprising of freaks and malcontents on the other. There was no right and wrong. No moral dimension. Only a simple choice: whose side were you on? One side had a tyrant with a throne, the other had a wannabe with designs on godhood. There had been heroes and villains on both sides. Some were Minuidon's victims. Some Dadarro's. It disgusted Killean that Kindean kept pretending otherwise.

'Go back to sleep,' he told Ash. 'We break camp at a dawn.'

'Why didn't the two of you fight?' Ash asked, sounding aggrieved. 'I thought you were sworn enemies.'

'Sworn enemies?' Sammia scoffed. She shot him a sly look and asked, 'Did you pinky swear it?'

'Absolutely. And then we carved an oath in the trunk of a tree,' Killean replied, with a grave nod.

'You know what I mean,' Ash grumbled, embarrassed. 'Everyone says you hate your brother worse than anyone, but you don't act like it.'

'Sorry to disappoint you. I'll be sure to rant and rave next time we meet,' he promised. 'Now go to sleep. We've a long trek to reach Cockle Shore.'

'I thought you could turn into a dragon,' Ash complained. 'Can't you just fly us there?'

Sammia whistled. 'Now, you've done it, boy.'

Killean rolled his eyes at her. Did she think he was made of glass? It was hardly a secret he'd been stripped of the ability to turn scale. Not that it surprised him that Ash didn't know. This kid didn't know much.

'Nothing says I come in peace like a fifteen-foot dragon landing in the middle of the town square,' he told Ash mildly.

'Oh,' Ash was almost certainly blushing in the dark. He ducked his head and wriggled back under his cape, meaning he didn't see Killean's smirk. It was so easy to score points off this kid.

Sammia nudged him. 'I'll take watch. If I see anything with feathers, I'll skewer it,' she promised. Killean didn't argue. Fatigue dragged at him.

'Wake me when you get tired,' he told her settling down in the scratchy grass and pulling his coat tightly around him. Maybe when they reached Cockle Shore he'd find a tailor who catered to his kind. It would be nice to wear clothes that had more cloth than holes in them. Then again, Sammia *liked* the shirtless look. Maybe he'd keep it a little longer.

Dawn brought heavy cloud and frequent showers that did little to cut through the humidity. The parched roads soon became swampy with rain and all three of them were covered in mud by the time they crossed the border into the Barley Lands.

Flatter than Potbelly, the territory of Barley Lands had been coveted for its prized crops for centuries, ensuring its people were prosperous and plentiful. During their descent from the hilly border, Killean spotted several small towns scattered across the plains as well as a patchwork of fields, the barley crop just beginning to turn pale gold under the leaden sky. Shading his eyes, he squinted into the horizon where the land rose steeply into two harsh escarpments creating a narrow valley that the Uswe River cut through. Beyond the valley was Cockle Shore.

'But that's miles away,' Ash complained. 'I'm already soaked. Can't we stop at that village down there?' he pointed to the settlement, the thicket of chimneys pushing smoke up into the wet air.

'No one is making you travel with us,' Killean reminded him. 'If you want to stop in Malt-on-the-Valley you can.'

Ash shook his head, shedding droplets of water like a dog. 'I need to follow you and gather information,' he said.

'On what?' Sammia asked. 'You were at the meet with the Carp elders. You already know more about this job than I do,' she pointed out.

'That's exactly why I need more information. I look implicated,' he said putting particular stress on the last word.

Killean met Sammia's gaze and shrugged, hiding a smile. 'Oh dear,' Sammia sing-songed. *'Implicated.* Sounds painful. Maybe we should stop at Malt and see if they have an ointment for that.' She paused thoughtfully, 'Or an enema.'

Killean snorted. 'We'll go to Malt and see if the coach is running,' he said.

He was tired of travelling by foot. If it was just him and Sammia he'd shift and ride the currents, settle down on a rooftop and do a little recon of the town, before circling back. He didn't trust Sammia alone with Ash, however, and as he had plans for the kid, he'd need to keep him close. Mamie Cat had gone out of her way to ensure he wouldn't have the element of surprise on his side, so he might as well arrive in Cockle Shore in relative comfort.

He nodded to Ash, 'Go on ahead, kid. Make sure the coach is running. We'll be right behind.'

The boy scowled. 'You could run away when my back's turned,' he said.

'I could fly away with you looking right at me and you couldn't stop me,' he pointed out starkly. Then he sighed and promised, 'I won't run. I have an appointment to keep in Cockle Shore. Mamie Cat has my money.'

'That's true,' Ash said, brightening. 'Money is all you villains care about.'

Whereas Ash's motives were pure as sunshine. Not for the first time, Killean wondered if he'd overestimated the kid's age. He seemed very *young* to be running around accosting people with fireballs. Then again, he couldn't believe there were too many circus kids as naïve as Ash. He was an oddity. Killean wasn't all that interested in unravelling his story. He didn't care if the kid was a liar or just addle-pated. He was keeping him around for his own purposes and thankfully those didn't require Ash to be smart. The opposite in fact.

The boy took off down the slope road, sandalled feet slip-sliding through the mud.

Sammia lamented, 'Riding coach like a civilian. How the mighty have fallen.'

Killean wasn't sure if she was speaking for herself, him or both of them. It didn't much matter. 'Better than sloshing through the mud like beggars,' he replied.

'I miss my old charger,' she said. 'And our army. The travel never seemed so long when we had ten thousand men marching at our backs.'

'That's because we weren't doing the marching,' Killean pointed out. 'We did plenty of cross-country scouting missions when it was just the four of us,' he reminded her. 'You didn't complain then.'

'That's because Bodai did it for me. Starry Night, he could whine like no one's business.' She was quiet for a beat before asking, 'Do you think he and Yuri survived?'

'It's hard to kill the wind,' Killean said. 'And the god cursed don't die easy.' A fact Sammia knew better than he did.

'You never saw them, after you were captured?' she pressed.

He shook his head 'No. I don't even know for sure if they were captured after the final battle.'

'You never asked?'

'Who would I ask? I was put in a magical coma right after they slapped me in irons.'

'But I heard they gave you a trial,' Sammia objected.

He shot her an incredulous look. 'You don't really think Three Rivers wanted me *talking*, do you?' he asked her. 'There was a trial. I wasn't present. I was already in the Timeless Realm sleeping my life away.'

The last weeks of the war were a blur to him. An angry blur. He remembered the hunted, boxed-in feeling that had clawed at the back of his throat as everything started to fall apart. He'd been filled with a wild, restless energy, driving him on even though he could see it was futile.

He remembered the screaming fury curdling under his breastbone as it became more and more obvious there was no winning the war. Any victory he might cobble together, his uncle would surely squander before they could rebuild their forces. He remembered sleepless nights fighting despair, afraid that if he slept, he'd be haunted by his dead. The shame of disappointing them had eaten him up inside. Of course, his misery could have been his dragon heritage, slowly alchemising his blood into molten fire. Either way, he'd been distracted.

'Did you ever think to look for them?' Sammia demanded. He heard the unspoken question – *did you ever look for* me.

He sighed. 'It's been six months.' Six months back in the world after half-a-decade locked away. 'All I've had time to do is survive.'

'Five years in the Timeless Realm,' she mused thoughtfully. 'I expected to find you looking as fresh faced and youthful as you did then. But you've aged. Not much, but some. How is that?'

Killean's jaw clenched. He relaxed with effort. 'I wasn't always asleep. Don't,' he held up a hand when she started to speak. Less harshly he continued, 'I'm not going to talk about it. So don't ask me.'

He was never going to talk about the horror of waking up in the Timeless Realm, trapped in a place where the only thing that lived or moved was him. He'd existed in a half-way state, somewhere between alive and not. There was no hunger, no thirst in the realm without desire, but nor was there direction. He'd had nowhere to go because there was nowhere *to* go. Just a formless, colourless, unfinished landscape with nothing in it but him and the stone plinth his sleeping body had been laid out on like some kind of dead offering to an absentee god.

He didn't remember how his torment had ended. He couldn't have escaped, which meant someone from the real world had come looking for him and put him back under the sleeping curse. He had feeling it had happened more than once, because Sammia was right. His body had matured in the years he'd been locked away, which meant he had to have wandered far enough to find marooned islands of progressing time in the Timeless Realm. He just couldn't remember doing any of it.

What might he have achieved in that realm had he retained his wits? Time only moved in the Timeless Realm when in close proximity to portals connecting to the Temporal Realm. Killean was left to wonder bitterly how many times he'd come within touching distance of escaping his prison before someone or something had put him under once more.

The speculation fed his suspicion that Torvin High King hadn't pardoned and released him out of some misguided spirit of altruism, but because he knew he didn't possess the power to keep him imprisoned forever. Which was interesting, because to the best of his knowledge no mortal had ever had the power to escape the Timeless Realm on his own. Only demi-gods and the spirit born could do that. Last time he checked, Killean was neither.

Chapter Seven

'I haven't been able to find either of them,' Sammia said, dragging his attention back to the present. 'I can't imagine either one of them without the other. Those two are a pair. Juri couldn't function without Bodai.'

'And Bodai wouldn't want to live without Juri,' Killean agreed softly. The sprite would refute him fiercely if he was here, but the truth was undeniable. Without Juri, Bodai had no reason to resist the call of the wind and simply float away.

'Who knows, maybe they'll find us,' Sammia said with forced cheer. 'It'll be nice to be the Dread Four again. Solo gigs are hard to come by. Everyone in the Magic nations is a chauvinist,' she added darkly.

Killean side-eyed her. 'There is no Dread Four. This is only one job. Don't get ideas.'

Sammia smirked. 'Now who's being soft-headed,' she mocked him softly. 'After we're done with the Blue Crab no one is going to believe you're not back in the rebellion business.'

'There is no rebellion business,' Killean objected but she did have a point.

Killean fully expected that Obawai and his consortium would be betray him at some point, if he gave them the chance. Jumping Carp's most influential mage elders would make irritating enemies. Disappearing them would result in a political incident. Jumping

Carp might call it an act of war. That was to be avoided, considering he was down an army of his own at present.

The Blue Crab were also a problem. Assuming he managed to gut their leadership and steal their prize, the Crabs were not the only crime syndicate operating in the Fish Archipelago. The other sea lords would come after him if only to uphold the fearsome reputation of pirates everywhere.

Suddenly, Killean had powerful enemies on all sides. He could refuse to fulfil the job for Carp, break ties with Mamie and hide out in some landlocked country on the mainland. He was good at hiding. He could manage for a while.

Eventually boredom would drive him out of hiding and then he'd have to deal with his problems. Even if Obawai let the matter drop, he'd have the Silk Paw to pacify. He didn't relish taking up arms against Mamie Cat.

Killean could see the outlines of the nasty little trap being built around him, but he didn't see a way to back out gracefully. He was already in it; the blades simply hadn't come down on him yet. The only way out was through. He'd have to hope that when his enemies showed their full hand, he'd have picked up a few aces of his own. He'd been lucky before; it could happen again. And if not? Then he'd take down as many of the bastards as he could on his way to hell.

He shot an oblique look Sammia's way. Ash was just ahead of them, prancing from one foot to the other on Malt's cobble-stoned main street, but Killean ignored him for the moment. He was more interested in Sammia.

Was she the first of his aces, as she had been during their war, or the first blade aimed at his back? She'd already admitted she'd expected to see him again. An admission he was sure she'd regret if she realised. He hadn't decided what to make of that slip up. It could mean nothing, or it could mean everything.

'What are you plotting?' Sammia asked him suspiciously, catching his look.

'Nothing,' he said looking away and thinking, *what are you plotting?*

She snorted. 'As if I'd believe that. You can play the defeated all you want, but I know you. The war didn't break you. And you *are* planning something. The boy is part of it.'

The boy *was* the plan. Sammia was grossly overestimating him if she believed he had some devious masterplan to restart their lost war. Still, it was gratifying that she could look at him as he was now and think he had a plan at all. He kept his mouth shut to build his mystique. If he said too much, he might reveal how little he was really working with.

'Come on,' Ash said impatiently when they reached the idling coach. 'You walk so slowly. What were you talking about?' he added, returning to his default suspicion.

'World conquest,' Killean drawled as he dug in his pack for his meagre funds.

The coach driver didn't want to take them. A long-haired beggar in rags, a woman with a spear and an excitable boy doing a poor job of hiding the magical gauntlet weighing down his arm.

Eventually Killean was forced to give the driver an ultimatum. 'Take us to Cockle Shore and get paid. *Or* we thrash you soundly on the street, steal your coach and leave your body for the gulls to fight over.' He spread his arms, knives drawn, as Sammia leaned on her spear and grinned wolfishly at the driver. 'This isn't a difficult decision,' he told the man. 'Income or evisceration. Make up your mind.'

Barleymen were made of stern stuff. The driver scowled at him, grumbling, 'You pay double. And if you nick the upholstery with that thing,' he pointed to Sammia's spear, 'I'm reporting you to the Cockle guard.'

THE LIFE AND TIMES OF THE TRAITOR KILLEAN ONRYN

Killean loved his countrymen. This was the kind of man he wanted in his army. If he still had one. He agreed to the man's terms and the three of them piled inside the coach. 'You know he just ripped us off,' Sammia murmured. 'He hasn't had a fare all day and now he gets double rate to take us to Cockle Shore. He's laughing at us.'

'Let him laugh,' Killean said, leaning back into what was, actually, very nice upholstery. 'Barley's economy was hit hard in the war,' he added with a shrug, 'And I'm about to come into serious money anyway.'

Ash had been suspiciously quiet during their altercation with the driver and he'd immediately curled up on the seat opposite Killean and Sammia, promptly falling asleep. Whether that was due to adrenaline crash or an epic sulk, Killean neither knew nor cared. He propped his chin on his fist, elbow leaning on the door as he watched grey-washed greenery slip past him.

Sammia fussed with her spear, arranging it so that the sharp end stuck out of the opposite window, the shaft stretching over the floor and getting in the way of both their feet.

She'd absolutely refused to lash it down on the luggage wrack. Killean knew for a fact that she had a terror of letting the damn thing out of her sight for more than a minute at a time. The habit was so noticeable that a rumour had spread among their enemies during the war that the spear was the source of Sammia's power. They'd caught more than a few assassins by using her spear as bait.

The driver's savvy aside, he'd expected to feel more of a sense of homecoming as he watched the Barley Lands roll on around him. Perhaps the lack was because this part of the territory had never really been home to him. His clan's ancestral seat was miles to the west.

Killean could still see Dragon's Ascent in his mind's eye, a square keep hewn from the gleaming white stone of the cliff itself, standing proud and aloof, like a thumb in the sky's eye. A wide flat lake below the rough cliff used to spread like a perfect mirror glass, reflecting back to the sky a picture itself. Mists had draped the lake at dusk and the angry high summer sun had turned the water into molten gold. The nearby towns and villages had all used the thick, mysterious evergreen forests as camouflage so that successive invaders and spies had a hard time believing anyone lived there at all.

Life had been harsher in the west than it was here in the east, where the bounteous fields that gave the land its name, ensured the living was easy. It didn't surprise him that Kindean had chosen these rich pickings as his homebase. The landscape was apiece with his personality.

Of course, there was a more pragmatic reason Kindean had chosen Cockle Shore as the site of his new protectorate. Dragon's Ascent, the escarpment it perched on, the lake and the forests of home were all gone now. Most of the landscape was a barren crater, as magic scarred as the Nameless Plain. Which somewhat put a crimp on any nostalgia for home.

Killean did feel a stirring of something, like a quick hit of adrenaline, as the coach rumbled through the narrow pass and Cockle Shore came into view. He sat up straighter on the bench, dropping his fist and leaning forward to peer through the window. The largest town in Barley, Cockle Shore had grown since he'd last seen it, which was surprising and pleasing to see.

Rising from the pebbled shore of the Uswe, the town walls were hewn from austere and imposing grey stone. Industrial chimneys rose above the walls and a spill of squat, wooden buildings had grown up outside along the cart road, all jammed together into the shadow of the walls' protection.

Despite their obvious newness, the buildings were cheerfully painted, their awnings daubed with colourful paint and carved with frills as if cut out by a cookie cutter. The higher floors tended to overhang the foundations and boxy, decidedly unsafe, wooden balconies cluttered the skyline above street level, casting the cart road in shade. People and live-stock clogged the road and if it wasn't for the Three Rivers' banner festooned to the city walls, Killean would have been very happy to see Cockle Shore looking so prosperous.

They were stopped at the gate upon entering. A guard in Three Rivers colours peered into the carriage through the window. He frowned when he spotted Sammia's spear, but it was only when he spotted Killean that he blanched like a sickly almond. Killean leaned further back into the upholstery and quirked a brow. Sammia gave the guard a little wave.

'You're...*him*,' the guard stammered. His eyes were wide and round.

'I am,' Killean agreed. There was an outside chance the guard thought he was some other infamous war criminal with a history of terrible deeds longer than Sammia's spear, but for the sake of his ego, Killean decided that the guard knew exactly who he was.

The guard swallowed audibly. 'His lordship says you are to be allowed in,' he said not sounding happy about it. 'I am to escort you to the Rhubarb and Duckling.'

Killean cocked his head. Either the Rhubarb and Duckling was a public house or his day was about to take a strange turn. 'How nice of Kindean to arrange a guide for us,' he drawled reaching for the handle of his door and pushing it open, incidentally knocking the guard back a step. On the other side of the carriage, he heard Sammia and Ash scramble out.

'You can't take that in with you,' the guard announced, voice shading with alarm as Sammia came around behind the carriage with her spear in hand. The guard's hand went to his sword belt. 'I have orders to confiscate all your weapons,' he said.

Killean exchanged an incredulous look with Sammia. He turned back to the guard. 'No, you don't.'

Grabbing two fistfuls of the guard's scaled breastplate Killean spun him and slammed him into the side of the carriage, startling the horses and making the structure shake. He leaned into the man's space and breathed into his ear, 'I can rip out your throat with my teeth before you can draw your sword. Do you really think taking my blades makes a difference?'

The heady aroma of fear rolled off the guard. Killean was aware of several of other guards emerging from the gatehouse to converge on them. Sammia whistled sharply, letting him know there were archers on the wall.

Killean drew back just enough to look the guard in the eyes. He smiled. 'We keep our weapons and enter peacefully. You try and take them from us and you and your friends will die. My brother knows this, which means he told you to let us pass unmolested. What do you think he'll do when he learns you went against his orders?'

'We will not allow you to harm a living soul, Killean of the Eternal Flame,' said one of the guards at his back. Killean looked behind him, curiously. No one had ever given him that sobriquet before.

'The *what* flame?' he asked.

'Honey,' Sammia purred, cocking her hip toward the guard provocatively, 'You couldn't stop him if you had a thousand men guarding this gate.'

That might be overselling it a bit. Killean was not a dragon anymore. Releasing the guard he stepped forward, eyeing the men arrayed around them. Three of them had pikes as long as Sammia's spear. One appeared to have a flintlock rifle. Killean held out his hands. 'I didn't come here to harm anyone,' he told them truthfully. 'But I'm adaptable. The real question is, are you?'

The guard who had called him Eternal Flame shifted his stance. 'I don't trust you, traitor,' he sneered most of his face obscured by his helmet and owl-shaped faceplate.

Now that was just rude. 'I'm no traitor to true Barleymen,' he said quietly. Most of the populace had risen with him in the war. True, his subsequent failure might have soured them a bit. Still, Cockle Shore owed a lot of its defences to Killean's preparations during the war. They could try and be a bit grateful.

He strolled forward, stopping just in front of the man. 'If I can't be trusted, Riverman, then why did your High King release me?'

'It is not my place to question my High King,' the man said but he sounded unsure. Killean didn't blame him. 'Why did you call me Killean of the Eternal Flame?' he asked, curiously.

The guard stiffened, his reaction so pronounced Killean reassessed his view of the man as a senior guard. 'I fought at the battle of Very Large Rock,' the man said, real heat in his voice. 'I saw what you did.'

'You saw nothing if you can't tell the difference between me and my uncle,' he snapped. 'I was never at Very Large Rock.'

Either the man was lying, or he'd picked up on Killean's mysterious new title and misattributed it, because Dadarro had never successfully managed to wield the Firefly's power. That had been the problem. Myron's relic had rejected Dadarro. Had it been otherwise, they would surely have won the war and his uncle would be god-king now.

Shoving passed the guard he walked toward the gate, his coat flaring out behind him. Two more guards shuffled hesitantly forward to block his path, lacing their pikes together. 'Don't,' he warned them softly. 'Just don't. This is not the day to play misguided hero.'

The guards exchanged a worried glance and then lifted their pikes. The men were torn between their instinct to strike him down and their orders to let him in. Duty could be a real pain in the arse.

The desire to acquiesce to a single authority warring with the will of the individual.

Killean understood. If he'd been a little more dutiful and a little less self-determined he might have made different choices toward the end of the war, like admitting to his uncle that *he could* wield the Firefly. Of course, doing so would have been a death sentence. Dadarro had tried to snatch out Nadil's still beating heart because he'd believed Nadil had the power and Killean didn't delude himself that family loyalty meant more to Dadarro than it had to him.

He addressed the soldiers. 'I appreciate your dilemma gentlemen. I wouldn't want a war criminal like me walking freely through the streets if I were you. But that's nepotism. Even scum like me get to take advantage. If it makes you feel better, I'm only here to meet the wanted criminal you already let in.'

It was a foregone conclusion that the gates would open for him. The guards had their orders and their moral outrage clearly weren't strong enough to fight over. Killean supposed there was a chance he'd pay for humiliating the guards, but frankly this was so low down the list of his sins he wasn't worried. He could only die once, and the line of contenders waiting for the honour was a long one. These guards didn't stand a chance.

Sammia and Ash moved to join him as the great gates creaked open. Sammia was laughing softly at his back but it was Ash he checked on. The boy could easily have shifted the balance of the encounter had he sided with the guards at the gate. But he'd done nothing and now walked through the walled gateway with a distinct hunch to his shoulders and his gauntleted fist, hidden by his cloak, was tucked protectively against his chest.

Killean hid a smile. Poor kid. He'd learn the hard way that inner conflict was a sure path to failure. Ash's problem was he didn't know what he wanted. He'd had ample opportunity to make another attempt on Killean's life and he'd acted on none of them. True, his chances of success were basically nil, but if he was committed to revenge he'd try anyway.

The boy wanted adventure. He'd likely convinced himself he was on a grand quest battling dragons and black and white evil that would result in him being proclaimed a hero. He thought he had control. He thought the gauntlet gave him leverage to turn the tide when it suited him. He was wrong on both counts. To the world he was nothing and to Green Peaks he was a thief, which in someways was worse than nothing. Travelling with two of the Dread Four wasn't going to help his case either, but if the kid hadn't worked that out yet, Killean wasn't going to tell him.

'This place reminds me of home,' Ash murmured softly as they prowled through the open market just beyond the gate. The smell of cow and horse dung hung in the damp air along with the more pleasant aromas of fresh baked bread and the silty ripeness of freshly caught fish. Killean breathed in the taste of burning coal, smiling as it stuck in his throat. The drizzle continued to fall like a cobwebby mist that turned the smoke from the open cooking fires cottony white and glazed the rooftiles dark.

Cockle Shore was a crowded hodgepodge of narrow streets and mismatched buildings all squeezed into the girdle of the city walls. The white plaster and dark cedar of older buildings looked flimsy in comparison to the kiln fire baked brick of the newer structures pressed close to the walls. The dark green roof tiles unified the buildings, along with the crossed barley stem emblems embossed on the eaves.

Rain chains glittered with droplets of water in the dank light and sturdy shutters covered the windows. Colourful cloth awnings flapped from the covered porches of seafood eateries and stores selling goods such as cast-iron pots and fine quality knife-ware. The factory district by the wharfs was part of the new town, outside the old town walls.

Killean had ordered construction on the wall and water defences that now defended the town's dirty, industrial heart. The urge to go and take a look was strong, but he resisted. If everything was as he remembered it, it would at best be bittersweet, but if Kindean had ruined what he'd made then he'd rather not know.

He did stop in his tracks, his breath catching sharply in his throat, when he spotted the Onryn emblem – a black dragon on a green background – flying from a flagpole outside the town hall alongside the trio of wavy lines that formed the emblem of the Three Rivers.

Sammia poked him gently with the tip of her spear. 'There it is,' she said nodding her head toward a sprawling inn, its roof sagging with crawling begonias, 'The Rhubarb and Duckling.'

Killean glanced at Ash. The boy had not left his side, even though they'd passed within sight of several guard boxes and the town's administrative offices. 'If you come in with us, you'll be implicated in whatever comes next,' he told the boy patiently. 'Now would be a good time to report us.'

The boy startled. He'd been looking around at their surroundings with wide-eyed fascination. 'But I want to know why those old guys hired you,' he blurted.

Killean met Sammia's eyes over the boy's head. She arched her brows, lips twitching in suppressed amusement. 'Circus boy,' she mouthed.

Killean suppressed a sigh. 'Follow us inside and you become part of this job,' he said. 'There is no going back. I will expect you to pull your weight and do what I tell you, when I tell you. Is that understood?'

Ash baulked as Killean had known he would. 'I don't work for you.'

'Then leave,' he said. 'Because if you follow us inside and try and stop me from completing this job, I will kill you. And it won't be quick like your father,' he added meeting Ash's eyes head on.

Those eyes widened with fear even as his face flushed with rage. 'You said you didn't remember,' he bit out, a whisper of smoke rising from the neck of his cloak, along with the sudden scent of burning. Killean wondered if he'd self-combust right on the street.

'I don't,' he said, smiling cruelly. 'That's why I know he died quick. Had I made it slow, I'd remember him.' He eyed the boy. 'By the way. Your clothes are on fire.'

Ash yelped as he reacted to the green flames that burst to life over his cloak, spilling down the cloth like emerald water. Killean left him on the muddy street, hopping from foot-to-foot as he tried to beat out the flames. They wouldn't hurt him. The gauntlet was spelled to ensure its wielder was immune to the fire it produced even if the magic wasn't the wielder's by birthright.

'You knew that would happen. You threatened him on purpose,' Sammia murmured as they mounted the steps and stepped under the covered portico toward the curtained entrance. 'If I didn't know better,' she mocked, 'I'd say you want that kid to get away.'

'The boy is nothing to me,' he grumbled. So what if he was stoking the flames of the boy's hate? It was all in the name of his plan. He scanned the bar looking for Mamie. They had not set a time to meet but Killean knew Mamie. She'd have paid spies to watch the gate and inform her the instant he arrived.

The taproom was a large, poorly lit space resembling a murky wooden box. The walls, floor and long bar at the back of the room were all built from the same type of wood. As were the long bench tables scattered around the room. The ceiling was low and fogged with pipe smoke. The floor was sticky with spilled beer. The room smelled like woodsmoke from the fire, wet clothes and meat stock soup. People stared at him, but whether that was because he was missing a shirt and Sammia was carrying a spear, or out of recognition he couldn't tell.

How many people in here were true Barleymen? Did they remember the years when they were free during the war, or had they swallowed down Three Rivers propaganda and now believed themselves to have been liberated from occupation? There was no way to know.

He spotted Mamie in the far-right corner of the taproom, sitting in the dark, smoking a long thin cigar. Ignoring the staring silence that descended as he and Sammia made their way across the room, Killean focused on the Silk Paw matriarch.

'I know that look,' the old woman grouched, breathing smoke like a dragon. 'Before you start, there was nothing in our agreement precluding me from telling your brother how to find you.'

Killean hooked a foot around one of the spare chairs drawn up to the table and dropped into it. 'And if I wanted to make such an amendment?' he inquired.

'Too late,' she told him brightly. 'Kindean beat you to it. My agreement with him supersedes yours,' she added smugly.

'You've been spying on me,' he said softly.

''Course I have, boy. I've your mother's memory to think of. She'd want me to keep an eye on you.'

'And would she want you dealing with a blood traitor?' he asked, voice low.

Mamie Cat winced, hiding it by turning her head and blowing out a perfect smoke ring. 'He's her son, just the same as you are. Kaeda loved you both,' she said just as quietly.

But only one of us helped kill her, he thought. He was distracted by Sammia as she propped her spear against the corner wall and sank into the chair between him and Mamie Cat. The two women eyed each other in distaste. They had never gotten along. 'I see you've brought help,' Mamie said tartly. 'What happened to the boy?'

'He's smouldering outside,' Killean waved her off dismissively. It didn't surprise him that she'd seen through his ruse about killing the boy. She knew him. While they both knew he was *capable* of killing the kid if he had to, that didn't mean he *wanted* to do it. 'Give me the information Obawai left with you,' he demanded.

'Oh, it's like that, is it? Straight to business.' Mamie smashed the cigar butt into a large, upturned shell set on the table and rummaged in the dispatch bag sat on the table beside a bottle of barley wine. 'You'd better watch yourself, boy. I can hear the commander coming out in you,' she grumbled him, gimlet eyes hard. She warned him, 'You don't want to go down that road again.'

Chapter Eight

'You don't know what I want,' he said, flipping through the slim portfolio she handed him. After a moment skimming through the papers a startled laugh escaped him. 'Starry Night. That little minnow, Rhodu, stole a prison.' He looked up and grinned at Mamie. 'I have to admit, that is impressive.'

'What are you talking about? Let me see that.' Sammia snatched the papers from his hands. Killean held Mamie Cat's gaze while she read. The older woman met his gaze with equanimity. But then again, she'd never feared his uncle either. Killean wasn't sure the smuggler feared anything. That wasn't likely to change either. She was too old and too wily for fear to get a foothold.

'Night with No Eyes, you're right,' Sammia breathed, dropping the file onto the cluttered table. 'It says here that Rhodu Gakai was one of Carp's mages. An inventor. He made magical weapons. Says he created an object that contained a "Virgin Realm". According to your pal, Obawai, Rhodu stole the object.' She shot Killean a sceptical look and asked, 'What's a "virgin realm" when its at home?'

'Don't worry, it's not as chaste as it sounds,' he drawled. 'Unless Carp's virgin realms are different, all it means is that this object gives access to a part of the Timeless Realm that can't be accessed by portal.' He picked up the folio and tucked the papers neatly away. 'I can see why Jumping Carp would want a Silent Hell all their own, but it doesn't warrant dragging *me* into this mess.' He was known for having a personal interest in collecting – some might say stealing – objects of power for his own ends, after all.

'Silent Hell? Isn't that what the Rivers call the place they stashed you?' Sammia asked.

'Yes,' Killean hissed irritably. The name was impressive, the reality was worse. And he was pretty sure he'd already said he didn't want to talk about it. Then again, Sammia lived to poke men in their sore spots figuratively and literally. Her smirk said she knew exactly how good she was at it, too.

He focused on Mamie. 'There's more to this you're not telling me.'

'I don't know what you mean, boy. I'm just the messenger.' Mamie fussed in her voluminous jacket made of decidedly lumpy yarn. She pulled out a mother of pearl and enamel cigar case, selected a slender cigar and lit up. She puffed determinedly for a moment, shooting him the side eye. 'Not buying that, are you?' She huffed. 'You know that's your problem? You can't ever leave well enough alone.'

'I was completely willing to leave Jumping Carp alone,' he argued. '*They* kidnapped *me*. With your help, Mamie dear.'

'Don't smile at me like that boy. You're not as clever as you think you are,' she grumbled. 'This doesn't have to be complicated, boy. Get the do-dad back from the Crab and everyone can walk away happy.'

'When has happiness ever been one of my lifegoals?' he asked her, incredulously. 'Obawai and his mages will kill me as soon as the job's done,' he added darkly. 'That's not a happy ending in my book.'

Mamie's jaw was crooked in an odd position as she wedged the cigar into the corner of her mouth, lips mouthing at the end like a fish sucking on a baited hook. Except that Mamie was always on the right end of the line, ready to reel in a sucker. 'Now boy, we both know there's been times when you've fancied death your happy ending,' she told him, pointedly. 'Why else would you spend seven weeks pretending to be a bird?'

Killean rolled his eyes and asked, 'Are you feeling alright, Mamie? Your barbs aren't landing well today.'

She tilted her chin, blowing a double smoke ring. 'Who says I'm trying?' She pulled the cigar from her lips and examined the end between her fingers. 'You don't need to worry about Carp. Truth is, no one wants you dead 'til they figure out what Torvin was doing, letting you go. Torvin's got the whole world wondering about that.'

Killean sat up a little straighter. 'And do *they* think *you* know the answer?' he asked.

'Claws in boy, of course I don't. I'm just a little old woman with a business in collecting difficult to acquire items.' She winked at him. 'Rhadu Gakai made off with more than he realised when he escaped with the Realm Pearl.'

Killean absorbed the significant title in silence. Since Myron's day there had been many mages who had crafted many an object of power and given it an impressive name, but few earned the right to be remembered. Mamie Cat spoke the object's name with the same level of reverence usually reserved for Myron's creations alone.

'A mage who can cage a realm is more valuable than the cage itself,' Killean murmured. 'Who wants Gakai, Mamie?' he asked, voice sharp. If he knew that, he'd have a clue what Mamie's real interest was in all this.

Mamie snubbed out her cigar. 'I don't know what you're wittering on about. You should focus on the task at hand. The Realm Pearl is trouble. You're a bright boy, you can guess what Blue Crab will do with it, should they figure out how to use it.'

The Pearl was both a doorway to a realm and a container with nearly infinite capacity, depending on how it was used. It wasn't just people that could be sucked inside and held indefinitely. Blue Crab could walk into any armoury in the Fish Archipelago, activate the

Pearl and whisk away every weapon inside, no matter how big or heavy. They could steal entire naval fleets. Starry Night, if the Sea Lord was really inventive, he could drain an ocean, then pop the Pearl in his pocket, carry it to the mainland and drown any nation of his choosing.

'You can see why those old fish were desperate enough to seek you out,' Mamie said.

He didn't actually. If anything, the threat the Pearl presented was reason to keep a man like him away from it. It wasn't just that a weapon like that would help kickstart a rebellion against Three Rivers. If the nations of the mainland learned that Jumping Carp had engaged him to retrieve it for them, it could spark an international incident.

That was not something a group of circumspect mages, eager to avoid public embarrassment, would go out of their way to seek. Still, it was clear Mamie wasn't going to tell him the truth.

'I'm more interested in what the Silk Paw gets out of all this,' Killean admitted. Just because he wasn't going to get answers didn't mean he couldn't put Mamie on the spot.

She scowled. 'Didn't you hear me, boy? The clan doesn't want Blue Crab having that kind of power.'

'Very noble,' Killean drawled. 'I misjudged you, Mamie. I had no idea you were such a humanitarian. I thought you were seizing an opportunity to use me and Jumping Carp to break Blue Crab's monopoly on trade in and out of Shipwright Island. How very wrong I was.'

Mamie gave him a droll look. 'You're so sharp you'll cut yourself, boy. The Clan has an interest,' she admitted, 'But it's not one I've an *interest* in sharing with you.'

Well, there it was. At least he'd forced her to admit that much. He slouched in his chair. He had his back to most of the room, a position he did not like but one that was necessary. Showing any weakness would be a terrible idea in here. He knew he was being watched by a least one Three Rivers spy, as well as a bar full of people, some of whom had legitimate reason to hate him.

Mamie fussed with her bag again. 'Silk Paw wants the waters around Shipwright open again, it's true. But we're hardly alone in that,' she muttered.

'True. But the Kakalan and Ikoi Clans don't have your reach. And they don't have me,' Killean added drily, watching Sammia under his eyelashes. He was trusting her to watch the room. Back straight and head up, she kept her gaze straight ahead, outwardly doing her job. He also knew she was analysing every word he and Mamie spoke. She'd reacted when he mentioned the names of two of Blue Crabs enemies on the south coast. She'd spent time on the coast, had she worked for the Kakalan or the Ikoi? What was her interest in all this? Because as sure as he was of his own name, he was sure she hadn't found him by accident.

'Are we safe?' he asked her softly, noticing the tiniest shift in her body language.

'Torvin's daughter just walked in.'

Killean cursed and swivelled in his seat, his line of thought cut dead. Mishka Silverfloe was at the bar and Killean could barely believe his eyes. Her hair, a shade of blue-grey that should have been unnatural but wasn't, was gathered up on top of her head. Her strong, athletic body was wrapped in a silk tunic embossed with silver roses. She spoke to the barkeeper and half-turned, giving nothing away when she met Killean's eyes. She said something else to the barkeeper, who was also looking Killean's way and then strode toward the table.

Killean turned back to Mamie, whispering fiercely, 'Did you know about this?'

'No.' The closed look on Mamie's face was genuine. Hurriedly she packed the paperwork away looking less than pleased.

'Hello, Killean.' Mishka's voice was exactly the way he remembered it. Husky and unexpectedly deep. Her oval face was dominated by large grey eyes the colour of river ice. There was a golden hue to her skin, which contrasted sharply with her cold-hued hair. She looked him up and down and quirked one whisper-thin eyebrow. 'I'd say you're looking well, but that would be a lie. You smell like you've been living in a sty. Or is it a swamp?' she smiled cattily. 'I've heard some interesting rumours you've developed an interest in cormorant fishing.'

'Prissy little princess,' Sammia sneered. 'You haven't changed a bit.'

Mishka's lip curled contemptuously. 'I'm not surprised to see you here,' she told Sammia, barely looking her way. 'You've always been a bottom feeder.'

Sammia stepped forward, pushing into Mishka's space. 'You want to say that again?'

The sporadic conversation that had picked up around the room stopped dead. The hush that swept in to fill the void was roaringly loud. Killean stood slowly, positioning himself between the two women. 'Sammia is a warrior of renown,' he said loudly enough to be heard. 'The High King of Past Tiger personally awarded her the Medal of Valour.' More quietly, he told Mishka, 'I really don't give a damn what you say to me, but I've never known you to treat a woman with disrespect. It's beneath you.'

All that practice with the fishermen must have paid off, because his barb landed. Mishka couldn't hide the tiny, perturbed frown that furrowed her brow. Her lips pursed. She wouldn't apologise, but everyone in the silent taproom knew she'd been shamed.

Even as a child Mishka could be highhanded, particularly when she was feeling insecure, which she often had. Growing up the bastard daughter of a celebrated but eccentric Three Rivers' mage, Mishka had always resented Torvin for never marrying her mother or acknowledging her. It had been uncharacteristically crass on his part. Mishka had grown up in the city fully aware that the father she idolised was raising two orphans, while still claiming to be childless himself. It hadn't helped that Mishka had inherited her father's natural gift for magic, necessitating her instruction in the craft. She'd joined Killean and Nadil in training sessions, working as hard for her father's affection as she had at her wielding.

No one in Delta City understood why Torvin refused to acknowledge Mishka as anything other than his gifted apprentice. Some thought it was because Mishka was a daughter and not a son. Some astute commentators thought it was a transparent attempt to protect her from Torvin's foreign enemies who might seek to kidnap and use her against her famous father. Killean wasn't sure that anyone, Mishka included, had realised that the dangerous enemy Torvin really sought to protect her from was High King Minuidon himself.

Minuidon had been a jealous and petty man in every way. With no acknowledged heir to the Camry throne, it was natural that the high born in Delta City would look around for someone else to replace Minuidon when the time came. Torvin-the-Spark was not especially high born, but he was an immensely gifted mage, a phenomenal soldier, and a general with a proven knack for tactics and strategy. Thus with the Camry line producing duds, he became the rival Minuidon couldn't kill off. Mostly because he needed him. Minuidon had driven off or killed everyone else with any competence in the kingdom.

No king wants to need his underlings more than they need him, so Minuidon targeted Mishka and her mother instead of going after the man with better magic than his own. Accidents happen, and children are more prone to mishaps than adults. There were a thousand ways Minuidon could make it happen, all nastier than the last, and Torvin knew it. He kept his daughter at arm's length to appease the king and endured the gossip and slander for years.

Killean had little reason to sympathise with Torvin, but even he wondered how the man had borne his daughter's heartache and bitterness for all those years. Truthfully, the only reason he didn't resent the fact that he hadn't offed Minuidon himself, was the grudging acceptance that Torvin had a claim himself. He'd served Three Rivers faithfully all his life, and the king had used him abominably. Of course, Torvin had been handed a throne as a reward for regicide, while Killean had gotten five years in a Timeless sleep for giving him the opening, so his sympathy wasn't *that* great for either Torvin or his daughter.

Mishka looked at him hatefully. Her large, pretty eyes glowing with anger. 'Everyone knows the king of Past Tiger was your puppet in the war,' she snapped.

Killean smiled without humour. 'Your own father recognises King Harkiv, Mishka. Every nation from here to Icicle recognises his rule. Whatever point you think you're making, you're failing. Go home before you embarrass yourself further.'

Hands shaking around a large tray laden with rice bowls and beer glasses, the barkeeper stopped just in front of the table. He cleared his throat nervously, 'My lady? Your food is ready.' He watched Killean with fearful eyes.

'Thank you, Taman. Please set it down on the table.' Mishka's transformation was miraculous. Gone was the eternally bitter girl, still smarting from her years of neglect and in her place was a gracious woman with a warm smile and lovely almond eyes.

No one spoke as the frightened barkeeper arranged four bowls on the table and placed a pitcher of beer and four glasses in the middle. Mamie Cat snatched her bag away as the man reached out to move it. The barkeeper left. Killean watched him hurry back behind the bar as Mishka drew a chair up to the table. The other bar patrons reluctantly returned to their drinks and conversation as Killean raked his gaze over them.

'Let us sit. We have matters to discuss,' Mishka announced regally.

Technically she still wasn't an acknowledged princess, existing in the same nebulous state close to Torvin but still too far for her liking she'd existed in all her life. Killean suspected there was some illicit substance pumped into the water in Three Rivers that allowed the citizenry to accept and simultaneously ignore so many overpowered bastards in their midst without question. To the best of his knowledge, Torvin had explained everything to Mishka now that Minuidon was long dead, but as a man who cherished his grudges, Killean doubted it made much difference to her.

Killean shared a look with Mamie and Sammia. They could leave, but to do so would be admitting they were afraid to eat with Mishka. Killean wouldn't put it past Mishka to have placed men at the door, in any event. She was very determined when she wanted something.

He sat down, examining the rice bowl. Thin slices of beef were layered over the top along with a tangy brown sauce. Killean's stomach growled quietly. It had been hours since he'd last eaten. He cocked his head at Sammia. Rolling her eyes, she picked up her two-tined fork and skewered a slice of beef from first his and then Mamie's bowls. She chewed and swallowed and then forked up a heaping of his and Mamie's rice, repeating the process.

Mishka sighed loudly. 'The food isn't poisoned,' she muttered irritably. 'What do you take me for?'

'You don't want me to answer that,' Killean retorted never taking his eyes off Sammia as she licked a thick smear of the dark sauce off her fork.

Sammia's expression was appraising as she poured a glass of beer and took a sip. 'The sauce is on the salty side,' she announced, 'but the beef is melt-in-the-mouth tender. The rice isn't bad either. The onion slivers running through it give it a bite.'

'I'll be sure to give Taman your compliments,' Mishka remarked cattily before continuing in more normal tones. 'You're being ridiculous. I'm hardly likely to murder my own future brother-in-law, am I?' she asked offhandedly as she picked up her cutlery.

Killean almost dropped his fork. 'Excuse me?'

Mishka paused; fork poised delicately above her bowl. Her eyes widened comically, lips parting in exaggerated surprise before a wicked smile sliced across her thin face. 'Kindean didn't tell you.'

Killean stared at her flatly. 'You're marrying my brother,' he said, disgust tainting his words. 'The daughter of Three Rivers is marrying the last legitimate heir of Onryn.' He shook his head, hands balling into fists on the table. 'So, this is how you plan to finally destroy my clan,' he muttered.

Assimilation was as good as death. Submerged within the new royal bloodline in a generation everything that had made his clan unique for centuries —the entire culture of the Onryn —would be washed away and forgotten.

He sensed Torvin's subtle hand in all of it and shot Mishka a look. 'I'm surprised you'd let your father sell you off like a prized cow.'

'You're a hateful shit,' Mishka told him. 'Believe it or not, not everyone lives their life like they're a piece on a gameboard. Kindean and I are in love. Unexpected, I know, but war can bring people together sometimes.'

'Oh, I can see it,' he assured her. 'The embittered scorned daughter and the turncoat bootlicker. You and my brother make a charming couple.'

Mishka set her cutlery down. She smoothed her hands over her thighs under the table. 'I realise you're terminally twisted, Ilin, but you know how much Kindean still loves you. He begged my father to pardon you. You have no idea how much it pained him to know you were locked up in Silent Hell.'

Killean shook his head. 'I'm actually impressed. I had no idea you could talk that much crap and keep a straight face.' He leaned in and whispered, 'You were there during the last battle, Mishka. You *know* why your father was never going to kill me.'

It was the last great secret of the Age of War. It hadn't been Nadil Shiny Scale who had landed the last blow against Dadarro. It had been him. He'd killed his uncle. He'd done it to save Nadil. And that harebrained moment of idiocy was the reason he hadn't been executed. But of course, no one knew that. No one save the people who were there.

It was one thing to accept that Kindean might not know the truth. His brother hadn't had Mishka's front row seat to the final moments of that disastrous battle between him, Uncle Dadarro and Nadil. Mishka was the who had dragged Nadil's broken body out of the way as he faced down his uncle for the final time. She was one of a select few people alive who truly understood that Three Rivers hadn't won the war. He – *Killean* – had lost it. That he'd done it more or less on purpose didn't take the sting out of defeat, however, and he was not about to let one of the few witnesses lie to his face about it.

'I do know Torvin, remember? He did a half-arsed job raising me too,' he reminded her cruelly. 'The man never does anything without a plan. Sweet-worded appeals for mercy wouldn't move him. Your father released me because he wants something he thinks I can get him.'

That last he said for Mamie and Sammia's benefit, and he saw the moment Mishka recognised that fact. He still didn't know why she'd decided to ambush him today, but he was sure she'd report back every detail of their meeting to her father. They'd learnt double talk from the same source. Even Mamie Cat couldn't pick up on everything they weren't telling each other.

'We love each other, Killean,' Mishka said giving an excellent performance for the benefit of the room. 'You and Torvin can scheme and plot all you like. You won't stop us from bringing true peace to Barley and Three Rivers. The warring must end,' she insisted, voice thrumming with saccharine sincerity. 'It helps no one and hurts everyone.' She looked at him beseechingly and asked, 'Didn't your time in Silent Hell teach you anything?' There was a keenness to her gaze, sharp as a blade.

Interesting. Just what did she think he could have learned in the Timeless Realm? He smiled blandly. 'I was asleep, remember,' he told her. 'Blissfully unaware of the passing time.'

He was lying, naturally. And both Mishka and Sammia knew it. Mamie Cat probably suspected as much, but only because she knew him well enough to assume he was lying at least fifty percent of the time.

He asked pointedly, 'Why are you here, Mishka?'

Her expression was earnest. Her eyes wide, her lip may have wobbled. 'I wanted to see you and make peace between us,' she declared. 'We were friends when we were children. You, me, and Nadil, I used to think there was nothing we couldn't do together.' She smiled sadly only for the smile to drop from her face like a stone when she told him, 'I hated you for leaving us for the longest time. Then I hated you more for the things you did in the war. But that's over now. Nadil has convinced me to give you another chance.' Her eyes shimmered with unshed tears.

'Nicely done,' Killean drawled. 'I think you missed your calling on the stage. You came here to spy on me for your father and for the pleasure of rubbing your engagement in my face,' he told her.

She smiled sweetly at him, eyes dry as old rocks as she finally dropped the act. 'You'd do the same to me. I might be a bitter bitch, but you're a bigger one.'

He laughed out loud, remembering why, once upon a time, they really had been friends. 'Where is my brother?' he asked.

'He was summoned back to Delta City hours ago,' Mishka said coolly.

Killean's grin was sharp. 'Let me guess, his little meeting with me in Potbelly went against Daddy's plans.'

Mishka shrugged, refusing to deny it. 'Look,' she said briskly. 'I'm staying out of father's scheming. I don't know why he's letting you roam free and I don't want to know either,' she added sharply. Interestingly, Killean couldn't tell if she was telling the truth or not. 'I am warning you – whatever you're up to, leave Barley out of it. I know you love this place – I do too – I also know that loving something won't stop you from using it.' She glanced obliquely toward Sammia. 'Consider this a request to get out of town,' she told him firmly, 'before you fuck everything up.'

Killean smiled, it was one of his more genuine offerings. 'I accept your request. Let us finish the meal you so graciously provided and clean up in the inn and we'll be gone by mid-afternoon.'

Mishka nodded and rose from the table. 'Nadil will be pleased to hear you're being reasonable,' she said loudly enough for the room to hear. She fixed him with another of her stage-worthy, insincere looks and told him nonsensically, 'He still believes there is goodness in you.'

Killean snorted. This was the third time she'd namedropped the Hero of Three Rivers and he was getting sick of it. 'What does goodness have to do with anything?' he asked.

Good men could kill just as surely as bad. An honourable man could act dishonourably. A villain could act selflessly under the right conditions. A hero could appear the villain and a villain could seem like a hero depending on what side of the line you stood on. The labels meant nothing in a battle of winners and losers. In the end, victory or defeat were the only things that truly defined a man.

Mishka sighed. 'I knew you were going to say that. You're as cynical as my father.' She added, 'Kindean wanted me to pass on a message. He said to tell you that the legacy of the Striking Talon lives on in you. The memory of what the clan was and was not will be defined by your actions from this moment on.'

'You can tell him, I think he's an idiot,' he replied cheerfully.

Now she rolled her eyes, a quiver of a smile on her lips. 'Goodbye, Killean. I hope you don't get yourself killed or condemned as a traitor before the wedding. We so want you to be there.' She threw him a wave over her shoulder as she walked toward the door, every gaze in the room rooted to her back.

Chapter Nine

Mamie Cat slammed her bag onto the table in poor temper as he and Sammia finished off the food, including her share. 'I'm surprised at you, boy. That food could be doused with slow acting poison,' she grumbled.

Killean piled food on his fork. 'It isn't. Torvin wants me for something. His people will protect me until he has it.'

Mamie frowned at him. 'The High King doesn't control everything.'

'Thank the gods,' Sammia murmured. Pushing her plate away she sat back in her chair, casting a lazy glare around the taproom. 'We're being watched. An odd cove in the far corner. He's not even trying to hide it.'

'There you are then,' Killean told Mamie. 'We're being minded. Any third-party assassin will have to go through Torvin's man first.'

'How can you be so certain Torvin wants you alive, boy?' Mamie asked him, genuinely curious.

Killean's smile was slight and sharp, 'I don't have an interest in telling you, Mamie dear. This is a game. And we're both playing. He's setting the board and defining the terms, but I'm determined to win.'

Sammia said irritably, 'Nothing you just said made a whit of sense.'

'Good.'

'Don't get distracted playing games with your foster father, boy,' Mamie snapped, sticking the knife in for fun and profit. 'Your focus should be Blue Crab. The Pearl is powerful. Buyers will be lining up across the nations, should you get hold of it for us.'

Killean looked at her. 'Buyers and enemy armies looking to crush you. The Silk Paw aren't reckless. You know better than to fence goods too hot to handle.'

For an instant, Mamie's expression froze and something real and shaken flickered in her eyes. It was gone in an instant as she plastered an indulgent smile on her face. 'True enough, and now you've said it aloud all Three Rivers knows it too.'

Killean finished eating and neatly set down his cutlery, filing that momentary break in composure away for later reflection. 'Let's talk about my money. It's fake, isn't it?'

'Half the gold is base and the bonds are forgeries,' Mamie agreed.

Killean sighed. 'I knew it. Honest employers dicker over price. Only the dishonest ones stump up the cash up front.' A tip he'd been given by his friend in the Sly Fox mercenaries. If money was no object to a potential employer, it was because he did not intend to pay up.

'The forgeries are good,' Mamie admitted. 'They could easily pass for the real thing.'

'And they will,' Killean agreed thinking ahead. 'I'm going to need a ship and a crew ready to sail from Tuna Quay.'

Sammia plunked her beer glass down on the table. 'We're doing this then?' she asked, wiping the foam from her top lip.

'We were always doing this,' Killean said.

'Why? The pays no good and the job is a suicide run.' Sammia narrowed her eyes. 'You're not doing this for Carp, I know that much. What beef do you have with the Crab?'

'I don't have any. Yet,' he said blandly. 'But I'm sure they've caught wind of Carp's plans by now. A meeting between me and Sea Lord Sikuzo is inevitable. I want it to be on my terms, not his.'

Sammia went very still. 'You know who runs the Crab?' she asked, incredulously. 'How? You spent a month hiding in a swamp.'

'Lotus peninsula has harbours overrun with pirates,' Killean reminded her. 'I might have had feathers at the time, but I promise you, my ears worked fine. Sailors like to gossip.'

Sammia narrowed her eyes. 'What sort of gossip?' she asked.

'Why the sudden interest, Sami?' he asked, cocking his head curiously. 'The gossip I heard was just gossip, but I did pick up a few names. Sikuzo was one of them.'

Sammia scowled. 'You're keeping secrets again.'

He smiled. 'Always.' He drained his glass. 'You can walk away if you want. I'm not holding you here.' He turned to Mamie who had been watching the whole exchange with keen interest. 'Can you get me my ship?' he asked.

She nodded slowly, jowls wobbling. 'The bonds will stand as a deposit, but you'll need real collateral to keep real sailors happy. Most honest sea folk won't sail into Blue Crab waters. And pirates make obstreperous allies.'

'So do I,' Killean murmured. 'Secure a ship. I'll ensure you get the funds.'

'How?' Mamie demanded.

'I'm going to ask a friend for a loan.'

'Since when do you have *friends*?' Sammia asked, sounding moderately outraged.

Killean frowned at her. 'I know how to make friends,' he told her.

'You *did*,' she argued. 'But then you lost the damn war. Who would want to be your friend now?'

Interesting question to ask, considering she'd thrown her lot in with him with so quickly on that roadside. Killean filed the observation away in the back of his mind and shrugged. 'I lost a war, but I'm free now and I've no shortage of people looking to use me. That attracts a certain type of...entrepreneurial spirit.'

She sniffed. 'So this person who's going to loan you money isn't exactly a friend then, are they? Just another sucker looking to hold Killean-the-Swift by the tail.'

Killean shrugged again. He wasn't sure he saw the distinction she was trying to make. He couldn't recall a single person in his life who hadn't wanted to use him for something. That was just life. Everyone had an agenda. 'I never said my friend would agree. Only that I'd ask. Mercenaries tend to up for an adventure,' he added flippantly.

Mamie hissed, sounding surprisingly like a real cat. 'You can't trust a Fox, boy.'

'I can't trust anyone,' Killean retorted. 'Still, unless the Paw are willing to stump up the money, the Sly Fox clan are my best shot of getting the funds we need.'

He'd need a ship with a friendly crew waiting in Shipwright's harbour for the return leg of the voyage. Assuming he survived his inevitable meeting with Sea Lord Sikuzo. He had no intention of sailing out to the island, of course. That would be suicide. The Blue Crab would sink any ship he sailed out on, but if by some miracle that didn't happen and he sailed into Shipwright in one piece, Obawai and the Jumping Carp navy would make certain he didn't survive the return journey aboard the same ship. He trusted Mamie to charter a vessel to sail out to Shipwright on seemingly unrelated business and then wait for him, which would hopefully make it much harder for Carp to pick him out on open waters.

He fixed Mamie with a look. 'I need the location and spell codes for all the Silk Paw portals linked to the islands of the archipelago,' he said.

Mamie curled her lip. 'I thought you were going by ship,' she grumbled.

'No, you didn't,' he replied easily. 'Don't skimp me, Mamie. You profit from this, no matter what.'

Not that he knew precisely how, but if there was one thing he was sure of, it was that Mamie had this mess stitched up in her favour no matter what he did. And if she didn't? Well, shame on her.

'We've connections to Sea Snail and Gull islands,' she grumbled. 'Snail would be safer, but its farther out. Gull is a pirate hive but it's a stone's throw from Shipwright and rife with news.'

He nodded slowly. 'I want both,' he said. He had no idea how to manage his approach in truth, but he didn't want Mamie to know that. Better to leave everyone guessing what his next move would be than suspecting he didn't have one.

Mamie clutched her messenger bag to her chest, an oddly defensive gesture from a woman he knew had nothing to fear from him. 'The clan want Blue Crab broken and the Pearl out of Carp hands. Is that understood?' she asked him tersely.

'So, you *are* playing politics,' he murmured. 'I won't waste time asking why. I know you won't tell me. What does the Paw offer me in exchange for this radical redrawing of the socio-political map?'

'Safety,' Mamie bit out sourly. 'You'll not get far without our protection.'

'If I gut the Crab I'll need more than the Silk Paw to protect me,' he scoffed.

'And you'll have it. There are bigger wheels turning than you know, boy.'

He rolled his eyes. 'There always are.'

Perhaps it was the fact that his uncle had named him his second-in-command and a General in his own right at seventeen, in an act of nepotism every one of his allies had expected would end in Killean's death, but people seemed to think he wasn't aware of the fact that he'd spent most of his life a piece on a gameboard controlled by others.

Just like then, he was more than the grand puppet-masters believed him to be. He'd proven himself in war and survived where his uncle and his cronies had not. He was the puppet who outlived his masters time and again and he knew the secret to surviving puppet-masters was to always carry big scissors. All this dickering for protection simply gave him time to sharpen his blades.

'I'll trust in your protection for now, Mamie,' he told her, 'but screw me over and there will be nowhere, in any land, where you can hide from me.'

Mamie feigned shock. 'Now, boy, is that any way to talk to your mother's dearest friend? When have I ever not had your best interests at heart?'

'Laying it on a bit thick, there,' Sammia drawled. 'The dear old granny act isn't fooling anyone.'

Mamie cat glared at her. Killean rapped his fingers on the table to draw her attention. 'Do you have some of the bonds with you?' he asked.

'Yes,' Mamie admitted.

'Give them to me. If they're as good as you say, they could be useful to the Fox.'

If only as a template to make more. The Sly Fox were an assassination outfit mostly, but Vilari really was an opportunist at heart. He'd see the worth in a bit of counterfeiting.

'The Blue Crab must be broken,' Mamie insisted with odd vehemence, withholding his bonds.

'I'll crack the shell and you and whoever you're working for can feed on the meat,' he promised smoothly. Out of the corner of his eye he could see Sammia watching him intently. He avoided her eyes, keeping his focus on Mamie Cat.

Mamie's whiskered old face creased as if she'd bitten down on something sour. 'You'll be wanting our agreement in writing, I suppose?' she asked him tiredly.

He nodded. 'And blood.'

Mamie sucked her teeth. 'Kindean was easier to bargain with,' she muttered.

'My brother is a deluded idiot,' he reminded her. 'He believes in good faith agreements.'

Mamie's dark eyes twinkled as she peered at him, 'And what do you believe in, boy?'

'Not much now,' he replied softly. He tapped the table. 'Use the back of the Carp bonds to write the contract. And don't forget those spell codes.'

Mamie scratched out the form of their agreement, Killean read it through and passed it back to her for a signature and a bloody thumb print before affixing his own. Mamie used a separate page to pass on the location of Silk Paw's hidden portals and the magic words to use them.

The old cat was still in a snit when she left shortly thereafter. Killean stored the contract in his pack and asked Sammia to inquire about a room. They wouldn't be staying, but it would be nice to wash the road dust off his skin. He was sure Mishka had already asked the landlord to give him whatever he wanted. The agents of Three Rivers were being awfully obliging.

'And what will you be doing while I'm talking to the help?' Sammia snapped.

'Sitting here,' he said, spreading his hands over the table. The atmosphere in the pub had relaxed somewhat since Mishka's departure. Killean wasn't sure if that was because a war criminal was less interesting than a not-quite-princess, or if everyone in the taproom was in fact a plant supplied by Torvin. One could never be *too* paranoid. That spy in the corner still hadn't made his move.

He didn't have to wait long for that to change. In fact, the spy was up and out of his seat the moment Sammia left her spear in the corner and sauntered up to the bar, very ostentatiously sticking her butt out as she leaned against the bar and favoured the terrified barkeep with her best smile. Predictably, most of the taproom's patrons found the sight very interesting indeed, which somewhat suggested they weren't spies.

The real spy was *also* interesting to look at. A dark-skinned man with a long face and features so severe they looked carved from ebony, he had long hair woven into soft fuzzy strands and dyed multiple colours that swung passed his shoulders. He wore a blue cotton vest and loose cotton trousers that cut off at the knees. His feet were strapped into sturdy sandals.

Wiry and leanly muscled, the man moved like he knew how to handle himself and with an odd, loose hipped gait Killean recognised from his time in Lotus. A sailor's gait. The man slid into Sammia's vacated chair without a by-your-leave.

'They call me Cactus,' he said, his voice a deep and resonant baritone.

Killean noted the lines of old tattoos covering his arms. Some of the ink was faded, blending with his skin tone, some were not. Tattoos were not popular on the mainland, but seafaring folk loved them. 'A pirate called Cactus,' he mused quietly. 'How quaint. I'm guessing you know what they call me. What do you want?'

Cactus smiled, flashing strong white teeth. 'I'm from the islands,' he said evading the question. 'I know how the Blue Crab operate.'

'Do all Islanders have your hearing?' Killean asked drily. 'We weren't talking that loudly.'

He hadn't been talking all that quietly either, but Cactus had been across the room the entire time. There had been an Accursed spy in the war who had been infested with a colony of highly intelligent, demonic fleas he used to gather information for him, but that man was long dead now. Killean had *not* been able to make friends with him – much to his misfortune. Still, he doubted Cactus had a similar power. He didn't look nearly as mangy.

Again, Cactus smiled. He seemed to be a man with a lot to smile about, or at least he wanted Killean to think so. He reminded him a bit of Kindean. 'I'm not telling you who I work for,' he said. 'But I will tell you this. My employer wants you to succeed.'

Killean regarded Cactus thoughtfully. The man had a faint, almost invisible scar running down the left side of his face from the corner of his eye to the hinge of his jaw and another shorter, deeper scar bisecting his right eyebrow near the bridge of his nose. Shrewd intelligence gleamed in his eyes.

'Mage?' he asked.

Cactus shook his head, hair shifting over his shoulders. 'No,' he said softly. 'I have no magic.'

Killean arched his brows. 'Are you cursed?'

Again, he shook his head. 'I am human,' he said, 'No more and no less.'

'Do you sail?' Killean asked him.

Cactus' smile returned. 'That I do,' he said. 'I once sailed with Olan Kinna. Though now he likes to call himself Sikuzo.' Cactus' smile became a sneer.

Interesting. The self-styled Sea Lords of the southern waters liked to fashion themselves after the petty lords of the mainland, save for the part where they swore loyalty to a high king. The men who followed the Sea Lords owed their masters fealty and breaking oath tended to shorten one's life expectancy, considerably. The Blue Crab had a reputation for treating its members well and rewarding loyalty, meaning that most did not want to leave.

Killean cocked his head and asked, 'What did he do to you?'

Cactus looked surprised. 'He did nothing. I have no quarrel with Sikuzo or the Blue Crab.'

'But you'll help me destroy them?' Killean asked doubtfully.

Cactus shrugged and spread his large hands. 'I sign on with the man with the deepest pockets,' he said.

Killean frowned. 'You're a mercenary.'

'So are you,' Cactus retorted. 'And worse besides.'

True enough. 'I only trust the loyalty of mercenaries I pay for myself,' he said. 'And I doubt I can afford you.'

Cactus laughed, a rich, deep belly laugh. 'No, you cannot, Killean Onryn. You have no true title. No lands. No army.' His expression was disdainful as he looked him over. 'You have nothing.'

'If you're looking to insult me with the truth, you're going to be disappointed,' he said blandly. 'I'm well aware of what defeat has cost me.'

Cactus' eyes were gimlet bright and twice as shrewd. 'So you say, but broken men don't carry themselves like you do.' He tapped his hand over the cluttered tabletop, causing the plates to rattle. 'I'm to help you find Rhodu Gakai and claim the Pearl. And I'm to watch you, learn how you work and what you want.'

Claim the Pearl, he said. But claim for whom? Killean knew better than to ask. Cactus had already told him he wouldn't answer.

He asked a different question. 'Why spy on me?' Killean asked. 'If your employer wants to hire me, he can kidnap me like everyone else.'

Cactus grinned as if he thought Killean was making a joke. 'My employer would say you already work for him,' he added slyly. 'And he would prefer it if you did not know it. The dog who does not feel the leash fights it less.'

That was illuminating. There were several very wealthy merchants and petty lords residing in the coastal regions of the mainland who had a vested interest in weakening the sea lords, but most of them would want to claim the glory also. The Lands of Magic may have fallen into an uneasy peace in the last five years, but power and prestige was still earned through military prowess and bold action against one's enemies. Very few people in power liked to act through back channels.

He said as much to Cactus. 'But what lord would want to associate with you,' the Islander asked. 'No one knows what you will do. Most think you should have been executed after the war and those that once supported you are waiting to see if you have the means to lead them in another rebellion. Some say you are broken, some that you are planning something. None are willing to make a move before you do.'

Interesting. 'Is your employer one of them?' Killean asked carefully.

'My employer wants to know if you still seek power,' Cactus told him, boldly sidestepping an answer.

Killean met his eyes and said, 'Power is a tool. A means to an end. I no longer have a cause so power is no use to me.'

'Causes are like breezes, they come and go easily,' said Cactus. His gaze was very level, almost knowing, 'Especially for a man looking for something to believe in.'

Killean smiled with just his lips. He was fighting the urge to growl low in his throat. 'If I see you again Cactus, I'll rip out your throat and leave you for the crows.' He rose from the table, scraping his chair back. He grabbed Sammia's spear. Immediately the taproom went deathly quiet.

Killean rolled his eyes. 'Oh, for fuck's sake, get out and get a life, all of you,' he snapped causing half the patrons to flee the taproom like a flock of frightened pigeons. Sammia was at his side instantly, taking her spear from him. She never had liked anyone else handling it.

'I've got us a room,' she murmured, swinging a key on a chain around her finger. 'Do you still want to use it?'

'Yes,' he hissed. 'I won't be harried off my own lands.' Technically, this was Kindean's land. He was the first born. But a quick spot of fratricide could fix that niggle right up.

'Do not be hasty, Killean Onryn,' Cactus intoned from his chair.

THE LIFE AND TIMES OF THE TRAITOR KILLEAN ONRYN

Killean curled his lip. Bracing his hands on the table he leaned down and pushed his face into Cactus's space. 'I think you're a liar, Cactus, and I don't like liars. Make sure and tell your employer *that* next time you see him.'

Chapter Ten

The inn room was clean and simply furnished. Killean ignored the embroidered Three Rivers emblem pinned to the wall above the sleigh bed for his own peace of mind. He did note where the floorboards creaked as he crossed to the window and drew the inner shutters closed. The room smelled of pine and candlewax. A small adjoining washroom contained a filled metal tub.

With a sigh, he gestured to the tub. 'Ladies first.'

Sammia grinned. 'Naturally. You know I'd kick your arse in a fair fight.' Carefully laying her spear over the counterpane she shucked her clothes with a lot less reverence. Killean sat on the bed and watched, easing his boots off carefully.

'It's Torvin,' she told him stepping into the bath. 'Your brother turning up, then Mishka spilling all that childhood memories crap. Cactus was the capper though. It all stinks of one of Torvin's schemes. Too neat. Too tidy. Too pushy by half.' She slid down in the water, submerged up to her shoulders. Squeezing out the sponge, she ran it down one arm before dragging it across her collarbone and down the opposite arm. Water sluiced over her smooth skin, making it gleam; a shimmering waterfall spilled down her breasts. Her nipples were erect, just peaking out of the water as she sank down to wet her hair.

Sitting forward on the bed, chin in hands and elbows braced on his knees to get a better look, Killean hummed in agreement. 'Mamie's in on it too.'

'A regular old conspiracy,' Sammia said rising up in the tub just enough to nock her shoulders against the rim. She extended her right leg, toes en-pointe, and swept the sponge from the nub of her ankle over toned calf muscle to her inner thigh where both sponge and hand disappeared from view, hidden by the side of the tube.

Killean experienced a pang of deep regret the tub was not see-through. 'Hmm,' he mumbled, trying to remember what they were talking about. It had been more than five years since he'd been this close to a naked woman.

'You're very calm about this.' Pausing in her ablutions, Sammia peered at him.

He smiled at her. 'I'm always calm.'

Hiding a smile, she turned her face away. The weight of the water had forced her hair to lie flat and it plastered her shoulders. She ran her hands over her scalp, squeezing out the excess water. Killean watched the rise and fall of her chest. A single bead of water chased down her throat, dipped into the divot of her collarbone and slipped down the narrow ravine of perfect skin between her breasts.

'Are you even listening to me?' she demanded crossing her arms over her breasts, moulding them together deliciously.

'Yes,' he lied.

'Then what did I say?'

'You wanted to know why Torvin's doing this,' he bluffed. 'There's more to this than Jumping Carp's missing goods.' He might not have been listening, but Sammia would have the same questions he did.

'Lucky guess,' she grumbled, retrieving the sponge. 'Do you know what he wants?' This time when she squeezed out the sponge she made sure to make a show of it, covering her chest and then swirling the sponge over one breast before the other.

He laughed softly. 'I don't know.'

'But you suspect.'

'I suspect everything. You missed a spot.'

'What? Where?'

He got up and crossed the threshold into the ensuite. He sank to his knees beside the tub, slowly, maintaining eye contact. Their faces were only scant inches apart. 'Just...there.' He waited until she nodded permission before leaning forward and placing a kiss on her right shoulder. She shivered. He reached for the sponge. 'May I?'

She let out a soft sigh. 'We haven't done this in a while.'

'Six years,' he agreed. Taking her hand, he pressed a kiss to her palm, then to the pulse point at her wrist. 'For what it's worth. I thought I was protecting you,' he murmured. 'After you escaped Three Rivers custody during the war, our spies found you. I could have come for you but I thought...'

'What?' she asked, voice raw.

He brushed his lips to her knuckles, taking a moment to just let himself breathe her in. 'I thought I was giving you a chance to get out.'

She pulled her hand away. 'Liar. You couldn't be bothered with the inconvenience,' there was heat to her words, but no deep anger.

'No,' he said catching her eyes and holding her gaze. 'I thought I was giving you a choice. If I'd come for you, even if you turned me away, our enemies would hunt you down. If I didn't come for you, I thought they'd let you be.'

'So you swanned off to invade my homeland and left me out – for my benefit?' she asked bitingly.

He sighed. 'The invasion of Green Peaks was a feint,' he said. 'I was never going to take the capital.'

'Not the point, Ilin.' She drew away from him, leaning into the far side of the tub. 'What about Shrimpton? What really happened back there? Why didn't you come get me?' There was a weight to her gaze. Did she really not know? Had she spent all this time thinking he'd abandoned her?

'Kindean caught me,' he told her sincerely. 'If not for his terminal idiocy, he could have bound my magic right then and there. But he wasted his shot because he wanted to *talk* and I got away. Just. I only learned that you hadn't made it out when I rejoined my uncle's forces a week later.'

He shifted around to the head of the tub. Reclaiming her hand, he kissed the back of it and then returned his attention to her shoulder and then her neck, savouring the softness of her hair against his cheek. Leaning back against his shoulder, she tilted her head back, extending her neck. He chased kisses along her throat, brushing her jaw, his hand slipping down her slick skin, over the jut of her collarbone to her breast. He traced her nipple.

She sighed. 'I know what you're doing,' she told him.

He chuckled. 'I should hope so.' Curving his other arm around her back he reached around scissored her left nipple between two fingers, idly brushing his thumb over the bud. He used his right hand to cup her cheek and turn her face toward him. She turned away from the kiss at the last second.

'You're trying to distract me from what's really going on here.'

'Trust me, conspiracies are the last thing on my mind right now.'

She pulled away from him. Rising to her knees and shifting in the tub, she turned to face him, looping both arms around his neck. He pulled her closer, flattening his palms against her back. Her skin was smooth, slick and cool, firm, supple muscle moving like silk under the run of his hands. The divot at the base of her spine was deep, her buttocks firm.

There was nothing especially soft about Sammia, she was lean, corded muscle, tension humming under her skin, taut as a spring, but all of it was wrapped in the most perfect skin in creation. She was at her most beautiful in motion, fury within and fury without, but these quiet moments, when she let herself relax were exquisite. He really had missed her.

Kissing her was exactly the way he remembered. Bittersweet, with just a hint of terrible idea thrown in. He had never regretted being with Sammia and the wanting hadn't gone away. In fact, it was coming roaring back with the fervour only five years imprisoned in a world without sensation could produce. But this was still a bad idea for a multitude of reasons. He just didn't care.

He reached out to press a hand to the back of her head. Rising on his knees, he pulled her higher out of the bath, their bodies flush against each other. Breaking the kiss, he dropped smaller kisses to the corner of her mouth, her cheek, fingers trailing down her belly, slipping lower. She gripped his shoulders and then shoved the coat down his arms. Pushing him back, she raked her fingers over the sparse hair covering his chest, lightly scratching her way down his stomach. To his mute horror, she stopped there and withdrew. Smirking like she knew exactly the agony she was causing him, she tossed the wet sponge in his face. 'You haven't washed my back, yet.'

Peeling a strand of wet hair off his cheek, he shook his head, smiling. 'How right you are, Lady Sammia.'

'Pfft, I'll never be a lady.' She sloshed around in the tub, presenting her back, in all its slinky perfection.

'Captain? Lieutenant? *Colonel*?' he suggested, shrugging all the way out of his coat. He dunked the sponge and dragged it slowly over her skin.

'Queen,' she said.

'Queen,' he repeated. 'That could take some doing.'

She glanced over her shoulder, managing to look very haughty as she looked down her nose at him. 'For you, perhaps. I might have a king on the hook already.'

'He's not good enough for you,' Killean said confidently. He dropped the sponge back into water and reached his arms around her, pulling her back into his chest. He let his hand slip passed her shoulder and downward, returning to its earlier travails.

Sammia shifted a little higher out of the water, canting her hips, obliging both of them. She quivered gratifyingly when his questing fingers found their mark. 'How do you know?' she asked breathily.

'Because you're here,' he said, pressing a kiss to the side of her neck. 'And I know you as well as you know me. If we were done not even the promise of a crown could make you come after me.'

'Excuse me? You're the one who stumbled onto me, remember?' She wriggled against him, spreading her legs a little.

'Hmm. Then its fate,' he said, nipping her shoulder. 'Turn around, Sami. Your back is sparkling clean.'

She turned her head, knocking into his jaw lightly. 'I don't take orders from you.'

She never had. Not really. The Dread Four had always worked together because they wanted to, even if none of them would admit it. He kissed the shell of her ear, nuzzling her hair out of the way and murmured, 'Please, Sami dearest, won't you turn around?'

She sighed happily but said, 'You're filthy.'

And planning to get more so before he was done. 'Shift over and let me in the tub, then.'

They made a tremendous mess. By the time Killean was reluctantly pulling his boots back on, hair bound in a still damp tail at the nape of his neck and freshly washed skin crawling under his filthy coat, the floor was covered in puddles of water. The counterpane was halfway across the room and they'd knocked the cross-stitch Three Rivers emblem off the wall.

Sammia stretched her arms over her head, popping her spine as she stretched. 'That was fun. Think we horrified the good citizens below? We weren't exactly quiet.'

Going over to open the shutters he said, 'I hope so.'

'You know,' she told him. 'You used to have a reputation for being repressed.'

'Enemy propaganda,' he scoffed. 'How repressed can I be when I waged war on the strongest nation in the world at seventeen?' Admittedly, he'd lost the battle by twenty, but the point remained. He'd rarely repressed any part of himself, on or off the battlefield. He lived his life on his terms because he really didn't care for anyone else's.

'*And* you scored with me and I don't do shy boys,' Sammia agreed.

He nodded. 'Exactly.'

A lot of the things his detractors said about him were true. But some were outright baffling. They said he was cold. Fair enough. They said he was taciturn. Only with his foes, whom he'd come to kill, not engage in small talk. They said he was stiff and grim in countenance. That was because they only met him on the battlefield. What did they expect him to do, crack jokes in the lulls between cannonade fire? He wouldn't call himself amiable by any stretch but the lie that he lived only to make war and whine about revenge was mildly insulting. He rarely whined. It was a waste of time he could be spending smiting his enemies.

He had the sneaking suspicion that the gossips maligned his character just to make a contrast between him and Nadil, Three Rivers all-loving hero. If Nadil was irreverent and laid back, then his great nemesis Killean, had to be serious and uptight. If Nadil was charming, Killean must be abrupt and ill-mannered. If Nadil was strong and forthright, then Killean must have an obsessive and vindictive spirit that would be his downfall. If he was being magnanimous, he'd give a partial point to that last one, but the rest was hogwash.

'What are we going to do now?' Sammia asked him.

'Get out of town and head for the nearest portal,' he answered.

'What about the kid?'

Killean froze in the process of shrugging on his pack. 'Shit.'

Sammia burst out laughing. 'Starless Night, did you forget about him?'

He had. He'd forgotten all about Ash. He rubbed a hand over his face. He couldn't quite believe it. 'Damn it.'

He'd left the kid smouldering outside the inn hours ago. He was surely long gone now. In fact, it was suspicious he hadn't come barging into the taproom during his meet with Mamie.

Sammia was enjoying herself and suggested, 'Who knows, maybe he's still outside, shivering on the street like a lost puppy.'

Killean rolled his eyes. 'I can't waste time hunting the kid down now,' he grumbled. 'He'll have to wait.'

'Like I did?' Sammia's mood changed in an instant. If he hadn't been used to her sharp edges and razor defences, he'd have been more worried. 'Are you going to tell me what your obsession with this kid is about?' she demanded.

'It's not the kid,' he muttered, still annoyed. Losing the kid was a setback. A pretty major one. But if he deviated from the path his enemies expected him to take, he'd only draw their attention to Ash, which he did not want. He wouldn't put it past Torvin to recognise the gauntlet immediately. He'd sooner let the kid get away for now, so he could hunt him down at his leisure when the present mess was dealt with.

'Obviously, it's not *really* about the kid,' Sammia retorted. 'It's the magic in the gauntlet you want. I just can't figure out why.'

'You missed out on the trip to Green Peaks,' he said with a shrug. 'That was the first time I came up against that gauntlet.' He knew she was waiting and he knew he had to give her more. No, he *owed* her more. 'You know Green Peaks is possessive about its magic,' he said. 'At first, I thought the guard's gauntlets were normal mage armour. I learned the hard way there's a reason the Peak's king only hands them out to his favourite guard. The peridot gauntlet, the one Ash stole, absorbs magic from its target and stores it.' He met her eyes and waited for understanding to dawn.

A huge grin spread over her face. 'The fire in the gauntlet is *yours*,' she said delightedly. 'You want to steal it back to get your magic back.'

'It's not as simple as snatching the gauntlet from his hand,' he said, turning away to adjust the strap of his pack.

'Torvin's curse,' she mused. 'It puts a limit on how much magic you can wield.'

'Something like that,' Killean agreed vaguely. He rolled his shoulders. 'We should head out, before the town guard crack out the pitchforks and flaming torches.'

'Or the housecleaner,' Sammia surveyed the state of the room with something like satisfaction.

They left quickly, ignoring the barman's wide-eyed staring. Killean swallowed a smirk, fairly sure he'd added another footnote to his reprehensible reputation. Repressed, indeed. Kindean would be appalled.

A frisson of something like excitement sang through his veins. He ticked through his agenda, knitting plans together in his thoughts. There were so many game pieces yet to take their proper place on the board and he still didn't know what he was truly playing for – *or against* – but the old thrill was back. The exhilaration of campaigning. That wonderful feeling of having a purpose again. Or at least, the start of one.

What was it, Cactus had said? Everyone was watching him now. All the petty powers in all the nations of the land, watching and waiting to see what he'd do next. And him without even a shirt on his back. He'd commanded that kind of power once, back in the rebellion's ascendency, when he kept confounding his enemies low expectations. The world had been his for the taking then and he'd truly believed anything was possible.

Stupid, adolescent hubris. He'd learned better since then. He'd thought he'd grown out of grand dreams and fanciful agendas. He should know better than to enjoy this. But that hunger was back. The desire to reach for the sun and risk the burn.

Torvin had handed him power when he'd tossed him back into the world without explanation. Killean could feel the world turning on its axis, feel the winds of change shifting his way. Opportunity. The mother of rebellion. The birth of ambition. The game was on and thanks to Cactus, Mishka and all the rest, he finally felt part of it again.

His ebullience lasted until they reached the gates and found them barred by pikemen. Killean sighed. Not again. 'I'm leaving,' he told the head guard, 'That's what you wanted.'

The head guard wore a full helmet designed to resemble a rooster's head crest. Killean assumed the man had on his family's ceremonial armour because that helmet was not fit for battle.

'What I want is your traitor head on my pike,' said the guard.

'Prepare for disappointment,' Killean told him.

At his back, Sammia murmured. 'We're surrounded.'

Killean released a deeper, louder sigh. 'I was given safe passage by Mishka Silverfloe. 'Your soon-to-be mistress,' he reminded the guards closing in on all sides.

The sounds of the market closing down for the day dwindled almost to nothing as stall owners fled to the safety of side streets, leaving behind a few squawking chickens and not much else. The market square was far from deserted, however. It was lousy with armed and armoured men and plenty of gawkers peering down from second floor windows.

Killean chuckled. 'You must really hate me. Public insurrections are hard to live down. Trust me, I know.'

The metal chicken in front of him, defied his appearance by standing his ground. 'You deserve to die,' he said.

'Probably,' Killean conceded. 'But then death comes for everyone, deserved or not, so what does it matter?' He looked the man in the grill plate and said, with steel hardened confidence, 'I won't be dying today.'

If the Onryn Massacre had taught him anything, it was that doing the right and just thing was no shield against cruelty and death. Once he accepted that the concepts the good and well behaved held fast to, like honour and justice, were nothing more than a fine veneer painted over the abyss, he'd realised that just about any action was open to him, because in the end, no matter what kind of man he was, he'd wind up worm food in the ground.

Letting his pack fall to the ground he transformed in the blink of an eye, visualising the word of power in his mind that would transport his clothes to a tiny fold of the Timeless Realm to wait for him to need them again. His wolf form was a powerful beast. Standing on hindlegs he was taller than the guard. He braced his front paws on the guard's shoulders, almost buckling the man's knees and deftly opened his jaws to clench his teeth around the metal frill sticking out of the top of his helmet.

The man's fear was a beautiful bouquet he didn't have near enough time to savour. With a twist and jerk of his head, he wrenched the helmet off the man's head, snapping his neck in the process.

He dropped to all fours, prancing around to face the next wave of attack as the rooster collapsed in a dead heap on the ground. He dove under one spear thrust as Sammia moved to counter, dashed forward, and tore open the guard's femoral artery. He barrelled into his comrade as the man collapsed screaming. Knocking the second pikeman down, he sprang away as Sammia skewered him with her spear.

A man in practical leathers, hunkered low to the ground with two thin blades, one in each hand, squared up to him. He moved with Killean as he darted right and then left, trying to zip around the man to reach the gates. Killean huffed. Were these fools really willing to fight this out to the death? He bared his teeth experimentally; a warning growl trickling up and out of his throat. The guard grinned back at him, tauntingly.

That was the warning, Killean needed to drop into a roll and dodge away from the fireball launched from his blindside. The gout of fire spread over the cobbles between him and the dual-wielding soldier. Killean leapt over the flames, slammed into the soldier's chest and used his diaphragm as a launching pad as he leapt at Ash, who'd broken cover and was now trapped in the no-man's-land between the gate and the high wall.

Ash froze, gauntlet smoking and arm still extended. His face was a picture of shock. Killean didn't know why. The boy ought to know how fast he was on all fours. He ploughed into the boy, knocking him flat and sending them both careening over the cobbles.

Snatching the boy's arm in his jaws, he gave him a quick shake. He wasn't trying to dislocate or puncture anything in particular. He just wanted to give him a good scare. And provide him with a clear target. He started to release the boy, worried he was too stupid to take the shot when scorching pain ignited over his fur.

The pain was intense, locking his muscles. He felt the heat permeate through his body, blazing a trail to his brain. The shock was awesome, but the pain soon gave way to something else, a brief sense of completion, as if the flames had come home. *Again kid*. He willed Ash to discharge the gauntlet a second time. As many as it took to drain its reservoir. It hurt like nothing else but it was working. He could feel it. He could have his magic back in less than a minute.

He sensed something through the white-hot pain and ecstasy painting the backs of his eyelids. A shadow, like a swathe of darkness moving horizontally through the air, inserted itself into the tiny spaces between him and the boy pinned beneath him. Somehow the shadow managed to balloon in size and send Killean flying backward. He landed hard on his back before flipping over onto his paws, thoroughly confused.

What the fuck was this thing?

He saw the shadow, flush to the ground, race across the cobblestones like a moving carpet. It's target was Cactus, stood near a collection of abandoned wood and canvas market stalls. The man wagged one finger at him, as if scolding a misbehaving puppy. The living shadow slithered up his legs and melted into his silhouette, vanishing completely.

Killean bared his teeth, a dangerous growl leaking out between his fangs. *Normal*, his furry arse. The man was Accursed and hiding it.

'What are you doing,' Ash yelled. 'I'm not the bad guy. He is!'

Killean whipped around to find that the town guardsmen – the one's Sammia hadn't poked holes in – had converged on Ash, weapons drawn. He cocked his head, amazed at the guards' fickleness. Then again, Ash had managed to set fire to a few market stalls and a hayrick leaning up against a wall. He dropped to his haunches, preparing to leap, while the guards were distracted.

Cactus' shadow raced across the cobblestones toward him. Killean rolled out of the way, whirling about to face the threat. The shadow had no scent. No mass until it wished to. He lunged at it anyway, just to see what happened, and his teeth clicked closed on empty air. The shadow withdrew, returning to Cactus.

'Leave,' Cactus told him. 'The boy is not for you.'

Killean snarled. The guards were massing, ignoring Cactus in favour of closing in on he and Sammia. Ash was already in custody. Killean could dispatch the guards, but he didn't yet have the measure of the shadow.

It had squeezed into half an inch of thin air and expanded with enough force to throw him three feet backward. Was that the limit of its strength, or could it expand to eclipse all the light in the open marketplace and smother him in darkness? He had no idea and until he knew one way or the other, he could not risk a fight. He transformed, reclaiming his man skin and his clothes.

'This isn't over,' he told Cactus.

'Never is with the likes of you,' he agreed.

Killean heard the clank and whirr of a crank being turned. Sammia barked, 'Gate's open.'

He turned and ran. This was not how he'd wanted to leave the city he'd once dreamed of making his capital one day. He couldn't help but wonder if Cactus had set up the ambush at the gates for this end, a subtle reminder of all he'd lost to defeat. That was a score to settle for another day. He knew when to retreat and regroup. He knew that in time, he'd get to take his shot against Cactus and his puppet master, Torvin.

Chapter Eleven

He and Sammia hot footed it along the bank of the river. The Uswe was wide and deep, impossible to cross except by bridge and the stony bank dwindled to nothing as the land flattened out. They joined the road as it tracked alongside the fast-flowing muddy waters.

'What was that about?' Sammia asked, grumpy from the run.

'Torvin flexing his muscle.'

He looked behind him. The town walls loomed against the grey skyscape, taunting him. But at least no one was firing cannon. Anger simmered under his skin when he thought how close he'd come to getting his magic back. If Cactus' little stunt had cost him his only chance to drain the gauntlet, he'd figure out a way to take it out of his hide, shadow and all.

It started to drizzle again as the sky darkened to the shade of a fresh blackeye, evening threatening on the horizon. Lush green pastures fringed the road and stands of bamboo forest rose in patches in the distance toward the foothills, all dripping wet and bowed under the rain.

'The pirate will be back,' Sammia warned him. 'We need a plan to deal with him. I suggest the tried-and-true skewering.'

He smiled thinly. 'Did you see his shadow?'

'Yeah.' She snorted. 'Some magic, huh?'

He shot her a look. Surprised that she seemed so unbothered by a type of magic he'd never even heard of before. Had she seen the like before? 'That shadow can act independently. And it's strong.' He told her how he'd been tossed away from Ash like scrap paper.

Sammia hummed. 'I thought you were going to kill the brat.'

Killean snorted. 'I barely scratched him. I needed him to fire point blank. That way no one would see when I drained the magic out of the gauntlet.'

'Did you?' she asked him.

He pursed his lips. 'No.'

While he'd felt something begin to give as the fire had coursed into him without doing any permanent damage, he hadn't been able to retain the flame or break the curse Torvin had placed on him. 'I just needed more time,' he said frustratedly.

The gathering gloom had leeched the colour from the environment, soaking everything in a damp greyscale. Sammia was mostly in shadow, only the tip of her spear and the shimmer of her scale mail catching the dwindling light. A gust of wet wind swept up the road. Killean turned his face away from the spray and shook the loose hair out of his eyes.

'Which way?' Sammia asked. She held her spear horizontally by the middle of the shaft, sharp end thrust forward. 'Are we headed north to Cow or doubling back to the second portal location in Clover Cove?'

It was a good question. Cow was the obvious choice. The portal site was just over the border. The oligarchs of Cow, once his allies, would happily sell him to the highest bidder now, but they would also look unkindly on incursion by Three Rivers' agents. If he was fast and avoided attracting attention, he could reach the portal site and be gone before the oligarchs knew he was there. He had contacts in Dairydale that might be willing to trade with him still.

On the other hand, he still needed funds. Reaching Frolicking Squirrel from either the Barley Lands or Cow would mean crossing back into Three Rivers. The second portal location was in the west Barley Lands, in an isolated locale that Killean knew well enough but a Three Rivers agent like Cactus who had not fought in the war did not. Caution suggested, staying in Barley made the most sense, but...

'Cow,' he said firmly. 'I'm tired of delays.'

Sammia snorted. 'Liar. You want to stay on the main road in case Cactus and the boy follow us. You want to lure them across the border. Cow still likes you more than it likes Three Rivers.'

'That's debatable,' he muttered.

'Whereas the Barley Lands have been nicely suborned,' Sammia argued back, twisting the knife just a little. 'Bet that sticks in your craw,' she added smugly.

It did. It really did. Ungrateful bastards. But then there had always been a lot of Rivers sympathisers in the south. 'Just because Cockle Shore is Rivers territory doesn't mean the rest of Barley feels the same way,' he said.

Sammia wasn't impressed. 'Word has spread about your release, but I don't see any uprisings springing up in your name,' she pointed out.

'Why would they? I haven't raised a banner.'

'There's no one left to follow it,' Sammia retorted sharply.

There was that. Uncle Dadarro's army – *his* army – had been built on a backbone of the lost and the damned. When Killean had failed them, most would have slunk away to isolated corners of the continent to lick their wounds and hide away from the world, like they had for most of their lives. He'd need more than a banner to entice the Accursed out of hiding again.

'There's a rumour you turned coat,' Sammia said softly, her words almost lost in the drizzle. It was true dark now. The air thick and muffled by the soft fall of rain. The wind falling still under the downpour.

Killean was quiet for a long moment. 'I know,' he said. 'I've heard the rumours. There was no *deal*,' he said fiercely. 'I didn't barter an early release on my uncle's life.'

Sammia sighed. 'I didn't want to believe it,' she admitted. 'Not the part about you offing Dadarro,' she clarified. 'We kept telling you to do *that* since the fiasco at Very Big Rock. Still. They say you took him out at the last to save Shiny Scale.' He could feel her gaze on him. He heard the question she wasn't asking, and the incredulity behind it.

'That part is true. Somewhat,' he admitted. 'Dadarro tried and failed to use the Firefly. He went into a rage and risked what was left of our campaign to capture Nadil. He performed a magical ritual that cratered Dragon's Ascent. If I'd let him finish, he'd have turned all of Barley into a wasteland and still failed to become a god.'

Telling Sammia this was dangerous. She hadn't been at the final battle. She hadn't seen the destruction Dadarro unleashed. She couldn't know that at the last, the battle stopped being one of sides and became a matter of survival. It had been Dadarro against the rest of them. The uprising had already been in shambles.

Cow betrayed him in the end, her generals refusing to take the field at the battle of Dragon's Ascent. Harkiv and his army had been tied down dealing with a rebellion raised by a Three Rivers puppet, unable to come to Killean's aid in time. He'd had to marshal a rump force of mostly Accursed to defend his home against an ascendant Three Rivers army led by a heroic dragon shifter and a newly minted High King who could split the ground with a single, magical lightning bolt. The army had been in rout even before Dadarro had scattered most of it by blowing everything up around them.

'The rebellion died in Shrimpton,' he said quietly. 'We were all trapped in the death throes of a dream after that.'

'Poetic,' Sammia retorted. 'Utter bullshit, but nicely put. You went from Shrimpton to Green Peaks and managed to take Harlin Hill and the port of Summerlee. Hardly the actions of an army in retreat.'

He conceded her point with a tired sigh. While his campaign in Green Peaks had led to a personal disaster, one he had hoped to turn to his advantage with the peridot gauntlet, his forces *had* made valuable territorial gains by taking Green Peaks and his enemies by surprise when he sailed into Summerlee and then moved into Harlin Hill.

A part of him wished he'd bedded down in Green Peaks and focused on a ground war there, rather than following his uncle's lead and going after another of Myron's relics. At the time, he hadn't wanted to spread his forces too thin, worried about a Three Rivers mounted invasion of Barley Lands. But considering how things had ended, he'd have infinitely preferred his uncle's maniacal meltdown to have occurred in Green Peaks and not his old backyard.

'You know Torvin's trying to trap you into acting in Three Rivers interests,' Sammia told him softly. 'He made an alliance with Jumping Carp last year. If you publicly end the Blue Crab, he can come forward and claim you were working for him in the name of the alliance.'

Killean stopped dead. 'Mamie never mentioned *that*,' he muttered, working his jaw.

Sammia shrugged. 'Still want to go after Gakai and this Pearl-thingy?' she asked.

'Yes. I'm boxed in at the moment. The only way to get out is to get my hands on that Pearl.'

Sammia hummed noncommittally but he thought there was just a hint of approval in her tone. He glanced at her quickly, without turning his head. He wished he could figure out her angle. She'd been asking him a lot of questions. Some of them he could write off as her wanting to know what she'd signed on for, but the rest – she kept probing him for his motives, as if assessing his answers for what she could use for her own ends.

He knew he was paranoid, but that was because everyone and their relics was regularly out to get him. And the Dread Goddess herself knew he'd given Sammia cause to want her pound of flesh. Could he trust her, he wondered. A stupid question. He already did. At least somewhat. He trusted her not to stab him in the back for now. But the future was an open book ready to be written in blood.

'You're thinking too hard. There's steam rising from your ears,' she said, proving her point when she casually tripped him with the end of her spear. He caught his balance and glared at her.

He hadn't seen her shift the spear across her body. That was dangerous. His night vision was good. He'd just been too distracted worrying about whether he could trust her he hadn't been doing the one thing he should have been doing, which was *watching* her.

Killean sighed and consulted his mental map. While they'd "rested" somewhat at the Rhubarb and Duckling, neither he nor Sammia had slept in hours and soon it would be too dark to keep walking. This road was good. He'd marched an army along it once upon a time. But it was also out in the open with large tracks of land lost in gloom on either side. It would be hard to spot ambushers in the dark. They needed to seek shelter for the night.

'There used to be a small settlement built around a post inn ten miles dead ahead,' he said.

Sammia groaned. 'What about a farmhouse?' she asked. 'I'm not too proud to beg for an hour by someone's fire. And if that doesn't work, my spear can be mighty persuasive.'

Killean nodded, looking up at the dark, moonless sky. 'I'll take wing and scout the area,' he said. 'You take shelter in those trees over there.'

He let the thermals decide his route. Dipping and rising on the current, he rode the air, wide wings spread. There was peace in his hawk form. A freedom found only in the air. The world was laid out below him like one of his uncle's military models, the topography of hill and valley, river and roads flattened and smoothed out by distance. Flying between cloud and ground he could see the shadows chasing the near non-existent breeze as the rain finally ceased, the slight breeze turned the patchwork fields into rippling traps for the eye. He could see the distant cluster of dark shingle roofs of the settlement and a coach headed their way on the lonely road.

Killean dove toward the trees, shifting to human, his clothes weaving around him as he drew them back into the realm of the real. 'There's a mail coach headed our way. We can hijack it.'

'Maybe we'll heist Kindean's private mail while we're at it,' Sammia suggested brightly.

The driver of the mail coach had a flintlock pistol but poor night vision, which resulted in him missing his one-shot firing at Killean in hawk form. Sammia knocked him off the carriage with the blunt end of her spear, harrying him along the ground with quick stabbing thrusts of the sharp end and driving him into a ditch on the side of the road. Killean reclaimed his man-skin and forced the passengers out of the carriage.

He directed them to the ditch and swung himself up onto the driver's bench, claiming the reins. Sammia joined him shortly after, clutching a string of pearls and two fat coin purses nestled to her chest.

'What?' she asked when she saw him looking. 'It's not a hijacking if no one gets robbed. I took this as well.' She brandished the driver's pistol, before tucking it away into the voluminous pockets of her red skirt. He was fairly sure she had a concealed holster strapped to her thigh and slit in her pocket for a quick draw.

'Did you remember the powder?' he asked driving the paired horses toward the edge of the road in an arc that would see them facing the opposite direction at the end of it, or possibly see the carriage tumble into the ditch if he misjudged the angle.

'Of course,' she scoffed. 'What do you take me for?'

'I don't like guns.' He said, focused on the reins in his hand and the horses in front of him. The carriage chassis rocked and jounced as it performed a U-turn on the road.

'Never understood why. You're normally up for anything gunpowder related,' Sammia said.

'They're too slow,' he muttered. 'I can bring down two men with tooth and claw before you can reload and aim that thing.' Plus his fire, when he'd had it, could immolate multiple targets with much greater ease.

'That was a fun. I like a good hold up,' Sammia announced changing the subject and asked, 'Are we racing to the border or driving until we find somewhere to bed down?'

'We'll see how far we get,' he said. The coach was poorly sprung and already he could feel the vibration radiating up through his bones.

'You'd think Torvin would spend a bit more on a coach with the royal crest painted on it,' Sammia grumbled.

'Why would he care? It's not his crest,' Killean retorted.

Despite having the mandate and a daughter with which to start a new dynasty, Torvin had made no attempts replace the trappings of the Camry line with his own. Killean suspected he intended for Nadil to replace him at which time, Three Rivers would finally stop pretending Nadil Shiny Scale was anything other than the last Camry.

Officially an orphan of no particular lineage, it was an open secret in Three Rivers and beyond that Nadil was the Camry bastard heir. He had to be. Only the Camry and Onryn bloodlines possessed the power to turn scale and the Onryn had always claimed their bastards, in both the literal and figurative sense, just to keep the power in the blood.

Killean had never understood how Nadil could have done so much for a nation that refused to grant him his birthright, while declaring him their hero. But very little Nadil did made any sense to him. He seemed content to be used, first as a living weapon, and later as a symbol of Three Rivers' moral conceit.

Killean couldn't throw too many stones about that. He'd done much the same with his uncle and got less out of the deal than Nadil. Maybe that was the nub of the problem. He couldn't understand how Nadil seemed to succeed without trying, while Killean schemed and fought and still had no choice but to accept defeat in the end.

Should something happen to Torvin before he could officially declare an heir, Three Rivers would be sunk into a succession crisis. The three main contenders to the throne would be Nadil, Mishka and his brother, Kindean, thanks to his upcoming nuptials to Mishka and the restoration of Barley Lands as a protectorate. Wouldn't that be twist. If, after everything that had happened, an Onryn sat upon Three Rivers high throne? Then again, Killean would be forced to kill his brother to assuage the insult if it did, so his brother's reign would be a short one.

Nadil as king would be a disaster. He was too good. Too forgiving. Too eager to make peace with his enemies and too soft on everyone else. He'd drive Three Rivers into the ground within a decade. Killean would back his claim just to see him do it. The one silver lining in his defeat was the knowledge that by saving Nadil, he'd condemned Three Rivers to a legacy of lousy kings.

In the dark, as they trundled along, a large shadow passing swiftly overhead, just below the low cloud line, was easy to miss. Maybe if Killean hadn't been thinking about Nadil right at that very moment he might have done just that. But he had, so he didn't.

Looking up, he saw the serpentine shape rippling through the air like a dull silver snake, a few shiny scales finding some form of errant light from the moon hidden by cloud, so that the dragon was just visible in the night sky.

'For the love of —,' Killean hissed, biting back his curse and drawing the horses up.

Sammia jolted out of a light doze. 'What is it?'

'Guess,' he growled.

Sammia looked up, saw the dragon twist like a streamer in the air and arrow down toward the ground, landing in the field on their right. 'By the nameless what does *he* want?' she snarled.

Nadil's dragon form was somewhere between white and silver and long as a ribbon. His head was as smooth as a salamander and his wings bunched like crimped paper between his stumpy front and powerful back legs. He stood on his hindlegs, spine and torso crooked and bent like a ferret as he waited for them. The horses tossed their heads, jangling their reins and flexing against the harnesses.

'We could just ignore him,' Sammia suggested.

Killean sighed and dropped down from the carriage. 'Wait here. This won't take long.'

Once Nadil was sure Killean was ready to meet him in man-skin, he shifted out of his scales. Standing in the crushed grass, Three Rivers hero fussed with his pale cape. His shock of blond hair, long on top and cropped close at the sides, was swept back in a wave off his brow. Killean could just make out the sheepish grin on his face.

'Sorry,' Nadil said brightly, 'I didn't mean to scare the horses.'

Killean responded in the only way a sane man could. He grabbed Nadil by the shoulders and headbutted him straight in the face.

Chapter Twelve

'Ahh!' Nadil staggered back, clutching his nose. Blood spurted between his fingers. Large, aggrieved blue eyes stared at Killean. 'Why'd you go and do that?' he slurred, words muffled by his hands and thickened by blood.

Ignoring his pounding head, Killean said nothing. His hands curled and uncurled into fists at his sides. Had he summoned the moron just by thinking about him? Did the gods really hate him so much?

Sadly, Nadil didn't bleed for long. He was a dragon shifter. He healed fast. Wiping off his mouth and chin, Nadil shook the blood off his hands, cleaning his palms on his no longer quite so pristine white cape. The bastard looked him up and down and then had the audacity to smirk. 'Mishka was right. You have let yourself go.'

A muscle ticked in Killean's jaw. *Murder him. Snap his neck. It might not take but Starless Night it'll feel good.* Killean counted down from five in his head, pushing down the homicidal little voice in his head. 'What are you doing here?' he asked through his teeth.

'I'm coming with you to Shipwright Island,' Nadil stated boldly.

What the fuck! 'No, you are not.'

Planting his feet and propping his hands on his hips Nadil mimicked his tone, 'Yes. I. Am.'

Killean's thoughts raced. Mostly just one word on repeat. *Fuck. Fuck. Fuck.* 'You are not,' he said again.

Nadil jerked his chin up, just asking to be punched. 'I am.'

'You. Are. Not.'

'I. Am.'

'Are not.'

'Am too.'

'No.'

'Yes.'

Killean delivered an uppercut to Nadil's guts. The draconic little weasel must have sensed something in his body language because he twitched to the side, taking some of the sting out of Killean's strike. He did end up wheezing like a bellows and half-doubled over, which was gratifying.

Hopeless optimist he might be, but Nadil was still a warrior. He caught hold of Killean's arm, jerking him off balance and twisting it violently. Killean broke the grip and Nadil kicked him in the side of the knee. He collapsed to one leg, wrestling Nadil down to the ground with him.

The tussle that followed was too undignified to recount. It ended with them both back on their feet and facing off, a growl trickling up Killean's throat while Nadil grinned wide just like he had when they were children after a long training session, the pair of them egging each other on to further and further annoyance in the name of competition and sheer devilry.

Killean drew a quick breath, swiping the back of his hand over his split bottom lip. He scrambled for a smidgen of self-control. It was an effort.

Nadil crooked his fingers and cooed, 'Here, wolfy-wolfy. Come get me.'

Screw it.

Killean transformed, barely maintaining the presence of mind to banish his clothes to safety first. In wolf form he lunged at Nadil. The absolute swine vanished. His body compacting and transforming into that of a lean hare, immediately lost in the long grass just beyond the dragon's landing site. Killean took off through the grass, chasing the tiny twitching vibrations through the stems left in the hare's wake.

His jaws snapped shut a scant breath away from a cute little bob-tail. There was a backwash of displaced air and magic as Nadil transformed again, taking the form of a pale wolf. He whipped around to snap at Killean's shoulder and the two tumbled down, rolling through the stalks. Breaking loose, Killean took wing, bursting out of the long grass in his hawk form. Nadil became an eagle and took off after him. His mass and wingspan dwarfed Killean's but the Hero of Three Rivers seemed content to harass him instead of closing in for the kill.

On the name of the Onryn, Killean *hated* this arsehole.

He dove for solid ground, reclaiming his man-skin and his clothes. He caught his balance on two feet, and spun around as the eagle dropped groundward with a piercing cry. What he wouldn't give for his fire magic right now. Nadil landed in the flesh, still grinning, teeth luminous in the moonlight breaking through the clouds.

In sheer frustration Killean yelled, 'Why hasn't anyone killed you yet!'

Nadil fussed with his cape. 'Someone came close. Then *you* stopped him.'

'So you're what? Punishing me for my mistake?' Killean shook his hair off his face, breathing hard and ground out, 'Words cannot express how much I hate you.'

Nadil beamed like he'd given him a great compliment. 'Admit it. That was fun,' he said cheerfully.

If Killean wasn't careful he was going to pop a blood vessel. 'I'm going to eat your liver,' he decided.

'Eww. Have you turned cannibal?' Nadil grimaced. 'I had no idea you were that hard-up. Wait,' he shouted. 'Don't hit me again. I didn't come here to fight.'

'Then why did you start one?'

'I didn't. You hit me first,' Nadil replied, sounding smug.

Killean covered his face with his hands. 'Will you just fuck off?' he asked. Asked, not begged. He'd never beg.

'Can't do that,' Nadil said brightly. 'I was called in to deal with your rampage.'

'My what?' Killean asked flatly.

'Rampage,' Nadil repeated helpfully.

'I'm not on a rampage,' Killean objected.

'Tell that to the guards you killed,' Nadil snapped losing his smile.

'I was illegally detained,' Killean snapped back. 'I was given safe passage and those guards ambushed me. One of them threatened to decapitate me.'

Nadil shook his head. 'You could have taken them down without killing them, Ilin.'

Technically, he only had one confirmed kill. But Sammia didn't tend to mess around with that spear of hers and neither of them were in the habit of underestimating men in armour making threats on their lives. Nadil must have insultingly little faith in the competency of Three Rivers' guards if he thought Killean could incapacitate over a dozen men without a single fatality with half his magic bound.

He curled his lip. 'Spare me the moral indignation. *That* was not a rampage.'

Nadil was deadly serious now. 'You killed civilians in Potbelly.'

'No, I didn't.' He was on more solid ground here. He'd hardly spoken to any of the natives, let alone killed anyone.

Nadil's gaze flicked behind him to where Sammia was standing back by the road, undoubtedly enjoying the hell out of all of this.

'Maybe you didn't kill those farmers, but you did nothing to help them either,' he accused.

Killean just stared at him. He couldn't possibly be serious. 'I'm a vagrant, not a roaming guard. It's never been my job to police Potbelly Hills.'

'You hijacked that mail coach,' Nadil pointed angrily behind him.

'True,' Killean conceded. 'But I did it in a controlled and orderly manner.' *And nobody died*, he thought but did not say.

'That's really not the point, Ilin,' Nadil said softly.

'It is when you're accusing me of rampaging through the countryside,' he said confidently. 'When I decide to go on a rampage, you'll know it.'

'Yeah. That's what we're all afraid of,' Nadil huffed, kicking at the grass at his feet like a little kid. 'You know, after five years in the Timeless Realm and these last six months, I was really hoping you might have calmed down. I mean, I'm not thrilled about your alliance with the Sly Fox, but you took most of your marks alive. I really thought you were turning a corner.' He threw Killean a reproving look mostly obscured by the gloom.

Killean reached behind him to tie his hair back only to discover he'd lost the strip off cloth to do it. Irritated, he shook his hair off his shoulders. 'You mentioned Shipwright Island before. Let's get to that,' he said.

'We know about the deal you made with Jumping Carp,' Nadil said.

Killean noted the repeated use of the word "we" but did not comment on it. 'No shit,' he drawled instead. 'Out of interest, what did Torvin offer Mamie to get her to set this sting operation up?'

Mamie Cat was working for Torvin. The High King was pulling all the strings. Somehow, he'd learned about Rhadu Gakai's theft of the Pearl and decided to use it to wipe out the Blue Crab, yank

Killean's chain and perhaps, get his hands on the Gakai. Why, Killean couldn't begin to guess. But Mamie and her clan had been the lever to get this scheme off the ground.

Now Torvin had sent Nadil after him to keep him in check. He should have known, after Kindean was mysteriously recalled to Delta City. In her own way, Mishka had been warning him – or perhaps taunting him – when she kept name-dropping Nadil in their earlier conversation.

'The Silk Paw are implicated in an act of treason,' Nadil told him gravely.

This did surprise him. 'Mamie wouldn't be that careless,' he said confidently.

Nadil was still uncommonly grim and still. 'Maybe you've overestimated her,' he said. 'She's in a lot of trouble. In a way, you're bailing her out,' he admitted.

Killean cocked his head. 'What the hell did she do?' he asked uneasily. Whatever it was, if *he* was her saving grace it had to be big.

'Yeah, I'm not telling you that,' Nadil said bluntly. 'I'm here to make sure you go through with infiltrating the Crab. I'm not giving you any ideas for anything else.'

'You tease,' Killean retorted flatly. 'You're just trying to trick me into thinking you got interesting in the last five years.'

Nadil snorted. He looked up at the heavy sky. 'It's getting late. We should get going.'

Killean smiled thinly. 'Nice try. You're not coming with us.'

'You can't actually stop me. I'm stronger than you right now,' Nadil remined him gently.

'Maybe,' Killean conceded. 'But as you've confirmed how very *necessary* I am to Torvin's newest scheme, I could set my mind to screwing him and you over instead of cooperating,' he pointed out equally pleasantly. 'You know how good I am at ruining masterplans.'

Just ask Uncle Dadarro. A casual observer might even say he'd ruined his own treasured plans by saving Nadil in the final battle. Any casual observer who did say that would be wrong, of course. Wrong and dead if he said it in Killean's hearing, but the point remained. From a certain vantage point, the only thing he was good for was making a mess.

Nadil sighed loudly. 'Can't you just do this one thing, take the money and, you know, not make everything more difficult than it needs to be?' he whined.

'You've met me,' Killean replied, 'What do you think?'

'Ugh,' Nadil groaned. 'You know, I think I hate Minuidon even more than you do,' he said, the non-sequitur leaving Killean momentarily speechless. Nadil didn't seem to notice. 'If he hadn't betrayed the Striking Talon clan, you'd never have had a reason to side with Dadarro. We could have kept you on our side and all of *this*' – he waved his hands in the air like a weirdo – 'would be so much easier now.'

'I have no idea what you're talking about,' Killean told him. 'But thanks for the reminder that I was justified in my rebellion.'

Nadil shot him a sharp-eyed look, the intensity of which he could feel even in the gloom. 'You were justified in wanting Minuidon gone,' he said. 'And in hunting down the mercenaries that killed your family. The rest?' He shook his head, words heavy as he demanded, 'Do you even know why you did it? You never cared about Myron's Relics.'

'I picked my side,' he replied. 'Just like you did. When you pick a side in a war, you're all in or you're dead.'

'You picked the wrong side, Ilin.'

'Maybe,' he said, 'but it's done now. Wishing it was different is a waste of time.'

'Just answer this one question: do you regret any of it?'

Killean didn't owe him an answer. Hell, Nadil was the one who owed *him* his life. There was no loyalty, no debts of honour compelling him to tell the truth. He did it anyway. 'Yes,' he said quietly. 'I have regrets.'

Nadil scrubbed a hand through his hair, which was flopping forward over his brow like a cockerel's limp crest. He let out a gusty breath. 'That's something,' he said softly. 'I mean, I always knew you had to, deep down, but it's something that you can admit it.'

'If you say so,' Killean looked at him. 'Not that I care, but you seem...stressed. Are you sure you want to be wasting time with me, when you clearly have more important things to deal with?' he asked.

Nadil Shiny Scale was a benign, grinning idiot. But he had his moments of depth and substance. There was pain and resentment hidden beneath the spit-polished exterior and Killean knew exactly where the fault lines were. But for the most part, the inane good cheer and manic determination to see the best in people was real. That was why he was so intensely irritating. Still, this new, jaded side of Nadil was oddly unsettling.

Nadil snickered and shook his head. 'Nice try, Ilin. I'm still not telling you what's going on.'

Killean hadn't been fishing for information to begin with, so he simply shrugged. 'You realise how it will look, the Hero of Three Rivers palling around with me while I do...whatever it is needs doing.'

He wasn't being coy. The truth was every participant in this rapidly enlarging cast of conspirators knew more than he did about what was really going on. He couldn't formulate any concrete plan of action when he still wasn't sure what the main players wanted of him, or what his enemy might be preparing. He enjoyed the danger, for sure, but it concerned him that Torvin would be so blatant as to team up his heroic heir with a down and out villain. The implications of the move were...disturbing.

'If that's your roundabout way of asking if Three Rivers are claiming you as our agent, then the answer is yes,' Nadil told him bluntly. 'We were always going to have to figure out some way of bringing you into the fold – Torvin had hoped you'd go home to Barley and make peace with Kindean,' he admitted. 'Yeah, I know. I told him pigs would fly first. This mess with Jumping Carp wasn't planned but it...works.' He shrugged.

It worked? Talking to Nadil was like dental surgery for the brain. Painful, unpleasant and left your head aching for hours after.

'You know what I do,' Killean reminded him. 'You just accused me of a rampage, but we both know Cockle Shore was nothing compared to what I'm capable of. Is the Realm Pearl really worth associating with me?'

Nadil didn't answer him. Something on the road had distracted him. 'Uh, oh,' he said.

Killean was running back toward the road before Sammia shouted an alarm. She had her spear in both hands and was jabbing at something Killean couldn't see, but as he drew closer, he realised Sammia wasn't fighting thin air alone.

Cactus' shadow was back. Almost invisible in the darkness, the only indication it was there was a faint warping in the air, like heat haze that floated five feet off the ground. Still too far to do anything or two feet or four, Killean could only watch as the shadow enveloped Sammia, spear and all. The shadow widened, resembling the ripping form of a great flat fish, it undulated over the ditch deposited Sammia's body in the grass.

Killean dropped to his knees beside her, touching her cool cheek. Her eyes were open and glassy, illuminated by a sliver of moonlight. Scooping her up in his arms, he snarled at Nadil, 'If she doesn't revive, I'll have your head for this.'

Nadil simply nodded, expression grim as he looked at the floating mass of black air. He called out, 'Call him off, Cactus. You were ordered not to hurt the Death Child.'

Two figures emerged from the behind the coach. Cactus and Ash. Both were illuminated by the green glow of Ash's gauntlet, the boy holding his arm aloft like a torch. The sickly, dancing light painted his face in harsh shade that couldn't quite hide the shocked look on his face.

Killean curled his lip. 'I was expecting an ambush at the border, not forty miles out of town.'

'I know,' Nadil replied sounding pleased. 'No way was I letting you get to Cow.'

Had Nadil carried the spy and Ash on his back as he flew through the air? Dragon flight was not exactly safe travelling for human passengers. It was freezing cold at higher altitude and dragon shifters didn't come equipped with reins and halters. But there was no other explanation for how the pair could be here now. No wonder Ash looked shaken.

Sammia returned to life in his arms. Her body spasmed. Her mouth opened on a rough gasp and her lungs filled with air. Killean shifted her back against his chest, supporting her and keeping her upright as she twitched and shuddered.

'What the fuck?' she choked out.

'Ambush,' he replied. 'Cactus and Ash are here.'

Sammia glared baleful death at the spy standing at the edge of the road. His shadow returned to him and vanished. She tried to surge to her feet. Killean didn't stop her, but her own weakness did. She fell back into his lap, rasping, 'What did he do to me?'

'Killed you. Don't ask me how,' Killean admitted. He watched Cactus too, thinking thoughts of bloody retribution.

Cactus bowed, shallowly, at the waist. 'Your reputation proceeds you, Sammia Child of Death. There are few, even among the Accursed, who can survive Jadek.'

Sammia jerked her head up to look at Killean, smacking him in the chin as she did so. 'Why aren't you killing him?' she demanded.

'Because he doesn't know how,' Cactus replied smugly.

'That's enough,' Nadil barked, a lash of command in his tone. He climbed up on the road. 'I told you to stay back and let me handle things,' he accused Cactus.

Cactus shrugged. 'The woman spotted us.'

'Only because you broke cover.'

'It was the boy's fault.'

'It's true,' Sammia said. 'I spotted Ash because he kept the gauntlet powered up.'

'It's not my fault,' Ash complained. 'The stupid thing isn't working right.' He shook his arm, yelping when the steady low flame spurted higher and nearly finished off the holey remains of his singed cape.

'Uh,' Nadil smoothed his hair back. 'Who is this?' he asked, warily facing Ash.

'The boy travelled with them,' Cactus said. 'The traitor ditched him in Cockle Shore. I freed him from the town guard because I thought he might be useful.'

'I'm not with them,' Ash insisted. 'I'm on a mission to bring the traitor to justice.'

'It's true,' Killean said blandly when everyone looked his way. 'He's on a proper revenge trip. He thinks I killed his father.'

'Did you?' Nadil asked tiredly.

'No idea,' Killean admitted truthfully. 'But let's be honest, the odds are good.'

Nadil prompted him, 'And you were dragging around some random kid who wants to kill you because...'

'If I'd left him in Jumping Carp he'd be dead now. The portal ambush sucked Ash into the top-secret meeting with Obawai and his cronies. The kid heard everything.' Killean shrugged. 'I could have slit his throat, I suppose, but I appreciate a good revenge tale. Plus, the kid isn't an actual threat —'

'Hey!' Ash shouted. 'That's not true. I blasted you good in Cockle Shore.'

'Of course you did,' Killean drawled.

Ash uttered an inchoate growl and pointed his gauntleted arm at him. Killean smiled. Cactus knocked the boy backward and he almost toppled into the ditch on the other side of the road. Killean lost his smile.

'What do you want to do with the boy,' Cactus asked Nadil.

Nadil did not sound at all happy when he said, 'We have to take him with us. He's under Three Rivers protection from now on.'

'Three Rivers...?' Ash trailed off weakly.

Killean grinned, as much in amusement as satisfaction that Nadil had just done exactly what he'd hoped he'd do. 'Meet Nadil Shiny Scale, kid. Nadil, this is Ashinue Rogu of the Dancing Deer clan. Son of Ashinue Rogu *Senior*. Who was either a member of Green Peaks elite guard or a fire eating acrobat – I'm not sure which. I will say that I've nothing against circus folk so if I did kill his father, he was definitely the former.'

Ash jerked sharply in surprise, turning away from Nadil to stare at him. 'How did you —?'

Sammia snorted. 'I'm a Peaker, kid. I *know* what the Dancing Deer clan are known for. You're all thieves and circus freaks.' Regaining her strength she sat up. She pulled away from him. Killean regretted the loss of her warmth.

'Alright,' Nadil said distractedly as he battled to repair his quiff, 'Thief, acrobat, dancing bear, it doesn't matter. I'm formally deputising you as an agent of Three Rivers,' he informed Ash.

'Dancing *Deer*,' Ash grumbled and then as Nadil's meaning filtered past his teenage moodiness, he squawked, 'For real? I'm your deputy?'

'Don't get excited,' Killean told him. 'I'm pretty sure he's about to deputise me and Sami too.'

'I am,' Nadil confirmed. 'From this moment on the five of us are a covert cell.'

Sammia chuffed a laugh. 'Oh, this is rich. I wish Bodai was here. He'd get a real kick out of this.'

'No, he wouldn't,' Killean said. 'Bodai doesn't have a sense of humour.'

'He'd make an exception here,' Sammia insisted. Twisting in the grass she turned to him and asked, 'Are you really going to accept this? Three Rivers is your enemy.'

Killean shrugged. 'We're getting paid, apparently, and if I'm going down for this I can think of worse things than taking Shiny Scale with me.' He addressed Nadil, 'I distinctly remember you mentioning something about money.'

'Of course you do,' Nadil muttered. In a clearer voice he said, 'Three Rivers rewards her agents. And protects them too.'

'This is some twist,' Sammia muttered.

Killean hummed in agreement. He stood up, swiping down his coat and then offering a hand to Sammia. She levered herself up without it. 'If we're not going to Cow, we've got to turn the coach around,' he said. 'The other portal site is in the opposite direction.' Truthfully, he was surprised the horses hadn't bolted already. The poor beasts were surrounded by vicious weirdos.

'Right,' Nadil agreed cheerfully. 'Cactus, you and Ash will ride in the carriage with the Death Child. I'll ride up front with Ilin.'

Sammia snatched at Killean's sleeve as Nadil moved forward to herd the other two into the coach. 'Please tell me we're ditching these losers at the first opportunity,' she whispered fiercely.

'Sami,' he murmured, shaking his head in mock approbation. 'What do you take me for? I have something much worse planned for all of them.'

Chapter Thirteen

They travelled through most of the night only stopping at a small coach inn on a long, lonely road in hilly country when the horses grew tired. He and Nadil had spoken little on the journey, which was a mixed blessing. No doubt Nadil thought he was being magnanimous in victory, sparing Killean more of his prattle. The quiet was nice, but Killean might honestly have preferred an awkward conversation about the war over a bumpy ride through increasingly rough and unpopulated land with only the silence of the landscape for company. There were signs of the ravages of his war everywhere he looked, from blackened skeletons of gutted stone houses to husks of dead trees along the roadside. It left him feeling depressed.

Nadil took care of acquiring them rooms for the night. Sammia and Ash were forced to bunk in a room across the hall while Killean had to bed down with Cactus and Nadil. It said something about how tired they all were that the arguments were kept to a minimum. Killean still added a notch against Three Rivers tally. His reckoning was getting expensive indeed.

Despite the company and having to share a double bed with Nadil, he fell asleep quickly. Consider who was waiting for him in his dreams, he would have preferred insomnia.

Dadarro sat on a golden throne. Its back wrought to look like a snarling tiger. The big cat's huge head and gaping jaws sat atop the throne, its contorted front limbs forming the throne's arms. The gold had been scoured and inlaid with stripes of glittering jet. A tiger pelt stretched over the seat, the vivid orange of the dead cat's fur faded by time and wear.

They were in the open, a wide expanse of dream world with nothing in it, except aching emptiness and a gritty breeze that smelled of battle, disturbing the red dust at Killean's feet. Thunder growled above him and the angry, swirling black clouds were lit with flashes of lightning.

His uncle had not been a big man in life. His frame was slim and compact, his features clean and handsome and his face long and angular. He wore robes of cloth of gold and silver and his long aristocratic fingers were laden with rings as he leaned on one elbow, his head cupped in his hand. His fine brown hair was swept from his face, revealing a pronounced widows peak. Sometime between his death and appearing in Killean's dream, he'd acquired a carefully sculpted beard that grew from his chin and was tied off with a gold ribbon. Which was certainly a new look for his uncle. Killean had never noticed before much alike Kindean and his uncle looked. It was disturbing.

Dadarro's eyes were not Kindean's eyes, however. They smouldered with a weak, golden brilliance. A mere ghost of the madness that had illuminated them in life flickered dully in their depths, like a guttering candle flame. 'We could have had it all,' he announced tiredly.

'There was no "we", uncle,' Killean told him, 'You would have killed me the second you ascended.'

Dadarro frowned but not as if he was angry. He seemed vaguely confused. 'Would I?' he wondered aloud. 'For what reason? You were my vassal. I had need of you still.'

'You disliked it when our allies praised my accomplishments, uncle.'

'Nonsense. I taught you everything you know. Your accomplishments were my accomplishments.'

Not when he acted against his uncle's orders they weren't. Apparently, death hadn't filled in the blanks of his uncle's ignorance. Could it be he really didn't know why Killean had killed him?

In death as in life, his uncle's moods were as uncertain and capricious as an Icicle Country snowstorm. In a blink, he went from morose to spitting mad. 'Weak,' he snarled at Killean. 'You were always weak. You lack courage in your convictions. You are easily defeated by minor setbacks.'

Killean quirked a brow. 'And yet, of the two of us, I'm the one who survived.'

'You betrayed me,' said his uncle.

Killean nodded. 'It's what we Onryn do,' he said. 'For all my weakness, Uncle, I have had a lot of time to think about the massacre and everything that led up to it. I've realised something. You deliberately provoked Minuidon knowing he'd attack the clan to get to you. You wanted my parents out of the way as much as he did.'

He'd figured it out sometime after tracking down the middling cutthroat gang who did the deed. His preparations for the battle of Shrimpton had been overshadowed by the realisation he was likely to face down the brother who had opened the gates to their parents murderers and on the orders of his uncle who had so extravagantly flaunted his power right under Minuidon's nose, knowing he placed his own kin in danger. Suffice to say, it hadn't left him in the greatest frame of mind for battle.

It had been far too late to simply walk away, of course. The war had its own pull at that point, its own momentum. But the revelation had decided him on his uncle. He'd wondered if he could trust his own flesh and blood, and finally getting his revenge on the clan's murderers had given him his answer. Onryn were treacherous to the last child and only the dead in the family were innocent. He'd vowed then and there that win or lose their war, his uncle would die.

'They were cowards!' his uncle blustered. 'Afraid of the power we were born to wield. My brother dishonoured our shared blood. They were *all* unworthy.'

Killean almost smiled. 'They were the best of us,' he said softly. 'Father and mother knew that the power you sought wasn't worth it. The Onryn have only ever used power to destroy ourselves.'

He looked around as the dreamscape transformed into the ruin of home. The upright spine of land his ancestors had built the castle on was still standing. Just. It rose above the parched and shattered ground like a finger bone, pointing at nothing. The lakebed was completely dry, filled with rock and grey ash. He breathed in the taste of stale destruction.

'You sound like Tinnian,' Dadarro complained. 'Defeat has made you just another snivelling coward.' Those reptilian, golden eyes narrowed. 'I raised you to be better than that. You were to be my heir. Not his. The child of my spirit, if not my loins. You were to be the last hope of the Onryn. My lieutenant on this mortal plain.' Rising from the throne Dadarro braced himself with one thin arm as he jabbed the air with a gnarled finger, his skin was scaled and grey. 'Your betrayal cost us everything.'

Killean bowed his head. 'I know.'

'*You know*? *You know*?' Dadarro parroted furiously. 'Is that all you have to say for yourself? Explain, nephew, why you still live. How is it that your shame has not killed you?'

Killean cocked his head. 'I'm not ashamed,' he replied.

'Not ashamed? Not ashamed,' his uncle shouted, voice mingling with thunder. In a quieter voice he asked, 'How can you not be ashamed?' Theatrics aside, he sounded genuinely confused.

Killean took pity on him. For a certain value of the word. 'I had been planning to kill you for a long time. I never saw myself as your heir. I saw myself as your successor. I did to you what you did to my father and mother. And I take only satisfaction in knowing you died at the claws of the last true Onryn.'

His uncle collapsed back into his ridiculous throne, as if Killean's words had landed a true blow to his body. His mouth moved soundlessly, miming Killean's words back at him. Then he started to laugh. At first merely a hiccupping chuckle, an almost involuntary giggle, that slowly grew into proud guffaws.

'There you are,' his uncle said, wiping a tear from the corner of his eye with one bony finger. 'Here is the boy I shaped in my own image. Here is the magnificent little shit who can stand here in the ignominy of defeat and declare he feels no shame for it.'

Killean could only shrug. He didn't put much weight on this figment's opinion of him. 'Your obsession with the Firefly was your weakness,' he told his uncle. 'What do you think would have happened if you'd ascended uncle? Do you really think the magical countries would bow to a giant salamander? Your grandstanding would have given Torvin exactly what he wanted. Uniting our enemies under Three Rivers banner just to end you. The Barley Lands, Past Tiger – all our allies would have been crushed in the rush to get to you.'

'My godhood would have saved us all,' Dadarro said dismissively, making it abundantly clear that he neither believed in his words nor cared what would have happened to the allies they'd gathered around them.

Killean made a derisive noise low in his throat. 'How many gods do you see ruling countries on the continent, uncle?' he snapped. 'Let me answer that for you: there are none. A total of *zero* gods. This world is not a storybook. A magic do-dad doesn't mean shit. No one in Cow Country, or Green Peaks is going to bow down to a fucking lizard. I had to lose our war to keep the dream alive.'

THE LIFE AND TIMES OF THE TRAITOR KILLEAN ONRYN

He'd had no ambitions of surviving when he'd turned his coat in the last battle. He'd run the odds, he'd calculated the losses his army had incurred and how many more could follow and he'd considered the benefits of keeping Past Tiger and the territories of the petty lords who had aided him in peace, so that at some later date they might rise again and kick Torvin's self-righteous arse. He'd decided that had just as much value as keeping Nadil's heart in his chest.

The choice to surrender at Dragon's Ascent had been calculated on a future dream. Just because he and his uncle had fallen didn't mean there weren't still powers out there targeting Three Rivers. Powers who could rise up in the future and carrying on the legacy of rebellion.

While he'd tied Three Rivers hands dealing with his surrender, Harkiv and the other petty lords allied against Three Rivers' had had time to fortify their positions and offer cease fire terms favourable to them. Torvin had little choice but to grant leniency in case any of Killean's allies decided to fight for his release. He'd always been a piece on a greater game board, and in his last-ditch effort, he'd turned himself into leverage for his allies to use. A part of him had even looked forward to exposing a few hidden skeletons in Three Rivers' closet on his way to the scaffold, but Torvin had out played him on that front.

'The difference between you and me, uncle, is that I live in the real world and always have. You believe in mystical powers created by old, dead men. I believe in a free Barley Lands. You believe power is magic. I believe in winning the game, even when the odds are stacked against me. And if that means I have to do it in disgrace, all the better. Fewer people will see me coming.'

He turned his hand, palm up and in a flash the Firefly was there, its gentle heat warming his skin. The flame turning a murky black.

Dadarro lurched forward in his throne. 'Is that —'

'The Firefly. Or well, my memory of it.' He held it out toward his uncle.

Dadarro was in raptures. His expression transcended. He looked close to tears. 'Give it to me.' He raked the air with his fingers.

Killean pulled the perfectly spherical orb away from him. 'Don't you remember what happened last time you held this, Uncle? It wouldn't flame for you.'

His uncle did not do the kicked puppy look well. He was altogether too maniacal. Stepped on snake, perhaps? Wounded newt? In any case, he looked hurt by the truth. 'It should have worked,' he whispered. 'I am Onryn.'

Killean hummed in agreement. 'So am I.'

His uncle's golden eyes rooted to him. Killean waited for him to figure out in death what he'd never even considered in life. It didn't take as long as he'd feared. Dadarro was out of his throne in a heartbeat and launching himself at Killean, hands outstretched and fingers hooked like claws. 'You!' he roared. 'You stole the power. You took it from me!'

Killean side-stepped his stumbling lunge and watched as Dadarro tottered to his knees in the dust. His robes billowed around him, dwarfing his emaciated body. Death had not done his uncle any favours, it seemed. In life he'd been in excellent fighting form despite being almost fifty. Now he looked like a doddering old fool near twice that age. In fact, he looked rather a lot like Obawai, old and gnarled and ravaged by desperation.

Dadarro twisted around to spit vitriol at him. 'You parasite. You worm. You took the power for yourself when you claimed the Firefly from those fool priests.'

'I did,' he said, 'but not on purpose. I only intended to test the relic to make sure it worked. I didn't know the power in it had chosen me until it wouldn't work for either you or Nadil.'

Another revelation that had come at an inopportune time. The heat of battle was a bad time for reflection, especially as it had hardly mattered then why he'd spent so many months feeling like he had molten lava bubbling under his skin. He'd thought the fever in his bones had been the nascent dragon in him – and it had been. It's just that his dragon form had also absorbed the essence of the Firefly when he'd used the stupid thing to toast Sakmon's temple in Potbelly.

The power might have come out in him earlier, had it not been for his run in with Green Peak's elite guard and their power sucking gauntlets. There was a certain irony that the very thing meant to depower him had actually saved his sanity.

Dadarro sobbed. 'Why?' he cried up to the sky. 'Why do you mock me? You gave power to *him* and he has squandered it.' He held up his hands, fingers plucking uselessly at the air like a man clawing at invisible bars.

'You really think, after all you taught me, I'd *squander* power?' Killean asked, astounded. 'Uncle, why the fuck do you think I'm alive and free? *Torvin knows what I am*, you idiot.'

Dadarro stared at him. His eyes widened like a fearful child, a naughty child who had first be told he can't have a treat only to then be told that he just might get one after all. His expression was poised between despair and hope. A decidedly treacherous place to be. 'What have you done, nephew?' he whispered.

Killean grinned. Starless Night, it felt good to get this off his chest. He'd wanted to gloat to at least one person for too damn long. He hadn't planned on it being a dream figment of his dead uncle, but then again, the dead told no tales. He confessed with relish, 'Torvin knows the Firefly chose me. He knows I'm Myron's fated heir, for whatever *that's* worth,' he added with a curl of his lip. 'But he doesn't know where the damn thing is. And that's my true power.'

The world thought it was Nadil who'd defeated Dadarro with the power of the Firefly, but four people knew the truth. Of that four, only Killean knew what had become of the Firefly after the battle. He told his uncle as much.

'I banished it to the Timeless Realm. The same incantation I use to banish my clothes when I shift. Trouble is, I don't entirely know where in the Realm I sent it, and I can't whistle it back while cursed.'

Which was why Torvin had cursed him in the first place. Killean wasn't sure if the Spark thought Killean himself was oblivious to what had happened to him, but he'd been plenty quick to make sure he had no chance of calling on his ascended dragon powers. Fair enough. But it did leave them with a problem. The Firefly was beyond reach of both of them now.

Killean still didn't know the nature of the new threat Nadil had hinted at, but it was pretty obvious it was the reason Torvin had sprung him early. That and the fact that he'd awoken in the Timeless Realm when he shouldn't have. There was a reason for that too, and Killean had an inkling it involved the Firefly. His memories of his waking moments in the were disjointed and unpleasant, but he still retained a lingering sense that something had been calling to him.

He and the Firefly were linked, its power was still inside him even if he couldn't access it. He believed it had been the Firefly that had called to him. It had been trying to alert him to its presence, draw him to it. Torvin had dragged him out of the Realm before he could gather the strength to escape his prison and go look for it.

'So, you see Uncle, I have been using the power I was given. Far better than you would have. I'm going to keep using it too. I'm going to use it to win back everything you forced me to give up.'

That was the thing about eldritch power. It worked the same way as extortion and threats of bloody violence. It worked so long as it was never used. You could keep a man on the hook with threats and blackmail for a very long time, but the moment you exposed his secrets, or hung him up by his ankles in a dungeon while you sharpened your long knives, you'd lost your power. Of course, that didn't mean the victim in this situation gained any. He was still dangling by his ankles with his dirty deeds exposed, but the nice little compact between you, the one that was keeping you both in the lifestyles you wanted – that was over. At that point the villain had to either kill or release his victim.

Dadarro had lost the war long before Killean had landed the killing blow. He'd lost the moment he squandered the alliances they'd built and the territory they'd claimed for the chance to transform into a big, shiny lizard and pulverise a mountain or two. There was very little political sway in laying waste to everything and everyone. Who was going to furnish your lair with gold and jewels when all the mines were buried under rockslides, the jewellers were all dead and the metalsmiths were starving because the fields had been scorched black? Failing to consider the practicalities always came back to bite you in the end.

'The uprising failed, Uncle, but I can still win through extortion.'

'You twice-damned *accountant*,' Dadarro sneered. 'Where's your warrior pride? You should thirst for conquest. You should use your power to smite your foes in fire and blood. You are Onryn! You are Striking Talon! Not some damn Silk Paw crook!'

'My warrior's pride is satisfied daily, Uncle. The life of a renegade isn't exactly peaceful,' he retorted dismissively. 'As for the rest of it. I'd like to draw your attention to the fact that Silk Paw *survive* to this day while the Striking Talon is *gone*.'

In Shrimpton, the heat of a burning town so intense Killean could barely breathe, he'd found himself surrounded by enemies wearing the Barley Land emblem, his brother at their head. He'd been wounded, his forces given a nasty surprise courtesy of Three Rivers mage units hidden in a town his intelligence officers had assured him was properly pacified.

Killean had been bleeding freely from his head and his right arm had been hanging useless by his side when Kindean had blindsided him with a cold so intense it shocked the sense right out of him. Magic ice was not really ice, of course, just like magic fire was not normal fire, but in some ways that just made it worse. He still dreamt of the cold that had stung his very soul and plunged him into a frozen sleep worse than death.

He'd awoken in chains, cursed symbols written in ink on his skin, preventing him from using his magic to shift or set fire to the prisoner wagon he was in. He'd woken to the sight of Kindean, sitting cross-legged on the other side of the iron cage, his knees awkwardly drawn up, his toes brushing the bars, his back pressed tight to the wall of the wagon.

Kindean's first words to him had been, 'Is this who you want to be, brother?'

Of all the questions a member of Three Rivers' elite soldiery might ask an enemy general, Killean hadn't expected him to take the philosophical route. But then again, this was *Kindean*. He'd said nothing, obviously. He hadn't wanted to deprive Three Rivers' torturers of their fun.

Kindean hadn't taken his lack of response as a cause to give up, unfortunately. 'Look at where you are,' he'd pressed, 'look at what you've become and ask yourself – where is it all going? Is the destination worth it? Is following in Dadarro's footsteps what you really want?'

At the time what he'd really wanted was to set Kindean on fire and get the hell out of there. But he'd mulled the questions in his mind much later, after Bodai and Juri had ambushed the wagon and gotten him out. Not that he'd ever tell Kindean that. The last thing he wanted was for his brother to think he listened to him. Ever. Still, he had asked himself where everything was going and whether he was entirely happy with his direction. He'd drawn several conclusions from that period of introspection.

THE LIFE AND TIMES OF THE TRAITOR KILLEAN ONRYN

The first was his plan to betray Dadarro at the first, best opportunity. But the question of who he wanted to be – he'd only decided that when he'd seen his uncle destroy Dragon's Ascent. That's when he'd decided that he wanted to be the person who fixed this mess. The man who restored his lands. The man who fulfilled the promise he'd made to his Accursed army when he'd offered them a homeland of their own in north Barley Lands.

Whether as a beggar, a thug, a traitor, a statesman, a deputy of Three Rivers or her greatest enemy, he would one day claim Dragon's Ascent for himself and the Accursed. No matter what it took, he would achieve his goal. That was who he was. Not only a villain. Definitely *not* a hero. A Barleyman. An Onryn. A cursed man who was going to get his home back.

'The difference between us, Uncle,' he told the fading visage of the man who had trained him, given him a purpose and helped him hone the skills he needed to achieve it, only for him to repay him with betrayal, 'is that you wanted the storybook version of power and I want the reality. Goodbye Uncle. May you find some peace in the Nevermore.'

Chapter Fourteen

Abrupt and shocking, a splash of cold water hit his face. Killean burst out of his dream and sat up in bed, face, neck and chest dripping wet. He had his knife drawn defensively before his wits caught up to his reflexes. He fixed his best glare on Cactus who was still holding the empty pitcher of water in his hand. 'You are a dead man.'

'And you are delaying our departure,' the ex-pirate retorted carelessly. He looked at Killean thoughtfully. 'You don't sleep like a soldier,' he said. 'You sleep like a corpse.'

'Blame the Timeless Realm,' Killean grumbled, kicking free of the wet blankets. Nadil was nowhere to be seen and daylight streamed through the small dormer window. 'What time is it?'

'Eight.'

Killean scoffed. 'I've only been asleep five hours.' That was good bit of time. Better than he managed on the road but hardly the catastrophic delay Cactus was making it out to be.

As punishment for having the audacity to actually give his body the sleep it needed to recover, he was deprived the chance to eat at the inn before they left in the stolen mail carriage. Sammia handed him a pilfered apple and a fresh oat biscuit before she climbed up to the driver's bench next to Cactus.

Killean flopped down on the thin cushioning covering the passenger benches inside the carriage, intent on finishing his meagre breakfast and then feigning sleep for the rest of the journey.

Nadil had other ideas. He wanted to talk. 'I thought you'd ditch us in the middle of the night,' he admitted.

Killean looked at him through his lashes, chin tucked low. 'Is that why you look like crap? Did you sleep at all?' he asked.

'No,' Nadil grumbled, rubbing at the golden stubble on his cheeks. Killean laughed. Nadil's glare intensified. 'You don't have to be an arsehole about it.'

'I don't have to be, but I enjoy it,' Killean retorted. He eyed the miserable looking teenager scrunched up against the carriage door next to Nadil. 'What about you,' he asked, 'did you sleep?'

'No,' Ash snapped. He tugged at his burnt and ruined cloak uselessly, trying and failing to pull it around his hunched body. 'I thought the Death Child was going to murder me.'

Killean rolled his eyes. 'You're not worth her time, kid.'

It said something about how tired the boy was that he didn't erupt as usual. Instead, he liberated one of his hands to make a one fingered gesture that the king of Green Peaks definitely wouldn't approve of. Killean chuckled, cracked open the carriage door and tossed his apple core out.

'You're in a good mood,' Nadil noted suspiciously.

Killean grinned at him. 'I had a very refreshing sleep.'

'I'm glad,' Nadil simpered back, ducking down in his seat, arms wrapped grumpily around him.

'That didn't sound very sincere,' Killean chided.

Nadil cracked open an eye to give him a very draconic look. 'I don't trust you when you're in a good mood.'

'You shouldn't trust me in any mood,' Killean told him. 'Sworn enemies remember?'

It was Nadil's turn to roll his eyes. 'You say that and yet when you had the chance to see me dead, you saved my life.'

Killean shrugged. 'I can save you a hundred times. I only need to kill you once to make it stick,' he replied.

Ash looked between them, a comically large and quizzical look on his face. 'What are you talking about? When did *he* save *you*?' he asked Nadil.

They shared a look. Killean shook his head minutely. Nadil sighed. 'We grew up together,' he lied to Ash smoothly, 'we trained in magic and shapeshifting. Growing up, we were close as brothers.'

'Closer,' Killean murmured. He quirked his brow at Nadil, 'I don't like my brother, remember?'

Nadil's expression lightened. 'Did you just admit you like me?' he asked, affecting shock.

Killean hid his smile. 'I don't hate you as much as I do Kindean, but that's not saying much.'

'Did you go on adventures together?' Ash asked thoroughly diverted. 'Is that when he saved you?' he asked.

'I guess,' Nadil said. 'Though there were lots of times I saved him.' He smirked at Killean. 'You remember that time you were going to throw yourself off Kindred Tower?'

Killean hitched his shoulder in a half-shrug. 'It would've worked. I *can* feather-shift.'

'Not then you couldn't,' Nadil shot back. 'If I hadn't talked you down you'd have pancaked all over Camry Square.'

He'd been twelve and frustrated at his lack of progress shifting and maintaining functional bird form. He'd been convinced jumping from a great height would shock his body into figuring it out. In retrospect, probably not his finest strategic moment.

'So in a way, you're responsible for all the terrible things I did after,' he mused. 'You could have spared Three Rivers a lot of trouble if you'd let me go splat.'

Ash looked pensive. He nibbled his lip. 'He couldn't have done that,' he argued. 'Heroes have to save people. Even arseholes like you,' he added darkly.

Killean snorted. 'How old are you kid, five? You can't really believe in heroes.'

Ash glowered at him. 'I believe you're a villain. That means I have to believe in heroes.'

'That's some impressive specious reasoning,' Killean commended him. 'Did you learn it in the Green Peaks guard?'

'Leave him alone,' Nadil warned. 'I remember when you used to believe good and bad were black and white too.' He looked at him hard, no doubt thinking about the many angry rants fourteen-year-old Killean had subjected him to about justice and hunting down criminals and getting even and defending his family honour before he'd finally snapped and run away to do something about it on his own.

Not taking the bait, Killean merely smiled blandly back at him. 'And look how well I turned out.'

Nadil grinned back at him, showing teeth. 'I know you're up to something,' he noted cheerfully, 'this is too much like old times.'

It was, wasn't it? He'd usually been up to something then, too. Killean settled back into his seat. 'I'm not up to anything right now,' he said.

Denying he had plans was pointless. Nadil would never believe it. His ex-friend was in the unenviable position of having to hope that whatever he was planning, he'd wait until after they'd reclaimed Rhodu Gakai and the Pearl to spring his trap. Poor Nadil. Life had not provided him with much natural leverage, despite his seemingly venerated position.

The three of them lapsed into silence as the carriage trundled over bad road. Ash fell asleep and Nadil pretended to doze, but his slumped pose was a little too stiff, his seemingly limp limbs a bit too close to his knife belt to be believed. Killean let him keep up the pretence. It was good that Nadil was restraining his natural optimistic idiocy and being pragmatic. It would improve his chances when he faced the Blue Crab.

Killean drew back the curtain and watched the scenery go by until the obvious scenes of blight and disrepair became too depressing and he closed the curtain again. The scars of war became more obvious on the landscape the further west they travelled. With nothing better to do, he let his thoughts drift, as they inevitably seemed to do, back into the past. He started thinking about Green Peaks and his first encounter with Ash's gauntlet. It was fertile ground for daydreaming.

After his successful acquisition of the Firefly, his uncle had consulted with various lesser gods lurking inside rocks, trees and rivers, to discover the location of the other two relics, Gendril's Flute and the Sapphire Clam. A stream goddess in Cow Country had claimed Gendril's Flute was hidden in Green Peak's royal treasury.

Killean had been less than thrilled when his uncle insisted the Dread Four infiltrate the Summer Palace. Green Peaks was known for stocking its armed forces with well versed mages, and certain notable Accursed, like Sammia, who were indentured to serve the royal family. Sammia, who had been long gone by this time, had told him enough stories about what Green Peaks did to ensure obedience from her magical slaves that he'd had misgivings from the start. The Onryn had always possessed the influence to command safety, but to Peaker eyes shapeshifters were Accursed.

He'd launched his campaign to claim Green Peaks territory around the capital as much as a delaying tactic as a way of distracting Peaks' intelligence from his planned infiltration. He'd worried that if the Peaks' king really did have the Flute he'd know Killean's next step would be to take it from him. By that time, everyone knew about Dadarro's obsession with Myron's relics.

THE LIFE AND TIMES OF THE TRAITOR KILLEAN ONRYN

Green Peaks was beautiful country and the nation's history was long and broad. Peakers had been building marble palaces while the ancestors of the Onryn and Camry were still fighting tooth and claw over uncultivated land. The capital of Green Peaks, Valley Good, was equal in size to Delta City and had been a major trading hub back when Delta was a tiny, gnat-infested fishing village. Killean had heard about the Great Library of Soshin and the thousand-year-old fighting arena where Accursed were pitted against bears, tigers and the occasional trapped and baited spirit. Sammia had escaped the arena as a girl. She'd admitted to him once while on campaign that she hoped for the chance to put it to the torch.

Had she been with him during his fateful incursion, he still wouldn't have been able to grant her request. The Dread Three had avoided the heavily fortified Valley Good and headed for the magnificent Palace of the Reflecting Pools, a gorgeous complex of gleaming domed buildings, icing-sugar delicate minarets and long tracks of lily pad studded pools, fringed by elegantly arched portico walkways where the fronds of palm trees whispered in a gentle breeze that barely rippled the surface of the water.

The palace was the royal family's summer retreat, a place where the king and his court retired for banquets and fetes while the seasonal plague swept through the teeming streets of Valley Good. A town in service to the migratory court had sprung up beyond the palace's high walled and magic secured gates.

A loose crosshatch of wood framed, wattle and daub houses, armourers, farriers, inns and at least one brothel, lined a long main road leading toward the gate while several small dirt roads spotted with houses meandered away from the main street on either side, nudging up to the drop into the moat that circled the walled palace. The town of Reflecting Pool was pitifully lacking in adequate defences while the court was away, which made it almost insultingly easy for the Dread Three to stroll up and settle at a table on the upper balcony of a tavern overlooking the moat.

They had come in disguise of sorts. Killean had donned the fine red and black silk robes of a petty lord's son, some minor noble from Cow or Red Mountain, unwisely travelling with only a retinue of two men-at-arms while Green Peaks fought a battle against an invading army to the south. It happened more often than one might expect. Killean's forces occasionally picked up additional revenue kidnapping and ransoming back noble idiots who thought their money and their family crests provided a shield and not a target.

Once or twice, Killean had discovered that the little lordlings had been sent packing by family hoping to see them killed off. He'd made a few unexpected allies that way when he set those nobles loose, armed them with what he had spare and unleashed them on their treacherous families.

The king of Green Peaks had failed to show up to his palatial retreat this summer as Valley Good prepared for a siege that would never come, and the innkeepers and souvenir sellers of Reflecting Pool were too grateful to receive customers to ask many questions. No one recognised Killean, nor looked more than twice at Bodai and Juri, although he was sure a few recognised one or both of them as Accursed.

Killean would wonder more about that, except that most of the population really had no idea what he actually looked like. He might dislike the heavy, restrictive helmets and armour sets he used for parley with the enemy, but they served an important function outside of battle. They hid his face, obscured his build and made it appear inconceivable that Killean-the-Swift would enter Reflecting Pool dressed only in silk with no army at his back.

'You can't expect the three of us to get in there,' Bodai grumbled, long, pale fingers ripping apart a pillowy soft flatbread on his plate. He glared sulkily at the view of the high walls across the water. 'The gates are barred tight. True, they've only got a skeletal force left to defend the palace, but what does that matter when the magic in the walls keeps us out.'

'Magic won't keep us out,' Killean said.

'What are we going to do, create a fire storm outside the walls? Them inside won't care if these folks burn,' Bodai grumbled. 'These people are the bellwether for an attack on the palace. The guards inside will watch a slaughter just to see what we're capable of.'

'I don't want to slaughter anyone,' opined Juri, worriedly.

'We're not here for that.' Killean swished his corner of bread in the sesame seed paste in the small, blue glazed bowl on the table. He kept his posture relaxed and his tone low and measured, affecting the look of a man talking about the weather, not an infiltration. 'Dadarro has called in a favour. Our contact is meeting us here. He'll have a way for us to get in.'

'Where is he then? We've been here over an hour and I'm bored,' Bodai complained.

'Bodai,' Juri chastised quietly and Killean caught the oddly intent warning look he shot his partner.

'What?' Bodai demanded. 'Oh. Right.' He sneered. 'I'm not allowed to upset our precious leader.' Bodai's look was baleful and a sudden stirring in the air rippled the table napkins.

Killean set down his water glass deliberately. He wiped his hands on a napkin and ordered, 'Whatever you're sulking about, spit it out.'

Dealing with Bodai was akin to handling a misbehaving toddler. Some of his attitude was simply for attention, but all the same, ignoring the signs of a tantrum could be disastrous. The sprite was as capricious as he was cantankerous and he had the means to cause serious problems if he put his mind to it. Killean didn't trust many at his back, and the choice to trust the Killing Breeze was always a risky one.

Bodai sat back in his chair, throwing on pale arm over the wicker and bamboo frame. 'We should have gone back for Sammia,' he said. 'This is her old stomping ground. She should be here. With *us*,' he added a note of real hurt in his voice.

Killean glanced at Juri, who ducked his head over his wiped clean bowl avoiding Killean's eyes. He could tell from the droop of the big man's shoulders he agreed with Bodai.

Killean spoke softly, evenly. 'Do you know where she is?'

'Three Rivers took her,' Bodai snapped.

'Where?' Killean shot back.

Bodai pursed his pale lips, his features drawn tight over his bones in anguish. 'I don't know,' he said breaking eye contact.

'Nor do I,' Killean said. Sammia had given his spies the slip weeks ago. 'I do know Three Rivers is counting on me looking. They know what Sammia is worth to me –' he corrected himself quickly, '– to the war effort. They won't execute her. They won't even try. If Torvin has eyes on her, his spies will keep their distance. She's too dangerous and too valuable a trading chip to risk losing her.'

This was not the first time they'd had this conversation. Once or twice Killean had ordered Bodai to shut up, but neither he nor Juri were regular soldiers. They couldn't be ordered into silence or flogged for insubordination. The pair weren't fighting for a cause, or the pay, or the distant hope of a land of their own. Those things didn't mean anything to them. They were fighting because they enjoyed it. But more than that, in recent months they'd fought for Killean and Sammia. They fought for the tiny number of Accursed they actually liked. It was a form of loyalty, but one that could be lost very quickly. Killean knew he was close to losing both of them just as he'd lost Sammia.

Bodai's lips moved soundlessly.

'What was that?' Killean murmured dangerously, eyes on Bodai. 'I don't think I heard you.'

Bodai looked up, anger causing the thin skin around his colourless eyes to bunch and crease. 'You heard me just fine,' he snapped. 'I said that if Three Rivers values Sammia then its more than you do.'

Killean's fists clenched under his folded arms. A muscle in his strained jaw twitched. 'Are you challenging my authority?' he asked quietly.

'Your authority? No,' Bodai jeered. 'I'm questioning your *sanity*. Why are we here, wasting time on a night-damned flute none of us can use while the war goes on without us?'

He threw out a hand and the doors leading out onto the balcony slammed closed, blown shut by a gust of air that swept on down the stairs, causing the hanging lamps to sway. 'We're this close to taking Green Peaks. Word is, there are Accursed in Valley Good just waiting for a sign from us to rebel. We could take the city from the inside out. Your Uncle Dearest's magical shopping list is taking us away from where we need to be.'

Killean pushed up from his chair. Bodai's eyes widened and he stopped talking, body tensing. Killean ignored him and focused on the dark-skinned man in the hot pink pantaloons and mirrored vest bounding up the stairs.

'I'm Jerrel Adiri of the Dancing Deer clan,' he introduced himself cheerfully, oblivious to the rising tension and odd atmospheric effects on the upper floor. He raised his right forearm and showed off the silver bangle with the single cabochon garnet set in it that Uncle Dadarro had told him would identify his contact. 'Welcome to Reflecting Pools. You three are to come with me.'

Juri rose and loomed over Jerrel. He looked to Killean for instruction as Bodai scrambled out of his chair, shame-faced that he'd spoken so freely without a thought to who might be listening in. 'Do we comply?' Juri asked, staring at Jerrel with the look of a very large man considering how best to disassemble a much smaller one.

Jerrel's eyes widened. He shot a quick look over to Killean but didn't dare take his attention off the huge man with the bulging forearms for too long. 'Uh, perhaps I could have phrased that request more delicately, my lord?' he suggested. 'If you gentlemen would be so kind as to come with me, I can take you where you wish to be,' he quivered into a flourishing bow.

Killean waved an imperious hand. 'Lead on.'

The Dancing Deer pranced away with alacrity. Killean met Bodai's eyes. 'Uncle Dadarro has forbidden the Fourth regiment from joining us and redirected our fleet to focus their efforts on the Albatross Straits,' he said softly. 'Our invasion dies here unless we can find the flute.'

'That fucker,' Bodai slammed his clenched fist against his thigh. 'He doesn't have the ships to hold the Strait. He should be helping us seize Green Peaks. And a navy on the verge of mutiny.'

'I did mention that to him. It didn't go down well,' Killean said, tone tinder dry with the smouldering resentment he was trying to keep down. 'Harkiv warned me my uncle is displeased with me right now.'

'Of course, he is. You're showing him up.' Bodai's expression was shrewd. 'What's the chances the Flute really is here and we can get to it?'

Killean pressed his lips together. 'Fair to good on the former. Slim to none on the latter.' He peered over the stair railing making sure Jerrel hadn't run off on his own.

'Dadarro's setting us up,' Bodai warned.

Just like the little lordlings whose form he'd taken, Killean thought. He had become a target to his uncle. Not that he could complain. He'd do the same to Dadarro given half a chance.

He said, 'Maybe. But we have to go through with this mission. Failure is not an option.'

Not only would it result in their deaths, but his uncle would happily sacrificing Killean's entire army if he didn't make it back in time. Ditching the mission wouldn't help. Uncle Dadarro would see such an action as an act of insurrection. Killean was under no illusions he could stand against his uncle's entire force.

Dadarro needed him, more than he wanted to admit, but Killean needed him too. Shrimpton had been a blackmark on his record, one his successes in Green Peaks could not entirely erase. No matter what Bodai said, Green Peaks was rallying their forces and he didn't have the supply lines to bed in for a long campaign. He had to get his forces out of Peaks safely and he needed his uncle's ships for that. Which meant he had to go after the damn Flute.

Chapter Fifteen

Jerrel led them into the sweating heat of the day, past the large fountain designed to look like a palm tree, a jet of water bursting from its top to splash down over the curving fronds to fill a blue tiled pool below. He led them along sun blanched, dusty side streets strung with washing lines upon which monkeys with long question mark tails scampered, to a narrow footbridge spanning the moat. There was a small door cut into the wall on the other side, invisible save for the haze of obscuring magic rippling in the air in front of it.

'The court refused to return to Reflecting Pool this season,' Jerrel explained. 'But the Vizier and his family still require entertainment. My troupe will cover your entrance into the palace. You will do what you need to do while we appear to set up for our act tonight.' He looked anxious, twisting the bangle around his wrist with worried fingers. This was not a man happy to serve the cause.

'What does my uncle have on you?' Killean asked him bluntly.

'That is a private matter between the Dancing Deer and your uncle,' Jerrel said stiffly, gaze darting away. 'My daughter has a man in the Vizier's guard. He knows nothing of you, but he is smitten with her. He will die for her and the bastard whelp he sired, should trouble arise.'

Good. Then Jerrel had an exit strategy. 'And the Flute,' he asked. 'Do you know where its hidden.'

Jerrel shook his head. 'I know nothing of what you seek. I am only doing what I am told. I am to get you inside. No more, no less. But if it is treasure you seek,' he added with an avaricious gleam in his eyes, 'then you should head for the treasury. But be warned, strong magics protect it.'

He looked Killean up and down. 'I have heard of you. The boy conqueror. The terror who lights up the world with his fire and is gone faster than a swift flies. But I think even you will struggle in your task here. I do not think you will make it.'

Bodai muttered, 'This is a bad idea.'

Of course it was. It was his uncle's idea. But Killean was bound to honour his orders for the time being. 'The Peakers must have a way to open the door,' he pointed out. 'Once we're inside we'll force one of them to help us.'

'What are you going to do, hold the Vizier's wife and children to ransom?' Bodai scoffed.

Killean shrugged. 'If that's what it takes.'

There was a good chance the stream goddess was wrong and Gendril's Flute was not here. What did a provincial deity in middle-of-nowhere Cow Country know about the contents of Green Peaks magical armoury, anyway? Killean thought he could placate his uncle with a tale of an ardent attempt that ended up in failure due to bad intelligence, so long as he could prove he'd made a good go of trying to find the Flute.

Bodai quivered where he stood, a motion no ordinary human could replicate. His form seemed to thin, blurring at the edges as the colour leeched from him, making him appear almost transparent for a blink-of-an-eye. 'You're serious,' he said.

'When am I not?' Killean remarked off-handedly. He turned to Jerrel. 'Tell me your plans for getting us inside unseen.'

'Your word that once I do this service for you, the clan's debt to your uncle is discharged,' Jerrel insisted fiercely.

'Your debt is with my uncle, not me,' Killean reminded him. 'I can't discharge it. But I will promise that if you betray me, it will be the end of you and your clan.'

'You think the Dancing Deer clan are weak simply because we make our living as entertainers,' Jerrel spat on the ground.

'I don't know anything about your clan,' Killean replied blandly, wondering what his problem was. The man had made a deal with his uncle. This was the price. Killean was not responsible for the cost. 'All I care about is my mission. Get us inside safely and I will tell my uncle what you risked to honour your debts,' he promised.

Jerrel bowed his cloth covered head. He was agitated, sandalled feet scuffing the ground. 'Your uncle is a grasping man. He does not let a debt go easily.'

'I could have your tongue for that slander,' Killean told him lazily. Jerrel stared at him, horrified. Killean smirked, '*But* as I suspect you'll need it to fulfil your promise, I'll leave it be. Just remember, no matter my uncle's character, it's mine you need to worry about. I've no reason to harm you, so don't give me one.'

Jerrel looked sullen. 'I have heard you are a man of plain intentions. There are some that say you make a fair bargain.'

'I keep my word where I can,' Killean replied. 'Do what I need you to do and I will vouch for you to my uncle. Screw me over and I promise you'll live long enough to watch your daughter and her whelp die first.'

Rage simmered in Jerrel's eyes. It was the look of a man trapped by the consequences of his own actions and angry about it. Killean had seen the look once or twice before. Sometimes when he looked in a mirror.

The leader of the Dancing Deer clan pivoted on his heel and strode across the bridge without another word. He set about writing magic words in the dust smearing the door.

Juri sighed sadly from behind Killean. 'A man catches more flies with honey than vinegar,' he said reproachfully. 'All you've done is give him reason to fear you.'

'Good,' Killean said. 'I want him to fear me more than the wrath of his Vizier.'

Despite the fact that the three of them did not look remotely like performers, or in any way related to Jerrel, the wiry, cagey old man was able to talk them passed the bored and too-hot guards standing on the other side of the obscured door.

He told them Killean and his companions were a three-man tumbling act from Frolicking Squirrel. He produced false paperwork from a pocket inside his baggy pants to prove that the Vizier had approved them.

Killean was a more capable liar than his reputation for bluntness gave him credit for, but he was no actor. He had no idea how a bouncing fool from Squirrel was supposed to look or act, so he surrendered to the guards scrutiny with a flat look, one hand perched on his hip, close to where he had a blade hidden. Bodai's otherworldly paleness and Juri's height and bulk should have given the guards pause, but this was Green Peaks, a land where the Accursed were often forced to perform tricks for the amusement of the bored and wealthy.

'What does he do?' One of the guard's pointed at Bodai. He favoured them with a wide and nasty grin, his dandelion fluff hair shivering around his head without the aid of a breeze.

'He can backflip through walls,' Killean answered before Jerrel could stammer out an obvious lie. The first guard chuckled thinking Killean was joking.

'And him?' the second guard nodded to Juri.

'Strong man. He lifts, we jump. If you have some palanquins spare, he can lift one in each hand with a third balanced perfectly on his head.'

The guards looked grudgingly impressed. 'What about you?' the first asked.

Killean smiled thinly. 'That would spoil the surprise,' he said.

Jerrel cleared his throat nervously. 'I promise Tahir, you will not be disappointed. My friend here is a master at his craft. His visit will linger long in the memory.'

Well, that was certainly true. Killean just hoped he would come to remember the raid on Reflecting Pool as one of his successes.

Entering under the shaded portico, Killean gained his first look at the palace's interior gardens and its rows upon rows of long, slender rectangular pools flanking a smooth marble path toward the main palace, a frothing confection of delicate towers, domed chambers and cut stone decorations.

It really was beautiful. Maybe, if things went very well and he found the Flute and convinced his uncle to back his Peaks conquest, he could claim this palace as part of his spoils. The whisper of the breeze through the palm fronds and the distant, musical lilt of flowing water was very soothing. Beyond the long walk lined with pools, was a semi-enclosed courtyard, framed by a colonnade just to one side of the main palace. This courtyard was crowded with wagons, colourful tents and animal cages.

'The servants' entrance is through there,' Jerrel pointed to a door-sized archway set into the side of the nearest building, a lookout tower protruding from the walls. 'If you take the first right passed the kitchens and follow the passage you will come to a guarded staircase. Below is the treasury.'

Killean glanced around. The tents and gauzy awnings of the Dancing Deer preparations hid them from view of the courtyard and the handful of guards stationed under the shadow of the porticos. He nodded to Bodai. 'Go and scout.'

Bodai shuddered into full transparency. Drifting toward the door he cast no shadow, his toes drifting above the ground.

Jerrel flinched violently, a curse bursting from his lips. 'What magickry is this?' he blurted.

'The magic of Icicle Country,' Killean lied casually. 'Bodai is abnormally talented even in this southern heat.' He glanced at Jerrel. 'Still think we'll struggle to get into the treasury?' he asked.

Jerrel shook his head slowly. 'No one can best the magic guard,' he said.

'We'll see. Juri stay here and wait. I'm going to look around.'

Removing the money purse and rounded paper fan that formed part of his useless, rich traveller disguise, he handed them off to Juri before transforming into a Golden Bellied Barn Swallow. He flew to the top of the ramparts and then performed an arc through the air, surveying the palace grounds.

An arrow-cut window midway up the tower gained him access. The guards packed into the small space reacted angrily as he flapped around. Deftly avoiding a barrage of swots, Killean counted the number of guards lying flat on the mat floor before leaving via the window and completing the same action in the other three towers.

Completing his swift-winged circuit of the walls, he reclaimed his human form behind the wagon of a sleeping baby elephant around the same time Bodai emerged and floated closer.

His wispy appearance did not bode well. He was still more breeze than man. Jerrel was gone and the courtyard had fallen quiet, the members of the entertainment troupe that had been hammering together the makeshift stages and erecting tents had disappeared and only the whickering of a few white horses tied to a wagon under the sun broke the silence. If not for the trio of servants in bleached white cotton sweeping the tiles under the porticos, Killean would have suspected an imminent ambush.

Bodai solidified long enough to give his report. 'Jerrel's instructions were on the money. I found the treasury, but it's bad news. The lower floor is heavily guarded. I counted twelve men in the central chamber. The treasury doors are at the end of the chamber. It's a sealed space. No antechambers or alternative ways in. And everything reeks of magic,' he added sourly.

Frowning Killean asked, 'The approach?'

'Clear. Too clear. This is a trap,' he said. 'It's got to be.'

Juri shuffled his feet. He looked worried. 'I don't want to break this place, Killean. It's too pretty to smash.'

Killean shook his head. 'Failure is not an option,' he reminded them.

'Beg to differ,' Bodai snarked. 'It is very much an option. In fact, I'd say it was a lock-set guarantee.'

Killean glared at him. 'The approach to the stairway is unguarded. How fast can you suck the air out of the lower chamber?'

'Quick as I can draw breath, but—'

Killean cut him off. 'There are guards in all the towers, more in the palace itself. Our only chance is to hit our target hard and fast.'

Chapter Sixteen

Predictably, half the servants in the kitchen were guards in disguise. The guards had time to draw their blades before Bodai drew in a deep and fast breath, hair streaming back from his face and sucked in all the air in the room.

He expanded like a human cloud, swallowing deep and creating a vacuum that ripped cast-iron pans from hooks and deep-red earthenware pots from shelves. Embers from the brick oven spread across the room and would have ignited the flour dust in the air had Bodai not drawn it all within him. Killean dropped to his knees behind a workbench and prayed his lungs didn't explode. Rising pressure roared in his ears as his vision winked out.

Breathing out, Bodai released all the air back into the room in a solid wall of force that smashed into the unconscious guards sending them flying into the walls. Killean got to his feet a little shakily, but there was no time for more than a single deep breath before the three of them were running for the corridor beyond.

Juri wrenched a stone bench from against the wall and slammed it in front of the kitchen door, the sound of stone scraping over stone teeth-gratingly loud. The windowless corridor was long and narrow. Killean looked up at the ceiling in time to see a slot in the wood open. A spear head almost took his eye out.

Ducking Killean hit the far wall, scrambling along it like a rat to avoid the thicket of spear thrusts from the ceiling. Juri grabbed a spear, shoving it back through the hole with elemental force. Killean heard a guard cry out in pain from the crawl space above.

He pushed his arms forward, fingers laced together, one palm covering the other. A wall of flame, so hot it was colourless, hit the four guards charging toward them from the end of the corridor. The men did not have time to scream as they died.

Killean dropped his arms. The mat flooring was burned away. The walls left black. The air tasted dry and smelled of burnt fat. Greasy curls of smoke rose from the four blackened bodies on the floor. He hadn't meant to release a fire that intense. He spared a moment to look at his tingling hands in surprise, before racing onward.

Ahead of him was the wide stairwell leading to the treasury. Killean heard the thunder of feet above him scrambling over the false ceiling as the spearmen rushed to get down. Bodai swirled into the passage, a cyclone of air whirling around his body. Killean released another jet of liquid flame upward, setting the false ceiling ablaze. He heard screaming above. By the stairs, Bodai took another deep breath, pulling the air up from the floor below.

Killean plunged down the stairs with Juri, bursting into the cool, stone chamber in the wake of the gale Bodai sent down the stairs ahead. The wind swept through the chamber, fluttering over the bodies of the three unconscious guards unlucky enough to have been standing at the base of the stairs.

Juri barrelled into the next three guards, tackling them to the ground as Bodai flew down the stairs and spun into the chamber, floating near the ceiling. He was almost completely translucent, the black-veined marble wall slabs visible through his body. Killean pivoted out of the way of a spear thrust, caught the man's arm and pulled him off balance into Juri's waiting arms.

The massive treasury doors were at the end of the corridor, gleaming dim gold. The double doors were inlaid with mother-of-pearl and a pair of blue agate peacocks, facing each other at the join. Carved into the gold in sunken relief, were the eponymous green peaks, a glittering trail of dark green-red bloodstone marking the outlines. Most of the magic in the room emanated from those doors.

A group of men, dressed in the vibrant green and gold robes and cowls of Green Peaks mages guarded the doors. They each wore a single, jewel-encrusted gauntlet on one forearm. The mage in the middle of the group raised his forearm. Seeing the raised gauntlet and expecting an imminent magical attack, Killean ignited the air between them, stifling a scream when his magic was sucked from the air. Pain exploded behind his eyes, like a vacuum opening up inside his skull.

He staggered off-balance, reaching out to grasp the wall for support. The mages were on him in an instant. Half-blind, Killean slammed his head backward into the face of the mage who tried to grab him from behind. Another punched him in the stomach. Still clutched in the arms of the biggest guard, Killean kicked his legs up and out, striking air and driving the mages away from him. Dropping his legs he hooked one foot around the burly guard's ankle, breaking his balance and forcing his way free.

Another wave of pain lit through him. Vision wavering, he saw the same guard as before pointing his gauntlet at him, the peridot stones set into the curled knuckle pieces glinting evilly. A haze of magic distorted the air around the man's fist. Killean's body was engulfed in dark flame. No, not engulfed. The fire hadn't come from the gauntlet. It was streaming out of his body; his magic was being siphoned from him by a hideous suctioning force coming from the gauntlet.

Roaring in rage, Juri charged the mages. Killean tackled him around the legs, bringing him down a split second before the air between them erupted in stolen flame. Killean ducked and covered his head as his own magic ripped through the chamber aimed at Bodai. The sprite howled in rage and pain as the flames ignited his protective cyclone. Bodai fled back up the stairs.

Furious, Killean sprang over the floor, rising up in front of the mage as he lowered his arm. He didn't bother trying to wrestle the gauntlet from the man's arm. Instead, he drove the spring-loaded blade hidden in his wristguard into the mage's throat. Grabbing the man around the chest, he used his body as a shield as one of the other guards raised his gauntlet. This one was studied with yellow diamonds and released a wave of invisible energy that slammed into the dying guard hard enough to crush his ribs. Killean was driven back into the wall, dropping the body.

Juri surged forward, grabbed the mage by the chin and jerked his head hard to the left, cracking his neck and coming close to severing skull from vertebrae entirely. Two mages remained. The big one held his pink tourmaline encrusted gauntlet down at his side. He jerked his wrist, manifesting a long, slender pink blade made of light. The other mage, an older man with a pattern of scar tissue running down his cheek resembling the feathering of creeping ivy vines, thrust out his white diamond gauntlet. Killean ducked and clapped a hand to his eyes as the room was engulfed in searing white light.

Instinct saved him. Blinded by the light, he kept moving forward, diving out of the way as he sensed another displacement of air. A bright line of pain opened down his right calf as the pink tourmaline mage's magical blade sliced open his leg. Killean drove his blade into the mage's groin while the man's balance was over-extended. He was back on his feet before the man had finished his collapse.

A fierce blast of air slammed into the last mage, propelling him along the corridor and into the magic sealed doors of the treasury. Magic breathed into the chamber, potent and dark and smelling like burning flesh. The mage's body disintegrated into ash and slightly larger chunks of shattered bone. The treasury doors blew open. Killean was in motion before the greasy residue filtered to the ground. He slammed through the doors.

'Reinforcements are coming,' Bodai shouted. 'Hurry and get the stupid flute.'

Easier said than done. One look around the treasury realised all his fears. The room was filled with jewelled urns, sets of ceremonial armour, vestments, sceptres, heavy gold torques, racks of ancient scrolls and swords. Glaives and spears mounted the walls. There were chests and lacquered masks, religious objects and paintings of Peaks royalty from years gone by stacked in the corners of the cramped space.

A life-like bronze horse sculpture took up one side of the room, decked out in fanciful tack and saddle. There were a few stringed instruments, lyres and lutes, and hide covered drums, half as tall as he was, littered about. But there were no flutes. Not a solitary one.

Fuck. All this for nothing. Killean thought quickly. It was all about damage control now. Never exactly his strong suit. Killean hit on an idea that was more to his strength. He'd rescue this disaster of an operation by making an unholy mess.

'Trash it all,' he ordered Juri.

'We're not going to take any of it with us,' the giant asked, looking disappointed.

Killean curled his lip. 'If you can carry it, you can take it. But I want this place wrecked. If we can't have the Flute, no one can.'

Bodai breezed up to him. 'Why don't you just roast it all?' he asked.

'There's still residue magic in the walls,' Killean lied. 'I don't want to risk an explosion.'

Bodai's expression turned sly. 'You're shaking,' he said, looking down at Killean's hands. 'Did one of them hurt you?'

Killean resisted the urge to tuck his hands into fists. 'Get in there,' he growled. 'Help Juri.'

Juri appeared to be having fun, if the sounds of destruction were any indication. There was a small possibility that he and Bodai might discover the Flute in a smashed chest, but Killean doubted it. Uncle Dadarro's lead had been a bust. Gendril's Flute wasn't here. He could feel it in his bones. He was sure if it was here, he'd somehow be able to sense it. It had worked with the Firefly.

Rage and shame warred inside him. Fury was a lightning cord lashing his insides, strangling his throat and filling his head with static. He hated failure. Hated that he'd been forced into it. Had Dadarro sent him on a wild goose chase on purpose? Was he meant to die here, caught like a common thief pilfering enamelled boxes and butter soft and useless golden swords?

'That's enough,' he snapped at the others, raising his voice to be heard over Juri's manic giggles and the more satisfying sounds of cracking wood and scattered jewels. 'Bodai, clear us a path out of here. Juri – this is a charging bull situation. Follow close behind Bodai.'

Juri came out of the treasury wearing a delicate crown twinkling with opal fire and several Green Peaks medallions of high office around his neck. He was smiling and flushed. Bodai's long fingers dripped with chunky rings and his pockets bulged conspicuously.

'I'll lose my glitteries if I spin up,' he complained.

'Better that than your life,' Killean retorted. He rolled his shoulders, preparing to shift. He was nervous, a paranoid fear digging its claws into the back of his mind that it might not work. There was a hollow ache behind his breastbone. When he breathed, he tasted loss. He felt like he was missing something. He decided to stay in his man-skin.

Bodai dashed down the corridor, hopping over the strewn bodies littering the floor. Juri thundered after him, considerably less elegantly. Foot slipping in blood, he ended up kicking one of the dead guard's in the head, adding insult to fatal injury. Killean followed more carefully.

What followed was an even bloodier fray than the fight in the treasury. Bodai's tearing winds hurled guards into stone walls, through false ceilings and, in one memorable occasion, into the points of several spears. Juri charged down the long narrow corridor with the burnt ceiling and barrelled through into the kitchen, moving so fast and so fiercely, even the trained guards gave in to instinct and leapt for cover.

Killean took care of the survivors at their backs, racing to the vanguard when they reached the door to the courtyard. There were guards streaming down from the upper ramparts and filling the courtyard. Someone, somewhere, was ringing a bell loudly. Killean prepared for action.

He *meant* to shift into the form of a bear to swat the guards away. Maybe even a baby elephant like the one still in its cage. That wasn't what happened.

The shift grasped him like a big black claw. Instead of his flesh and blood melting seamlessly between forms and his clothes vanishing to the Timeless Realm, this shift came on him like an invader, as if some alien intelligence had reached out from the Nevermore and started violently rearranging his limbs into a form of its choosing. Black, bony fingered wings burst from his back, sheathed in leathery flesh. His fingers shifted into scaled claws, resembling the ugly feet of a chicken. Fiery pain erupted in his chest. His throat filled with magic. His eyes bulged as he began to asphyxiate.

He burst through the door. He barely had time to clock the courtyard full of soldiers, the trampled tents and scattered detritus left over from the Dancing Deer preparations. His head snapped back, before cracking forward and he spat a gout of black flame through the air into the middle of the first line of pikemen.

His usual flames were impressive, burning hotter than regular flame, but this black stuff was something else. It spread like oil, splattering all the men in the line before burning through them like acid. Unable to stop, Killean vomited another ball of fire and then another. It hurt so much he wondered if he was burning to ash right along with the guards.

He couldn't see or hear anything as the fire erupted out of him. All he was aware of was the pressure in his throat and head. The terrible feeling of being slowly filled up with power he didn't recognise. His wings spread, beating the air and carrying him several feet over the heads of the survivors. He spewed fire down on the courtyard indiscriminately. He couldn't stop. He felt like he was dying.

As abruptly as the shift had come over him, it fled, like a connection had broken inside him. He crashed back to the ground, and only Bodai's winds cushioning his fall, saved him from crippling injury.

His body shifted back to normal. His clothes were strewn with holes. The tips of his fingers burned. He felt like gagging. Juri hauled him to his feet. He staggered drunkenly, stumbling into the bigger man. His legs had turned to water.

The courtyard didn't look so pretty anymore. There were bodies everywhere. Burned down to the bone and sinew, trapped in poses of abject agony. A rain of heavy, black ash sifted through the air. Even the baby elephant in his cage was dead.

'What in the name of the Never Hells was that?' Bodai demanded.

Killean stared at his shaking hands. Panic clawed at his throat. His heart hurt. His chest felt tight. Black and white spots danced at

THE LIFE AND TIMES OF THE TRAITOR KILLEAN ONRYN

the edge of his vision. 'Run,' he choked out. 'We have to get out of here.'

Chapter Seventeen

'I hear Lord Sikozu has a summer estate in Lotus,' Nadil announced, apropos of nothing, his words rudely interrupting Killean's nap.

Cracking open an eye he murmured, 'I wouldn't know.'

'You really didn't check in on the Sea Lord while in Lotus?' Nadil pressed, attempting to disguise his interest with an innocent tone.

'You are a terrible interrogator,' Killean grumbled. Stretching, he shifted on the bench. 'I spent most of my time in Lotus in bird form,' he reminded Nadil, leaning forward to flick the curtain open and peer outside.

They were driving through a wild plain, the dark green grass and ferns studded with outcroppings of rock in random formations as if a giant had flung bounders around in a tantrum. Leaning forward, Killean could see that the old road curved toward the entrance to an abandoned mine dug into the foothills. They were close to the hidden portal.

'Why'd you leave?' Nadil asked him.

'What?'

'Lotus, I mean. Why did you leave that life. It seemed...peaceful.'

Killean stared at him askance but decided to ignore for the now the implication that Nadil had been spying on him. 'I was pretending to be a *bird*,' he snapped. 'How long do you think I could keep that up?'

Nadil sighed. 'Sometimes I think life would be simpler if I stayed in shift,' he mused sadly.

'Sometimes I wonder how you manage to dress yourself,' Killean mimicking his thoughtful tone with his own sarcastic edge. 'Your intelligence doesn't seem high enough.'

Killean had been born a shapeshifter. It was as normal as breathing to him to assume the form of a bird or a wolf, and with a little effort any other animal he wanted, but he never forgot that his true form was that of a man. He could soar like an eagle and he could sing in the night like a wolf, but he would never be either in truth.

He was a man with a hereditary magical curse. The only difference between him and Juri was that his Onryn ancestors had managed to impress the right people and gain influence in the days before it became fashionable to hate the Accursed. The same was true for the Camry. Two accursed bloodlines with better press than the rest.

'Don't get lost in the call of the wild,' he warned Nadil quietly. 'That's what started my uncle on his path.'

Nadil looked at him sharply. 'I thought he was mad your father was named head of the clan and not him.'

Killean smiled thinly. 'That too,' he admitted. 'But the reason he was passed over was because everyone in the clan could tell he was unhinged. He enjoyed being a monster a bit too much.'

'What about you?' Nadil asked.

Killean quirked a brow. '"Monster" is more of a job title than a pleasure for me.'

Nadil rolled his eyes. 'Not what I meant. Don't you feel more alive when you shift?' he asked eagerly. 'When I'm in scale-skin the whole world is brighter – more alive. Didn't it feel like that to you?'

'I only turned into a dragon once,' Killean remarked flatly. 'And I didn't exactly have time to enjoy it.'

'Do you think you would have?' Nadil asked him shrewdly.

Killean stared him down. 'No.'

After Green Peaks he'd worked hard to keep down the dragon under his skin. Unlike the wolf or the hawk, his scale form didn't feel like a set of armour he donned for a specific purpose. It felt alive, like a trespasser lurking under his skin. The dragon part of him was separate from him, a distinct personality that he didn't recognise as a part of himself, even though it was more truly him than any of his other shift disguises.

Giving way to the full transformation in the final battle had been the riskiest thing he'd ever done. Admittedly, once he'd turned scale it hadn't been hard to assert his will. There had been no loss of control, no sudden onset megalomania as there had been with Dadarro. The mental dissonance between him and his dragon-self had diminished rapidly once he claimed his ultimate form, but the wariness remained. He was not in any hurry to transform again, even once he got rid of this damned curse on him.

'They say Sikozu is Gengo Anbi's bastard son. There are some in the Land of White Surf who believe he should succeed his father,' Nadil said, returning abruptly to their previous conversation.

Killean eyed him warily. 'I don't know why you think that's relevant to me,' he said.

'I can never tell what might sway you, Killean,' Nadil replied tiredly. 'But I know you have a thing for powerful upstarts. Harkiv in Past Tiger. The Sly Fox, Vilari. Even the Child of Death. They all have one thing in common. They'll do anything for power.'

'Sammia isn't interested in the kind of power you're talking about,' Killean argued.

'No, she wants the freedom to do whatever she wants and not pay the consequences,' Nadil retorted sharply. 'I know she was a slave in Green Peaks. I get why she'd want to rebel against all that. But she's a killer everywhere else.'

'You sound jealous.'

'I'm not jealous of a bunch of pirates and mercenaries.'

'Are you sure?' Killean asked him keenly. 'Every one of them has the one thing you don't.'

'Let me guess. Your respect?'

'Uh, no. Freedom.' Killean looked at him oddly. 'They're free to be who and what they want to be. The only thing holding them back is their own limitations in skill and daring. You've been shackled to Three Rivers all your life. And now you're their *hero*, they'll own you for the rest of your life.'

Killean would never know what Nadil intended to say in reply because either Sammia or Cactus hit the top of the carriage, startling Ash awake. The carriage began to slow. Killean braced himself, hiding his eagerness. 'We're here.'

Sammia shot him a keen, focused look as he climbed out of the carriage. He was relieved to see that she and Cactus had refrained from killing each other. Well, he was relieved about Sammia at any rate. He wouldn't mind if she'd managed to off the shadow-cursed. Killean brushed up against her, slipping the scrap of paper with the word of power written on it into her hand before Ash noticed.

'Is there really a portal down there,' the boy asked, peering into the darkness of the mine shaft. The entrance was little more than a hole bored out of the rock, surrounded by scrubby bushes and carpeted with the rusted remains of cart tracks. The darkness inside the shaft was thick as paint.

'We're about to find out,' Killean told him.

'We'll go through in two groups,' Nadil announced. 'Cactus you and the Child of Death will go through first. Remember, it's dangerous to head straight for Shipwright Island. The chances of

Sikuzo being there are slim to none anyway. We'll head for Gull Island instead.'

'Wait, why?' Ash asked, confused. 'I thought Shipwright was where the pirate lived.'

'Shipwright is the largest, wealthiest island in the group, pipsqueak,' Sammia told him. 'It's also a disease infested shithole. The Crab do business there, but no one with ambitions as grand as Sikuzo would *live* there.'

'Our intelligence states that Sikuzo likely has Gakai and the Pearl hidden somewhere else. He's using Shipwright Island as a blind,' Nadil explained. 'Which is why we shouldn't waste time on the wrong island.'

'Why head for Gull and not Sea Snail?' Killean asked. 'Snail is neutral ground. It'll be safer.'

'No. Snail doesn't have portal access to either Gull or Shipwright,' Nadil dismissed his idea. 'Sailing into either island is impossible, the Crab will blow us out of the water. We'll go to Gull, get the lay of the land and then portal into Shipwright only if we can't pick up Sikuzo's trail on any of the other Blue Crab islands.'

Killean wasn't sure that was the best plan. Yes, Shipwright Island was a dangerous prospect, being the largest of the Blue Crab's trading hubs, but its size was also an advantage for a motley group of infiltrators looking to stay hidden.

Sikuzo undoubtedly expected Carp to send someone to retrieve their property. Chances were good that Sikuzo was running a double bluff to lure enemy agents to one of the smaller islands to trap them.

If Killean was running this operation, he'd head to Shipwright with the express intention of causing as much disruption as possible, kicking as many hornets' nests as it took to dig up real intelligence, and working hard to disrupt Sikuzo's operations so his premade plans fell through. He'd shake down the island and force Sikuzo to throw everything at him or split his forces putting out endless fires, by which point Killean would have a good idea where the Pearl was and be halfway to fulfilling his promise to break the Crab for Mamie.

This *wasn't* his mission, sadly. Nadil was in charge. For the next five minutes at least. It didn't suit Killean's interests to spend that time arguing tactics. The whole thing would become moot when he sprang his trap, anyway.

It was dark in the pit, the ground pitching steeply under his feet. Killean experienced a pang of real envy when Nadil lit the end of a wooden torch with his blue-white fire, lighting the way. Ash was so eager to prove his worth, he almost set fire to an old mine cart in his rush to ignite his gauntlet. The shaft was lit by flickering green and blue flame, casting sharp, creviced shadows over the walls. The air tasted stale, heavy with dust and stone and whatever mineral had once been hewn from the rock down here. He scented magic on the air before the light found the portal at the bottom of the slope.

The Silk Paw had transformed part of the mineshaft's support structure into a portal at a point where the ground levelled off in a long passage that vanished into darkness around ten feet beyond the wood posts and lintel holding up the ceiling. Magic moved sluggishly between the struts, catching the light from the twin magical flames and winking in the gloom. The portal was crude but effective. There were a lot of knife-scratched magical symbols carved into the wooden struts, which suggested this portal was used often. And why not? This part of Barley was only good for bandit hideouts as it was.

Meekly obeying Nadil's edict, Sammia stepped in front of the portal doorway alongside Cactus. Killean watched her disappear through the haze of magic before turning to Nadil and asking drily, 'Are you going to trust me to go first, or do you want to hold hands?'

Nadil frowned at him. 'We go through together,' he said. 'I'll activate the portal. You hold onto the boy.'

Ash, predictable as clockwork, objected loudly to that. 'I don't need help.'

Killean dropped his hands on the boy's shoulders. 'I think he's more worried I'll run off if I'm not anchored to one of you,' he said.

Ash shook him off, turning to scowl at him suspiciously. 'Why would you do that?' he asked.

Killean shrugged. 'Villain, remember?'

Ash jutted out his chin. 'Don't worry,' he told Nadil. 'I've got my eye on him.'

'Excellent,' Nadil sounded a bit distracted, his focus mostly on the portal.

The magic had yet to die down from Sammia and Cactus' passage. Motes of blue and white light swirled in the doorway like water gurgling down a sinkhole. Usually that meant a transport was still in progress, or that someone or something remained in the small part of the Timeless Realm that connected this portal to its sibling on Gull Island. Nadil had to be distracted, or particularly impatient, not to notice that.

The three of them pushed through together. Killean braced for the disorientation he always felt when realm shifting, pushing through it with an act of will. His feet hit solid ground, even though he could barely see a thing through all the random sparkles exploding in the air like tiny fireworks, he knew in his bones they were in the Timeless Realm.

Next to him, Ash asked, 'Why have we stopped?'

Adjusting to his new surroundings, Killean saw that they were standing between two free standing portal arches. The one at his back resembled the portal he'd just travelled through. The other portal was a ramshackle thing, made from two sun-warped wooden posts connected by a string at the top hung with tiny clam shells and dried seaweed. The space beyond the portals was a shifting kaleidoscope of vague colours and ever-present sparkles, but Killean could just make out a number of crates and barrels a few feet away. Now he understood why the mineshaft was used so often. The Paw were using this tiny piece of the Timeless Realm as a secret cache for contraband.

Killean acted fast, grabbing Ash by the arm he swung the boy straight into Nadil, who had cautiously approached the second portal. The boy slammed into Nadil's back, causing him to stumble through the threshold. The magic ate him up greedily, a single ringing note ringing through the air, like a struck tuning fork. Sammia burst from her hiding place behind a stack of crates and shoved Ash through the portal before the boy had time to do more than yelp.

Killean pulled her back from the bulging magic of the portal and slammed his hand, with his own scrap of magic paper pressed to his palm, into the support beam of the portal behind him. Reactivating the portal, he and Sammia dove through before the Master Word Mamie had given him to overwrite Nadil's commands stopped working.

'Idiots,' Sammia grunted as they both watched the magic eddies fade away between the portal's struts. 'It's like they forgot whose portals we were using.'

'I don't think Nadil expected Mamie to give me different magic codes to the ones she gave Torvin,' he said. 'He really seemed to think Torvin had her tamed.'

'If he can't keep up, he shouldn't play in the big leagues,' she sniffed. 'It's an old smuggler trick to give an untrustworthy ally only part of a portal code and leave them stranded in the Realm.' She shook her head in disgust. 'Even Cactus fell for it.'

Killean shrugged. 'He's a pirate. A totally different kind of smuggler.' He glanced at her and asked, 'You didn't have any trouble giving him the slip?'

'Of course not, I used Mamie's real code to suck the idiot through the Gull portal.'

'Nadil wasn't hard to fool. He was convinced I wanted to go to the islands,' he said quietly. 'I think he was expecting me to turn on him *after* we found the Pearl.'

Sammia smirked at him. 'You do have form stealing magical do-dads.'

'Not for my own sake,' he said. 'There's something bigger going on. The Pearl is just part of it. Whatever Nadil's afraid of, he's half convinced I'm in on it. His paranoia had him looking for treachery from me in all the wrong places.'

Sammia sniffed disdainfully. 'He really doesn't get you at all,' she said. 'You're the type of ruthless bastard who invades entire countries as a *distraction*. It should have crossed his mind you'd use him as bait for the Blue Crab.'

'Nadil doesn't think like I do. He's one of those people who believes everything has to have some grand meaning and purpose behind it. It would be beneath him to ditch a mission before he'd even started it, so it didn't occur to him that I really don't give a shit about the Pearl.'

'Weird,' Sammia remarked. 'You grew up together. He should know you're a shameless opportunist. If you go after the Pearl, it will be for your profit, and no one else's.'

Killean was not entirely sure he liked the picture Sammia painted of his character, but he couldn't really dispute it. He *did* intend to finish the mission but for his own reasons. And he had just thrown Nadil, Cactus and a young boy into hostile pirate territory, hoping they'd be caught instead of him. He just wished Sammia wouldn't make him sound so...shallow.

'The portal's cooled down,' he said. 'We can use it to jump to Frolicking Squirrel.'

THE LIFE AND TIMES OF THE TRAITOR KILLEAN ONRYN

'You really want to see that mangy fox now?' Sammia did not sound pleased.

'Mamie needs her money,' he reminded her. 'Plus, I have business to discuss with Vilari.'

Chapter Eighteen

Killean had always liked Laidlow, Frolicking Squirrel's nominal capital. It was a wretched hive, but it was a colourful and generally cheerful one with a number of excellent inns serving good food, some of the best rice wine and ale a man could find anywhere on the continent, and underneath the apparent lawlessness, there was a structured orderliness to the gambling dens, brothels, music halls and pleasure gardens that appealed to him.

Laidlow's business was vice, but those in charge never forgot that vice was worthless unless it made a profit, and they kept a very keen eye on what happened on their streets. A visitor to Laidlow was actually less likely to have their throat slit by some random mugger than in Pork Cutlet or Valley Good. This was because the various crime syndicates effectively running the town had driven out or incorporated all the small-time criminals. If you died in Laidlow, you would at least know you deserved it.

'I hate this place,' Sammia grumbled as they pushed through the crowds thronging the paved main street.

The boardwalks were alive with entertainers, jugglers, trapeze artistes swinging from wires running between rooftops, fire eaters, contortionists and common hawkers all busily trying to attract the attention of the tourists who flocked to experience Laidlow's dubious delights for themselves.

Swerving to avoid an overly enthusiastic balloon animal seller with a manic grin, Killean asked, 'Why?' He hoped over a steaming puddle of vomit, then danced out of the way of the passed out drunk who'd made it.

Sammia, her spear politely lashed to her back, looked ready to start laying into the crowds with her bare hands. Even her hair, loose and framing her head like a corona, was crackling with anger. 'It's loud. It stinks. It's full of pervs and addicts — do I really need to go on?' she asked.

Killean looked up as one of the wire walkers took a tumble, landing heavily into the nets strung across the street. Screams and jeers rose from the crowds below, reacting to the near fatal mistake. There was even some sporadic applause. The performer, dressed in a green body smock that left little to the imagination, bounced to his feet, grinned proudly, and took several bows, playing off his error.

An accordion player, ensconced in a rocking chair in front of a saloon, started to play a lively, whining number. The old man's toothless grin to passersby who did not tip him was a subtle warning of future misfortune. Killean flipped the old man a coin.

'Where are we going?' Sammia asked him. 'Or are we going to spend all day turning over rocks looking for scum?'

'We'll be picked up soon enough,' Killean murmured, hiding a smile. 'The gangs have eyes on every street corner.'

He turned away a woman wearing a few too many shawls who rather aggressively tried to shove a tray of cheap souvenirs into his chest. The woman needed to get her eyes tested if she'd spied Killean in his old coat and tattered trousers and thought he looked like a man with the coin to waste on knockoff jewellery and poorly made trinkets.

They walked the length of the main drag, passed the grand facades of the music halls and freakshows, not stopping when the men and women inside various velvet lined doors tried to entice them inside with special offers and the promise of an unforgettable night. They continued walking as the lights and crowds dwindled, losing themselves in the plainer, narrower streets of lesser-known Laidlow.

The parts of Laidlow where normal people lived and worked looked a lot like Delta City or Cockle Shore or any other large town where people got on with the business of living. Killean and Sammia were stopped by the same woman with the souvenir tray before they could get more than a quarter mile from the main drag.

'Killean-the-Swift,' the woman called out to him in a low voice. She'd dispensed with the shawls and souvenirs, revealing a gaunt-face and iron-grey hair pulled up in a no-nonsense bun. Her body was wiry and built for action.

'Agna,' Killean nodded to her politely. 'I didn't recognise you under all that knitwear.'

'That's the point,' Agna told him dryly. 'It wouldn't be much of a disguise if every reprobate in the city recognised me on sight.'

'And am I a reprobate?' Killean asked.

'The worst,' Agna said.

Agna was Vilari's lieutenant. A woman who knew her way around a knife and enjoyed the chance the prove it. Her nickname was Slice'n'Dice Agi. According to Vilari, it did not do her artistry justice. Killean had no desire to find out for himself if her nickname was deserved or not.

'What's brought you and the Child of Death to our streets?' Agna asked him warily.

'An opportunity for mutual profit,' Killean said mildly.

Agna looked him up and down. 'You don't look like you have two coins to rub together,' she said.

'And you look too old to be taking orders from a stripling sell sword,' Sammia snapped, 'but you know what they say, appearances can be deceiving.'

Killean closed his eyes briefly. 'I'd like to see Vilari,' he requested politely. 'I'd have sent word ahead, but I don't suppose I need to tell you why that wasn't possible. I know how fast news reaches the Sly Fox.'

'Flattery gets you nowhere with me,' Agna told him, but she did relax her stance. 'Where's Shiny Scale hiding? We know you're working with him now.'

Sammia snorted derisively. 'Hardly.'

Killean met Agna's eyes. 'He's not here. I tricked him into a portal and sent him to Gull Island. He's either still there or dead.'

Agna cocked her head and squinted at him. 'Mutual profit you say?' She was quiet for a moment pretending to think things over. 'Alright,' she said, 'I'll take you to Vilari.'

As if there had been any doubt of that. It was a done deal that Vilari would see him the moment Agna revealed herself to him. If the leader of the Sly Fox hadn't wanted to see him, he'd have simply left Killean and Sammia to walk the streets of his city all night. They'd never find him on their own. Vilari didn't keep to one base of operations, preferring to keep himself mobile, switching from one backroom to another just to confuse his enemies.

Tonight, he'd set up in the manager's office of the Nutkin gambling palace, one of his favourites. Seated behind a monstrosity of a desk, a bank of mirrors at his back concealing either hidden spy holes or a safe or two, Vilari filled the manager's chair with regal ease. He wore a loose, open necked purple silk robe, embossed with a pattern of lean, athletic looking squirrels with a border hem of acorns. His glossy dark hair hung down passed his shoulders in large, loose ringlets. His face was narrow, his mobile mouth already stretching into a genuine smile, and his eyes, somewhere between a sunlit brown and a very murky gold had a familiar, keen light of intelligence to them.

He slapped shut the ledger on his desk and clapped his hands together as Agna ushered Killean and Sammia into the office before ushering herself out. Killean heard the key turn in the lock.

Vilari didn't bother with anything as pedestrian and traditional as a standard greeting. Instead, he launched into conversation as if he and Killean had seen each other only the other day. 'So, my friend, tell me, are the rumours true? Have you let Torvin-the-Spark put a leash on you?' Jovial to a fault, Vilari's expression was amused and expectant.

'The day he does that is the day I rip his throat out,' Killean replied easily. He looked over at the left-hand wall where a large aquarium took up most of the available space. Colourful fish drifted back and forth amid the planted waterweed. 'Is that new?' he asked. 'It looks bigger than the last time I was here.'

'Yes,' Vilari said with characteristic enthusiasm. 'I recently acquired some Rat Bottomed guppies and needed a larger enclosure for my collection.'

'I see,' Killean suppressed a smile. He pulled one of the forged Carp bonds from his backpack and held it out across the desk, careful to keep his movements slow and telegraphed. 'Here. Take a look at this.'

'Ah,' Vilari murmured appreciatively after a moment's study. 'Oh, yes. This is *very* good. Fake, of course. But an *excellent* forgery.' He looked at Killean with bright interest and said, 'This was made by someone in Carp. The ink gives it away. It's just the right colour. No one on the continent can replicate Carp Red this well.'

'Everything is right apart from the magic in the Royal Seal, I'm guessing,' Killean agreed. 'I got it from a royal mage. I've gold too. Base, but it carries the Carp crest.'

Vilari's smile was bright and hungry. As always, his expression suggested this conversation was the best entertainment he'd had in ages. He always looked like that. Killean had actually witnessed him giggling as he discussed a contract on the life of a high-ranking Meadow Lands politician. It was nice to meet a man who enjoyed his work.

'What, pray tell, do you intend to do with this unexpected wind fall?' Vilari asked him, sounding like he was on the verge of a giggling fit now. His sly expression hinted that he already knew the answer.

Killean couldn't help grinning back at him. 'Give it to you, of course,' he replied.

Vilari threw back his head and laughed, revealing the long line of his throat. 'Oh, my friend,' he purred, 'you are a delight!' His smile would make a courtesan proud. He was both winsome and dangerous. 'Make a habit of bringing me gifts and I'll have to invite you over more often,' he cooed.

Killean didn't bother to point out that he hadn't actually invited Killean this time. He liked Vilari. The young mercenary had begun as just another cutthroat in the ranks as a boy of nine and through a judicious application of charm and considerable cleverness, he'd climbed over the bodies of his superiors to lead the Sly Fox clan into a new era of prosperity.

At twenty-three, he was the youngest of the syndicate heads ruling Frolicking Squirrel by at least a decade. Vilari had vision, which was an attribute his rivals lacked. Vilari didn't want to stay in the shadows, doling out death for coin. He wanted to claim the throne of Frolicking Squirrel and fight his turf battles against the likes of Three Rivers, Cow and Green Peaks. To that end, he'd been carefully suborning his rivals, undermining their efforts through trickery or promised alliances, while casting his net outside Squirrel to bag a few unlikely allies.

Like Killean.

'This isn't a gift. It's a make good on our agreement,' he told the other man. 'I did promise that next time you saw me, I'd bring something worth your while.'

The first time they'd met, when Killean had hunted him down the hard way to warn him off sending more assassins his way, Vilari had reacted to his appearance with the same delight he showed now. He'd wasted no time trying to forge a deeper relationship.

'My dear, *General*,' Vilari had gushed. 'I am absolutely delighted you came to visit. Please, take a seat. Have a drink. No, no. Don't think it is poisoned. I would never. You see, I knew those men would fail. I sent them out to die at your hands to rid myself of a batch of bad eggs. You've done me a favour getting rid of them. Now let me make you an offer in return.'

Killean, who had come here expecting a fight with faceless men in hoods who relied on their blades to do the talking had been thrown off balance by this cheery, faintly obsequious, high-key flirtatious young man in his fine robes and carefully oiled curls, smiling and purring at him like an eager kitten.

'Give me one reason not to kill you,' he'd told him, while trying to back out of the room.

Vilari had beamed at him as if he'd said something witty and urbane. 'How does five thousand sound?' he asked.

Killean blinked. 'Just one will do.'

Vilari threw his head back, laughing with abandon. 'No, no,' he said swiping a tear from the corner of his eye without smudging the artful kohl lining his eyelids. 'I meant, how does five thousand in Three Rivers groats sound to you? Think of it as payment for your assistance.'

Killean narrowed his eyes. 'I'd rather take the money you received for accepting those contracts on my life,' he said.

Vilari looked utterly delightedly. It was mildly unnerving. 'Good for you,' he purred, voice deepening. 'That was a test, of course,' he added off-handedly. 'I wouldn't expect the great Killean-the-Swift to settle for a measly five thousand. You can have half the money,' he said breezily. 'And that's my final offer. I do need to pay all those men's widows, after all.'

'You didn't lure me here to give me money,' Killean told him warily. 'What is it you think I can do for you?' He was beginning to see the shape of the trap he'd walked into. A velvet lined trap, one that appeared to have a greater cost for Vilari than it did for him, but appearances were deceptive. Especially when dealing with assassins.

Vilari had finally lost the smile, but the eagerness didn't leave his expression. 'Once upon a time, there was a young rebel upstart who helped a certain king in Past Tiger win his throne,' said the assassin in sing-song tones of a dreamy storyteller.

'So what?' Killean had asked.

He'd been sixteen when his uncle had dispatched him to Past Tiger to learn guerrilla tactics from the entrenched rebels in the jungle. Killean wasn't sure, looking back on it, if his uncle had intended to support Harkiv right into his throne, or simply use the rebels to give Killean his blooding. Whatever the case, he'd learned a lot from his time in Past Tiger. But all that was in the past. He wasn't a soldier anymore. He was nothing. A vagrant. A spent force.

He said as much to Vilari, who exclaimed, '*Nonsense.* You are ever the soldier! But,' he said speaking so fast his words ran together, 'more than that, you have past form toppling regimes by backing dark horses. I know you backed Arlo Isshki against his father in Cow. The resulting upheaval allowed Dayone the One-Eye to ascend to the Chamber of Commerce. A very fortuitous result for your uncle when he visited the Cow Lands cap in hand.'

Killean cocked his head, curious where this assassin learned that. Not even Three Rivers knew about the Isshki coup. Not that it mattered now. Killean had helped a lot of upstarts to better themselves and gained nothing from it in the end.

'The past is dead,' he said, 'and you will be too if you don't get to the point.'

'Very well,' Vilari had said briskly. 'I want an alliance.'

Killean very nearly asked with whom. He stared at the Sly Fox. 'You can't be serious,' he said. 'Men like you don't go offering men like me terms.' Especially when he had nothing but his own viciousness to bring to the table.

'What sort of man do you think I am?' Vilari had asked, his smile not quite as assured this time.

Killean knew his answer needed to count. 'A clever one,' he said. 'I know of your exploits, Smiling Vilari. You've done many impressive things and I'm sure you'll do many more. If I had my army still, I would've sought you out with terms of my own,' he admitted and saw the flash of satisfaction in Vilari's quick smile. 'But I'm just a penniless traitor now. One who wears a leash poorly,' he added pointedly. 'I've never made a good follower, nor servant. The best I can offer you is that so long as you leave me alone, I'll do the same for your men.'

Vilari waved away his objections as if barely hearing them. '*Now* this is true,' he said disdainfully, as if the present was an insult to Vilari personally. 'But who cares about *now*? *I* am concerned with tomorrow and the next day,' he said grandly. 'Torvin let you go free. Try as I might, I cannot find out why. And this excites me.'

He certain did act excited, pacing his room between the bubbling fish tank and the fainting couch leaning against the far wall, like a tiger in a cage.

'He must want you for something. There is no other explanation for setting you loose,' Vilari insisted, speaking his thoughts aloud. He spun on his heels to face Killean. 'There are whispers in certain quarters of a new uprising. Someone has taken up your uncle's mantle and is seeking Myron's relics,' Vilari told him.

'Who?' Killean asked.

Vilari shrugged carelessly. Too carelessly. 'No one knows. The rumours are barely more than bad air, stinking up the inns in backwaters like Horseflesh and Lotus. It's the same old, same old, we've heard since you went down. I had discounted most of the rumours, until Torvin did the inexplicable and turned you loose on the gameboard again. Now *anything* could be true.'

'Do you seek the relics?' Killean asked coolly.

'Starless Night, no,' Vilari said, sounding honestly offended. 'I want real power, not mystical do-dads. And I think you do too. That's why I'm getting in on the ground floor. I foresee your rise, Killean, and intend to profit from it as that dimwit Arlo and the king of the tigers did before me.' He paused, face contorting into a look of true concern and asked, solicitously, 'You don't mind me calling you Killean, do you?'

Killean shook his head, biting back his smile. This oily, little fox was either a madman or a trickster, but he'd be damned if he wasn't enjoying the performance. 'It's not like I have a title anymore,' he reminded the other man. He'd been called a lot worse than his given name since returning to the waking world.

Vilari beamed at him. 'Marvellous. Here is my offer. I propose we help each other, *Killean*.' Vilari dragged out the rolling syllables of his name, making them sing.

'You're going to have to be a bit more specific than that,' Killean told him, intrigued despite himself. He hadn't met someone so obviously ambitious and imaginative in a very long time. Vilari was an odd duck for a Fox, but he was completely in control of the image he showed to the world. In full mastery of his own destiny and filled to the brim with ideas.

'Mutual profit,' Vilari said. 'We each have our own desires, our own ambitions. I flatter myself that they complement each other. At present your strength is in your potential while mine is more concrete.'

Killean nodded slowly. He certainly couldn't argue means with a syndicate boss. 'Go on,' he prompted.

Vilari spread his hands. 'I will aid you where I can, offering you information or funds – within reason – and in return you will find opportunities to repay me, and the Sly Fox, either materially or in your own *distinctive* style,' he said.

His *distinctive style*, was it? Given that Vilari had begun this little tete-a-tete discussing a stolen throne and an interclan coup he'd helped engineer, Killean could guess what Vilari thought his style was.

'And what are the bounds of this unusual agreement?' he asked.

Looking supremely pleased, Vilari had clasped his hands together like a man in raptures. 'Only the limits of our imagination, my dear General. In fact, allow me to plant a little seed in your fertile mind right now. I recently heard an interesting story about a young vagabond from Green Peaks who has somehow managed to acquire a very valuable magical gauntlet.

'My sources tell me it is known as the *Essence Drinker*, a weapon that can steal a mage's magical power. Except this one appears only to set things on fire.' Vilari shrugged carelessly. 'Oh well, most legends are lies. But the point of interest is this – the boy is looking for *you*. Apparently, he thinks this gauntlet gives him the mettle to kill you.'

Killean's mind raced. He could well guess what the Essence Drinker was. The rest of the story didn't interest him, lots of people wanted him dead. But the prospect of getting his hands on a gauntlet like the Essence Drinker certainly did get his mind working.

'Alright, tell me about this boy,' he said, knowing that he was essentially tying himself to Vilari by the bounds of this nebulous alliance. Which might be a truly terrible idea. He certainly didn't trust the Fox, but what did he really have to lose anyway? His life was worthless now.

'Not so hasty, my friend. First, I must ask what you will do for me, in return..?'

THE LIFE AND TIMES OF THE TRAITOR KILLEAN ONRYN

Killean thought about it. 'Tell me how to find this boy and the next time I come for you I'll bring gifts to further your power and glory,' he promised.

Chapter Nineteen

'You scheming bastard,' Sammia accused him. 'You've been canoodling with this fox the entire time!'

Killean exchanged a look with Vilari. 'There hasn't been any canoodling,' he said.

'Yet,' Vilari added brightly. 'But I knew my hunch to back you would pay off. I can make very good use of these bonds.'

Killean was sure he could and would. It was time to get to the reason he'd come here. 'I need money.'

Vilari paused in the process of placing the bond into a drawer in his desk. 'That's not really in the spirit of a gift,' he said pleasantly.

'But it is within the bounds of our agreement,' Killean replied. 'You knew when you offered me an alliance, I wouldn't come cheap.'

Vilari's eyes widened, his smile twinkling. 'Saucy.' He sobered and asked guardedly, 'How much do you want?'

Killean told him the figure Mamie had quoted him. 'I need to hire a ship and a crew to sail into Shipwright Island and wait for me there.'

'You're going after the Blue Crab?' Vilari asked. His smile was as sly as his namesake. 'Interesting. Did you know the Crab are implicated in those rumours I told you about when last we met?'

Conscious of Sammia glaring at him, Killean answered cautiously, 'I know that Three Rivers and the Silk Paw are invested in getting rid of them.'

Vilari laughed. 'Oh, I bet. The Cat was a fool to try and deal with those nasty little cultists, especially when she couldn't stump up the goods she promised.'

Killean ears pricked up, metaphorically speaking, but he knew better than to ask for details. If he hadn't come here for a specific purpose, he might have dickered over a price for the information Vilari had on Mamie's indiscretion. But the old adage about never asking a question he didn't already know the answer to, held true in this instance. Vilari was eager to help him, so long as that aid proved profitable for him, and Killean knew how easily he could become indebted to this smiling killer.

Vilari was visibly disappointed he didn't take the bait but got over it quickly. 'Very well. I'll make sure Mamie Cat gets the funds to hire you a ship and crew.'

'I want a cut from the bond profits too,' Killean said.

Vilari spluttered a laugh. 'Oh, now, really. That is *too* much,' he declared.

Killean raised his brows. 'It's fair,' he said flatly. 'It's a lot more than that, considering how much you stand to gain when the Crab goes belly up.'

Vilari smiled patronisingly. 'Really? And how do I profit from that?'

Killean crossed his arms. 'Our association is well known. My hand, your will, some will say. Any move I make reflects upon the Sly Fox.'

Considering the Sly Fox's stock in trade, this was a situation guaranteed to benefit Vilari more than him. There weren't many acts beneath the dignity of a Fox. Killean had avoided a meeting in person for weeks, but word had reached him that Vilari had started retroactively billing the enemies of the rogue assassins who had tried their luck against him, taking credit for Killean's kills.

Sea Lord Sikuzo's scalp would provide considerable bragging rights among the types of people Vilari dealt with. It might also open some doors usually barred to him. A fact that Vilari had likely already considered. Sometimes the only difference between an assassin and a hero was good press.

Vilari's chuckle was low and appreciative, coming from the diaphragm. 'Would you be my hand in this matter?' he asked invitingly.

Killean merely shrugged. 'I'm my own master, but you might as well take credit for what I'm being made to do.' Letting his act of indifference drop, he smiled a little. 'Torvin will be annoyed if rumours start that you and he are working together. I imagine you could get a lot of leverage out of that.'

Vilari stroked his chin, his tarnished gold eyes dreamy, his expression abstracted. 'Yes,' he sighed happily. 'I think – yes – I think this will work *very nicely.*'

Killean didn't expect Vilari to share his schemes. All he needed to know was that Vilari believed their arrangement served him so he'd continue to support Killean.

'Can we go,' Sammia snapped. Her expression was savage, '*Before* I skewer this prick for completely ignoring me?'

Killean realised she was right. Vilari hadn't acknowledged Sammia's presence once in the entire time they'd been here. He looked at the man askance. Sammia was the Child of Death, a woman well versed in the art of killing. That should have garnered her more than a little respect from the Sly Fox. Even Nadil and Cactus were grudgingly willing to acknowledge how dangerous Sammia was. Vilari's smile slid just passed her left shoulder as if she was made of glass. Plain, uninteresting glass that held no intrigue for him whatsoever.

It wasn't the fact that she was a woman either. There were woman like Agna of rank and respect in the Sly Fox. This disrespect was uncharacteristic.

'Have you two met?' he asked, confused.

Had Sammia swiped a contract from the Fox, or otherwise undercut Vilari? The explanation wasn't very satisfying given the fact that Vilari's response to losing several of his assassins at Killean's hands was to thank him. Had Sammia turned Vilari down before now? Was that it?

'No,' Sammia snapped. 'We haven't met.'

'But I have heard many things,' Vilari said, the pleasantness of his tone ringing false. He looked at Killean and said, 'Perhaps I should give a report?'

'Keep your trap shut before I open a new hole in your belly, Fox,' Sammia snapped.

Killean grabbed her arm. He'd heard something. Movement in the walls. They were almost certainly being watched by assassins hidden in hollow spaces between the walls. 'We're leaving,' he said firmly.

'If you must,' Vilari said blandly. And then, finally deigning to look at Sammia for one heavy moment, he turned his gaze on Killean and said, 'I do hope to see you again soon.'

There was a message there for him to decipher. Killean nodded sharply and drew Sammia toward the door just as it was opened by a granite faced assassin he didn't recognise. He and Sammia were hustled off the premises with alacrity, their welcome well and truly rescinded.

'Let go of me.' Sammia jerked her arm away. She was coldly furious, striding off down the main drag, her thunderous mood causing even the drunks to dodge out of her way. Killean followed after her, mood pensive.

'You could have defended me,' she snarled when they were out of the city limits and back on the road to the Laidlow portal.

The portal, hidden in a small wood full of feathery trees and thick underbrush, had been formed when an old tree had partially uprooted due to disease and toppled into the side of a thick bodied oak beside it, forming an unusual archway at an acute angle. A mage had imbued the trees with magic and created a rustic portal few knew existed.

'You could have kept your cool,' he retorted, swiping an arm through the swarm of gnats massing around him on the road. 'Vilari is a syndicate boss. He deserves respect.'

Sammia whipped her head around. 'And what do I deserve?' she demanded.

Killean looked away, expression pinched. *Everything*, said a little voice in his head, *if only I could trust you.*

'Vilari didn't trust you,' he said instead of the truth. 'He's not a man with high moral standards. Got any idea why he took against you?'

'He's a woman-hating perv?' she suggested hotly. He tried not to notice the gleam of tears in her eyes.

'He might be a pervert,' Killean conceded. 'I really have no idea. But I haven't heard he hates women.'

He focused on the road. It had rained earlier and now the air was heating up and the insects were in full song. The smell of decomposing vegetation tickled his nose and the overhanging trees along the route shed teardrops down on his head.

'He's jealous,' Sammia said quietly. 'I'm a better assassin than he is.'

Killean glanced at her. 'Definitely,' he agreed. 'Vilari tends to hire his competition, not insult them. What happened back there was...odd.'

The look she shot him was decidedly unimpressed. 'So you admit it, but you still didn't stop it. You acted like a besotted boy in there, you know,' she grumbled.

Killean rolled his eyes. 'Vilari is useful and I don't have enough allies to turn away help.'

'You like him,' she snapped.

'I like *power*,' he corrected her. 'And Vilari has it.'

The trees lining the road grew densely on either side, their branches straining to meet in the middle, creating a thick lacy canopy that cut off the murky daylight overhead. This stretch of road was known to be popular with bandits, but the chances of any bothering them was slim. More's the pity. He wouldn't mind a spot of violence interrupting this conversation.

'Why didn't you defend me?' Sammia asked him again.

He looked at her irritably. 'What was I supposed to do? Fur shift and rip his throat out for ignoring you?'

'*Yes*,' she hissed.

Oh, for crying out loud. 'There were assassins in the walls! You might come back from a chest full of poison darts, but I can't. A cold shoulder is nothing to die for.'

'Horse shit,' she snarled. 'He outright implied he had dirt on me. He wanted to drive a wedge between us.' Unlimbering her spear, she used the point to sweep aside a moss draped broken branch lying in her path. She sent the piece of rotted wood skidding into the weeds spilling over the side of the road.

'That's why I got us out of there,' he told her. 'I didn't stay and listen, Sami.'

'You listened,' she said darkly. 'You trust him more than me.'

He moved ahead of her so he could block her path. 'And do you trust *me*?' he demanded.

Sammia glared at him. The dripping canopy provided a soft percussion beat to their argument, the heavy foliage creating an enclosed little world just for them. She took her sweet time answering. 'I trust you enough,' she said warily.

'Enough to what?' he asked. 'Let you down again? Dump you as soon as the going gets tough? Or maybe you think I'll stiff you on your payment? Perhaps I'll hand you over to face Three Rivers judgement like you think I did before, is that it?'

She clucked her tongue in disgust but wouldn't meet his eyes. 'I don't think that.'

'Then what do you think?' he pressed, going on the attack. 'I've asked you no questions about where you've been these last five years, or what you've done. I never even asked why, when you got free of Three Rivers within hours of your capture, you never once tried to find me, even when you knew I was in Green Peaks. All *you've* done is pick and harry me for information. Why is that, Sami? What is it you really want?'

'You're blaming me for not coming back?' Sammia asked, disgustedly. 'I didn't come back because I was being hunted. Torvin had people watching me! He wanted me to lead him to you!'

Killean pinched the bridge of his nose. 'I never blamed you for anything,' he said quietly.

'You are now. You don't trust me,' she accused. She slammed the bottom of her spear into the ground. 'I'm supposed to be your night-damned *queen*!'

Killean turned away, he started walking, shoulders hunched. 'Fine,' he growled, 'when I've secured us a kingdom and an army to defend it, you can wage war on Squirrel if that will make you happy. Starry Night, why do you care if some guy insults you? You have to be used to it by now.'

It happened a lot. Sammia was an incredible fighter. She was a shrewd operator and she tended to be more ruthless than most of the men fool enough to challenge her. All of this meant that a cottage industry of nasty gossip had been spread about her, merely to tarnish her reputation and soothe fragile mercenary egos.

'That's why I need you to help me squash that bullshit,' she told him angrily. 'Did any of that crap you said in Cockle Shore mean *anything*?' she demanded.

'Every word,' he said. 'But Sami, answer me this – what were you doing in that inn in Potbelly?'

It was the question he kept turning over in his mind. The doubt that ate at him even now. He couldn't think of a single good reason for her to have just happened to find him there.

She frowned and asked, 'What do you think I was doing? I was giving those yokels a lesson in *respect*.'

'But why Potbelly?' he pressed. He might have believed in the coincidence of their meeting if they'd bumped into each other here in Squirrel, or on the plains of Cow country, but they had unhappy history in Potbelly and the country was surrounded on three sides by Three Rivers.

Sammia narrowed her eyes. 'What are you accusing me of?' she demanded. He only wished he could believe her confusion was genuine. But she knew. She knew exactly what he was accusing her of, that's why she'd reacted so strongly to Vilari's sly hints.

'Were you sent to find me, Sami?' he asked her softly.

'No,' she snapped. She looked away, sharply. He saw the corded muscle in her neck as she ground her jaw. 'If you must know, I was chasing up a rumour about the boys,' she told him coldly. 'You know, the rest of our team you abandoned?'

Killean scowled. 'I didn't abandon them.'

'Then where are they, Ilin?' she snapped. 'What in the Nevermore happened to them?'

He crossed his arms. They were both getting unpleasantly wet. The drumming patter of raindrops increased in tempo as the rain came down in earnest. 'You thought they were in potbelly?' he asked incredulously.

'Why not?' she threw out. 'I already checked everywhere else.'

'Potbelly is full of Accursed hating bigots,' he reminded her. 'They'd never settle there.'

Rain gathered like a scattering of tiny gems in Sammia's hair. It glistened over her bare arms, reminding him of happier times. Her shirt was damp and her scale-mail breastplate shone with moisture. She was breathing fast and light, anger making her features shine.

'You haven't forgiven me for Shrimpton,' he said. 'You don't forgive anything.'

'Starry Night, you've got an ego,' she sneered. He saw her fingers clench around the pole of her spear. 'Get over yourself, Ilin. I have.'

He smiled grimly. 'Then why are you here, Sami?'

She tossed her head, shaking her hair. 'I need the money, alright? Works been slow lately.'

He looked down at the wet road, because he couldn't look at her. *Lies,* a little voice in his mind whispered. *She's lying about everything.* Rain gathered on his eyelashes, making his cheeks damp and cold. He sighed. 'Let's get moving,' he said. 'I think we've giving the others enough time to attract notice.'

'Shipwright Island?' she asked him, tone curt.

He hummed in agreement and started walking. They made the next leg of the two-mile trek to the portal in silence. Eventually the canopy parted, exposing a leaden sky. They walked along the side of the road, hopping into the brush to get out of the way of passing carriages and palanquins carried by half-naked servants. The rain ended as abruptly as it began. The road became busier and they had to wait their moment to slip into the woods.

Squirrels leapt from limb to limb in the mulch smelling woods. Killean wasn't sure if that counted as frolicking or not. The woods had grown up in a natural basin, and the ground sloped inward toward the base. The portal was in the basin, the approach made difficult by bracken and ankle-twisting undergrowth. A few birds trilled in the trees above. A squirrel hurled an acorn at a neighbour and a cabbage butterfly, sheltering from the damp, fanned its wings on a lichen covered log just in front of the portal. Killean pulled out his knife and set to work cutting his marks into the archway post.

'Ilin,' Sammia called to him, abrupt and urgent. There was a ringing note of feeling in her tone. He turned his head to look at her.

'What is it?'

She took a breath. A spasm of expression zipping over her face too fast to track. '...Never mind,' she muttered, gaze skittering down to the ground.

Killean sighed, cut the pad of his thumb and daubed his marks with his blood. He braced himself as the magic in the archway ignited in pretty golden sparkles. Sammia hurried forward, suddenly eager to be away. Oddly, Killean felt the exact opposite.

Chapter Twenty

Killean had first met Sammia while roaming the lesser kingdoms of the continent for notable Accursed to join his elite forces. He'd already picked up Bodai and Juri when word reached him of an interesting Accursed causing a nuisance in Windchill Country.

Dadarro was waiting for him in Frog Song, the piddling nation west of Windchill and Killean had taken the opportunity to rest at the estate of a sympathetic petty lord, Ktaka, who along with peppering him for an introduction with king Harkiv, had also told him of a problem plaguing his lands. A spirit-born Accursed, some kind of water sprite, had declared himself the new master of the local riverways and set about flooding the lands. The sprite was apparently a fearsome giant capable of felling ten men with one sweep of his massive arm.

'Only ten?' Bodai sniffed. 'Juri can do drop double that with his bad breath alone.'

'That's not nice, Bodai,' Juri murmured, looking unhappily down into his trencher. He picked nervously at the greasy chicken thighs piled up under his nose.

Lord Ktaka had put up a bounty for the giant, but so far none of the adventurers who had showed up to claim it had proved up to the task. 'None of them?' Killean asked sharply. 'Are you sure this water sprite isn't a real god?'

'It is a man,' Ktaka had said. 'But you know as well as I do these Accursed adventurers are cowards. They come to abuse my hospitality and take advantage of the good women of these lands. And to a man, they leave the job undone.'

Killean had slowly lowered his wine cup. 'If you feel that way about Accursed, should my men and I take our leave, m'lord?'

Ktaka wasn't listening. He was too busy complaining. 'To make matters worse, I had a woman turn up! Said she could take on the giant,' he scoffed in disgust adding nonchalantly, 'I had my guards send her away. She was no doubt a whore and a cutthroat. She likely stole that spear of hers from a real soldier.'

'If he was so easily dispatched, he wasn't a very good soldier,' Killean said quietly. 'Where is this woman now?'

Ktaka looked askance at him. 'Why would you possibly care about that trash?'

Killean shrugged and pushed up from the table. 'Rebels, like beggars, can rarely be choosy, m'lord. And a woman armed and ready to face a giant sounds like one I'd like to meet.'

'Where are you going?' Ktaka demanded.

'To solve your problem, m'lord. And perhaps my own as well.'

The town under Ktaka's control was not large and it didn't take long to ascertain that the woman he was looking for wasn't here. 'Maybe Ktaka's poor welcome scared her off?' Bodai suggested, drily. He asked, 'Do we have to take on this giant? I'm all for letting the brute drown Ktaka.'

'He's supplying arms to my uncle. He can't die,' Killean murmured.

Juri spoke up. 'Do you think...' he trailed off.

Killean turned to him curiously. Juri so rarely spoke up. Whatever he had to say had to be interesting. 'Go on,' he prodded gently.

Juri scuffed his feet, wriggling shyly. 'I have heard of an Accursed woman who wields a polearm,' he raised his eyes from the ground to meet Killean's gaze. 'Sammia, Child of Death. She's a five-time winner of the Valley Good arena. People say she can't die.'

'Why would the Death Child waste her time on a backwater like this?' Bodai asked, derisively.

'Let's find out,' Killean said decisively.

He'd heard of the Child of Death as well but had never attempted to locate her as he'd assumed an Accursed of her reputation was likely already pledged to a mercenary outfit. The best Accursed – or at least the one's with the most established reputations – usually were, which was why Killean recruited from among the young and the hungry. Still, he was honour bound to go after the giant anyway. If his path should cross with this woman, the Death Child or whoever she was, he'd considered it a bonus. A statement he was sure few other people who'd crossed Sammia would share.

He hadn't known then, but Sammia had been in town all along. She'd struck up a useful acquaintance with the local barmaid who had hidden her when she heard Killean was looking for a woman matching her description, afraid that he'd been sent by Ktaka to run her out of town.

Sammia had spied on the three of them from inside a parked hay cart on the side of the road and followed them into the countryside to face the giant. Using her superior knowledge of the terrain to her advantage, she'd managed to get ahead of them, cutting them off at the overflowing banks of the glutted river meant to be the giant's home.

Killean's first impression of Sammia was of a young and lovely bandit, with hair as soft as a cloud and skin as smooth as silk, carrying a Green Peaks spear. He'd barely had time to think, *Pretty and could be useful,* before she was attempting to use that spear on him. He'd thrown himself out of the way of a gut-skewering lunge.

'You won't take my kill from me. I was here first.'

Killean had been working with Bodai and Juri for months by this point. They were a good team and had faced down several formidable opponents. Sammia still proved a challenge. She was fast. She was mean. And she wielded her spear like an extension of her body. It was like she bent her frame into and around every arc and thrust of her spear. She used it like a staff and like a pole for vaulting. She broke their formation, interrupted attacks and kept Killean moving defensively so he couldn't marshal his magic.

When all four of them tired, she faced them down fiercely, her back to the river and said, 'I was going easy on you before. Get lost before I decide to play hard.'

'Boss?' Bodai queried, urgently.

Wiping sweat from his brow Killean had nodded. 'Do it.'

Bodai had sent a sharp gust of wind straight into Sammia's solar plexus, knocking her off her feet and flinging her into the river.

Baited, the giant had wasted no time making his entrance. Exploding from up from the surface, the Accursed had flesh the greenish-grey colour of river silt and a mane of hair that streamed down his muscular back in the form of knotted riverweed. His eyes were wide and gelatinous like a fish and his skin was scudded with patches of iridescent scale. He was indeed a big fellow, with a gut to match. Throwing Sammia her spear, Killean and the others backed a little distance from the bank to watch.

She cursed him soundly. 'You bastard. You used me!'

Killean cupped his hands and shouted back, 'I'm just giving you what you wanted. Kill him in five minutes and I'll pay you double the reward money.'

It didn't go well in the beginning. The giant swiftly turned the current against her, causing the water to surge before pulling her under. She was swept further down river, dragged over submerged rocks and tossed head over heels by the raging waters. A normal person would have quickly drowned. Sammia drowned at least twice before the giant grew complacent and released his hold on the river, slowing the current. Body collapsing into water, he sank under the surface, reemerging just as Sammia's body surfaced, tangled in riverweed.

'So much for that,' Bodai grumbled. 'What a waste of time. I got my feet wet for nothing.'

'Wait,' said Juri, his focus still on the river. 'It's not over.'

Killean narrowed his eyes. There was something not quite right about the body. The spear was next to the corpse, as if it had travelled with her the entire time, clutched in her hand. The sharp blade was angled and pointed out of the water, the shaft still in her hand, its end sunk securely into the sloped bank. The likelihood of it landing like that naturally was incredibly small. Killean moved to the wooden bridge, giving up the safety of dry land to get a better look. The others followed him.

The giant either sensed something was wrong or intended to devour the corpse, because resurfaced and drew closer, coming into range of her spear, but still Sammia did not move. She played dead with the consummate poise of someone who had died for real several times over.

The giant, his lower body made of frothing surf, hovered over her, craning his upper body around the spear to peer down at her face. Killean only had a view of the giant's muscular back, so he missed the moment Sammia's eyes sprang open and she launched herself out of the water, a small skinning knife in her left hand.

She struck the giant in the eye. He reared back the blade still lodged in his eye, releasing a terrible roar and sliced open his own flank on Sammia's conveniently placed spear. The water rose in a cascading wave that slammed into the bridge support struts, almost bringing it down and chased over the surface of the river, growing in size until it crested at the giant's back, absorbing him and flooding over Sammia. She and the giant were lost in the water, which swirled down river and burst the banks, spreading into the standing pools of water saturating the land around the river.

Killean ran along the bank, splashing through the edge of the flood waters. 'Where's the spear?' he shouted. 'Find that and we find the girl.'

The spear, it turned out, had found a home in the giant's shoulder courtesy of Sammia. When they exploded out of the raging river, Sammia was caught in the giant's arms and he was shaking her violently, his motions jerky with pain and possible brain damage. Red water streamed down his chest, back and left arm and his ruined eye was a gored mess. Still, he had more than enough strength to crush the life out of Sammia.

Tossing her broken body onto the half-submerged bank, the giant was fool enough to roar his victory. Killean considered hurling a fireball at him.

On the bank, Sammia bolted upright, like a puppet jerked on the end of a string. The giant was too surprised to see his opponent spring back to life to do much as she launched herself back into the water and snatched at the end of her spear, driving the blade deeper into his flesh.

She shoved the giant off balance, but he knocked her away with a sweep of his arm. Sammia went under the water and popped back up again. Spitting bloody froth from her mouth, her breath wheezed like a broken bellows. There was a disturbing whistling undertone it, as if she'd sprouted a few unfortunate holes in places that really should be airtight. It didn't slow her down.

She tackled the giant from behind, leaping on his back and drawing her little skinning knife across his throat. The river surged and an arc of blood flew through the air like a hair thin sickle blade. Not content with simply slicing, Sammia changed her grip on the blade and drove it deep into side of his throat, jerking and twisting her wrist to rip a bigger a hole through his flesh and sinew.

The giant collapsed into the water, his body seeming to melt, until he appeared to be kneeling torso deep in the river. Blood spread through the water like ink, turning the frothing wavelets cloudy red. The giant, woozy with massive blood loss, remained upright for another several seconds, spitting dark, thick gouts of blood down his chin. His mouth moved silently; his remaining eye was unfocused. Sammia shoved him over, face first into the river. He dissolved into dark red fluid and spread through the water.

Sammia retrieved her spear and scrambled for the bank as the river surged one final time and swept the giant's remains downstream on a furious red wave.

Juri broke into enthusiastic clapping. Sammia, kneeling on the bank, body heaving for breath, turned and glared with enough venom to kill a giant dead. Unfortunately for her, she wasn't nearly close enough to sink her teeth in.

'Who are you?' she demanded when Killean drew closer.

'Killean Onryn, of the Striking Talon clan.'

She squinted at him. 'You're the arsehole that's been causing all the trouble down south?'

'Yes.'

Her eyes narrowed and she asked, 'What do you want?'

Killean studied her. Soaked and shivering, he could see all the places where her skin had been scraped raw by rocks. The rasp to her breathing suggested she had several broken ribs, some of which were probably poking into squishy places that couldn't take it. Her left shoulder looked to be dislocated and her eyes were bloodshot with broken capillaries likely caused by the dual threat of being squeezed to death and drowned. Yet here she was, upright, speaking, victorious and griping the shaft of her spear like she was seriously considering using it.

'I want to offer you a job,' he said. 'Lend me your strength, Sammia Child of Death, Victor of the Blood Arena and you can name your price.'

'Oh, yeah, and what if I want your smug head on the end of my spear?' she demanded.

'I might not be able to stop you,' he conceded, 'but my uncle would see you dead.'

She scoffed. 'Small threat.'

Killean nodded. 'True. But tell me, can you grow back severed limbs?' She stared at him. He continued. 'Kill me and my uncle will have you hunted down.

'Then, when he learns that you can return from death, he'll order your limbs cut off, all save your head, and have your helpless torso planted in the ground so he can watch how long it takes your limbs to grow back. When they do, he'll do it all again. My uncle has a twisted sense of fun.'

'Then why the fuck would I want to work for him?' she demanded.

'You don't,' Killean replied simply. 'And you wouldn't be. You're making a deal with me. My uncle won't touch you. You will never answer to any of his generals. You'll join my elite forces. Your name will be known from here to Icicle and across the ocean to the court of the Jumping Carp. No petty lord will ever turn you out again. You'll command a king's ransom from every town we conquer.'

'He's not lying,' Bodai spoke up. 'I've got the vestments of a Roedian priestess in my war trunk.'

Sammia's brow creased in confusion. 'What do you want with a priestess' clothes?' she asked.

Bodai's pale skin pinked with the faintest blush. 'They're pretty,' he said, 'and the tiara's loaded with diamonds the size of chestnuts.'

'I can pay you better than bounty hunter rates,' Killean said, ignoring Bodai.

She was still suspicious. Bitterly she said, 'You're some kind of noble, aren't you? Why would you keep your word to an Accursed freak?'

'Because he is one,' Bodai said before Killean could give an answer. 'He's a shapeshifter. Him and Dadarro. 'Course, they put on airs about it, but truth is, this is a freak rebellion. Kind of up your street, I'd a thought. If the rumours about you trying to kill the king of Green Peaks in the Blood Arena are true, that is.'

'Are they?' Killean asked interested.

Sammia tilted her chin. 'I'm not telling.' Digging the end of the spear into the saturated ground, she levered herself to her feet. 'I'm not saying yes,' she told him, 'but get me my money from that jumped up bastard, Ktaka – and get him to acknowledge I'm the one that killed his giant – and I might, just might, agree to travel with you for a bit,' she said grudgingly.

Killean inclined his head. 'Deal.'

She poked the sharp end of her spear toward him. 'I'm warning you, betray me in any way – turn me in, abandon me, use me as bait – and I'll make you sorry. I always repay injury done to me in kind.'

Chapter Twenty-One

The Gull Island portal spat Killean and Sammia onto an isolated beach shaped like a horseshoe, closed in on three sides by high, granite cliffs. Thousands of seabirds screamed from the nest-littered cliffside and the air stank of sea salt, rotting seaweed and bird guano. The contrast between the cacophonous bay and the airless nothingness of the in-between was jarring. Killean hissed through his teeth, five senses reeling.

Sammia turned to him, accusingly. 'This isn't Shipwright,' she said.

Killean shrugged. 'Must have used to the wrong power word,' he muttered, turning away to scan the ocean horizon. The sea was choppy and white-tipped wave after wave rushed the grey-sand beach in quick succession.

'Of course you did,' Sumie replied, not even trying to sound like she believed him.

Shielding his eyes from the glare of a bright, but cloudy day, Killean looked around. There was no sign of life other than the birds and no sign that any other humans had been here recently. Wherever Nadil and the others were now, they'd left no traces behind.

'Have you ever been to Gull Island before?' he asked.

'Once or twice,' she replied noncommittally. 'What about you?'

He shook his head. 'Do you know how we can get out of here?'

'Run out to the rocks out there and hail a passing ship?' she suggested, nodding to the backbone of dark, barnacle encrusted rocks that jabbed out from the beach into open water.

He looked at her sharply. 'The portal is here. There must be someway through the cliffs.'

She chuckled at his irritation. 'There's a cave that cuts through the cliff over yonder. It leads onto the main trade road circling the island.'

Killean looked in the direction she'd indicated but couldn't make out the cave entrance. 'Why build a portal in a place like this,' he grumbled.

'Gull isn't exactly a heaving metropolis,' she reminded him. 'It's a collection of fishing villages and a market town. A better question would be who thought it was a good idea to put a portal on the island in the first place.'

'No one can control where the Realm touches the material world,' Killean muttered following her across the crumbling sand. He scowled at a blue-backed crab as it scuttled out of a mound in front of him.

'Not true,' Sumie corrected him. 'Rhodu Gakai does. That's why you're here, remember?'

Killean looked at her sharply, noting her very specific use of language. "You" she'd said, not "we".

'Are you sure there isn't a better way?' he asked.

He could see the mouth of the cave behind a lumpy rock and a slimy belt of brown seaweed stinking up the air in front of him. Shrilling gulls dived low and disappeared inside. Killean sighed, realising that the noise would be deafening if the birds were using the cave to nest.

Sammia nodded. 'I'm sure.'

She sounded sure, but he didn't feel it. 'You sound like you know this island well,' he commented.

She shrugged, looking dead ahead as she walked. 'I've travelled a lot in the last five years,' she said evasively. 'It's not like the mainland was the safest place to be after the war.'

He didn't believe her. The certainty that she was lying sat in the well of his stomach like a rock. Sammia had managed to evade Three Rivers for all the time he was incarcerated in Silent Hell. She wasn't the type to live a hermit's life in the wilds, which meant that she had to have found a benefactor. Likely someone who would see the value in her particular talents.

Killean would have heard about it if she'd joined a mercenary outfit, begged asylum in Past Tiger or taken up a posting working security for a Cow oligarch. Any and all options having been open to her after the war. Instead, she'd spent time in Blue Crab territory.

Killean stopped walking. Sammia stopped as well. 'What's wrong with you? The way out is just through there,' she pointed to the dark, uninviting mouth of the cave.

Killean closed his eyes, drawing in and releasing a slow breath. Deep down he'd known all along that the coincidence of meeting up with Sammia right after Obawai had kidnapped him was too great. Sammia was not a forgiving person. Nothing in her life had given her reason to learn how to forgive or forget, and she'd told him when they first met that she'd pay him back in kind if he ever betrayed her. He'd believed her then. He believed her now. Somewhere deep inside, he wasn't even surprised.

'Call them out,' he said.

'What?'

'The men you have waiting to ambush me in those caves. Call them out.'

'Are you mad?' she asked, maintaining the act. 'How could I have men waiting for you here when we're supposed to be on Shipwright Island?' she demanded.

He smiled bitterly and reminded her, 'You know me. You knew I'd switch locations without telling you.'

She knew his tactics. She knew the way he thought. She'd used his paranoia, the doubts he had about her, against him. That's what their fight on the road had been about. She'd wanted him to doubt her so he'd walk into the ambush she'd prepared. Damn it. She'd done to him what he'd done to Nadil. He'd laugh if it wasn't so sad.

'Sami,' he said tiredly.

She dropped the act. All the animation, the life, left her face. Her features became stone, but he flattered himself that she wasn't happy when she said, 'You know why I have to do this. I can't forgive you. I've walked that road before. It never ends well. I can't just let bygones be bygones.' Her eyes were bright. Wet. She gripped her spear like her life depended on it.

The gulls wheeled overhead. The ocean sighed, or maybe it was just him. 'I know.'

They were both vengeful creatures. They'd carved their identities out of the ruins of old pain, past betrayals. They couldn't be other than they were. Still, he wished he'd seen it coming. More than anything, he wished there was some way he could have avoided this. Some sequence of magic words he could have said or penance he could have done to fix what was broken between them before they got to this point.

'I didn't betray you, Sami,' he said.

'You never found me.'

'And you didn't find me,' he retorted. They'd left each other waiting.

Sammia turned her face away from the breeze. She brushed her hair back. He saw her swallow. She drew in a shallow breath. 'He's not going to kill you,' she said, voice tight. 'He needs you.'

He flexed his fingers at his sides and asked, 'Sikuzo?'

She nodded. 'He got me out of a jam, a little while back. I owe him, and I really did think you'd ditched me.' She looked at him, asking him to understand.

'I get it,' he said. Betrayal was his life's work. Sometimes it came back to bite him.

Sammia drove the point of her spear at him. He hopped back, but that only gave her the opening she needed to hurl an ashy grey powder in his face. He coughed, doubling over. His eyes burned and his throat crawled with grit. He couldn't breathe.

Sammia struck him across the back with the shaft of her spear, then knocked his feet out from under him. His throat closing and his vision a burning mess, he couldn't do much to defend himself. The world narrowed down to a pulsing, blind heat. His throat was swollen shut. The pressure in his head was immense. His last thought before he spiralled into unconsciousness was that if this was his end, he was glad it was at her hand.

He came to inside a cage. A particularly small one. Too small to contain his human form. He must have shifted right before losing consciousness. Damn it. That meant his clothes were completely ruined. Cracking open his eyes, he took his first look around.

The floor of his cage was wood covered in rush mat. The bars of the cage were made of a light, reddish-blonde wood he didn't recognise and smelled faintly of cedar or some other resin-y wood. The roof of the cage was solid. Along with the more pleasant cedar scent, he could smell magic. The cage was enchanted, which was likely why he hadn't resumed his human skin when he passed out.

His cage was surrounded by men on all sides. He could only see their legs. Loose dark pants cinched in tight at the ankles, the men looked like they might be wearing some kind of uniform. He struggled to rise. He was in the skin of a fox, he realised and snorted at the dark humour. He very much doubted Vilari would get himself into a predicament like this.

He wasn't even angry, he realised. That was the truly puzzling part. He didn't take betrayal any better than Sammia did. He'd been punishing Kindean for years for the crime of being less than the perfect brother he'd wanted him to be. He'd been willing to lay waste to an entire nation to punish a corrupt king, and yet, he wasn't angry that the woman he loved had shafted him.

He just felt tired. And his throat hurt.

Kindean's words from long ago filtered back into his head. Was he any happier with the trajectory of his life now than he had been during the war? Was this really the cycle he wanted to keep perpetuating? No. It wasn't. He still wanted Sikuzo and his crabs dead. And he wanted his own free state of Barley Land. Also, killing Torvin was looking like a more inviting prospect every second. But the rest of it? The pettiness of paranoia. The tit-for-tat of being vengeful and unforgiving? He'd be glad to be shot of all that.

For the first time, he found himself really looking at himself and asking, did he like who he'd become? Nadil had asked him if he had regrets. Of course he did. He'd failed at everything he'd hoped to accomplish and succeeded at doing a bunch of stuff he really didn't care about one way or another. The problem was, he didn't really understand why. Could it be, he didn't really understand his own wants?

Take Three Rivers. Did he really hate the country, or was it just force of habit? If things had gone differently and it had been Torvin in chains and kneeling before him in surrender, would he have killed his old mentor then and there or would he have dredged up some mercy for the man who had never truly wronged him? He honestly had no idea. And if he'd managed to suborn Three Rivers, what would he have done with the place? He'd only ever had an interest in Barley Lands. He'd become incredibly successful at conquering countries he didn't want at the cost of losing the home he desperately wanted back. Clearly, there was something wrong with his tactics.

THE LIFE AND TIMES OF THE TRAITOR KILLEAN ONRYN

What would have happened, he wondered, if he'd offed Dadarro before he went too far and destroyed their home? What if he'd sued for peace with Torvin while at the height of his powers? Would he now be ruling a liberated Barley Lands with the Dread Three at his side?

Probably not. Sammia would still have a grudge against him for what happened in Shrimpton. But how much easier would it have been to make things right between them with a kingdom of his own and powerful allies in his pockets. Sammia would never have needed to make deals with pirates in the world he could have created, if only he'd had the courage to admit his mistakes earlier.

In a moment of shocking doubt, he asked himself if the reason he'd surrendered to Torvin five years ago was because he thought he *deserved* to lose?

He was so busy wrestling with questions of ethical philosophy he paid scant attention to the men who picked up his cage and carried it, draped in heavy oil cloth, up a gradual incline that grew increasingly steeper until they were traversing the narrow hairpin bends of a winding path up a cliff on the other side of the island from where he'd started.

Killean couldn't see much with a cloth over his cage, but he could smell the Crab men's sweat and hear the scuff and skitter of their feet over the hard-scrabble road. The soft murmur of the sea, so large and omnipresent its majesty wrapped around the whole island like a god's whisper, was almost soothing but its distance reminded him of the jam he was in. He was being carried up a cliff without a plan. He could feel the rising heat of the day in the air, but the cloth was too thick for light to penetrate. He settled down on his belly to wait, his brush tail sweeping against the bars of his cage.

As they continued to climb, he heard the call of macaques and the creak of swaying branches and dry, rustling leaves. The drone of insects came close to overtaking the more distant shouts of seabirds.

He smelled camellia flowers as the men carrying his cage slowed to a stop. The path they'd travelled had levelled out a while ago, and Killean imagined that they'd arrived near the crest of the cliff where trees and flowers grew in abundance. He couldn't see it, but he suspected they'd come to the walled entrance of a large villa and the floral scent was coming from the gardens on the other side of the wall.

A human voice asked, 'That him?'

'Aye,' one of his bearers replied, gruffly.

Killean heard a scuff of heavy boots scraping over the ground and a rough huff of breath as the original speaker squatted in front of his cage and flipped up the cloth. He had to twist and bend his upper body low to the ground to see inside the cage and his fleshy, creased face was red from exertion. Killean skinned his lips back from his wrinkled muzzle, baring his delicate fangs.

The man responded by flashing his own rotted teeth in a savage grin. He rose swiftly to his feet. The cloth was dropped over the cage again. 'Put him with the others. Our lord isn't ready for him yet.'

Killean's ears perked up. That could mean only one thing.

'Not you woman,' the guard barked abruptly. 'Our lord wants to see *you* in his chambers.' There was a hint of a leer in the man's voice that raised the hackles on the Killean's back.

'Your lord's about to learn a lesson in disappointment then,' Sammia replied sharply. 'He's crazier than I thought if he believes I'm setting foot in his bedroom.'

The guard bristled. 'No one defies our lord.'

Sammia snorted. 'Sure, they do. You've got a couple of prisoners in your cell to prove it.' Killean knew she'd said that last for his benefit. At least he knew Nadil was alive. His newfound conscience had been bothering him somewhat. Sammia left him then and he wondered if he'd ever see her again.

Chapter Twenty-Two

His escort carried him through the perfume fogged garden and into the house. Killean could tell they were inside due to the change in smells and the echo his bearers sandalled feet made on wood laid floor. The quietude inside possessed the quality of a large house considerably under occupied. Several discordant notes were drawn when his bearers took him across a nightingale sprung wood floor. Designed to be deliberately creaky, the nails of the floorboards were set into clamps that produced a sonorous chirping noise when anyone walked across them.

Killean hadn't known they still made floors like these. This must be one of the traditional manor houses favoured by people in the Fish Archipelago. Built around an enclosed garden in a quadrangle shape, every room led onto the next almost as if the house had been designed as a series of interconnecting hallways and not individual rooms. The house would stand only one storey high, though he suspected there was an extensive basement complex carved out of the rock beneath them. Sikuzo needed a dungeon to keep his prisoners.

His bearer's finally stopped in a room with bamboo mat flooring. He heard one of the men accompanying his bearers lift a square of matting back. There was a metallic clink, as if that same someone was heaving on a metal ring and then a squeak of hinges as a trap door was dragged open.

His cage was abruptly knocked onto its side. Killean dug his claws in, but one of the barred sides was now underneath him and he couldn't find purchase. The cloth was pulled up and the cage opened. Killean sprang, twisting to avoid the gaping trapdoor beneath him, he sank his teeth into the thigh of the guard. He got a punch to the head for his efforts, but that only encouraged him to clamp down harder. One of the Crab's kicked him in the flank. Had he been in his wolf form, he likely could have repaid the man by biting his foot off. But as a fox, he lacked the strength. He tumbled down through the trapdoor.

He hit the bottom hard, his fox body just barely able to absorb the impact before he pancaked. The shock was still enough to trigger his transformation back into his human skin. He groaned, collapsing forward and tasting dirt.

'That looked like it hurt,' said a familiar, if subdued, voice from somewhere in the darkness.

Killean lifted his head, straining to see into the darkness as above him, the trapdoor slammed closed. Nadil's voice had come from somewhere to his right. 'It did,' he gritted out.

'Good.'

Killean bared his teeth in the dark. 'Arsehole.'

Carefully he pushed himself up on human limbs. He was relived nothing seemed to be broken. He had to assume the involuntary shift had fixed any impact breaks or pulverised organs. He was completely naked, the stagnant air of the basement petting his bare skin unpleasantly. He sniffed suspiciously. He tasted magic on the air.

'Yeah,' said Nadil tiredly, 'there's some kind of spell on the room. You'll feel it soon.'

'Feel what?' The darkness bloomed like black-brown roses behind his eyes. Dizzying in its completeness, it defeated even his night vision.

'Timeless magic,' Nadil said and Killean could hear an unusual note of bitterness in his tone. 'The spell taps the Realm, filtering through some of its magic. We're sealed in here and shifting doesn't work. That's why you're back in human form.'

Killean sucked in a sharp breath. 'Like Silent Hell.'

'I don't think we're actually in the Timeless Realm,' Nadil explained. 'But the energies are bleeding through. I think this is a side effect of the Pearl.'

'That means it has to be close,' Killean reasoned.

'Maybe,' Nadil murmured. 'Or maybe Sikuzo is forcing Gakai to make more toys for him.'

'He's wasting the man's talents if this is the best he can come up with,' Killean said. He sat up on his knees, shoving his hair back. Once he'd finished eviscerating Sikuzo he was getting a haircut. And some new clothes. Actually, that should probably come first.

'What happened to you?' Nadil asked him. 'Did your deal with Sikuzo fall through?' There was a nasty edge to the question.

Killean rolled his eyes. 'I wasn't the one making deals. Sammia was. She double crossed me.'

Somewhere in the velvet darkness, Nadil sat up in a hurry. 'The Child of Death is working for Sikuzo?' he asked in alarm.

Killean was a little irked that he seemed more concerned about that alliance than he had about the entirely fictional one he made up in his head between Killean and Sikuzo. 'She said she owed him,' he said. 'Sikuzo's just a means to an end. What she really wants is to get back at me for Shrimpton.'

'Because naturally everything is always about you, Ilin,' Nadil drawled.

'Naturally,' Killean agreed, blithely ignoring the sarcasm. He asked, 'Where's the kid?'

'I'm here,' Ash piped up from somewhere to his left. 'I'm ignoring you, traitor,' he informed him in the officious tone of an unhappy teenager.

'Noted,' Killean muttered. 'Good to know you're still alive. Don't suppose you have your gauntlet with you?'

'They took it along with my weapons when we were seized,' Nadil answered. 'Cactus got away.'

'Good for him. Think he'll come back for you?'

Nadil hesitated before answering, 'I think he'll come back for Sikuzo.'

'Ah,' Killean said, 'Revenge, is it?'

'Something like that.'

Killean crawled carefully to the far side of the basement. He figured he'd hit a wall sooner or later. The magic of the Timeless Realm could play havoc on ordinary physics and regular dimensions but this was still a basement. The Darkness had to be contained by solid walls, and Killean felt the need for something solid at his back right now.

'I...owe you an apology,' he said into the darkness.

'What?' Nadil sounded startled.

Killean grimaced, slumping back against the wall he'd finally found, and drawing his knees up to his chest. 'You heard me. I've done some thinking, and I've decided I really should have offed Dadarro a lot earlier. Things would have been better then.'

A strange, choking sound erupted from Nadil's side of the room. 'Are you choking on your tongue?' Killean asked him warily.

'No,' Nadil coughed. 'I'm just amazed. Do you really think that your greatest sin is murdering someone too late?' he asked incredulously.

'No,' Killean grumbled. 'But I knew Dadarro was mad long before I did anything about it. I...didn't want to murder family. But it occurred to me, if I'd given you the Firefly and sued for peace with

Torvin, things would be better for the Accursed right now. I really did want to give them a homeland, you know,' he added sullenly.

Nadil was very quietly. 'That's nice, and y'know, it's definitely growth of a sort. But...you did set fire to a lot of things,' he reminded him carefully. 'You can't really think we could just let you go free after the war.'

'I think that's exactly what you did do,' Killean retorted. 'Five years imprisonment isn't much of a punishment when you sleep through it,' he lied. 'And let's not pretend Three Rivers is totally innocent. Minuidon arranged the murder, displacement and land thefts of a lot of people,' Killean reminded him. 'We were at war. One side hurts the other. That's how it works. Or maybe you want the reminder that *Torvin* tried to ferment a coup in Past Tiger to get rid of Harkiv and nearly restarted a war that had already cost thousands of lives?'

'I told him that was a bad idea,' Nadil muttered.

'I've never claimed innocence,' Killean said, ignoring him. 'I'm just saying, there's a reason I had no trouble drumming up support against Three Rivers. Victory and influence don't equal moral purity, Nadil. What do you think will happen to Shipwright and Gull Island when the Crab are gone?'

'They'll be free from the rule of a tyrant.'

'You mean they'll be free to be torn apart by the other factions,' Killean scoffed. 'Face it, Nadil, sometimes the greater good does a lot of harm to lesser folk.'

'And sometimes it's worth the risk to give people the chance at better governance,' Nadil snapped hotly. There was a moment of pregnant pause and then Nadil exclaimed, 'You bastard. I didn't mean that the way it sounded.'

Killean grinned into the darkness. 'Uh-huh, no takebacks. The kid is my witness. We both heard the great hero Nadil Shiny Scale state that sometimes taking up arms against a tyrant is worth the collateral damage.'

'...That's not what I said,' he complained.

'But its what you meant,' Killean sing-songed, feeling very pleased with himself.

'I thought you were meant to be apologising,' Nadil grumped. 'This is supposed to be the part where you realise you were wrong and change your ways.'

'It really isn't,' Killean retorted. 'Changing the subject, can you or the kid move?' he asked.

'No, I'm shackled to the wall.'

Interesting. 'I'm not,' he said.

'I'd noticed that,' Nadil replied drily. 'Considering how you were tossed down here, I'm guessing the Crab were hoping you'd break every bone in your body and wouldn't need to be restrained.'

'I don't think that's it,' Killean said, thinking aloud. 'Have you seen Sikuzo?'

'Not since the ambush. Why?'

'Sammia told me Sikuzo wasn't going to kill me. He wants something from me. I haven't been restrained because I'm not going to be down here long.'

'I know what he wants you for,' Nadil said grimly. He sighed. 'While you were imprisoned a lot of subversive elements started looking for the Firefly. Everyone figured out pretty quickly you had to have stashed it in the Timeless Realm. That's why Obawai commissioned Gakai to build him a tool that would make it easier to search.'

'By capturing a part of the Realm in the Pearl?' Killean asked. That was certainly a novel way of managing a search in a near infinite space.

'Yes. Gakai got cold feet and sought asylum with the Crab. But Sikuzo got greedy and decided he wanted the power of the Pearl for himself. He doesn't care about the Firefly, but he must have learned that you're immune to the Timeless Realm's sleeping curse. He wants you to enter the Pearl.'

If he thought that he was very wrong. Killean wasn't immune. The reason he'd been able to temporarily break the sleeping curse was due to outside influence. It was interesting that Nadil knew about his waking moments but didn't seem to know that he'd had no control over them. Did this mean Torvin believed he was immune as well? Or was the Spark simply playing his cards close to his chest and only doling out partial information to his closest allies?

'What's inside the Pearl that Sikuzo could want?' Killean asked.

'Rhodu Gakai,' Nadil replied bluntly. 'Cactus' source inside the Crab told him the inventor hid inside once he realised Sikuzo was as bad as Obawai. I'm here to make sure *you* don't enter the Timeless Realm,' Nadil explained. 'I was *supposed* to secure the Pearl and return to Three Rivers where our mages could free Gakai safely. You were supposed to act as a credible threat to distract Sikuzo while I infiltrated his base. Thanks for wrecking that plan, by the way.'

'You're very welcome,' Killean told him sweetly. 'For the record, if you want my compliance with a plan, try explaining it first, instead of railroading me into missions and keeping me in the dark. I *can* follow orders, you know.'

'All evidence points to the contrary,' Nadil muttered drily and asked, 'Would you follow mine?'

'If it's in my interests, yes,' Killean retorted. 'These subversives after the Firefly, are they after me too?'

'Yes,' Nadil said quietly.

Killean hummed. 'Something woke me in Silent Hell,' he admitted. 'I didn't do it myself. It was like someone or something was trying to summon me. If these relic hunters can do *that*, I want them put out of business just as much as you do.' A new thought occurred to him and he asked, 'Is Mamie part of this conspiracy too?'

'She was, but she turned her coat when Torvin threatened the clan. She claims she was using them to spring *you*,' he added sceptically.

Killean shook his head disgustedly, 'She must be losing her edge in her old age. If this conspiracy is looking for me and the Firefly, why didn't Obawai try and capture me during our meeting?'

'Mamie said he didn't believe someone who looked as bad as you did could possibly possess the power of the Firefly.'

Killean scoffed. 'I look a damn sight better than that shrivelled sardine.' He stretched his legs across the ground. 'At least Sammia's plan has given us the opening we need,' he mused.

'What?'

'Sikuzo will let his guard down now he has me prisoner. He'll bring me and the Pearl together. All I need to do is figure out a way to also get him to bring *you* out of the basement and we've got him and the Pearl right where we want, all without having to do any of the tedious legwork.' He smiled. 'Sammia did all the hard work for us.'

'By betraying you,' Nadil reminded him pointedly. 'After *you* betrayed *me*.'

Waving him off he said dismissively, 'Whatever works. The point is, with us here and Cactus plotting to get in, we have all the ingredients we need to break the Crab and get away with the Pearl. We couldn't have planned this better if we tried.'

Nadil did not sound nearly as confident. 'You know that Sammia isn't on our side, right, Ilin? You can't trust her.'

'Of course, she's not on my side. She's on her side,' Killean said irritably. 'She's hedging her bets to see which side comes up on top.'

'That's quite a leap,' Nadil objected.

'I *know her*,' Killean insisted.

'Not well enough if she was able to betray you — wait. Oh, *starry night*. Killean. Did you know this was going to happen? Did you set *me* up knowing *she* was setting *you* up, just to make sure we'd all be in position to take down Sikuzo?'

Now *that* was a leap. Killean opened his mouth to say as much when Ash blurted, 'No way! There's just no way this backstabbing piece of shit planned all this. He's not that smart!'

Well, now Killean had to act like he *had* planned this. He might not have foreseen *all* the twists and turns this adventure had taken, but he was still the only one trying to make it work for them. Nadil had spent almost two days sitting in the dark feeling sorry for himself.

'Shh,' he said. 'I hear something.'

Looking up he could see a square of light in the darkness someway above his head. The trapdoor was glowing. He grinned despite himself. So much for this not being a piece of the Timeless Realm. The trapdoor was a *portal* and someone on the other side was pulling him through.

He felt the wrench on his limbs as the magic of the portal defied gravity and yanked him bodily into the air before he was pulled through the mouth of magic into who-knows-where.

Chapter Twenty-Three

The portal spat him out into a room made cavernous by removing the partition walls between several smaller rooms. Before he could get his bearings, strong hands pulled his arms behind his back and dragged him into a hard backed chair. In short order he was tied to the chair with thick rope tingling with magic. Killean lifted his head and met the eyes of the man ensconced in an elaborate chair of his own directly opposite.

Sikuzo, leader of the Blue Crab and bastard son of Gengo Anbi, lord of White Surf, was older than Killean expected, but younger than some of his seadogs. There was a hint of grey in his neatly trimmed beard and peppering his temples. His skin was a ruddy bronze, his features bold and sharply defined. He wore a deep blue robe trimmed with cloth of silver and patterned with crawling lines of spidery crabs. His most striking accessory, aside from Sammia, standing to attention to the left of his chair, was the living shadow pooling close to the floor on the man's right, resembling something between a congealed blob and a kneeling attendant.

The shadow looked exactly like Cactus' Jadek, a living fragment of pure darkness. Considering that until two days ago, he'd never seen a man with a living shadow, he highly doubted it was a coincidence that he'd now met two men with the same curse.

Sikuzo frowned at Killean, thick brows bunching. He turned to Sammi, exclaiming, 'He's naked.' He sounded almost accusatory, as if

Killean's naked body was a personal affront. Killean figured it might be, even with his robe hiding Sikuzo's form, Killean could tell he had the better physique.

Sammia smiled blandly, her dark eyes fixed on his lap. 'He certainly is. Thanks for dressing down for me, Ilin.' She winked at him.

'Anything for you, Sami.'

Sikuzo's face darkened. 'It is distasteful to converse with a naked man,' he said, his voice crisp as a lord.

'You're a pirate. I'm sure you're used to doing distasteful things,' Killean remarked.

'Silence! Do not speak until spoken to, traitorous dog,' Sikuzo bark was a bit much.

Killean's arched both brows. He looked at Sammia. 'You threw me over for this dolt?'

She rolled her eyes. 'My arrangement with Sikuzo is strictly business,' she said.

'How much is he paying you?' Killean asked. 'I'll double it.'

Suddenly, blackness descended before his eyes as Sikuzo's shadow filled his vision. There was a crack, the sound sharp as a pistol shot and Killean's head jerked to the side with the force of an invisible slap, a hot stain of tickling pain blooming over his cheek. The shadow withdrew as quickly as it had approached, spilling over the floor and returning to coil at Sikuzo's feet like a fawning pet. Killean tasted blood on his tongue and spat over the side of the chair.

'I warned you,' Sikuzo said fingers tented together and elbows on the arms of his whale bone throne. 'I rule here. You will obey me or suffer my wrath.'

Killean felt his lips twitch in disdain. Who did this stuffed shirt think he was talking to? Showing the man the opposite of respect, he made a performance of looking around the pleasant confines of the room.

The sliding screen doors on his right were open on a view of an interior garden. Sunlight pooled on the mat floors, setting the silver teleport circle on the floor to gleaming. The air was sweetened by the aroma of incense and some unknown herb growing outside. The incense came from an alcove altar set into the back wall near a collection of beautifully lacquered portable screens decorated with flecks of mother-of-pearl. The screen blocked off a section of the room laid out for entertaining with low couches, soft-looking chairs and a long table low to the ground.

Several dark wood end tables held miniature trees, grown in mossy soil and expertly shaped to resemble the wide and stretching canopy of real trees in a form of artistic futility Killean had never understood the point of. There were also several artful but rather sterile flower arrangements dotted around the edges of the room in large, tasteful pots. Heavy, dark wood beams striped the ceiling and the papery walls were interspersed with painted sliding screen doors.

The blurry shadows of guards stood outside the closed doors and two men, armed with short swords, guarded the garden veranda. Beside the man who had tied him up, he could sense the presence of two addition guards at the back of the room.

Turning back to the Blue Crab leader he asked, 'Shall we get to business?'

A muscle in the pirate's lean cheek twitched. He rose stiffly from his chair and snapped his fingers. 'Harnin.'

The Crab beside Killean's chair snapped to attention. 'Yes, Lord Sikuzo?'

Sikuzo's gaze flickered down to Killean's lap and then swiftly away. His lip curled. 'Find something for this wretch to cover himself with.' Turning away Sikuzo paced across the mats, his shadow tumbling after him like an anxious puppy. 'I will not converse with a man with no clothes. It is a disgrace.'

Killean laughed aloud. 'There's nothing disgraceful about my body.' Still standing by Sikuzo's abandoned throne Sammia grinned at him.

'You were once a high lord's son,' Sikuzo said as if his parentage had escaped him. 'The shame of your current state disgraces your parents memory,' he insisted.

There were several ways he could react to that and he was sure Sikuzo was hoping to get one of the more murderous responses from him. Killean was well aware he could be touchy about the legacy of the Onryn, but all he did was laugh. 'I think getting wiped out by two-bit mercenaries is a bigger black mark on their name than my loose balls. In fact, my package does honour to my clan,' he added thoughtfully.

Sammia snickered and then tried to disguise the sound as a cough. 'Killean is a shapeshifter, my lord, he doesn't have the same...attitude toward nudity that civilised folk do,' she told Sikuzo.

'You are a savage,' Sikuzo told him.

'And your very high strung for a bastard born with no real title to his name,' Killean retorted.

This time he was ready for the shadow's strike and braced himself before everything went dark. It still left him reeling, starbursts of static tinging through his skull. Rolling his jaw, he turned back to Sikuzo, expression bored.

'Are you going to tell me why you brought me here?' he asked 'Because the grandstanding is not working. You'll get no respect from me, so why keep wasting both our time with this act?'

Sikuzo's face was a picture of rage. His lips skinned back from his teeth in a mad grimace. The tension in the air racketed up a notch. 'You live on my whim alone,' Sikuzo told him. 'I hold the lives of Shiny Scale and the boy in my hands. You would do well to remember that. You have fallen far since the war. Your reputation will not protect you.'

Killean cocked his head. 'Do you know, I met your father once? He was a jumped-up self-absorbed fool too. He didn't have a living shadow, though,' he admitted. 'Does your little friend there, come from your mother's line?'

He was trying to figure out how he and Cactus were related. There wasn't much of a resemblance he could see, and if Cactus was another of Gengo Anbi's by-blows Killean was sure he'd have heard about it by now.

Sikuzo surprised him by breaking out in an impressively wolfish smile, quite at odds with his tantrum from seconds ago. 'You are right to be impressed,' he said, although Killean had not in fact stated that he was impressed. 'Iviana has been my guardian for much of my life. A gift, as you say, from my mother.'

Reaching down to the shadow with one hand, Sikuzo caressed the dome of its head and the shadow rose to meet him eagerly. Unlike Cactus' shadow, Jadek, Iviana appeared almost human as the shadow tilted its featureless face into the caress.

Killean exchanged a lightning-fast glance with Sammia while Sikuzo was distracted fondling his shadow. She nodded ever so slightly, letting him know that Sikuzo's erratic mood change was what passed for normal for him. Killean repressed a sigh. It was probably a holdover from his time serving as Dadarro's vassal but he had very little patience for mercurial lunatics. He just hoped Sikuzo's dramatic moods and living shadow impressed the pirates he commanded.

'My mother was a remarkable woman,' Sikuzo continued. 'Some called her cursed but she was blessed by a deity of the night with great gifts. She should have married my father and lived in peace and splendour, but the ignorant people of White Surf believed her to be a witch. They said she enchanted my father to leave his first wife. To keep the peace, my father exiled my mother and I.'

Killean cocked his head and threw out an educated guess, 'Is that when you and your half-brother formed the Blue Crab?'

Sikuzo's lips thinned. 'My father's other son has nothing to do with my enterprises,' he said.

'I wasn't talking about your *father's* true heir,' Killean said. 'I was asking about your mother's *other son*, Cactus.'

Sikuzo's face was a mask of displeasure. 'How do you know Cactus?'

Killean smiled slowly. 'Don't you know? He's working with Three Rivers.'

'Traitor,' snapped Sikuzo.

'It happens,' Killean remarked coolly. 'But I imagine he'd have a different take. He helped you build up the Blue Crab, didn't he?'

Sikuzo didn't have the temperament to muster an organised syndicate. He acted like an entitled lordling who thought his dubious parentage was enough to command the respect of men who had earned their reputations the hard way. His shadow and his obvious violent tendencies would get him quite far in the pirate life, it was true. People tended to be cowed by mystical powers they didn't understand. Still, Sikuzo would have needed a solid, reliable first mate to manage his crews and stave off mutiny. Killean would happily throw Cactus overboard to the sharks, but having met both brothers, he knew which one was the sane one and it wasn't Sikuzo.

A traitorous little thought flitted through his mind. Had his soldiery looked at him and seen a man like Sikuzo. A mad, entitled lunatic harbouring a grudge? He shook off the thought. He was perhaps more willing to entertain his faults at present, but there was no way that his soldiers would have considered his *uncle* the sane one during the war.

Sikuzo turned on Sammia, fury whitening his lips. Sammia shrugged indifferently. 'I didn't tell him,' she said. 'Killean's good at figuring out these sorts of things. He doesn't get on with his brother either,' she remarked blandly.

'The tip off was your guards,' Killean told Sikuzo. 'They're all either too old or too young. Your little spat with your brother split the syndicate, didn't it?'

That would explain why Sikuzo was camped out here in Gull Island and not ensconced in Shipwright's Red Fort. There were strategic advantages to seclusion, but Sikuzo didn't have nearly enough men in this villa to defend it properly. He was hiding out here, pretending to be in command, but the truth was the only thing keeping him alive right now was the threat of the Pearl.

Killean's gaze cut to Sammia, 'That's why you're here, isn't it? He hired you to protect him.'

Sammia laughed. 'He hired me to bring you in,' she corrected. 'The rest is a wounded bird ploy.'

'Ah,' Killean nodded in understanding. 'Draw your enemies in with a display of weakness and then wipe them out. I'm guessing you came up with that plan *before* Gakai got away from you?' he asked Sikuzo.

Sikuzo ignored him in favour of Sammia. 'I deigned to make a deal with you, woman, because you said you could bring me Onryn, but you are fast outliving your usefulness,' he warned.

'Funny,' Sammia replied. 'I was just thinking the same about you, you stiff-necked wannabe. While you were stealing your brother's crew and begging daddy-dearest to please, oh-please, accept you, I was earning my crust fighting bigger monsters than you,' she sneered.

Sikuzo lost it in a moment of silent rage. Iviana erupted in the air around him, flailing tendrils of darkness like an irate sea star, her powerful aura spilling through the room like black ink. Sikuzo's soldiers ran forward, fanning out behind their master.

Sammia hefted her spear, assuming a fighting stance. 'Don't be a fool, Sikuzo. You can't kill me.'

Maybe not permanently, but Killean wasn't interested in seeing him try. He tested the ropes binding him but the magic was too great for him to slip a wrist.

Strolling into the rising tension like a lamb to the slaughter, Harnin returned, carrying a piece of sack cloth. His eyes widened and he stuttered to a halt as he took in the scene. 'Um, my lord? I brought something to cover the prisoner like you asked.' He held up the cloth.

Sikuzo pivoted smoothly on his slippered heel, Iviana flowing with him in perfect synchronicity, her tendrils lashing the air. 'Finally,' the pirate ground out. 'Quickly. Cover him.'

The strategic intervention of the sack cloth seemed to calm Sikuzo. The man smoothed his hands down the silver hem running along his chest and turned his back on Sammia. A suicidal act had he not had a living shadow to protect him. He eyed the sack cloth covering Killean's lap as if its presence was ensuring the survival of all decency in the world and Killean was left to wonder how a man such as this had survived so long among pirates.

'Iviana,' Sikuzo addressed his shadow. 'The Realm Pearl if you would.'

Iviana retracted her tentacles. She pulled loose of her master's shoulders. The shadow pulsed once before expelling a palm-sized milky-grey sphere into Sikuzo's waiting hands.

'This, Onryn, is what you are here for,' he said holding up the Pearl. 'Gakai's sealed realm.'

Light swirled under the surface of the Pearl like grey clouds. There was a sheen to its reflective surface. It really did look like a very large pearl. 'Actually,' Killean told him, 'I'm here to kill you. The Pearl doesn't interest me at all.'

There was a heavy pause, broken by Sammia's aborted laugh. 'Starless Night, Ilin. At least wait until after he's done gloating. He's waited days for this moment,' she chastised.

Sikuzo ignored her with great forbearance. The presence of the sackcloth really did seem to have settled his flighty nerves. Killean had to assume he was severely lacking in the trouser department, if the sight of a limp dick was the cause of his bad mood.

Speaking as if reciting a well-practiced speech, the pirate explained, 'Rhodu Gakai is the greatest mage Jumping Carp has ever produced. Thanks to Gakai, Carp have stockpiled an arsenal of magical weaponry to rival Myron's relics.' Holding the Realm Pearl to the light, Sikuzo obligingly turned it in his hand. 'This beautiful trinket is only the beginning. With Gakai under my control, soon I will have an arsenal to match.'

'If you survive,' Killean murmured. 'And if you can get Gakai to help you. I'm guessing he's the only one who can fully control the Pearl?'

Sikuzo's expression twitched at the interruption, but he controlled it. 'I had hoped you would be reasonable in defeat,' he said with false regret, 'but I prepared for this very scenario. You clearly know why you are here. You are going to enter the Pearl and retrieve Gakai for me.'

'And if I refuse?' Killean asked mildly.

'I will torture you until you relent. I have the time. My enemies have proved themselves cowards who dare not attack me in numbers. While I hold you and Shiny Scale I am perfectly safe from Three Rivers.'

That was probably true, but Cactus was still at large and the Blue Crab was not at full strength. Torvin wouldn't send more men to be captured, but the Spark would have other ways to deal with one upstart pirate. He already had an alliance with Carp. The High King would lean on Carp to send in its navy to blast Gull Island off the map.

'There is something else you should know,' Sikuzo told him slyly. 'When Gakai fled Jumping Carp, he did so with more than just the

Realm Pearl. Would you like to see one of the other wonders Gakai developed for the Carp?'

Killean knew better than to trust that smile. 'No,' he said flatly.

'A pity,' Sikuzo replied blandly. 'I intend to demonstrate anyway.' He addressed his shadow, 'Iviana. Release the spider.'

'Wait,' Sammia said a note of true alarm in her tone. Her gaze cut sharply from Killean to Sikuzo and back again. 'Break him too badly and he won't be any use to you,' she warned.

'Then let us hope your lover doesn't break too badly,' Sikuzo jeered. Killean braced himself, knowing that whatever was about to happen he was not going to like.

Flicking his hand in a wordless command to Iviana, the pirate lord's expression was avid with a sick excitement. 'Previous test subjects lasted but minutes,' he explained as Iviana convulsed in the air, mass expanding and contracting like a palpitating heart. 'I expect you to put up more resistance, Killean of the Striking Talon.'

Something silvery and vaguely metallic dropped to the floor on eight, spindly legs. The spider stood about six inches off the ground, its round body looking like a blob of liquid mercury. Its long pointy-jointed legs rose above its body and looked like they were made from clear glass. The spider had no eyes, but it did have a set of chelicera equipped with fangs and a shorter pair of glassy limbs to assist with eating. It looked hungry.

'What do you think of my spider, Onryn?' Sikuzo all but purred.

Killean licked his lips, tasting a little dried blood and looked from the spider jouncing on its joints to Sikuzo. 'What does it do?' he asked.

Sikuzo's grin would have made any dragon proud. 'It devours years.'

Killean blinked. 'What?'

Sikuzo looked inordinately pleased with himself. 'In Silent Hell time moved so slowly you aged barely two years in five,' he said.

'Through his experiments, Gakai learned that beings native to the Timeless Realm develop an insatiable hunger for our mortality once delivered to this realm. This spider eats *life*, Onryn.' Sikuzo smile was supremely smug. 'I think it fitting to have my spider pull those three preserved years of youth from your bones.'

Well, Killean thought succinctly. *This was going to suck.*

Chapter Twenty-Four

Uncle Dadarro had possessed a keen interest in putting Killean through rigorous and sometimes downright sadistic endurance training in the early years of their partnership. He had been a firm believer that pain was the best teacher and one must break early to avoid breaking irrevocably in enemy hands. Yet nothing Dadarro had put him through prepared Killean for the spider.

It started badly as the spider made an impressive leap from the floor and landed on his chest, the sharp points of its dagger-like feet digging shallow gouges into his flesh. It bit down on the skin over his heart. The pain was indescribable. Yet, worse than the pain was the sensation of loss and grief that swept over him.

Every sorrow he'd ever known ripped through him anew. He saw his mother and father lying dead in front of Dragon Ascent's grand fireplace. The image was so powerful, drawn from a child's nightmares, it was easy to forget that the memory wasn't real.

He had not been there. He hadn't seen the bodies. He had never seen the ruin of his mother's opened throat, or his father's limp limbs. He had never choked on the abattoir reek of old blood painting the walls, nor tripped over his uncle Myda's body in his rush to escape the scene.

The spider didn't care. It feasted on his imaginings, reviving his childhood nightmares and revelling in the worst corners of his imagination, just as readily as it feasted on his true memories.

The sights of battle. The moans of soldiers in the medics tent. The screams as the field surgeon got to work. The exhaustion of training his body hour after thankless hour for one battle after the other. The terror of Tiger's jungles. The night chorus of insects and monkey jeers he still heard in his sleep even now. Hiding in foxholes surrounded by volatile explosives, as the rain slowly filled the hole. The long painful hours of marching. Poring over maps and charts as the bodies of his men lay strewn across the last battlefield, knowing there was no time to bury them before they pushed on to the next fight.

Faces flashed before his eyes, people he had known. People he had loved. People he had lost. His parents. His aunt Minigan and his favourite cousin Ina. Bodai and Juri. Nadil. Mishka. Kindean. He saw the men and women of his regiments fly by, each face a reminder of his broken promises. And the truly sad part was, he didn't know what had happened to most of them, his cursed soldiers.

An ache like tired fire, caustic and bitter, coated his bones. His blood moved acid-hot through his veins and a crushing weight centred under his breastbone left him gasping as tears drenched his cheeks. The world narrowed to nothing but the flash of light and shade behind his flickering lids and the sorrow clenching his throat. He may have screamed. He may have whimpered. He couldn't tell. His dignity was the least of his concerns. His world was only pain.

Sikuzo said the spider devoured years, but this was much worse than losing a little off the top of his life span. This was his life unspooled before him as a parade of pain, defeat, failure and betray.

It was broken promises, compromised ideals, twisted obsession. It was burned villages, defiled shrines, desperate searches, and hours spent with his quartermaster, plotting how to put their resources to best use before his uncle squandered them all.

It was Reflecting Pools scorched courtyard and a dead baby elephant turned to leather and blackened ivory in its cage.

It was a stupid boy who had every reason to hate him, whom he was using even now for his own ends.

Something stirred in him. The sleeping dragon within, locked down by the curse, held back by his own will, awakened. It's power surged. Outraged, the dragon wasn't shamed or cowed by anything they had done. His dragon-self believed only in the fight. The dragon wanted to fight now. It seized on Sikuzo's image in his memory and vowed they would be avenged. Bloodily. The dragon seethed under his skin, pushing against the spider's poison fangs, disgusted that such a little thing could have driven Killean so low.

Sharp, bright pain, new and fresh, jerked him back to awareness. The connection between him and his dragon-self was abruptly severed as the spider's spurred feet were yanked out of his flesh.

Head lolling forward, all he could do was breathe, sucking in great rasping gasps of air that did nothing to help steady him. His skin was slick with blood. The spider's bite pulsed in agony and he felt so weak, he'd be a boneless pool of flesh on the floor if not for the chair. Exhaustion dragged at his limbs. *Sleep*, he thought. If he just closed his eyes and went to sleep everything would be better.

'Damn it, Ilin. Snap out of it.' Sammia yanked his hair, wrenching his head back. His eyes snapped open.

He looked at Sammia as if seeing her for the first time. Her hair was a cloud. Her skin, flawless. Her almond eyes dark and steady. Her features lovely. Her expression immensely pissed off. The spider, legs limp, dangled from the sharp end of her spear. Evidently, her deadly cold steel offered nothing for the spider to feast on. Silvery blood seeped down the shaft.

It occurred to him, wonderingly, that Sammia hadn't appeared in his parade of regret and loss. Not because he didn't regret Shrimpton, or the choices they'd both made since, but because he didn't see Sammia as someone in his past. He didn't see her as the ex-lover that had betrayed him. He didn't see them as history.

'What the hell are you smiling about?' she demanded, giving him a look that said she was wondering if she'd been too late pulling the spider off him and feared his mind was already gone.

'You,' he whispered, or tried to. His voice was a wreck. Much like the rest of him. Had he not just experienced a fate worse than Silent Hell, he'd have cared about his ruined image a lot more.

Sammia impatiently shook the dead spider off the end of her spear, hurling the body across the room and dropped the pole. She crouched beside his chair, tilting his face to look at him. 'Sikuzo really got you there,' she said, aiming for a conversational tone and falling short.

Killean chuffed a laugh. 'Yeah,' he breathed shakily, 'if you hadn't pulled that thing off me when you did, I'd be a goner.'

Surprise bloomed over Sammia's face. 'I never thought I'd see the day you'd admit needing help,' she marvelled. More quietly she added, 'Sikuzo said the spider doesn't just eat years. It eats regrets too.'

'It does.'

'I've never heard you scream like that,' she said softly.

'I've never felt anything like that.'

He hoped he never would again, but it seemed like a vain hope. Even if he was lucky enough to avoid another encounter with a regret eater, the course of his life had been set years ago. His future would have its own sorrows.

Sammia caught his chin and turned his face sharply toward her. Her fingernails dug into his skin lightly. She pressed a firm kiss to his lips, the pressure a sort of warning. 'Cactus is on his way,' she whispered before hurriedly getting to her feet. Snatching her spear she moved swiftly to the back of the room as the main doors opened.

He looked up tiredly to see Iviana spreading across the ceiling like a stain. The Blue Crab guards filed back into the room followed a moment later by Sikuzo himself, a jaunty spring in his step. He stopped just in front of Killean's chair, posing with his hands propped on his hips.

'Well, Onryn, have you learned respect?'

Not for you. Killean tilted his aching head back against the chair. 'I can't enter the Pearl like this,' he said and if he'd been able to, he'd have gestured to the various new leaks he'd sprung courtesy of the spider. 'If I enter the Timeless Realm with open wounds the magic of that realm will contaminate my blood and I'll never be able to leave.'

It was true. Legend had it that most of the creatures native to the Timeless Realm were descended from beings that had been corrupted after tumbling into the realm accidentally.

Sikuzo hid his flash of dismay poorly as he looked over Killean's bloodied torso. He'd lost the modesty cloth at some point and that was most likely why the man swiftly looked way before getting his fill of his pet's bloody handiwork.

The pirate paced. The look on his face was a picture. He had no one to blame for this but himself.

Killean said, 'Nadil can do it.'

'I will never trust Shiny Scale.'

But he did trust Killean? His opinion of the Sea Lord's competence continued to plummet. He was beginning to think he'd be better off keeping the man in power and letting him destroy his syndicate on his own. Then again, he owed Sikuzo for the torture he'd just endured.

'He can do it,' he repeated. 'Nadil is a dragon shifter like me. He'll last longer inside the Pearl than anyone else you can send. And he has a pathological need to save people. He won't be able to resist even if it means helping *you*.'

'He does not have your immunity.'

There was no immunity. Killean told him as much, adding, 'As long as he's fast, he doesn't need it. Nadil's nature will help him stay awake. And let's be honest. Gakai is much more likely to trust *him* than *me*. This is the kind of job you need a real hero for,' he lied with all the conviction he could muster.

Sikuzo did not like it and if he'd been a little less desperate and better hinged, he likely would have seen through Killean's paper thin logic, but the truth was, he had no choice and he knew it. He was running out of time. Even he didn't realise how little he had left.

Cactus was coming, Sammia had said, but how could she know that unless she was the mole inside Sikuzo's camp. All those hours Sammia had spent up top of the mail coach with Cactus must have given them plenty of time to hash out their plan for after Sammia had delivered him into Sikuzo's hands.

Sammia was clever, she'd have realised immediately that Sikuzo was weak and set about making side deals to her advantage. For all he knew, she was on Torvin's payroll and had been the entire time, though for his pride's sake he hoped not. That she'd let Killean know Cactus was on his way let him hope she hadn't given him up for good. She still thought he could win this.

Sikuzo's snapped to his guards, 'Harnin, Inoue. Summon the prisoners.'

'Yes, my lord.'

Harnin, the Crab who had fetched Killean's modesty cloth, crouched on the ground in front of the metal ring set into a square of concrete in the middle of the floor and activated the portal. He and Inoue stepped into the circle one after the other, returning a minute later with first Ash and then Nadil.

Nadil sported wrist shackles, but Ash was free. 'Hey,' he shouted, eyeing the gauntlet on Inoue's arm. 'That's mine!'

He lunged at the younger Crab, trying to wrest the gauntlet away from him. A day in the basement, breathing in enervating Timeless air and the fact that he was built like an adolescent scarecrow meant that his efforts were in vain. Inoue knocked him on his arse, but Killean admired Ash's gumption all the same.

'You should give it back to him. Those gauntlets carry a curse. Only those chosen by the Peak's king can wield them safely,' he told the guard.

Inoue cussed him out, making it very clear what he thought of Killean's advice. He smiled wolfishly. 'Got a headache? Chills? Are the ends of your fingers hot and tingling? Yeah. That'll only get worse. Give it up now, before you lose the arm.'

'My lord?' Inoue asked worriedly.

Sikuzo hissed in annoyance. 'Is this true?' he asked Sammia irritably.

'Yes,' she said from the back of the room, near the door. 'If it wasn't, everyone would have one.'

'Take the damned thing off and toss it over there,' Sikuzo ordered.

'My lord —'

'Once I have the Pearl under my command you'll have your pick of Jumping Carp plunder,' Sikuzo snapped at him. That seemed to assuage Inoue's objections. He tossed the gauntlet across the room.

'Hey!'

'Make one move,' Inoue warned Ash, pulling an oyster knife out of his sleeve, 'and I'll gut you where you stand.'

Quietly Nadil asked, 'What happened to you?' He looked Killean up and down and winced.

'Time spider,' Killean told him.

Nadil grimaced, as if he actually had any idea what that was. 'You can't go into the Pearl like that,' he said.

'No,' Killean agreed. 'Hence, why you're here and not decorating a wall in the basement.'

'Ahh.' A slight smile touched Nadil's stubbled face.

'I have an arsenal of Timeless weapons at my disposal,' Sikuzo told Nadil. 'Refuse me and I'll punish the boy with torment unimaginable.'

Nadil looked from Killean to Sikuzo and back again, his head cocked to one side thoughtfully. 'Alright. I'll do it,' he said decisively.

Sikuzo, who clearly had several more threats cued on his tongue and ready to go, blinked and stuttered, 'What?'

Nadil looked back at him innocently, his blue eyes pure as a spring sky. 'I said I'll do it. Show me the Pearl.'

He might have overplayed his hand with that last bit. Sikuzo looked highly suspicious. 'You're supposed to be a warrior,' he objected. 'Yet you give up without a fight.'

'I'm not going to let you torture a child,' Nadil said simply.

Killean had the distinct impression Sikuzo was disappointed. He clearly liked his spiders a lot. Personally, Killean thought Nadil should have dickered a bit longer, just to sell the act, but then again, he hadn't spent two days in a basement cell. And they were on a time crunch.

Sikuzo snapped his fingers. 'Harnin, Inoue, tie the boy down and guard him. He will be our insurance in case Shiny Scale decides to double cross me.'

Nadil rolled his tired blue eyes. 'That's more your stock and trade than mine. Show me the Pearl,' he ordered, commanding more respect in rumpled clothes and with two-day old stubble fuzzing his jaw than all Sikuzo's tantrums and Iviana combined.

The shadow spat out the Realm Pearl into her master's waiting hand. Nadil extended his shackled wrists. 'Release me and give me the Pearl.'

'Sammia,' Sikuzo barked.

Killean bit back a smile, looking down into his lap. Nadil, lips twitching, made a point of looking around the room. 'Uh,' he said helpfully, 'I don't think she's here.'

Sammia was gone. She'd slipped out of the room while Sikuzo was distracted. Killean tested the give on the ropes around his wrist. Sammia had broken the magic on then earlier and now they were only fibre holding him back.

Sikuzo summoned two more guards into the room. 'Find Sammia,' he ordered, 'bring her to me. You,' he ordered one of the men from the garden to come inside, 'unshackle Shiny Scale.'

That was three guards occupied. Harnin and Inoue had their hands full dealing with Ash, who was putting up a spirited, if ineffectual, struggle in the corner. He'd even managed to bring down one Sikuzo's oversized vases.

Demonstrating more self-awareness than Killean had first given him credit for, Sikuzo asked him urgently, 'Has she gone to my brother?'

'How would I know?' he asked. 'She threw me over for you, remember? It's not like this entire sequence of events has been an elaborate ploy to get you to bring us inside your defences.'

A muscle in Sikuzo's cheek twitched, joining his quivering eye in a little dance of nerves. He turned to his remaining spare guard, the one left in the garden. 'Send word to the men outside to secure the walls. I want scouts on the cliff paths. The first man to kill my brother will be rewarded with a ship of his own,' he instructed.

And that was the last guard taken care of. Killean was beginning to feel quite good about this venture. Especially when the entire house was shaken by the firework squeal and thunderous boom of an explosion outside the main gate. The redolent aroma of gunpowder wafted into the room from the gardens.

'A shadow!' Someone cried from the front of the house, their voice and any subsequent supply swallowed by another detonation that rocked the room and threatened to topple Killean's chair.

'Fire!' A guard yelled.

Most of the building was made of wood. The walls were paper. Sikuzo's palatial retreat had transformed into a tinderbox with him in it. And he knew it. He spun on his slippered heels; expression bleached white. 'Onryn,' he said quickly, 'protect me and I'll make you, my second-in-command. We'll lay siege to Carp harbour together. We'll be equals!'

Killean pretended to think about it. He could already smell smoke. 'How many ships would I get?' he asked.

'Half the fleet,' Sikuzo said quickly, well aware that he wasn't in a position to haggle.

Even in diminished circumstances, Sikuzo commanded a fleet of some fifty or more vessels. He had in his possession some of the best warships sailing the seas, commandeered from Jumping Carp, Lotus and White Surf. Killean could do a lot with a fleet of twenty-five sailing vessels and a handful of warships, especially if he used them to blockade Delta City's only seaport.

'*Ilin*,' Nadil snapped.

'Relax,' Killean told him irritably. 'I'm not going to take the offer.' He turned to Sikuzo and countered, 'Your title of Sea Lord for your life.'

Sikuzo stared at him. 'You can't be serious.'

Killean shrugged. 'You're asking me to go up against your brother and Shiny Scale. I think fifty sailing ships and whatever's left in your war chest is more than fair compensation. The question is, what do you value more? Your life or your reputation?'

THE LIFE AND TIMES OF THE TRAITOR KILLEAN ONRYN

There was quite a lot of noise coming from the front of the house. It was the sort of ruckus that suggested anyone in the back of the house had better pick up a sword or run before it reached them.

Killean could see Sikuzo doing the maths. He made the only sane choice, presumably for one of the first times in his life. The irony of which was certainly not lost on Killean. He hurried forward to cut away Killean's bindings.

Killean stopped him with two words, 'Say it.'

Sikuzo's face twisted in anger, but his fear was greater than his pride. 'My rank and title for my life,' he hissed. 'You are Sea Lord now. The Blue Crab are yours.'

'Excellent.' Killean jerked his shifted hands free of the already severed ropes, leapt to his feet in front of the shocked Sikuzo, grabbed the man by his face and rammed his elongated, scaled and clawed thumb nails into his throat.

Sikuzo made a noise like a frog someone had stepped on, twitched violently enough he almost wriggled out of Killean's grip and expired with a gurgle. Killean held him in his talons until the man's body was dead weight and the startled light had left his eyes, before dropping him. Bending to retrieve the Realm Pearl from the large pocket of Sikuzo's robe, he tossed it to Nadil.

'Go, now. Leave the Crab to me.'

Nadil likely would have objected, either to his killing Sikuzo or his suggesting that he leave him unsupervised, but he didn't get the chance. Iviana, Sikuzo's subservient shadow launched herself at Killean, dropping from the ceiling with an unholy shriek.

Killean dove and rolled out of the way, crashing into two large pots and taking out an arrangement of white lilies as he came to land, sprawled on his belly, near the far side of the room. Iviana burst from the floor, spreading through the air like a very angry oil slick. Her speed was so great Killean would have died then and there, choking on shadow, had Jadek not burst through the shattered doors of the room and flown straight into Iviana.

Chapter Twenty-Five

There was nothing quite like a free-for-all brawl between supernatural forces to upset the rhythm of even the most seasoned soldiers. The Blue Crab pirates spilling back into the room were anything but disciplined.

With Sikuzo dead and a furious ex-crewmate blowing up the walls looking for revenge, the pirates left in the mansion were caught between the basic instinct to fight or flee. Seeing as these were sensible pirates and not navy men every one of them chose the latter, escaping into the garden and through to the east side of the building.

Killean spied the Pearl on the ground, pulsing with power. Nadil was gone, presumably inside the Pearl. Killean grabbed it and scrambled over to Ash. He intercepted the boy before he could make a wrist-bound grab for the discarded gauntlet.

'Get off me!'

'Hold still and let me untie you,' he snapped back. 'You don't want me slicing a hand off.'

Ash coughed. The room was beginning to fill with smoke, spilling in through the shattered doors. It was getting uncomfortably hot. 'Why are you helping me?' he asked.

'Because I need you to do something for me,' he said honestly. 'Don't worry. You'll like it. I want you to fire the gauntlet at me. Every bit of magic stored in there.'

The poor kid didn't get it at all. Had no one sat this boy down and explained things to him? 'Kid, what I said about the gauntlet being cursed is true. The gauntlet chose you, just like it chose your father. I need you to discharge the magic stored in it.'

'Why?' Ash asked in alarm. 'The building is already on fire!'

He had a point there. 'Let me worry about that,' Killean said quickly. 'The Essence Drinker is the only thing that can stop *them*,' he gestured with his head toward the tussling shadows. 'It was designed to absorb magic. But only when its empty.'

Bursting through the broken doors brandishing a rifle, Cactus came to an abrupt stop as his gaze landed on his brother's body congealing on the floor. Sammia burst in behind him, breath catching. 'Shit,' she hissed meeting Killean's eyes, her own wide and worried.

Cactus looked like a man hit by lightning. He twitched on the spot, the muscles of his face contracting in a strange dance. He looked stricken. Until his gaze found Killean. 'You!' he cried, choked fury in his voice.

'Now, kid!' Killean yelled.

For once, Ash did exactly what he told him when he told him to do it. Possibly because he had long harboured the desire to roast him alive. He powered up the gauntlet and blasted Killean with everything he had. The force of the magic knocked him backward across the room and through the open doorway to the enclosed garden, before Cactus could fire off a shot.

His back ploughed into the pedestal of a stone birdbath with crunching force. Had he been entirely human, he'd have been paste. As it was the blow stunned him badly enough that he couldn't move, see or hear for a precious handful of seconds. His insides were alight with magic. His dragon-self thrashed against his cursed bonds as Torvin's magic frizzled out.

Cactus roared from the doorway, 'Out of my way, woman. His life is mine!'

'For fuck's sake,' Sammia shouted back, preventing him from charging Killean. 'Dead is dead. Who cares who did it? It's what you wanted isn't it?'

'My brother's life was mine to take,' Cactus insisted. He shouted, 'Jadek! To me!'

Sammia ducked and swept his feet out from under him. She took off across the mossy paving stones to Killean's side. 'Get up, arsehole. We're in real trouble now.'

Killean staggered to his feet. He felt none too steady. 'What about a trade,' he suggested. 'I killed your brother, you can kill mine.'

Beside him, Sammia groaned. She held her spear out crossways in front of both of them. 'Not helping, Ilin.'

'Do you think this is funny?' Cactus shouted. 'You have deprived me of my revenge.'

Cactus had ditched the rifle for two, sickle-like blades, one in each hand. Killean wasn't sure how practical a weapon they were and he wasn't in a hurry to find out. He was healing at a pace now he was free to shift scale, but he was feeling the toll of his injuries. He had experienced three years of torture already. That was quite enough for one day.

Walking out into the shaded sunlight of the garden, the air ashy with smoke, Cactus intoned solemnly, 'I promised Torvin I would not kill you.'

'I hear a "but" coming,' Sammia murmured. Killean hummed in agreement.

'I will not let you take the Blue Crab,' Cactus continued. 'It is mine. It was always mine. To have the syndicate stolen from me by blood is one thing. But I will not let trash like you steal my victory. Torvin will not go to war with me over your corpse,' he declared confidently.

'No, but he will for the Pearl,' Killean said holding out the object in question. 'Nadil is inside. Torvin might not care for me. But he does love his *other* surrogate son.'

Cactus froze. His face contorted in an angry twitch. 'You planned this,' he said.

Killean nodded. 'Nadil should never have told me he was here to stop me getting inside. It made it too easy to trick him to do it instead.' He hadn't been lying when he'd told Sikuzo Nadil was hamstrung by a compulsive need to be a hero. Now he had the best possible leverage to keep Cactus at bay.

Sammia cackled. 'Starry Night, Ilin. Sometimes I think you must be the luckiest bastard alive.'

'It's not luck,' he grumbled. He kept his focus on Cactus, who looked a lot like his deceased brother when stymied. 'Tell me, Crab, do you think Torvin will let bygones be bygones with both me and Nadil dead and you holding the Pearl?' he asked.

Cactus's grin was nasty. 'After I kill you, I'll hand the Pearl over myself. Torvin will have nothing to complain about.'

'You can't hand it over if I destroy it first.'

'A weak bluff,' said Cactus. 'You don't have the power.'

'Don't I? Take a look at my hand, Cactus. See the scales? The claws? I think you'll find I have more than enough power to destroy the Pearl and trap Nadil in the Timeless Realm forever.'

Cactus lost his smile. There was a dull weight of fear to his voice when he said, 'Your curse is broken.'

Killean grinned, showing all his teeth. They were somewhat sharper than usual. You see, the thing is, Killean had known all along he couldn't plan his approach to Sikuzo's lair when everyone he was working with was deliberately keeping him in the dark about their plans, motives and allegiances. But if working with and against Uncle Dadarro had taught him anything, it was how to build a plan of his own to undermine the schemes going on around him. He'd had plenty of time to set up his plan to break his curse, regain his true power, and use all his so-called allies secrets against them, all while they fell over themselves trying to use him. All he'd had to do was wait for the right timing. His alleged 'friends' had done the rest themselves.

Sammia had given him his way in. Nadil had presented the perfect hostage. Cactus had provided the firepower. And Ash...he'd been the key to unlock the door. Killean could never hope to empty the Essence Drinker's reservoir unless the gauntlet's chosen bearer specifically wished it so. Ash, desperate to be a hero, eager to both hurt him and be useful for once, had jumped at the chance when he'd offered it.

Smile on his face he called out, 'Whenever you're ready, kid.'

Cactus whirled around. Killean couldn't see Ash around his body, but he could clearly imagine the kid's pose, arm extended, gauntlet aimed, precocious look of concentration on his face. Cactus jerked on the spot as he was hit by the Essence Drinker's magic. His body was limned by darkness as Jadek was pulled through his skin. It looked painful. Almost as painful as a bite from the time spider.

'Stop!' Cactus shouted. 'I surrender. Do not take my soul from me.'

His soul? *Ouch*. No wonder Iviana had reacted so poorly to the death of her useless master. Considering he hadn't seen or heard from the other shadow since crashing into the garden, he had to wonder what had happened to her. Had Jadek destroyed her? Had Ash?

He pocketed the Pearl. 'It's over Cactus. Either the boy takes your magic and I take your life, or you surrender and keep both.'

Cactus glared at him. 'I don't fear death,' he said.

'Then you lose your soul,' Killean replied chipperly. He called out, 'Suck away, kid.'

'I can't,' Ash shouted back. 'The gauntlet's full. I used it to eat the other shadow!'

Well, that explained the mystery of what happened to Iviana.

'Fine,' he said. 'Roasting it is.' He tipped his palm, grimacing a little at the weird chicken leg scaly skin covering his hand. With a little concentration he was able to kindle flame in his palm. It burned with a familiar dark light. Dragon flame.

'Wait,' Cactus said hurriedly. 'What about the Blue Crab?'

Killean extinguished his fire and shrugged. 'Mamie wants them broken. Seems to me they already are. Give me two good warships and five merchant vessels and you can have the rest. Assuming you can find the crew to run your fleet,' he added drily.

Cactus looked like he was considering his generous offer. 'And the Pearl?' he asked.

Killean grinned, savouring the sharp sting as his slightly too long teeth cut the thin skin of his lips. 'I'm feeling magnanimous. I'll do you a favour and deliver it to Torvin personally.'

Cactus's eyes widened. 'You can't seriously intend to kill the High King on his own throne?' He sounded somewhere between horrified and impressed. It was an interesting reaction. Killean wondered what kind of relationship he and Torvin had.

Enjoying himself, he shrugged cheerfully and reminded Cactus, 'It's no concern of yours what I do. You're not in a position to stop me.' Jadek might give him some trouble, but the shadow would lose his way if he burned Cactus to a crisp.

Cactus stared at him shrewdly. 'You're not going to kill Torvin,' he said confidently. 'There is something you want from him.'

Killean said nothing. He wasn't going to admit the man was right when he had him on his knees.

'Go,' said Cactus, as if he had any authority here. 'Leave the island and never return.'

'And my ships?'

'What do you want with sea vessels? You're no sailor.'

'I'm thinking of going into international trade,' Killean told him drily. 'I'm headed for Shipwright. Come find me in twenty-four hours to settle up or I'll set the harbour on fire and end the Crab's dominance on the seas once and for all.'

'Agreed,' said Cactus, although he didn't sound happy. Killean was confident he'd honour his word, however, if only because he knew if he didn't, Killean would keep his promise to burn Shipwright off the map. It felt good to have the power to back up his threats again.

He looked over to Sammia, who had remained silent, a pensive look on her face. He cleared his throat. 'You're free to do as you please, Sami,' he told her, 'but if you choose to come with me, I'd like that.' He winced internally, wishing he was better at this kind of sentiment. Making threats came so much easier to him.

Sammia's eyes were bright, a hint of humour in their depths. She nodded. 'There's nothing left for me here.' It wasn't exactly the enthusiastic and forgiving response he'd been looking for, but he'd take it.

'What about me?' Ash asked, he'd squeezed his way around Cactus and out of the door and now stood in the no-mans-land between them. A place he'd been trapped all along. He looked supremely uncomfortable about it too. Which was fair, Ash was a mostly good kid with mostly good intentions stuck between two villains and a pirate. He must be missing Nadil.

'You can go or you can follow me,' Killean told him.

'Seriously?' Sammia sounded surprised.

Killean supposed his offer was odd. The kid's gauntlet was more of a threat to him now than it had been when it was clogged with his stolen power. Whether the kid knew that or not was another matter, however.

Ash looked overwhelmed. He'd jumped into the deep end and found himself swimming with sharks. Killean was surprised to realise he felt sympathy for him. He'd done the same thing once upon a time. The results had been...mixed.

'You'll let me go?' Ash asked, his dark eyes shiny with the knowledge that the villain had won and he was in trouble.

Lucky for him, Killean didn't feel like playing to type. 'Yes. You can go. I'll give you the magic word to portal back to the mainland. I suggest you take the opportunity to return to Green Peaks and get some proper training before you come after me again.'

Ash's eyes widened in understanding. He knew Killean's words were a tacit confession that revenge was warranted. His bottom lip wobbled. 'You really did do it,' he whispered. 'You killed my grampa.'

And here it was. The kid's pain had always been real. Just not for the reason he'd given. Killean remembered that courtyard. The scorched and destroyed remnant of the Dancing Deer's tents. He thought about the nervous man who had helped him get inside the palace. A man he'd never intended any harm toward. The man who had a daughter who'd given birth to a guard's bastard son. Who else but a lowborn woman determined to give her son his best chance at life would give him his father's exact name?

Ashinue Rogu senior had died so quickly at his hands Killean didn't even remember him. He wasn't sorry either. The man would have killed him just as quick. But Jerrel Adiri's death he did regret.

'Your grandfather was never my target,' he said. 'I took your father out in a fair fight. But Jerrel was an ally. Killing him was an accident. I never wanted to hurt a single member of your clan.'

'I don't believe you,' Ash whispered. 'What you did...you...you...'

He knew what he'd done. 'I don't expect you to believe me,' he said. 'And when the day comes that you can best me in a real fight, I'll take the consequences gladly.' He meant it. He *believed* in revenge.

'I don't understand you,' Ash said, pained. 'Are you...' he trailed off only for his expression to firm and light with renewed anger. 'You act like your sorry,' he said close to tears. 'Sometimes your almost...*not* a *complete arsehole*...but I know what you did. You killed my *clan*.'

Starry Night. The words hurt. They were true, of course. But, damn it, with the memories of his parents death raw in his mind it hurt like hell to acknowledge it. But he'd never been one to shy away from ugly truths.

'I did,' he said. 'And I am truly sorry for it.'

'You're just saying that to confuse me!'

Killean sighed. 'If it will make you feel better, kid. I can just kill you now and send your soul along to your clan,' he suggested tiredly. He didn't mean it, of course. He'd put a lot of effort into keeping this kid alive, up to and including making sure Nadil knew who he was. But Ash had nothing left but his anger. He needed it more than he needed to know that his family had died in a night damned *accident*.

'Arsehole,' Ash spat at him. 'I hate you.'

'Good,' Killean said meaning that too. He rose creakily to his feet. 'I'm glad that's settled. Now let's go. Before our lungs turn black.'

Chapter Twenty-Six

Fourteen hours later, sprawled comfortably in a chair set out on the oversized flowerbox that passed for a balcony in the Herringbone Inn, overlooking the sagging grey shingled roofs and puffing chimney stacks of Shipwright Island with a bottle of stout in his hand, Killean felt something close to contentment. 'You know, I quite like it here,' he said.

'That's because you have no taste,' Sammia retorted, seated on her chair beside him, with her feet propped on the balcony railing. 'This place is an even bigger shithole than Laidlow.'

'You're right,' he said happily. 'And it smells worse.'

Sammia snorted. 'Weirdo.'

Killean glimpsed her out of the corner of his eye. She looked relaxed. A big indicator that her state of ease was more than skin deep was the fact that she'd left her spear leaning against the wall inside the room. 'So,' he said aiming for a light tone and likely failing, 'are we good or are you going to turn me over to the next petty tyrant who wants me dead?'

Sammia turned her head enough to glare at him. 'You know why I did that. Torvin's got a long reach.'

'Torvin might have asked you to spy on the Blue Crab, but you set me up for your own reasons,' he said. Long reach or not, if she'd wanted to, she would have defied the Spark. 'I want to know if you still hate me,' he admitted bluntly.

He'd tried to come up with less direct ways of asking the question, the answer of which was his single biggest preoccupation, but giving up, he'd decided to risk getting an answer he wasn't going to like.

'What does it matter?' she threw out flippantly. 'You're all-powerful now. I'd be a fool to betray you.'

He pursed his lips. 'And you're basically unkillable. If anyone has the courage and cunning to best a dragon it's you.' Killean was very far from all-powerful and she knew it. Being full dragon hadn't helped Dadarro in the final battle.

'Give it a rest, Ilin,' she rolled her eyes. 'I know you. You only crank out the flattery when you're worried.'

'Do I have reason to worry,' he pressed.

Why wouldn't she just answer him? 'I know I hurt you,' he said quietly. He hadn't shown her how much she mattered to him when he had the chance. He'd taken her for granted both during the war and after. He should have sought her out when he was freed. 'I'm...sorry for leaving you behind.'

'I'm over it,' she told him breezily. 'You were right before. I could have tracked you down. And,' she said more seriously, 'I wouldn't have been so angry if I'd known you were caught too.' She glanced at him slyly. 'I'd've still turned you in on principle. But I probably would have acted faster to get that spider off you, if I wasn't still mad.' She shook her head, expression pensive. 'Seeing that thing munch on you was really upsetting for me. That's when I decided I was done being mad at you.'

He twisted in his chair to stare at her. 'I was *tortured* Sami,' he snapped. 'Being eaten by that spider *hurt.*'

Sammia threw up her hands. 'It was the principle of the thing!' she exclaimed. 'I told you back in Windchill what would happen if you let me down! If I'd let you off the hook just because I love you, I'd look weak!'

He was still gaping at her. 'That thing ate three years of my life! How long did you wait before you pulled it off me?'

'Around three minutes.' Sammia rolled her eyes again. 'I've been stabbed, shot, burned, beaten, crushed under rubble and drowned. *Twice*. All in the name of your damn crusade for revenge. Or an Accursed homeland. Or whatever the fuck it is you think you're fighting for. I think that makes us even,' she told him.

Killean tried to speak but he had no words. His head was filled with a white hot-static. He was stunned. He was confused. He was really, really happy. Sammia had just said she *loved* him. She'd also set him up to be tortured over a night-damned misunderstanding. One he'd already apologised for – hence his confusion.

'Finish your beer, Ilin,' Sammia told him, while he was still floundering. 'We both know if you were mad, I wouldn't still be here.'

He looked at her sharply, 'Do you think I could hurt you?'

'Yes,' she said. 'That's what love is, Ilin. It means you can hurt me and I almost hate you for it.'

'I don't think that's how love is supposed to work,' he said.

She smirked at him. 'How would you know? You're as crazy as I am.' She leaned across the space between them and stole his beer. 'Face it, we're both broken. We're going to cut each other up. You're going to chase your big dreams and leave me behind. I'm going to make you pay for it when I catch you. It's how this works with us.' She tilted the bottle and took a long pull. Killean watched her throat move.

'You love me?' he asked.

She pulled lowered the bottle. 'Starry Night. You just caught that?' She wouldn't look at him, her eyelashes fluttering in a nervous dance as she looked down. He couldn't be sure but he thought her skin was just a little ruddier, heated by a subtle blush.

'You did turn me in to a bunch of pirates,' he reminded her.

'Pish-posh,' she scoffed. 'You tossed me into a river to fight an angry fish god the first time we met.'

'I knew you could handle it,' he lied.

Now she looked at him, gaze shrewd. 'Ditto.' She smiled at him without her usual edge. 'That's the thing about living broken,' she told him gently, 'when we get hit, we take it. We don't shatter.'

Maybe, maybe not. He didn't think she was talking about torture. She was talking about who they were and how their cracked edges fit so neatly together. Like cogs in a mechanism, they couldn't chew each other up so long as they worked together. A smile twitched his lips. He shifted in his lounger so he was fully turned toward her and she mirrored him.

There was only a small gap between them. He reached out and trailed his fingers down her bare arm in a gentle dance, before swiping his bottle back. He set it down on the floor between their chairs. When he looked up, Sammia was still smiling.

'I'm still holding you to that queen thing,' she told him. 'And we're going to find Bodai and Juri. *Together.*'

'Already have an idea about that,' he said. 'I think Torvin has them.' He reached out to brush her cheek with his knuckles. 'If they were free, you'd have found them. If anyone else was holding them, they'd have sent a ransom. Their Torvin's last bargaining chip.'

Sammia pulled away. 'He needs to pay for that. Night damned Rivers mage, thinking he can play with Accursed lives anyway he likes,' she muttered darkly.

'He will,' Killean promised. 'I'm thinking extortion for starters.'

Sammia seized his hand, holding it to her cheek. 'And how will you finish?'

'With a kingdom of our own. Someone out there has the Firefly. That scares Torvin. He needs me now. I'm going to use that to make him bend until he breaks on my demands.'

'I love it when you talk politics,' Sammia drawled. 'Why not just kill him?'

He pushed his fingers into her hair, feeling the soft resistance. 'Because I don't want a war. Yet.'

'And the ships?' she asked. 'I've been trying to figure out what you want with those.'

'Brand new countries need imports,' he said simply. 'With the Blue Crab in my pocket I know my goods will be safe.'

She chuckled. 'And just like that, everything works out the way you want it. I swear you have a god or two in your pocket.' She shook her head, dislodging his hand. He let it slip to her neck, brushing his thumb over the underside of her jaw.

'No gods that I know of. Just Torvin,' he retorted. 'If the Spark hadn't freed me, none of this would be possible.'

In fact, his present could be much worse if the conspirators had found him in Silent Hell. He'd have agreed to almost anything they asked if it meant getting out of there. Of course, he wasn't a stickler for keeping his word, so there wouldn't have been much stopping him from using the conspirators and then disposing of them when he had what he wanted, but that came with risks of its own.

There was something about the flavour of the magic they'd sent after him that left him unnerved. He'd rather not have anything to do with the conspirators if he could help it. He didn't know if the Firefly's power was still within him, or if his connection to the relic was just residue, and he was in no hurry to find out. His days of chasing relics were over. The boy warlord wanted peace for now.

'Make sure you tell the Spark that when you deliver our demands,' Sammia murmured, leaning forward to bridge the gap between them.

'I intend to rub it in to an obnoxious degree,' he assured her. Cupping the back of her head, he leaned in.

The kiss started chaste, a simple brush of lips. They parted quickly parting and then closed the gap again in a flurry of soft kisses that deepened gradually, heat building between them.

Killean pulled her body across him, rolling on his back on the recliner. Sammia broke his hold and sat up, straddling his hips with her feet on the ground on either side. She pushed her hands up his torso, dragging his new shirt up over his belly. Her smile was wicked. Killean reached for her and —

Magic filled the room behind him. The scent and texture of the Timeless Realm flooded his senses. Two loud thumps sounded in the bedroom, an unfamiliar voice utterly a muffled curse in the language of Jumping Carp before a more familiar voice exclaimed, loudly and angrily. 'Oh, for the love of little fishes! What are you doing? She betrayed you, like, five seconds ago!'

Sammia climbed swiftly off him, hurrying into the room to grab her spear. Killean stood more slowly, but no less irritably. He straightened his shirt, scowling at Nadil standing in the space between the twin beds and the ugly vanity table carved into the shape of a giant clam shell. There was another man with him, somewhat mousy and bent backed, whose bald head was shiny with perspiration and whose small dark eyes darted around the room like a man already missing the safety of Realm Pearl.

Killean crossed his arms over his chest. 'Rhodu Gakai, I presume.'

The mage flinched back a half-step, heels hitting the bed. He lost his balance and fell onto the mattress. He said something in the lilting, fluting language of the Carp.

Nadil grimaced. 'He doesn't speak our language,' he said. 'That's why it took me so long to get him out. He didn't know who I was.'

'Aww, that must have bruised your ego,' Sammia mocked sweetly.

'Shut up, Death Child.'

'Hey,' Killean objected mildly. 'Don't speak to my queen like that.' Sammia beamed at him. He grinned back.

Nadil face-palmed. 'What happened,' he groaned. He looked around. 'Where's Cactus?'

'Chasing crabs,' Killean said. 'He's the new Sea Lord. If he can find anyone to follow him,' he added drily.

Nadil relaxed fractionally. 'He's alive?'

Killean shrugged. 'He was when I left. I'm not responsible for anything that happened to the fool after.'

'How long was I gone?'

'Twelve hours or so,' Killean told him. 'I thought you'd take longer. Well done.'

'Thanks. You sound like you meant that.' Nadil sighed. He looked back at the bed where Killean had tossed his coat with the Pearl still in his pocket. The pocket was shredded and the Pearl was now glowing faintly on the counterpane. 'You took the Pearl?' He stared at Killean accusingly, 'What are you planning?'

Killean rolled his eyes. 'To deliver it to Torvin. *Naturally.*'

Nadil snatched the mystical do-dad up and clutched it to his chest. 'Well,' he said trying to cover his actions with good cheer, 'I'm back now so I can do that for you.'

Killean grinned at him. 'Where's the trust, Nadil? I was nice enough to let Cactus live to take over the Crab, just like Torvin wanted.'

Nadil flushed. 'It's not like we want a bunch of pirates running around —'

'*Sailing*, not running,' Sammia interrupted helpfully.

'— but it would be chaos if the most powerful faction in Shipwright Island was wiped out just like that,' Nadil finished his sentence, ignoring Sammia. 'With Cactus in charge we have a chance of steering the Crab onto a better path. A more *peaceful* one.'

'And if that doesn't work, you've got a pirate fleet in your pocket just in case Jumping Carp act up,' Killean said brightly. 'It's not like I missed the part where Torvin conveniently signed a treaty with a member of the conspiracy you're so worried about. Torvin wanted Sikuzo gone so he could put his puppet in charge of the Crab.'

Nadil sighed. 'I like my explanation better.'

'Of course you do.'

Nadil narrowed his eyes. 'Where's the kid?'

'Back where he belongs.'

'What's that supposed to mean?'

'It means he's back, safe and sound, on the mainland with a handy-dandy pet shadow, you self-righteous prig.'

Nadil sagged, slumping down on the side of the bed beside Gakai. 'You can't blame me for thinking the worst,' he said.

'I can blame you for whatever I want,' Killean assured him. 'Now get out and take your mage with you. Sami and I have things to do.'

'Like what?' Nadil's blue eyes were bright with suspicion even in the gloom of the unlit room.

Killean just looked at him impatiently. Even he couldn't be this dense. Sammia made a noise of disgust, 'Do we need to draw you a picture, Shiny Scale?'

Nadil jumped up off the bed. 'Ugh. No.' He clutched the Pearl. Then hesitated, shooting Killean a suspicious look, 'Where are you going to go next?'

Killean shrugged. 'Home.' There was more naked longing in that one syllable than he'd intended to reveal.

Nadil's expression softened in understanding. The sap. 'Alright,' he said softly. 'Just remember, Torvin will send me after you again if you act up, so for both our sakes, don't. I'm sick of your face already.'

'Get lost then,' Killean chirped.

Nadil did, taking the very confused Rhodu Gakai and the Realm Pearl with him. Killean wondered if Gakai had any idea he'd signed over his liberty once again. Three Rivers was good at providing its political hostages with the illusion of freedom, but the truth was, while there were conspirators at large hunting down relics and those with the power to make them, Rhodu Gakai was a marked man, too dangerous to be left to his own devices. Especially when those devices had a tendency to be bloody dangerous.

As soon as they were out of the door, Killean turned to Sammia. She made a performance of stretching, arching her lithe spine and reaching her arms toward the low ceiling, her chest thrust out as the honed muscles in her calves flexed when she bounced onto her toes. Her shirt rode up, revealing the toned plane of her stomach. 'Well, well, what *are* we going to do with our time? Cactus won't be here for *hours*.' She winked at him.

Killean grinned, snaking his arm around her waist. 'I have some ideas.'

'Me too,' Sammia shoved him down on the nearest bed and climbed up his legs to settle over his hips. She grinned fiercely. 'Let's see whose are best.'

Chapter Twenty-Seven

Two days later, Killean was back on the mainland. Delta City was exactly as he remembered it and completely alien. He perched in his hawk form on the copper domed roof of one of the many watchtowers overlooking the muddy delta where the Uswe and the Gillimot rivers fed into the Bay of Solace. Large sailing ships sat in port, their sails stiff, and gulls wheeled over the red tiled roofs of the factories and warehouses fronting the docks. Westward, the Aspmouth river branched off from the Gillimot and streamed passed the city limits as if escaping the call of the sea.

The High King's Palace was built on a tiny island formed where the Aspmouth left the Gillimot that was cut off from the rest of the city by the Aspmouth's snaking path of escape. The gleaming white plaster, dark wood beams and black tiled pitched roofs of the castle peeked above the stony grey outer walls like a fancy cake bursting free of its box. Smaller river boats, barges and fast-moving ferries streamed up and down the twin rivers alongside the palace and a wide drawbridge connected the royal sanctuary to the rest of the city.

The air in Delta City tasted like coalsmoke and rain, reminding him of Cockle Shore. Dirty, grey-white clouds scudded above his head, large enough to cast shadows onto the city below. Several domed watchtowers dominated the skyline at strategic positions, more than he remembered from before the war, which made sense, he supposed. Most of the extra precautions had probably been erected because him and his uncle.

The watchtowers had competition from any number of tall, cupola-topped buildings made of cloudy grey stone or fired-red brick, pock-marked with banks of windows that reflected the colourless sky. From above, the city looked like a thicket of blunted needles striking up from the ground, forbidding and unfriendly. There were patches of greenery here and there; parks hewn out of the warren of brickwork. Killean remembered games of tag in Prospect Park that he, Nadil and Mishka had insisted were essential training exercises and toy boat races on the flat waters of the boating lake.

The path of the Aspmouth travelled through the westward outskirts of the city; including the Tanneries District where the waters were so polluted there were rumours a man could walk across the surface and not sink. The Temple of the Sacred Tilapia looked like an oasis of green and blue to the east of the city, the sapphire-glazed pitched roofs standing out in sharp contrast against the clusters of low, mean, tar-blacked houses spreading around it.

Killean cocked his head, looking beyond the smoke stakes of the industrial district to the mages barracks where Torvin had reigned supreme before he made the jump to the throne. The broad circular main tower looked smaller than he remembered as a child first entering the hallowed compound to visit his brother.

This city had been both home and cage to him back then as he chafed against the expectations and impositions placed upon him. For years after it had been a target for conquest. Now it was just another place to visit. Strange how that worked.

During the war, his memories had twisted this crowded, dirty, thriving city into a symbol of everything he despised in the world. He'd dreamed of watching it burn. He'd longed to start the fire, imagining the tiger roar of flame leaping from the wooden rooftops of the poor neighbourhoods and climbing the stone walls of the watchtowers until the entire city was lost in a basin of orange-gold sparks and lethal black smoke. The idea still had some appeal, but it was a dull temptation he could easily chalk up to his dragon's influence.

Killean twitched his feathers, shifting his balance on the dome. Sammia was waiting for him in one of their old bolt holes in the backwoods of Cow Country. They'd both agreed that it was better he visit Torvin on his own. His shapeshifting powers provided him a better chance of sneaking in unnoticed.

He'd spent the previous day scoping out the palace in his bird form, fluttering from guard post to guard post as a sparrow or starling and learning the layout of the keep's many floors as a mouse, scampering close to the walls.

The castle's weak defences against shapeshifters had made him suspicious until he remembered that Nadil had rooms in the royal apartments. The guards had likely become complacent to the presence of oddly curious wildlife flitting about. He was confident he could make it all the way to High King's private audience chamber without being caught. He was only idling here now to build up his nerve. He hadn't seen Torvin since his surrender at the end of the war. The Spark had sent unknown mages to free him from Silent Hell and they had never been alone after his capture. It was going to be strange meeting the old man again face to face.

He dove from the roof, taking wing and wheeling through the air toward the palace. He shifted from bird to rat after cresting the walls and scurried down old, spiralling stone stairs from one tower to the ramparts and then along the walls to another tower and into the barracks.

He jumped from trap doors, narrowly missing the rungs of wooden ladders, and descended to the castle bailey. He had a close call with the wheels of a munitions cart as he dashed around it and through a servants entrance into the main keep.

It had occurred to him that this could be a trap. Torvin knew him. He might be expecting a visit. In fact, he *had* to be, all things considered. Perhaps this was Torvin laying out the welcome mat. Or maybe the old fool expected Killean's visit to come in scale form, announcing his presence with a well-placed fireball. Five or six years ago, he would have done just that. But not today.

He was Killean-the-swift and he had a new goal now. Nothing would stop him from achieving it, not with Sammia waiting for news in Cow Country and Bodai and Juri waiting for him to spring them. He thought of Dragon's Ascent and the ruined, desolate lands of north-west Barley and knew the risk was worth it. He'd pay his debts and collect on some more while he was at it.

The main keep was a stacked rectangle, each floor much like the layers of a sandwich tower, getting progressively smaller as he ascended. The High King's audience chamber was at the top of the keep and visitors were required to progress through an endless parade of waiting and receiving rooms before reaching that vaulted locale.

Killean's goal was not the uppermost crust of the sandwich. There was an antechamber where Torvin did his paperwork. It was reachable by trapdoor from the throne room and via a secret service passage on the floor below. Killean had once paid a Rivers palace defector a tremendous amount of money to find out about that entrance but had never had the opportunity to make use of it. He was putting his faith in the information still being accurate. He didn't want to go to all this trouble only to infiltrate the chamber of some palace notary going about his boring business.

He had to hide in a hallway, hidden by the loose fringe of an old tapestry, waiting for his opportunity to breach the passage on the heels of a servant with a tea tray. He skittered into Torvin's inner sanctum as a rat. He'd bet Mishka would have some choice things to say about *that*, if she ever found out.

THE LIFE AND TIMES OF THE TRAITOR KILLEAN ONRYN

The room still bore the crest of the Camry, a white dragon tussling with a black wyrm – no doubt an Onryn ancestor – and several knick-knacks from Minuidon's time, including several suits of armour standing sentry against the wall. A tapestry depicting Delta City centuries ago, dominated the opposite wall. The woven sky was filled with wheeling dragons, which seemed like artistic licence gone mad to Killean. The Camry had never had that many dragon shifters at any one time.

The High King sat cross legged on the mat floor on a faded lilac cushion, a ledger open in his lap, his head, bald as an egg, was bowed low over the pages and a slender bone pipe, unlit, was clenched between his teeth. He wore a simple tasselled silk stole over his shoulders, decorated with the Three Rivers crest, over the top of a loose light blue tunic and baggy trousers. White soaks and simple cork soled sandals covered his feet. He looked more like a clerk than a king, which was exactly what made him so dangerous. Only the supremely confident and the supremely powerful needed to waste so little time advertising either.

Torvin thanked the servant who set the tray on the cluttered desk at the far end of the room and swiftly departed, clearly used to this routine. Killean skittered into the light, scampering over the mats toward the king.

The sun weathered skin at the corners of Torvin's merry blue eyes crinkled. 'A rat? That's a novel form to take for an assassination. Are you planning to kill me with plague?' he asked cheerfully.

Killean had forgotten his voice. It was surprisingly light and high, with a natural rasp to it that was only partly the fault of pipe-smoke. The rasp and the lack of depth in his register should have undermined his authority and opened him to mockery. That it didn't said a lot about Torvin.

Reclaiming his human form – including the new enchanted clothes he'd purchased on Shipwright Island – Killean settled on the floor, mirroring Torvin's pose. He didn't bother to answer the man. Instead, he studied him openly, really looking at the surrogate father he hadn't seen in more than a decade. 'You've gotten old,' he remarked. 'Kingship is clearly taking it out of you.'

Torvin lit his pipe and puffed casually. 'Hello, Killean. It's good to see you looking so well.'

He had dealt with a lot of liars in his time, but Killean knew few who could fake sentiment quite so well. Killean almost believed the old man meant it. 'I'm not here to kill you,' he said, getting to the pointy end of things first. 'I'm guessing you already knew that.' If Torvin had been truly worried, he'd have greeted him with a lightning bolt not a smile.

'That's good,' Torvin replied. 'I have a three o'clock appointment with the Carp Ambassador I really shouldn't miss.'

Killean quirked a brow. 'I'll bet. Are they after Gakai or is it me their mad about?' he asked. 'Obawai is part of this dread conspiracy you're worried about, isn't he? Is Carp using the hunt for relics as a means of regaining their lost power?'

Torvin smiled chuckled, 'You always did ask a lot of questions. And you so rarely had the patience to find the right answers.' He shrugged. 'Who's to say what Carp truly want? Diplomacy is much more interesting when I don't know the outcome.'

Killean did not roll his eyes. He couldn't even pretend to be surprised at the non-answer. 'You owe me,' he reminded the older man.

Torvin's blue eyes were aggravatingly innocent. 'Do I?'

'I did your dirty work.'

'Ah,' Torvin puffed on his pipe. 'But you see, technically you are a citizen of Three Rivers and therefore subject to my rule. I'm not required to offer you anything for your service.'

'I can revoke my promise not to kill you anytime,' Killean informed him flatly.

Torvin chuckled. 'You have more restraint than that,' he said, adding drily, 'at least now.'

'I came here to state my terms,' he said, ignoring the dig. He remembered well enough Torvin's teasing from his childhood. The best way to deal with it was to ignore it and keep focused on his purpose.

Torvin affected a look of mild interest and asked, 'In regards to what?'

Killean smiled thinly. 'A working truce between the newly autonomous state of West Barley and the kingdom of Three Rivers,' he said.

Torvin didn't have to feign surprise this time. 'I wasn't aware there was an autonomous West Barley,' he said.

'Consider yourself duly informed,' Killean replied in terms that brooked no argument. 'I'm taking back what is mine. All the land west of the Ishma Hills and north to Dragon's Ascent. What I want from you is simple. My trade fleet are to be granted access to Delta's port and rights to use the rivers and canals for a discounted rate of tax for five years. In exchange I will acknowledge your sovereignty and enter into a pact of non-aggression.'

Torvin tapped the bowl of his pipe out into the tray beside his cushion. He set the empty pipe down on the lip of the flattened porcelain dish. 'So that's what you wanted the ships for,' he murmured.

Blue eyes sharp he fixed Killean with his full attention. 'Non-aggression isn't enough. You take the same terms as your brother and become my vassal. This is non-negotiable, Ilin,' he snapped when Killean opened his mouth to object. 'You scare my counsellors. Bend the knee and promise to behave and then you can build your Accursed homeland as you see fit. Yes,' he added coolly, 'I know about that. If you'd bothered to visit the northwest, you'd have seen that I sent the remnants of your army to settle the land.'

Killean scowled. 'Why?' he asked warily.

Torvin sighed. 'Because I knew I couldn't keep you locked up for long. I put you in Silent Hell to calm you down, boy. Your dragon side was too volatile. I didn't want another Dadarro on my hands.'

'You could have had me executed,' Killean pointed out, unimpressed.

Torvin's expression was tired. 'Yes, I could have. And there are many who wonder why I didn't. I suppose I took a gamble. You were Dadarro's greatest asset. When you turned on him and surrendered, I had hope you could be an asset to Three Rivers instead.'

Killean looked away. The angry kid he'd been and still was in a lot of ways, wanted to leave in disgust, shouting threats that he'd never work for Three Rivers interests. The realist in him knew that he already had. He'd come here to be paid and he'd banked on Torvin wanting to use him still when he'd come here seeking amicable terms.

If one good thing had come out of the time spider making a meal out of him, it was that the ordeal had helped him accept that he was well and truly done with war. It helped him keep his temper now.

'You want to use me as a stalking horse against the people looking for Myron's relics,' he gritted out.

'These people want to do what Dadarro failed to. They want to unite the relics and subjugate all the Lands of Magic,' Torvin justified himself.

Killean rolled his eyes. 'My uncle was a nutbag whose biggest dream was turning into a giant reptile. Why not let these relic hunters have what they want and destroy themselves?' he asked.

'Because this is a group with greater ambition than personal power. They threaten us all.'

'So you *are* setting me up to be their first target,' Killean pressed.

'The power inhabiting the Firefly chose you,' Torvin countered. 'You have the best chance of besting its new owner.'

'Do you know who they are?'

'No.'

Killean nodded bitterly. 'So, I was right. All this, setting me free, placating me with my own lands, it's all just a ploy to put me in position to take the hit meant for you and Three Rivers.'

'I'd remind you that you came to me demanding your own lands, but I don't want this meeting to devolve into one of the temper tantrums you used to throw as a boy,' Torvin retorted drolly.

'I'm willing to let you rearm and rebuild, Killean, at great potential risk to Three Rivers, because I believe we have a *mutual* enemy. And that, you, despite all evidence to the contrary, actually learned something from your failed rebellion.'

Oh, he'd learned something alright. He nodded slowly. 'I'll accept your sovereignty, but I want a complete waiver on import and export taxes for ten years.'

'That's steep.'

'It's cheaper than getting blown up by a would-be god and you know it.'

'Two years.'

'Seven.'

'Two years tax exemption and three years reduced rates.'

'Five years exemption. Two years reduction – and that's my final offer.'

'I'm not sure what you have as leverage here,' Torvin mused. 'I really don't have to offer you anything. The conspirators will come after you on their own. They already did while you were in Silent Hell. You can face them alone, or with Three Rivers aid. *That* is your only choice.'

Killean smirked. 'Accept my terms or I put a sign out on my lawn welcoming all would-be conspirators and Firefly wielders to my home and country.'

Torvin widened his eyes. 'You realise that the new wielder likely wants to kill you?'

Killean shrugged. 'That's as likely with our alliance as without it, which doesn't give me much reason to go easy on you,' he said. 'I could side with the conspirators against you and fight it out with them in Delta's burning ruin.'

'Yes, you could.' Torvin pursed his lips, unhappily. 'My counsellors think you already have such an alliance.'

Killean heard the question Torvin wasn't asking. He relished that little hint of fear and doubt in the man but set it aside. He really had come here to build a future; he wasn't going to waste that on the petty pleasure of tearing the old man down. 'All I know about these conspirators is what I've been told. If Mamie was in with them, she kept me out of it.'

Torvin nodded. 'I suspect that was the Silk Paw's motivation in the first place. Mamie Cat has invested a lot in you. She's not likely to throw that investment aside now. She thought to find out the conspirators identities, but they were too wily for even her.'

'A likely story,' Killean rolled his eyes and scoffed. 'Not everyone is as sentimental as you.'

Torvin ignored that. 'You know,' he suggested mildly, 'Kindean may object to having his country bifurcated.'

'Kindean is an obsequious toerag and your soon-to-be son-in-law. He'll do what you tell him to do.'

Torvin smiled widely, just short of full-blown laughter. 'You should try and be a bit more understanding. Kindean has always done what he thought was best for both of you.'

He wasn't here to talk about his brother. His wedding present to the happy couple was letting them keep Cockle Shore and the nicer parts of Barley. 'I want one other thing from you,' he told the man.

Torvin nodded. He already knew. He'd given the game away when he'd admitted to having resettled his army. 'You want your lieutenants. But you see, my counsellors have been very firm on this point. The Dread Four absolutely must not reform.'

'Give me their names and I'll change their mind on that,' Killean suggested.

Torvin looked amused. 'No, I don't think I will. Your methods of persuasion tend to be...fiery.'

He picked up his pipe, playing with it in his hands. 'I can't be seen to release Bodai and Juri, you understand,' he said regretfully. 'There is, however, little I could do if they were to mysterious free themselves, perhaps through the machinations of an unknown third party?' His voice rose provocatively at the end, turning the suggestion into a question.

Killean resisted the urge to sign loudly. Night damn the man and his games. 'Tell me how to find them and I'll arrange the rest,' he said.

'First, tell me, your magic...'

Killean looked at him hard. 'Why are you even asking? Cactus has to have tattled already.'

Torvin dropped the paternal amusement entirely. 'You are a dragon shifter once more,' he said flatly.

'So is Nadil. Do you give him that look too?'

'You aren't Nadil. And the Firefly chose you.'

'I didn't choose *it*,' Killean retorted. 'Remember old man, when it came time to choose, I gave up power to save your heir.'

'Yes. And it was because of that I almost sided with my counsellors and had you killed. Ah, that does surprise you, doesn't it?' Torvin nodded grimly. 'A thinking foe is more dangerous than a fool and his magic,' he said. 'I wish I could believe you acted on sentiment. I know you care about Nadil. But I also know you. You are always looking for advantage. You do nothing without a plan.'

'And I learned it all from you,' Killean snapped. 'You can't kill me now. You need me.'

Torvin surprised him again by smiling, big and bright and mirthful. Sadness remained in the worn creases around his eyes, however. 'You have always been the wolf at my throat, Killean, from the moment I took you in.' He said, 'My greatest hope is that our détente will hold a good long while. I would sooner have you at my side.'

Killean ignored the heat building behind his eyeballs. He hated how the wily bastard made him feel. What made everything worse was that Torvin sounded completely sincere. He meant it. Even after all these years. The war. The schemes. The conspirators looking to turn them against each other. Torvin would plan for the worst and hope for the best, just as he always had.

Looking into his blue eyes, Killean felt seen and transparent, as if every thought he had and every plan he devised had already gone through the old man's mind. The urge to do anything to throw him off was almost too much. But he wasn't a rebellious child anymore. If he wanted what was his, he'd have to swallow his pride and accept that his future required him to be exactly what Torvin had shaped him into.

'Here,' Torvin said, extending a slip of paper toward him.

Written on the paper were instructions and a map to a series of portals that would eventually lead him to where Bodai and Juri were held. Killean glared at Torvin. 'You make it very hard not to hate you,' he said.

Torvin smiled. 'Mishka says the very same thing.' He waved his hand. 'Go now. Before the servant comes back for the tray. I'll send an envoy to hash out the formal terms of our agreement one week from now. I'd advise you have your lieutenants well hidden at that time.'

Torvin could take his high-handed advice and shove it where the sun never shines. Killean tucked the piece of paper carefully away in his enchanted pocket and reminded himself that letting the old man get the last word in was a small price to pay for all he'd won. It was one of his least convincing self-deceptions. He transformed back into a rat before he lost his grip on rationality and set the smug bastard on fire.

Chapter Twenty-Eight

Sammia looked around the lumpy, desolate Nameless Plain, with its ramshackle ruins and mournful wailing winds and exclaimed, 'Torvin imprisoned Bodai and Juri *here*?'

'There's a kind of thematic poetry to it,' Killean said tiredly. 'The portal we're looking for is the same one Jumping Carp used to kidnap me. Plus, Torvin is an arsehole. I really should have guessed.'

Sammia turned her face away as a scudding, dust-laden breeze swept passed. She hissed through her teeth and asked, 'You think he's playing us?'

'If he is, I'll kill him,' Killean bit out.

The Spark's instructions had led him on a merry trek through several countries, connecting disparate portals together in an intricate bit of ritual magic that was far too complex for anyone to stumble on by accident. Torvin had used the nebulous laws governing the Timeless Realm to his advantage, sealing Bodai and Juri away in a sliver of timelessness, trapped between portal jumps. The only way to free them was to follow the pattern exactly.

'The portals here are ancient, part of a network fallen to ruin. It's actually the perfect place to hide someone.'

'Then why don't more people do it?'

'Because most people aren't as clever and devious as Torvin.'

'Careful. That sounded almost admiring.'

Killean shrugged. 'What can I say? I admire cleverness no matter the source.'

'Even when its used against you?'

'Especially then.' He grinned at her. 'I *did* make you my queen, remember?'

'You didn't *make* me anything,' Sammia told him. 'I *consented*. Ugh,' she spat out a mouthful of grit. 'Can we get on with this? I want to get out of here before I'm flayed alive. Trust me, the experience is overrated.'

Killean pulled his new coat around him, hunching his shoulders against the biting wind. 'Over there,' he nodded. 'That's the last one.'

They trudged across the broken, sandy ground. 'Still can't quite believe you agreed terms with Three Rivers,' she remarked. She cut him the side-eye adding, 'It's even weirder that you seem happy about it.'

Reaching the ancient arch, Killean ran his hands through his newly shorn hair. 'I'm fine with draining Three Rivers' coffers to rebuild my home,' he told her.

As an act of benevolence that Killean recognised for the bribe it truly was, Torvin had extended him a loan at a staggeringly low rate of interest to help get his fledgeling nation off the ground. Literally in some respects. Dragon's Ascent looked very flat right now. Killean had stood on the banks of the dried lakebed in the shadow of the broken escarpment and apologised to his parents memory before setting about spending the money.

He handed the paper with the instruction to Sammia. 'I think you should be the one to do this last part,' he said.

She rolled her eyes. 'Only because you think Bodai will murder you for leaving them stuck for five years.'

He shrugged. 'That goes without saying. I thought you might *want* to do this,' he added pointedly.

Sammia had been looking for them a long time. She'd told him the number of times she'd used any number of the portals in the sequence during her searches, never knowing that for want of the right pattern she would have found them.

'Tell me this much, are you really planning to side with Torvin against this new lot, whoever they are?' Sammia asked.

'What do you think?' he asked her honestly. 'You are co-ruler.'

Sammia swept a hand through her hair, shaking grit out of the mass. 'I think we see if the conspirators can make us a better offer. We'll get rich as our enemies fight over us.'

Killean chuckled. 'My thoughts exactly.'

The truth was he wasn't convinced this new threat was anything more than the old rumblings of discontent that had always been present in the inns, taverns and low places across the continent. He and his uncle had failed to create lasting change on the continent with their rebellion and he couldn't see how this alleged new threat, too timid to declare rebellion directly, was going to do any better.

Sammia approached the worn stone of the standing pillar. Its surface mutilated with so many shallow cuts of magic it looked like it had been designed that way. 'Same procedure as all the others?' she asked him.

'Yes.'

Not trusting Torvin's magic entirely, they'd added another step to the process, using blood magic to make a safe barrier between them and the suctioning magic of an active portal in case Torvin had set a booby trap. Killean couldn't think why Torvin would do this, but just because he couldn't see the logic in it didn't mean there wasn't any. No one stayed alive long expecting their enemies to be honourable. And he and Torvin were still on opposite sides, no matter what it looked like from the outside.

Using a paring knife to prick her finger, Sammia smeared blood into the ancient grooves cut into the stone. The magic of the pillar seemed to like the taste of Sammia's cursed blood. Magic breathed through the air, warm and eager. Sammia hurriedly stepped back as the air under the lintel and between the two standing pillars turned opaque, rippling like cloudy water.

They both looked into the portal. 'How long are we going to wait?' Sammia asked.

They'd come to the mutual decision that neither of them would enter this last doorway. Instead, they'd wait to see who or what came out. If Bodai and Juri didn't make it out themselves, that meant they were either dead or long gone, lost to the spell of the Timeless Realm. In either case, they would be beyond any help Killean and Sammia could give them.

'Hard to say,' he admitted. 'Time is...basically meaningless on the other side.'

'A whacking great door opening in your prison cell sure isn't,' Sammia argued.

'I agree. Let's just hope Bodai and Juri do too.'

They hadn't talked about it, but there was a real fear that Bodai, at least, might have given into the call of the Timeless Realm and transformed into one of the strange, inhuman creatures that called the realm home. Killean liked flesh and blood monsters more than he did most humans, but even he drew the line at working with the capricious, unknowable entities of the other side. Most of them made the time spider look tame.

As the wait crawled on and he grew progressively colder in the wind, Killean began to worry. Sammia would be bitterly disappointed if they couldn't find them. So would be he, if he was being honest. As the trek had gone on, he'd started to look forward to seeing his lieutenants again.

He and Sammia remained silent, not even looking at each other as they waited. Both of them fixated on the strange lights that strobed across the surface of the magic portal. Vague, dreamlike colours swirled in a marbling effect, but nothing human surfaced behind the magical surface.

Until...

'Look. There,' Sammia exclaimed pointing at the portal with the hand not clutching her spear. 'Do you see?'

He saw. The span of colours skimming the surface of the portal shifted, becoming a hundred faceted and distorted reflections of a single face. Half a face actually. A huge round eye, the hint of a lank strand of hair falling across it, the bridge of a nose. It looked like someone had pressed their face against the magic on the other side of the portal and was trying to peer through.

Sammia flung down her spear, waving her arms. She shouted, 'Juri! Juri! Its me, Sami. We've come to get you out!'

The face in the portal vanished. Sammia dropped her arms, dejectedly. She turned to him. 'Screw it. I'm going —' Before she could finish her sentence, the magic in the portal became violent, spinning into a vortex until the reflections across its surface looked like the baleful eye of a cyclone.

'Crap!' Sammia yelped, leaping out of the way as the tearing whirlwind burst out of the portal.

Killean darted out of its wobbling path, watching as the mass of air swept up anything not weighted down into its wake and sent bits of shrapnel flying in all directions.

'For fuck sake, Bodai,' Sammia yelled. 'Quit that. It's us, you fool.'

Out of the tumult came a huge, hulking figure, staggering onto the solid ground of the Nameless Plain. Sammia squealed in joy, a noise she'd never made on seeing *him*, and hurled herself into Juri's arms. The confused giant just about managed to avoid crushing her reflexively. He turned his head and looked at Killean.

His expression was tragic. 'Is this real?' he asked.

Sammia clasped his head, pulling his face around to her and squeezed his cheeks between her palms. 'We're real, you moron. Starry Night! Its good to see you!' She kissed him, quick and sisterly.

The spinning cyclone slowed to a complete halt, revealing Bodai in all his washed-out glory, standing in the middle of a small rain of debris that pelted the ground around him. He and Juri were still in the tattered remains of their armour from the last, fateful battle.

Bodai fixed him with a furious glare and demanded, 'What in Silent Hell is going on?'

Sumie's laughter was sweet as a nightingale's song. 'It's a long story,' she told him. Releasing Juri she smacked Bodai on his shoulder, forcing the reedy sprite to take a big step forward to steady himself. 'Just be glad we got you back, air-for-brains.'

'Got us back?' Bodai asked, puzzled. 'Sami, you're the one who was gone.'

Sammia swiped at her wet face with a grit-covered hand. 'The war's over,' she told him gently. 'You've been stuck in a Timeless prison for five years. Him too,' she jacked her thumb toward Killean before either of the others could ask the obvious question. 'Ilin got out six months ago. He worked out terms with Torvin to get you and his lands back.'

Killean arched his brows. While that was true, Sammia was leaving a lot out, like how most of what had happened had been accident over design, and how, without her prodding, he might not have gone looking for either of them at all. Sammia was doing him a big favour glossing over the details.

Juri's face crumpled mournfully. 'If you negotiated with Torvin, does that mean we lost?' he asked.

'Let's call it a draw,' Killean said, not meeting his eyes.

Bodai dropped into a heavy crouch. 'I feel like I've been run up a flagpole in a gale,' he whined.

'You look like it too,' Sammia grinned.

'So it's over, then?' Bodai asked. 'No more wars. No more rebellion. No more enemies to vanquish?'

All three of them looked at him with various degrees of expectation. Killean felt a smirk crook the corner of his mouth. 'There are always more enemies to vanquish,' he promised. 'Now come on. We've got a long road back to Barley and a lot to do.' Not waiting to see if they followed, he turned and strode away across the plain.

'That's it?' He heard Bodai complain behind him, the wind obligingly bringing to his ears every nasal strain of his annoyance. 'No explanation. No welcome? Just new marching orders. *Starry Night*, I did not miss this.'

'I did,' Juri said and Killean heard his big heavy footfalls eating up the ground between them.

Killean ducked his head, ostensibly against the gritty winds but mostly to hide the grin lighting his features. The last time he'd crossed this plain he'd been a broken man with nothing to fight for, living out of force habit. Guilt and bitterness had been his only companions. His heart numbed by defeat, his ambition trampled into dust, he'd been a shell of himself. What a difference the murder of a pirate lord could make on his outlook on life.

He didn't know what the future held, or what new enemies might be waiting to try him. He didn't know if his new alliances would hold. It didn't matter. He felt whole again with Bodai and Juri whispering at his back and Sammia striding at his side. His hope contained as much in them as in the schemes born in his mind.

Revenge was a lot like life, he decided. It could be lost in a single battle or squandered in doubt. Like the victory that had eluded him too long, it did not always take the form he expected. He knew that while the fire burned in him, the old adage was as true for vengeance as it was for life itself. If at once you don't succeed, try, try and try again.

THE LIFE AND TIMES OF THE TRAITOR KILLEAN ONRYN

Killean Onryn, traitor, warrior, failure, monster, orphaned son and fallen general, lifted his head into the wind and bared his teeth in a victor's snarl, knowing full well that a dragon's shadow unfurled behind him in the dust and ruin.

Whether his future lay in villainy or some other path, he hadn't decided, but he did know he was going to have a lot of fun finding out.

Coming 2025...

Did Killean's adventure leave you with burning questions? *Such as...*

Why did Mishka Silverfloe turn up in Cockle Shore just to buy Killean lunch?

What is the exact nature of Sammia's deal with both the Blue Crab Pirates and Three Rivers?

Who are the conspirators seeking Myron's Relics and what really happened to Killean in Silent Hell?

...Then turn the page for a sneak peek into the next book in the series, where answers will be revealed in Book Two of the Relics Saga: *Mishka Silverfloe and the Secrets she Learned*

THE LIFE AND TIMES OF THE TRAITOR KILLEAN ONRYN

A.R CUNNINGHAM

Mount Haze, Northern Three Rivers:

Another day, another rebel faction raid. Mishka Silverfloe hitched a sigh as she picked her way, carefully, through the dense, dank jungle covering the lower reaches of great Mount Haze. Everything was dripping and stinking in the fetid heat trapped under the canopy. The staccato beat of raindrops on leaves thrummed through her head, echoing the steady pounding of her footsteps and the almost inaudible groan of old trees breathing in the damp.

This close to the border with Past Tiger and the wildlife in the region grew some very sharp teeth. But it wasn't chittering monkeys or lone prowling panthers Mishka was on guard for. Death stalked her steps, creeping through the knee-high undergrowth with a phantom's grace. Mishka had been leading her on a merry trek for the last fifteen minutes, skirting boggy waterholes and criss-crossing the raised, spidery roots of massive, hollowed out trees just to give her hunter a workout. But her patience for the game was wearing thin.

She could be back in Delta City now, enjoying the clement weather. She could be reclining on pillows and blankets laid out on the grass, sipping chilled white wine while nibbling on lacy wafer biscuits as the Delta City Philharmonic played Nebadiah's Seventh Symphony with intended cannonade accompaniment. Kindean had bought the tickets weeks ago and a bottle of '52 Diviner's White, just to make the prospect of a well-deserved day off irresistible. '52 had been a particularly fine year for her favourite vintage. She could almost taste the sweet but sharp wine on her tongue and smell the gunpowder in her nose.

She shivered hungrily, imagining the thunder of the cannon as the orchestra swelled to crescendo. A rapturous harmony of bombast and skill, the vibration thrumming through her bones like the best kind of magic. And beside her, quietly soaking it all in, fingers laced with hers, the man she loved. Total heaven.

But she wasn't in Delta City, was she? No. She was stuck in the stinking northern jungles, ankle deep in rot and leeches waiting for death to get a freaking move on. Ugh. That was it. She'd had enough. The time for fun and games was over. Those rebels weren't going to arrest themselves and she needed to get to the meeting spot before the idiots got too drunk to say or do anything incriminating.

She raised her voice to be heard. 'If you're going to attack me, Sammia, get on with it already. I *do* have things to do today.'

A normal person would never have heard the attack coming. Sammia, Child of Death, knew how to use the trees, the undergrowth and the dripping condensation to her advantage. She'd spent plenty of time hiding out with the rest of the Dread Four in Past Tiger's jungles and the other woman's movements were as graceful as they were economical. Alas, against Mishka, none of that mattered.

Mishka didn't *see* Sammia leap down from the sturdy bough of the tree behind her, but that didn't matter because she *heard* her just fine. She heard the rasp of her boot sole slip ever so slightly on the moss covering the branch as she launched herself through the air. Before that she'd heard the creak of the bough, the tremble of the leaves at the end of the branch, the otherwise imperceptible intake of breath before Sammia committed to her leap. A normal person wouldn't have heard a thing. But Mishka wasn't normal. Thank the Torch Bearer.

She struck out with a low leg sweep the instant Sammia landed behind her, using her momentum to complete her turn and back up the grazing jab she aimed at the other woman's head. Sammia rolled to the right, lunging with a hooking kick of her own for Mishka's ankles as she came out of her roll. Mishka hopped over the kick and side-stepped to the left, fists up.

Sammia bounced to her feet, her grin a wet flash of white in the emerald gloom surrounding them. They circled each other, the ground slick and spongy underfoot. Sammia, Child of Death, wore the colours of the jungle well. Clad in tight fitting green silk trousers and smock with a dull leather jerkin crossed with straps for the weapon missing from her back. Not a complete surprise that Sammia had decided against leaping from a tree with a six-foot spear strapped to her back, but still, Mishka wasn't used to seeing her without her weapon of choice.

During the war a rumour had spread that Sammia's immortality was tied to her spear; take it and she would be rendered powerless. Needless to say, it wasn't true. All the same, Mishka cast a quick look around the treetops for any place the other woman might have stashed her spear. It might not be the source of her power, but she sure was prickly about people handling her polearm.

Sammia held out her arms, crouched low in a wrestler's stance, and twinkled her fingers invitingly. 'Come at me, princess.'

Mishka grinned back at her, showing all her teeth. 'Drop dead, *Sami*.'

The Child of Death lost her smile. 'Don't,' she grumbled.

'Aww,' Mishka drawled, 'what's the matter? Don't you like your pet name anymore?'

They continued to circle. Around and around the same tiny patch of free ground. Beyond the canopy, the wind shifted direction, causing a fresh deluge of raindrops to thunder down overhead. Mishka heard the shriek-squeal of an animal at the exact moment it became a panther's dinner someplace else in the jungle.

Sammia narrowed her eyes. 'No one calls me that.'

Well, not anymore. Killean was gone. Hopefully for a long time to come. Mishka's childhood friend turned enemy was currently sleeping his life away in Silent Hell and had been for the last five years. Which was something of a sore spot for his ex. Sammia was the only member of the Dread Four still free to roam the Lands of Magic. And her freedom was something of a *technicality*.

'I'm sorry,' Mishka simpered, 'that was insensitive of me. I'm sure you must be – *frustrated* – with the way things are. I mean, who else but a blood thirsty lunatic would ever lie with you? And there just don't seem to be enough of *those* around right now. It must be *so sad* for you. No one to call you pet names. No one to give you back rubs. No one to —'

'Oh, that's it.'

Sammia launched herself forward, head low and arms wide in a front tackle that ploughed Mishka into the trunk of a tree covered in phosphorous toadstools. As the breath whooshed out of her lungs, Mishka did wonder if goading the notorious killer in front of her had been her best idea to date. But not for long. Riding out the impact as her spine collided with trunk and fungi, she pressed her fingers together and cupped her palms, clapping them hard over Sammia's ears.

The other woman yelped and leapt free. Mishka licked her lips and curled them over her teeth before bringing her fingers to her mouth. Sammia's eyes widened. She threw up one hand. 'No, wait!'

Mishka did not wait. She took a breath and gave a sharp whistle. The shrill sound tore through the dank jungle like a musket rapport. Sammia was thrown backward by a solid wave of sound that sent her flying across the narrow clearing and into the undergrowth growing up between two trees. She landed in an undignified heap on her back.

The jungle was alive with sounds. Monkeys screamed. Panthers coughed out yowls of protest and a symphony of warm-blooded critters hidden in the ferns broke into a chorus of complaints, scampering deeper into the forest. Birds took wing, blasting free of the canopy and the branches shook in their wake.

Oops. Not exactly stealthy behaviour, Mishka. She needed to remember she still had a job to do. Torvin would have words for her if she blew the mission scuffling with Sammia. She sighed, rolling her shoulders and scraping fungus stains off her back.

'You okay?' she asked, as the other woman hauled herself out of the thicket.

Sammia rolled her eyes. 'It's not like you can kill me.' She cocked her head, smacking the side of her skull. 'I could do without the ringing in my ears, though.'

'You attacked me first,' Mishka reminded her.

Sammia plucked a broken stem from her froth of hair. 'You told me to do it.'

That...was true, actually. Darn it. Mishka grimaced. 'We need to quit messing around and get on with the job,' she said briskly, deciding her remaining dignity demanded she ignore that remark.

Sammia's look was droll. 'You know this is a waste of time, right?'

Of course, she did. She was supposed to be sipping wine with her beloved while the sky over Delta City rang with music and cannon fire. But that wasn't the point. It was never the point. At least according to Torvin.

'There's been an uptick in subversive behaviour in this region. As agents of Three Rivers Intelligence its our duty to investigate,' she said.

Sammia was not impressed. 'It's going to be the same as last time. A bunch of drunk yokels and Tiger ex-pats talking big in some disused mine in the mountains.'

Mishka sighed, shoulders sagging. 'It would be nice if just once they chose somewhere else to have their clandestine meetings. There are a couple of very good hunting lodges not far from here.'

'These're amateurs,' Sammia scoffed, crossing the clearing to retrieve her spear from its hiding place in a patch of feathery ferns. She expertly strung the spear to her back without a mirror. 'They're playactors, not real rebels. It's not like in my day. Back in the war, we knew how to do things right.'

Mishka wanted to argue with that on principle, but Sammia wasn't exactly wrong. The Onryn Uprising had upended the balance of power across the Lands of Magic. Things could so easily have ended very differently for all of them had Dadarro been a little less deranged and Killean...well, never mind. That was all in the past. Right now, it was her job to make sure none of the disgruntled rebel groups popping up around the country harboured the *next* Killean Onryn in their midst.

She eyed Sammia warily. 'Just remember you work for us now,' she warned, 'get too misty eyed about the glory days and it'll buy you a one-way ticket to Silent Hell.'

'And you'll be the one signing the ticket, right?' Sammia's smile was caustic and nasty. Almost a provocation in itself.

Mishka crossed her arms over her chest and reminded her, 'Torvin put your life in my hands.'

When the war had ended with Dadarro dead, Killean and the other members of the Dread Four locked away and Killean's army of Accursed falling apart without a leader to follow, it had made sense to hunt down Sammia.

Three Rivers' Intelligence had been tracking her since her split from the Dread Four during the war, in the vain hope that she might lead them to Killean. That hadn't happened and in the excitement of their abrupt victory, Rivers' Intelligence had lost track of the Child of Death.

Mishka had spent three months chasing whispers and hunting down leads until she finally caught Sammia in middle-of-nowhere Cow prairie lands. The collar should have been her crowning moment of victory and the final nail in the coffin of the Onryn Uprising. The least her father could have done to reward her for her good work was properly punish the war criminal.

Instead, he offered her a job.

Worse. He offered her the *exact same job* he'd granted Mishka after the war. The job of a Three Rivers' spy, working in the shadows to keep the country safe. A position that should be granted only to the most trusted patriots and citizens of the land, not a Green Peaks mercenary who made her name killing her fellow Accursed in the Valley Good Arena.

Once again, in a single thoughtless act, Mishka's father had managed to disrespect and invalidate all her hard work for the sake of his never-ending schemes. Yet, despite this being the pattern of a lifetime, Mishka never could shield her heart from the blow of disappointment.

'An enemy in the hand is an excellent shield against our enemies hiding in the bush, Mish,' her father had told her when he first announced his intention of having Sammia work under her supervision. The inanity of his delivery, puffing on his pipe as he sifted, listlessly, through the endless pieces of paper his clerk kept handing him, only added to her mounting fury.

They were in his private study, hidden behind a secret passage on the second from top floor of the Royal Palace. The room was still full of Minuidon's junk. Elaborate swords in jewel crusted scabbards whose blades couldn't cut paper. Suits of armour strung together with wire, moth-eaten tapestries depicting a fabled draconic past that never really existed. Mishka wondered how her father could stand it.

Former High King Minuidon had been a tyrant and petty bully who had blackmailed her father with threats against her life for most of her childhood. If Mishka had her way, all evidence of Minuidon's reign would have been purged from the palace within a half hour of the monster's death. She didn't understand how her father could spend all his time surrounded by keepsakes of the man who had oppressed them all, while acting like a squatter in his own castle.

THE LIFE AND TIMES OF THE TRAITOR KILLEAN ONRYN

'That's not how that saying goes,' she ground out, clasping her delicate teacup with shaking fingers. The truly disgusting thing was, if she tossed her lukewarm tea in his face the guards stationed at the corners of the stuffy room would arrest *her* for treason. 'Sammia, Child of Death can't be trusted. In the name of the Light, she even abandoned *Killean!*'

Not that he hadn't deserved to have his beloved ditch him, but the point remained. Sammia had proved she couldn't be trusted. She had no creed and no cause beyond her own self-preservation. Those were lousy traits in a friend and lover, but honestly terrible traits in a spy.

A spy had to be willing to give up her life and honour in the name of king and country. She had to be willing to stomach any indignity and shoulder any insult in the name of Three Rivers' continued safety. Mishka understood that, so why didn't her father?

'We can't let a potent symbol of the failed rebellion walk free, darling,' her father soothed.

'Then lock her up! For crying out loud, that's what we did with the rest!'

'Well, that's true,' Torvin temporised, 'but Silent Hell is getting a *bit* crowded...'

Mishka put her cup down before she shattered it in her bare hands. 'Daddy. Silent Hell is part of an infinite expanse of magical energy outside the reach of time and space,' she reminded him through gritted teeth, 'it doesn't get crowded.'

'Weeell, almost,' Torvin tapped his fingers against the drum of his pipe. His blue eyes were smiling when he focused on her. 'I want you to work with her. *Watch* her. If the war taught us anything, it's that we can't keep pushing our Accursed to the sidelines. So many of them are looking for a cause to believe in. I believe with your guidance, Three Rivers can be that cause.'

Mishka believed her father was full of it. There was no point in calling him out on it though. Torvin-the-Spark had multiple reasons for everything he did and he delighted in keeping all but the most trivial hidden from his closest advisors. Mishka wasn't foolish enough to flatter herself into thinking she counted as one of those.

Abandoning yet another failed teatime with her father, Mishka had risen from her cushion with a familiar ball of bitterness festering in her guts. 'I want full authority to pass judgement on her conduct,' she warned. 'If I say she goes to Silent Hell, she goes, Father. No arguments. You may think a criminal can do this job as well as I, but I'd like to see how well you rule without *me* in your corner.'

Her father beamed at her, outwardly proud, but Mishka, who had wiled away her adolescence longing for such a look, knew how empty it was. He wasn't proud of her; he was proud of the reflection of his own cleverness he saw in her place. He delighted in his manipulation as he forced everyone and everything to dance to his tune yet again.

'Of course, sweetheart,' he promised, 'you are my Princess of Whispers. You know I trust your word above all others. Now let me tell you about this group in the mountains. The rumours coming out of the region are alarming. They say this group know where the Firefly is. I want you to go and find out the truth...'

Don't miss out!

Visit the website below and you can sign up to receive emails whenever A.R Cunningham publishes a new book. There's no charge and no obligation.

https://books2read.com/r/B-A-SGPOC-OZPCF

BOOKS 2 READ

Connecting independent readers to independent writers.

About the Author

Born and raised in the UK, A.R Cunningham has always been interested in life's big questions. Such as - is it better to be eaten first in a zombie apocalypse or last? And what would happen if heaven outsourced its paperwork to hell? Naturally pursuing answers to these fundamental(ly daft) questions has helped make her a writer!

Read more at https://aldlischronicles.wordpress.com/.

Milton Keynes UK
Ingram Content Group UK Ltd.
UKHW042004281024
450365UK00003B/159